'RILLAS AND OTHER
SCIENCE FICTION STORIES

Borgo Press Books by A. R. MORLAN

The Amulet: A Novel of Horror
Dark Journey: A Novel of Horror
Ewerton Death Trip: A Walk Through the Dark Side of Town
'Rillas and Other Science Fiction Stories

'RILLAS

AND OTHER SCIENCE FICTION STORIES

A. R. MORLAN

with John S. Postovit

THE BORGO PRESS

MMXII

'RILLAS

FIRST EDITION

Published by Wildside Press LLC

www.wildsidebooks.com

DEDICATION

To **Kevin J. Anderson, Jerry Oltion**, and **Darrell Schweitzer**,

for supplying me with copies of a "lost" page of the story "'Rillas" (incomplete contributor's copy) after I lost my original manuscript of the story during the September 2, 2002 F3 tornado which damaged my house—most specifically my office!—I couldn't have created this collection without your help!

CONTENTS

ACKNOWLEDGMENTS

THESE STORIES WERE previously published as follows, and are reprinted (with minor editing, updating, and textual modifications) by permission of the author:

"The Best Lives of Our Years" was originally published in *Full Spectrum IV*, ed. by Lou Aronica *et al.*, Bantam Spectra, 1993. Copyright © 1993, 2012 by A. R. Morlan.

"Contingencies and Penti-Lope-Lope," with John S. Postovit, was originally published in *The Fifth Dimension* (e-zine), Edition 3, Issue 4, August, 2001. Copyright © 2001, 2012 by A. R. Morlan and John S. Postovit.

"Ciné Rimettato" was originally published in *Sci-Fi.Com/ SciFiction* (e-zine), August, 2000. Copyright © 2000, 2012 by A. R. Morlan.

"Boog'/4 and the Endicaran Kluge" was originally published in *Once Upon a Future: The Third Borgo Press Book of Science Fiction Stories*, ed. by Robert Reginald, Borgo Press/Wildside Press, 2011. Copyright © 2011, 2012 by A. R. Morlan.

"Robin Williams, Speaking Spanish" was originally published in *Challenging Destiny*, #17, Dec. 2003. Copyright © 2003, 2012 by A. R. Morlan.

"What Falls from the Life," with John S. Postovit, is published here for the first time. Copyright © 2012 by A. R. Morlan and John S. Postovit.

"Etamin at East 47th" was originally published in *Challenging Destiny*, # 16, June 2003. Copyright © 2003, 2012 by A. R.

Morlan.

THE BEST LIVES
OF OUR YEARS

...sociologists of the time predicted initially that if there was to be any so-called "positive" effect of the Esperme Virus Plague (EVP) in 2007, with its resulting drop in the male birth rate (down 59 percent in North and South America from 2007 to 2009 alone and dropping between 45 percent and 70 percent worldwide, with Africa and the South Pacific-Australia-New Zealand areas experiencing the most significant decreases in live male births), it would involve the overall shape of future civil and world wars. While there remained no doubt—thanks to Operation Desert Storm in the preceding decade—that women were capable of waging war, under the circumstances of EVP (and the eventual barring of all fertile males from active combat in 2012), it *was* believed that those women already in positions of power in government and the military would be more likely to rely strongly on negotiations rather than overt military action in potentially explosive diplomatic and territorial situations, due to their innate maternal and familial protection instincts (which, after EVP, were exacerbated by the added need to protect the ever-dwindling male members of society), with all previous notions of women's rights, equality of the sexes, and rejection of the "Mommy Track" to be cast aside by those women now experiencing the onus of possible human extinction within the next 200 to 300 years. (According to the initial projections of Dr. Olivier Dreyfus, discoverer of the first strain of EVP; those figures are currently undergoing intense world-wide scrutiny.)

Unfortunately, sociologists—like practitioners in any speculative field—can be wrong....

> —Dr. Coriane Katan, *The War of All Mothers* (Double-day/Warner, 2085).

I.

red

I didn't look at the letter as I fished it out of the narrow slot of the opened post office box; that Tyvek envelope they send the notices in says it all, the second your fingers touch the damned thing. After ten years behind the window, I've seen enough draft notices stuffed into the router's bags to just about know those suckers by *smell.* By the almost antiseptic sort-of-plastic stink of them; the odor of bandages and suitcase linings and those little rain bonnets with the flimsy ties that always broke when Grandma tried to take them off in a hurry. And the reek of the plastic kits they issue to new recruits, the War Bags designed to be worn Velcroed around a waist, or around a thigh or upper arm if your waist is ballooned from within by child.

Enough of the returning War Bags come through the post office for me to know their scent as intimately as I know the odor of my own menses. That slightly acidic, slightly *warm* redolence which somehow manages to permeate the oversized Tyvek envelope they stuff the War Bags in after plucking them off the bodies of the fallen.

So...trusting my nose, and my fingertips, I wasn't about to

waste my eye's time by reading my own name on the draft notice. It's always been a *given,* I suppose, that I'd be called; Tashia is five, and Alan still makes his deposits at the *s* 'bank on a monthly basis (thanks to me taking the filled, vacuum-bottle-protected vial to the *s* 'bank myself—His *Uniqueness* hasn't ventured out of the flat since '16 or so; he's still got the raz from the last time he got *s* 'mugged, and won't go *near* any woman other than me bearing an *s* 'vial in her hand).

At least he hasn't gone full-blown EVP; they can still use his *s* ' in the banks, or so the credits for withdrawals he gets in the mail tell me. I know more about his payments than he does—I do every step of his banking except for signing the backs of his checks—so even without my P.O. check, they'll be set should I have to go.

When I go, now. I resist looking at the letter during the sub ride home; just the presence of it in my bag is enough. I know without bending down to smell it that it is already stinking up my bag, infecting all my civilian personal things with that syntho-blood aroma. Across from me, another 'muter's paper is folded in her hand so that I can read the inner front page headline, the one closest to the spine of the paper:

"WAR IN MANDELIA CLAIMS 15,000 U.S. TROOPS"

Another war-euphemism, like "fallen" for the *dead*, this one outstripping the Penta-Pret's propaganda department. "Claims," instead of *kills.* Like war is someone who plucks up the foot-groaners, collecting 'groans like seashells on a tide-washed beach, claiming the best ones for her store of soldiers. Like, "This here 'groaner is mine, I've *claimed* her."

Maybe "envelopes" would be a better word for what war does to 'groaners. The envelope taketh you away, the envelope giveth you back.

The 'muter folds her paper yet again, to swatting size, and gets off at the stop before mine. Through the opposite window, I see her (young, thin, hair puffed 'n' piled, suit 'n' tie improbably bright olive) slide through the crowd, waving her paper like a scythe. I try to imagine someone like her getting a draft notice, showing up at the 'cruitment center, losing that piled puff of hair with just a few swipes of the razor, standing in line with gov'issue uniform parts in hand.... Midway through the scenario, I give up. 'Muters in suit 'n' tie are just too valuable back home, got to keep the corporate machines clicking along. Today's version of Joe College from Grandma's teen-hood, when the 'groaners were grunts, and only guys burned their draft cards.

Minutes before my stop comes up, I try to picture Alan going through the draft notice routine, but it's just too improbable. No man goes farther into battle than having his voice issue orders from a safe bunker, miles from real action. And those 'groaners are oldies, past worrying about EVP further messing up the chances of the boy-*s'* making it past the tough hide of the egg, past worrying about making girl babies whose kid-machines are defective. And past *s'*bank donation checks, too.

No, even if His *Uniqueness* back home were a *woman,* like the other eighty-five percent of us in the world, I still couldn't see him making it as a 'groaner. He'd have to leave our flat first....

My stop; elbowing past the 'muters and on-leave 'groaners and palm-outs huddled behind their "My man's EVP, no *s'*deposits" signs, I reach the stairway leading up to my street. More palm-outs; men in the last stages of EVP—no-colored behind beard stubble, mucus running out of their eyes, nostrils, past mosaic-parched lips, and women whose clothes are cut away to show the scars where they'd been de-repoed, de-kid-machined. I feel around in my bag for the draft notice, wave it around, let them catch a whiff of its reek. I walk the last block unimplored by the palm-outs.

In the lobby, I press the buzzer one-handed, peeling open the envelope's gummed flap with the other hand, pressing the notice against my thigh for leverage. The gov' seal is there, over the computer-standard greeting—"Dear Ms./Mrs. Ingram"—but I am buzzed through before I have a chance to read more. No voice confirmation, no Alan fearing some *s'*mugger will barge into the flat, knock him on his back, yank down his pants and *s'*rob him at knife-gun-fist point because she can't make a legal *s'* withdrawal due to being a (take your pick) felon, drugger or ex-'groaner mustered out for a non-repo-related infraction. Maybe he thinks they can smell the live *s'* on his breath as he speaks, I tell myself, riding the elevator to our floor. The 'vator is empty, for once; I have a clear view of myself in the round convex security mirror in the upper corner, a leftover from the days when women had to worry *about* men, rather than just worry *for* them. I take myself in, as I am now, freshly post-civilian: hair pulled back in P.O.-reg flowing tail, light-over-dark uniform, shoes thick-soled enough for stand-on-your-feet comfort. I still have the unfolded letter in my hand; it has a date for my arrival at the 'cruitment center, but I will look at that later on. For a few more precious seconds, this is *my* life.

For the space of time it takes the elevator to travel up, up to my floor, I am still a *woman,* in the old sense, as if any female today can *ever* be a complete woman anymore (considering how we're all mothers not only to our young, but to our spouses or whatever man we have to defer to at the job, on the streets, or wherever one happens to encounter a *unique* member of an increasingly female society)—each step I take is for *me,* not for the Pentagon-Pretties in their leather chairs and uniforms with pants and half-inch-long hair under their uniform caps.

The 'vator reaches my floor. Doors slide open, wait for a few seconds, then start to close again. Sliding sideways through the diminishing open space, I catch a last glimpse of myself—hirsute, skirted, *female*—before the 'vator closes itself to me and descends to the lobby.

Smoothing the skirt against my legs as I walk, savoring the feel of air circulating around my moving limbs, I tell myself that Tashia will be fine while I'm gone; Alan is a good mother, and once I'm gone, he can have a messenger carry his *s'*deposit to the *s'*bank. They have men with vaccine-arrested (but not cured) EVP just for that purpose.

Not wishing to make Alan take an unnecessary trip down our hallway, I get my keys (already scent-tainted) out of my bag and begin to unlock the six deadbolts set into the edge of our door. Alan has never had to do this; he hasn't been out of the flat since we had the fifth and sixth deadbolts installed. Through the fine gaps where the door and the door frame don't seal perfectly, I hear an odd sound coming from within the apartment. Too even to be crying, too loud to be moaning—opening the door, I see something rippling *over* the nap of the carpeting within. Radiating out in a sun-like formation from a central bare spot. The low yet persistent noise is coming from farther down the inner hallway, but the bright-color ripples on the carpet have command of my attention for the moment.

Bending down, I run my fingers over one of the rays of color, feeling the strands separate under the pressure of my finger-tips, splaying out against the carpet's springy fibers. Hair...still smelling faintly of mild shampoo, the kind Tashia uses—

A pound of footfalls coming toward me, coupled with Tashia's "*Mommy*," attacks my ears. Looking up I see Tashia's legs first, encased in *pants*, oh *God* wherever She is, a little pair of *overalls* like little *boys* used to wear, like Alan wore in the days when he was a child and actually saved in the hope that his own little boy would...and then I slowly raise my eyes, to take in her little-boy pullover shirt, the one with the blue and red rugby stripes and the little white collar—and instinctively *stop* looking after one glimpse of Tashia's head, of the whitish scalp showing through the places where Alan's electric razor clipped too close, leaving almost no stubble at all.

Tashia stops short of the spot where her hair is resting, fanned out in an approximation of the shape of her head, saying in a voice I hear only faintly, coming like static through the pound of blood in my ears, "Mommy, Daddy *said* it was gonna be like Hallo'een, but 'stead of candy I was gonna get a big *s'prise!*' 'long as I closed my eyes an' layed on the floor *there*—" she may've been pointing at the rays of her hair, all I could see was red and black, hazing before me "—only it buzzed and tickled and then Daddy went 'way without giving me my *s'prise*—"

Fainter still, I hear Alan, babbling either to me or to himself or to God, from somewhere down the hallway, "—fixed it, don't you *see*! They don't take little *boys*, not for the war, little boys are too *unique*...saved the bibbies, and the shirt, *knew* I'd have a boy someday, little *boy,* with a buzz cut like I'd get every summer...'fore little boys were *special*, and never left home any, *any* more. Like their Mommies do...see, Tash's a *boy*'s name, and little boys don't go away...*they*'ll never look, never check, boys are too *special*, have to protect the *sper*— keep *it* safe, from the *dis-ease*—"

And Tashia...my *girl,* my *Na*tashia, she doesn't care that she's dressed like a boy, or is shorn like a first-day 'groaner in the 'cruitment center barber chair. *She*'s boo-hooing about not getting that "*s'prise*" Alan promised her...*he*'s congratulating himself for finally becoming a boy-maker...and I glance down at my draft notice, praying for an early date of recruitment on that sane-smelling form....

II.

white

30.08.46 (*eleven hundred hours/thirty minutes*)

From: T. Sgt. Natashia Ingram
c/o SC Box 987760
APO AP 96266

To: Captain Janet Ingram (Ret.)
P.O. Box 5490342
FDR Station
New York, NY 10150-0342

Dear "Capt." Mom,

Got this machine* to myself for don't know how long, so this will have to be brief. (*Usually EVP'ers are chained to it!)

Looks like the 'Delas are in retreat; their antique SCUDs are no match for our MOAWs, but that could change any sec, as you remember from your hitch here. Wish I could be more specif; but the CO would rip off both my tits if I said more (not that they don't have pens to black out classified info!). Needless to say, we're **XXXXXX**, so don't expect to take the gold ribbon off the doorknob any time soon!

Went to **XXXXXX** to see the Li'l General; your grand-daughter weighs over fifteen pounds, and measures over twenty-five inches long. Tall like you. Should make a great captain eventually, *you* know how the tall ones are automatically officer material. (I don't think Gen. Boles would be what she is today if she were a Size 6 Petite!) Wish I knew who the gen-dad was; tried pulling in a few favors, but all I've heard on the wire is that he was (is?) of Mid-East descent, which is unusual, since EVP hit harder there, 'specially since it split off into EVP I and II. Like Leia, the 'ner on **XXXXXX** always says, tho: "All gen-dads look the same...smooth, white, and bald as a rubber bulb on top." My CO calls 'em "loaded tampons," but considering that only **XXXXXX** 'ners in the squadron are carriers now, I'm inclined to think of 'em as *blanks*!

Don't know how you and the rest of the 'ners in your squad made it through the POW camps without monthly gen-dad blasts; it's still bad for the POWs, but they will go easy on a carrier. Might be *with-unique,* fresh source of gen-dad for *them.* One of our 'ners brought back some of *their* gen-dad (same make of blaster we use, only the bulb is softer, more like wet Tyvek) she'd 'vaged off a fallen; it was confiscated, tho, and **XXXXXX** so we won't know for a while if it took. Only hitch is wearing the gen-dad *belt*; the cold element in there some-times leeches out, and causes chem burns. Last night, I had a dream about you and Dad; he was telling me what a good *boy*

I was, only it wasn't like we were in the old apartment, but I was in a 'cruitment chair, getting my first shave, and you were just standing there with a draft notice in your hand. Not saying a word, just holding out your free hand as my hair drifted down, like you were catching leaves in the fall.

I wonder if that's how guys used to feel when they were drafted or enlisted. I can't picture it; the EVP's in the offices are all so old they're natural shine-heads. Got to thinking. When it came to the whole war process before EVP, were we women jealous of what the men were able to do in war, or secretly proud that we didn't really *have* to get in there and fight? Once there was EVP, was it then "put up or shut up" time? Tried to bring that up once, in the bunker, but for all of us, it was like trying to figure out what the world would be like without sunlight, after we'd lived all our lives *with* it. Sort of a fairy-tale life, where women took pills *not* to have children, and men wore rubber sheaths on their *s'*rods to *stop* them from blasting the women, and not just to try and stop AIDS or EVP. I can read about it, talk about it, and know all the while that it was true, but for *me* it *wasn't*, period.

I *know* you remember what it was like. Just like you remember Dad before EVP, and him eventually dying from it like just about all the men who got it and didn't respond to the vaccine. I'd ask you, but I know I'd never get my answer....

You asked about the POW situation; we only see them for a short time, before they're shipped out to **XXXXXX**. Looks like their army is treating the 'ners on their side 'bout the same as us, maybe a little worse. Some of the POWs that come through here are only twelve, maybe less. No hair down there when they're stripped for delouse. Don't know how they 'spect to get results from the gen-dads the youngest 'ners carry. Probably give 'em blanks.

Lights are flickering; happens every time a **XXXXXX** flies overhead. Which means that **XXXXXX** is coming back, either more POW or more wounded. Least I hope it's just wounded. I hate seeing what they do to the fallen 'fore our 'ners can get to them. Hacked, or ringed with burning tires and always split open if they're carrier due to evacuate soon. Most of the time they're totally *claimed* when we find them. Worse if they aren't; we have to **XXXXXX** them.

I wonder, honestly, if even pre-EVP male 'ners had to do that. Even if you won't—or can't—answer.

Lights again, almost out, taking the keys of this thing with them. Insane to send electronic machines; too susceptible to brown/blackouts. An EVP just toddled up, wants *his* toy back.

Salutes and hugs, Tash

04.09.46

From: Major Emi Takei
c/o PSC Box 976591
APO AP 96266

To: Captain Janet Ingram (Ret.)
P.O. Box 5490342
FDR Station
New York, NY 10150-0342

Re: T. Sgt. Natashia C. Ingram

Dear Captain Ingram,

It is my sad duty to inform you that on 31/08/46, your child Natashia was injured/<u>killed</u> in the line of duty during a MOAW missile attack on her bunker.

Her War Bag will be sent to you under separate cover, along with her Purple Heart and Bronze Star.

Her <u>daughter</u>/son Diee will remain in Army custody, per Property Regulation 5499872-C, as outlined in the standard enlistment forms Natashia signed upon joining the Army in 2034. You will be informed of the child's progress as *she*/he advances in military training. Again, I am sorry to inform you of the injury/<u>loss</u> of your child. May God comfort you and look down upon you in this time of sorrow, and may She comfort your daughter Natashia.

With regret,

Maj. Emi Takei. C.O.
U.S. Army

Captain Ingram,

Please excuse the form letter above; it is regulation, and you & I know reg is God around here. I knew your daughter, and while she and I did not always agree on principle (or procedure—a habit of hers I seem to have posthumously inherited!) I found her to be a *woman* with a questioning, insightful mind— not a prickle-headed 'groaner blindly following orders (in my case, *touché!*) despite their logic or their true necessity. Not that she ever disobeyed any order given by myself or any of her superiors, but Tash was aware of the purpose (or lack thereof) behind day-to-day Army life, and chose to rationally and intelligently question the *why* of this woman's Army.

Would that I had had the answers she was so desperately seeking.

Maj. Emi Takei (Soon-to-be-retired)

LIST OF CONTENTS:
War Bag, T. Sgt. N. C. Ingram:

Dog Tags
Genetic-donor receptacle belt (empty of donor syringes)
Diary (edited to conform to regulations 87943-A and -B)
Emergency MRE's (three packets)
African-American phrase book

Misc. photographs (Infant Recruit D. M. Ingram-Hussam)
Letter dated 30.08.46 (unmailed at time of death)

III.

blue

Norma was taking ears again. We were bunkering, cleaning out abandoned subter dwellings of the enemy fallen, burying those who'd been left by *their* evac units, but ears (and noses and lips—upper and lower) were off limits—unless your mother was a lieutenant colonel, and *her* mother was a *ma*-frucking-*jor*. Norma can fillet the whole frucking *hide* off an enemy 'ner and wear it over her uniform, if she wants. Claims she's a pre-EVP relation to ol' General Norman S. hisself.

She *is* big enough.

"G'eee *over here*," Norma barked, stretching the "G'eee" out hard and fast, like when you give an order to a K-9'er.

I didn't know if that was her way of saying "Get" or a corruption of my name, Diee, but I sure as *fruck* wasn't answering. I may be an I.R. born to a draftee tech sergeant, raised in Mandelia's kibbutz-*cum*-boot camp, but I don't lick *any* lips. Upper *or* lower.

Staying where I was, I shook powdery grayish snow off a Mongol-English phrase book, watching Norma through lowered lashes as she raised the fallen 'Gol 'ner by the meaty scruff of her neck (her rounded yellow-brown head was covered with a quarter inch of stubble), took out her laser-knife from her parka, and with a hum and a flash of rod-focused light, the right ear, followed by the left, rested in Norma's wide palm.

"Lieutenant Ingram-Hussam, g'eee *over* here!"

I put the phrase book into the 'Gol 'ner's War Bag, taking the time to untangle the straps before approaching the earless corpse. Patting the Velcro male section onto the softer, female patch on the 'Gol's outside belt, then resting the straps across her body (I wasn't strong enough to lift her and secure the straps under the uniform back), I leaned back on my heels, asking, "What, Norma?"

Glaring, yet unable to protest (we shared the same rank), Norma said, "I think this one's a *he.*"

"I think not, Lieutenant." Rocking back 'n' forth before I built up the momentum to rise in a long, fluid movement (loving Norma's narrowed eyes and puckered lips as I did it), I dusted semi-melted snow off my pants before walking away from her, adding over my shoulder, "I don't see the wisdom in using a nonexpendable member of any society as missile-munchie."

Muttering "*Thesaurus*-tongue," Norma opened her parka pocket—the rasp of separating Velcro carried far in the cold, dry air—and hid her latest ear harvest.

Norma wasn't the first to call me that. Once I gained access to my mother's War Bag effects, after *her* mother died in '63 when I was seventeen, I started to talk (and *think*, which no one can ridicule) like her. My mother was one of the last voluntary lifers. Why she kept re-enlisting I never could figure out, even after reading her censored diary. Black lines, passages, all inked out to protect long-declassified information. What was left was her first weeks in boot, her first carrier term (aborted male EVP-positive), MRE gripes ("Mucus Regurgitated Everyday!") and her thoughts, about everything else.

Those passages I memorized; there's little room in a War Bag for your own gear, let alone someone else's. Also I don't have to worry about harvesters like Norma going through my bag should I die, and misreading my mother's words.

My mother came from a real family, something even Norma can't lay claim to. A mother who eventually had to work once EVP began *s'* busting every man on the planet; a father who started out full of male-bonding hope and wound up drippy-eyed and -nosed, curled in a ball in a room he hadn't left since he found out his wife had been drafted. And whose grand-daughter would be born into army-sanctioned servitude, in a society that demanded each member do her duty—be it by serving the Pentagon machine, or by endlessly bearing future cogs for said machine.

Or, as my mother wrote:

> I guess being army-doc blasted beats trying to do it on your own, month after month, in the privacy of your home—the latter way means reporting back to the *s* 'bank within a week of withdrawal, empty vial in hand, ready to pee on a strip of treated plastic. In the army, there's something in the latrine water—once you're a carrier, you know immediately. As long as you don't flush prior to rising.
>
> If you prefer being blasted so hard it feels like the tip of the gen-dad probe will burst out of your navel (I swear all medics have balls somewhere on them!) it is *surely* worth not having to pee on a wand of chemical-treated plastic!

I would've liked to have spoken to her. My mother. I've an old picture of her. Looked like every 'groaner since the War Protection Act of '12. Round bare head, squinting eyes from too much combat in the sun, tanned face, and a blur of a smile. Same as me, save for my naturally darker skin. Not much opportunity to tan in Mongolia come winter. It's always winter after those bomb "tests" over the Ukraines.

Norma—her ears safely hidden in her parka—was rooting around in the fallen 'Gol's uniform; the rending of fabric brought me back to reluctant reality.

I closed my eyes until I heard her whisper, "*Diee.* G'eee over here...*told* you."

Oh, God, it was true. They were sending *men* into battle. Some *how*, some way, the 'Gol's had a surplus of men, enough to sacrifice new sources of gen-dad. How many? I asked myself. Ten, fifteen percent? I've never lived in (never *known* of, period) a time where men made up more than five to seven percent of the North American population. And most other countries were worse off than the U.S. and Canada.

Norma was about to switch on her laser-knife when I opened my eyes and asked her to wait. Crawling over to the earless 'ner, I peered down at the patch of exposed flesh between Norma's circling hands.

It was and it wasn't like a gen-doc: the long thinness was right, but there were two lightly haired bulbs of flesh above. And it was all attached, seamlessly. It was real...and sadly defenseless. Pointing the laser-knife at it, Norma remarked, "Just think...a world's trouble centered around a little virus getting into such a little organ," as she used the turned-off knife to lift the *s'*rod from the rest of the body. The whole thing was so opaque I couldn't see where the *s'* was hidden. Even the bulbs were deflated.

Norma was clucking, moving the dead bits this way and that, while I sat back on my heels, rubbing my face and scalp with my palms, wishing my mother was here, now, with me, Norma, and the dead man.

A few weeks after I was born, she'd written in *her* diary:

> It puzzled me as a child, and it still makes me wonder—when it came to EVP and men, which was the real enemy of womankind (as opposed to *human-kind*)...EVP, or the male organs it attacked? And once the war on man's ability to reproduce himself (i.e., *man*) was waged—and all but lost—were we women attacking each other because of what had happened to the men, or because there were no longer any men to attack? Is that why the women's army (and navy, and marines, and air force, *and*—) became more stringent, more basic, more *butch* than the old army, navy, and so on ever were? When men waged war, they took the time to *not* wage war; time to take R & R for the sake of Rest and *Relaxation,* not Rest and *Recuperation* (what yours truly's doing now: feet up, hair growing in, womb free of gen-docs for at least three months).

Do we wage war so vigorously, so joylessly, so grimly, because it's always been so, or because we must do it better than it was done before? And in our case, must "better" mean...*meaner*? Shiny-headed killing wombs-on-legs, with little sense of bonding, of comradeship—just one-upmanship and "we'll show *them*" attitude, all directed at the *unique* men we have to both protect and better?

I wonder—are we waging war for the sake of humanity, or to forsake *humanity?* To prove forever and ever that even if we can lick EVP—not that the female doctors seem as driven to conquer it as their (dwindling) male counterparts seem to have been—we're still the better "men"? That real men only need exist on any level as gen-doc donors?

Were we women so put down that we need to forever fight to prove how strong, how capable, how *indispensable* we were all along?

"Well, Diee, make up yer mind—off or on?" Norma's thumb rested on the knife's switch—and said knife was resting, "blade" up, under the limp *s'rod* of the fallen 'Gol. One flick of her thumb and the *s'rod* would be severed, two more knife flicks and the 'Gol 'ner would be as good as female. Good as *us*.

"*No.* Better put a marker by the claim, so's the docs at the base can check it—*him*—out later. Might be able to analyze the *s'rod*, and the bulbs."

Norma—puffed up with importance over finding the first *male* 'Gol 'ner in the history of at least *this* war—waddled out of the bunker, into the drifting snow outside, in search of a red flag marker. Alone in the empty-walled bunker, I started to roll up the 'Gol's bedroll—until something fell out at my booted feet. A book, filled with carefully printed lines, in phrase-book English, no doubt penned in hope that if he was taken prisoner the 'Gol could prove to us American 'ners that he was ready and willing to learn the American way, to side with us if necessary. I'd seen this sort of thing before: copybooks filled with stilted English phrases, some written over and over, schoolgirl-fashion.

But this 'Gol—this *guy*—had something different on his mind, aside from learning English:

> Morning of each day I sit, wait, as day become noon, noon become night, as I wonder "Why *I* fight? Why my mother? Why her mother? Must I fight harder, because I man in woman world?" I one of few men, but we grow in number. Women, they try hard next to me, more hard than with other woman. And always, I hide manness, other soldier tell me, "*They* know you man, they kill you harder." But they woman too—so, then, *my* women, they do same to *their* man, if any? If that so, who is enemy?

I slowly paged through the thin diary, looking for a name, an age, *something* to identify this man lying behind me. I didn't want to touch him again, couldn't violate his War Bag. All I found was "I" and "me." Perhaps that's all I needed to find.

For my mother, in her diary, never mentioned *who* she was, never needed to use her own name. She knew herself, or tried to, considering that she belonged to a generation born to alien roles, and to an alien situation which reversed the roles of the sexes.

Yet my mother knew of this lost past, and took the time to discover pasts lost well before that of her own mother was devoured by an invasive virus:

> I remember reading a sociology textbook, how back in the early 1900s, baby boys wore pink, because it was such a healthy, robust color, while girls were dressed in blue, a delicate, gentle hue. It wasn't until after one of the world wars—I forget which one, they were spaced so far apart then—that the norm switched

around, and blue became the "masculine" color. Considering the mess we "pinks" are in, perhaps that older assignment of colors for babies of different genders wasn't so wrong after all.

Outside the cave, I heard Norma swearing, "Where the *fruck* is that damn flag?" as I reached the last page in the 'Gol's diary, where he'd had the time to write one final line:

"Snow today—cover land. Soon cover me."

Closing the book, the pages falling together with a soft *chuff*, I rocked back and forth on my heels, eyes shut, but still seeing what my mother had written in *her* diary, not long before the MOAW missile fragmented her like so much shrapnel:

Lull in the fighting—I don't like it. Don't know what will happen next. Better to either be in a battle or be coming out of it. This way—too much uncertainty. Get too relaxed. My mind is racing, racing. Remember a war movie I saw in basics, really an after-war film from the 1940s. No color, like old TV. *The Best Years of Our Lives.* Three men-grunts, coming home from one of the world wars. Second one, I think. Yes; no movies during first world war.

Anyway. The three—one was maimed, navy one— couldn't adjust to life without war; war had given them all purpose, justification, glory. Came home to uncertainty, rejection, degradation. Seemed to me that the war years weren't the best years of their lives, but had instead sucked away the best lives of their years. Oh, the movie had a sort-of-happy ending, but the maimed one was still maimed, and the poor one was doing work on junked war materials. The one who was rich before got to be rich again, but his daughter was in love with the low-life one. Strange to see a war actually end. And the women had stayed at home. Must've been why it finally ended.

Watching, I kept thinking it was all a dream-life, with women razzed about *having* to stay home and take care of the home front. Thought maybe EVP must've gotten into us women, made us hard, tough, mean—everything the men have lost. But seeing the play-soldiers of old, I think: They have lost something we women can never have—the ability *not* to be manly under certain circumstances. We women are so wrapped up in being wo-*men,* both in one, that we are neither.

And later, during history class in my last year of school, while learning of Desert Storm, I read a microfiche of an old pre-EVP newspaper, and an article about the first instances of bunkering (high-tech scavenging) in the Kuwaiti desert. This reporter who wrote the article came across one fallen soldier, named Mardy. Mardy had a diary, like mine, like all of ours. He hoped the war of his people and ours would be over soon, He asked God to make it so. He felt betrayed by his life. He had a girlfriend, Diee, whom he never saw again. And when the American reporter found him, Mardy was dead, mouth open, hand over his heart. And the reporter read of Mardy's words: "I open my eyes and cry, sitting, thinking, 'O God, will you accept me?' I close my eyes and remember. Then I cry again. There is sand on my face. It is about to cover me. It is my destiny. I want to shout in my loudest voice but life doesn't follow me."

And before he left Mardy, the reporter buried him in those same sands. Reading that, I realized, in war there *are* no real enemies. Only victims—of our countries, of our races, and of ourselves. We need no other adversaries.

War, politics, EVP and AIDS before that—all shadow boxing partners. Only we do the actual moving.

My mother died a couple of days after writing those words. Oh, she did write a letter to her mother, but it only skirted the questions gnawing at her, perhaps in deference to her mother's rank, more probably in deference to her own un-faceable fear. Yet hers was a war of equals, of women hurting other women. No fear of being killed faster and dying slower. My mother fought a war, not others not quite like herself.

"...*who* is *enemy?*"

Sitting by the earless 'Gol, his soul resting cloth-bound in my hands, I wish I knew the answer to his—and my—question. Just as I wish I knew who was doing the real moving—me, or my image on a snow-flecked earthen wall.

AUTHOR'S NOTE: The newspaper article mentioned in this work appeared in the Tuesday, July 30, 1991 edition of *USA Today,* and was written by Jack Kelley. The diary passages quoted were written by Hussam Malek Mohammad Mardy, to whom this work is dedicated.

Afterword for "The Best Lives of Our Years"

Looking back on the genesis of this story, I suppose it amounts to my overwhelming disgust over the events which made up the end of the Gulf War (senior), including the treatment of those enemy soldiers who tried to surrender, only to be literally buried alive by their own military vehicles, driven by our soldiers...somewhere along the line, even the barbaric rules of war had been hideously breached, and the horrors of the second Bush ("Dubyah") Presidency's Gulf War were yet to come, even as they had been anticipated by the events of the 1990s war. That war marked one of the first instances of women being used on the battlefront in a supporting role, a situation which blossomed into the current Middle East war(s) creating female vets coming home *sans* limbs, or worse. Now, I've read that women will probably be in combat soon. Never have I hated to see something I once wrote about in a fictional sense coming to fruition more than I hate this current military turn of events.

Getting back to the actual writing of this story, I had the first two sections outlined in my head long before I finally wrote it in 1991; I knew part one would be "red" and part two was "white" but I had no idea what "blue" was going to be. I had an inkling it would involve the granddaughter of the woman in part one, but I couldn't come up with a viable scenario for her part of the triad of war stories. Then, I read the account in the July 30, 1991 issue of *USA Today* of the live burial of those enemy soldiers, and I had my ending for the tale. But when it comes to war, and war, in any century, all I can eventually do is hang my head after seeing or reading accounts of what actually happens in battle, and ask myself: How can any civilization do something so stupid so many times?

But I think I know the answer to that earless 'gol's query: *We* are the enemy. We always have been, and as long as we fail to figure out how not to settle arguments through battle, we'll never cease *to* be the enemy.

CONTINGENCIES AND PENTI-LOPE-LOPE

WITH JOHN S. POSTOVIT

Day 93:

The 'lopes watched us from their self-imposed distance as the six of us gathered in a circle on the flat-grass around the box holding the last of the spacer 'slop. I could see them craning their necks, oddly wide and flat heads jerking, flared ears twitching, as they scrutinized our movements. And Penti-Lope-Lope's canted amber-orange eyes were focused on my hands, my face, as I tore open my last dinner packet and pretended to enjoy it. At the best of times, the 'slop was a poor replacement for real food. This sure wasn't the best of times. Even if I *hadn't* been preoccupied, I still wouldn't have enjoyed it. My sinus medication had long ago run out, and without my pills, I had little sense of taste.

And Nutraform ('slop's official moniker) wasn't much to brag about even when I *could* taste it. It was nothing more than a flavor-enhanced, textureless, gloppy substance with the consistency of adipocere flesh; a nutritious, amino-acid, vitamin, mineral, carbohydrate, and damn me I can't recall what else that was just bulky enough to provide proper elimination, neutral enough not to cause heartburn, indigestion, or allergic reactions after ingestion.

Spacer swill; compatible with any and all human digestive systems, made palatable by loads of flavoring designed to fool the taste buds into thinking it was getting something real. If I ever got back to Earth, I'd start a campaign to impeach the politician who got the stuff on the official provisions list. Him and the moronic food-processing company that makes the stuff. Probably owned by the politician's second cousin.

Well, he's safe from me. I don't expect I'll ever make it back to start that campaign....

The others half closed their eyes as they moved the 'slop around in their mouths, oblivious to the watching 'lopes, savoring whatever packet they'd saved for their last meal. Their last real meal, before descending into that lonely abyss that yawned before us. I lowered my eyelids, pretending to enjoy 'slop I found as appetizing as nose drippings.

The 'lopes bunched closer, shifting from thickly muscled feet to half-squat in place, elongated torsos supported by their extended tails. They patted each other with their great hairy hands, all the while making those rumbling grunts and semi-mewls. But they came no closer to our meager supper circle. The Last Supper, as it was. If only Christ was here, to change water into wine, and those pole-fruit into bread. Made from safe, Earth-grown wheat....

Finally, Jimmie opened his eyes, and said, "We can't avoid it, not now. That's the last of the reserves—"

Huoy gulped down her utterly fake, perfectly bland Cambodian pork then snapped, "Not as long as the vitamins hold out. The water's safe, so there's no need to—"

(Beside me, Reba—paying no attention to the spoken words of her fellow esper—kept glancing at the surrounding 'lopes, an unreadable expression on her lightly freckled face. And for their part, the 'lopes likewise remained unreadable, or—at least to us incomprehensible....)

"Ever see a heart after starvation sets in?" Elizabeth asked in that mild, dreamy brogue of hers, face pale beneath burning-brown eyes. Huoy was suddenly engrossed in the crumbling soil and in the brown-to-tan-ombre spotted pebbles resting near her lotus-positioned feet, as the doctor continued, "It becomes like leather, brown leather. Not red. Not soft. Not very big."

Elizabeth held up her fisted right hand, the skin red-gold from the light of the too-small sun above us. "The body eats itself, attacking the muscle once the fat is depleted. The heart grows *hard*—"

Huoy stopped shifting the dirt particles between her stubby fingers. "So?" For a second I thought she was going to throw the dirt at Elizabeth. "Either way, we're dead. Matter of time. We know the anatomy of death by starvation."

"But once we eat this"—soil-stained fingers pointed at the fleshy tubers and foliage around us—"who knows?"

Jimmie crushed the remains of his packet against his chest, sighed deeply then replied, "Ecology here is certainly carbon-based. Right-handed sugars. Digestible at any rate. No toxins showed up in the tests I ran, least so far. Not many of the aminos we need but I can cob up whatever else is missing. At least we didn't run up against any left-handed sugars or—"

"None of the animals have died," Neil added, scooping up pebbles and rattling them, gourd-like, between cupped palms.

Huoy's head whipped around so quickly I heard one of her vertebrae pop softly. "'None of the animals have died'? My, my...oh *brilliant*, dear Mr. Aaron. How utterly perceptive of you.... Wait a minute, Mr. Aaron, *perhaps* I'll clap for you. Now, do you remember how rats can grow immune to almost any poisons? Or cockroaches? *Remember*, Neil? Their physiology is *not like ours*." Then Huoy's conversation went silent, her voice taut with unvoiced argument; the others leaned slightly forward, in the unconscious way of espers, and once again I felt like a child—too young and too stupid to be included in the conversation.

Reba suddenly dropped out of silent argument and gave me a little look of sympathy. Poor esp-mute, little boy lost! She leaned closer against me, chin level with my shoulder, and gestured. "That tree over there. Me Eve, you Adam, 'kay,

Scott?" She rose to her feet with a graceful motion that made my heart jump. Damn, she was beautiful!

Padding over to one of the two-meter high plants we dubbed "trees" for lack of anything else tall and tree-like on the horizon, Reba reached up and pulled one of the brownish, stick-shaped fruits off of the tree, before carrying it back to our "circle" of two.

The fruit's peel was husk-dry, faintly pebbled with bumps a shade darker than the rest of the dappled surface. Like 'lope fur, I thought, as Reba dug into the peel with a blunt thumb. The interior was meaty, seed-laced pulp, stringy, yet glistening with juices. It smelled wonderful; a heady, musky, tart pungent aroma which made it past my painfully blocked sinuses, as if it were a sign of virtue. Scooping out some pulp with her index and middle fingers, Reba handed the rest of the fruit to me, her freckled face aglow with an impish smile. Before awareness of our absence had time to register on our crewmates, Reba softly said, "Look the other way, God," before taking her first dripping taste.

"No, Reba!" Huoy screamed, flat face furrowing as she dashed to where we stood. Jimmie called after her, "Come back, Huoy, what other choice do we have—" but Huoy already had her hands on Reba's cheeks, shouting; "Spit it *out*! Spit-it-out-*now*!" As Huoy tried to force open Reba's lips, I leaned over and yanked the geologist's forearm away, warning, "Leave her alone. You know that a biologist like her knows the risks better than anyone—unless biology is *also* your specialty now—"

Then Reba swallowed, stuck her tongue out at the other woman and spat, "And it's good, Huoy. Not processed sludge in a damned *pouch*. It's *good*. And I know the 'lopes eat it—*they* haven't keeled over yet."

Huoy stood up, hands fisted against her sides, and snapped, "Since when did you grow a tail and a spotted pelt?" before turning on her heel and running back to the ship. Watching her leave, I raised my eyes to the heavens and took my first taste of fruit. It felt cool sliding down my throat, cool and mild.

Running my tongue over my teeth, I found that the fruit's taste was piquant; a little like kiwi, yet smoother; all I could think to call it was *red*, that odd flavor peculiar to crimson gum drops or cheap jelly beans.

Wordlessly, I handed the husk to Neil Aaron, commander of the grounded *Sagittarius IV*. Solemnly he scooped out a dripping finger full of the pale orange pulp and deposited in his mouth, before passing the husk to Elizabeth. Jimmie finished the last of it, and after we'd all had a taste, we sat there, expectant, waiting for someone to keel over in agony—until the inherent ludicrousness of our situation made Reba giggle behind a hand pressed against her lips.

From their semi-hiding place in the tubers beyond our circle the 'lopes chittered, watching us with what seemed to be 'loper expectation.

Then Jimmie—clown prince of dieticians—rolled his eyes, stuck his tongue out until he could almost lick the cleft in his brown chin, and toppled over, laughing and drumming the flat grass with the heels of his booted feet. Even Elizabeth joined in the laughter, forgetting her Irish martyr act for a few minutes.

Our prolonged laughing fit scared the 'lopes; they took off *en masse*, kicking up billows of acrid dust with their powerful hind legs. By the time we looked in their direction, all we saw were upraised tails flailing madly, like a cat's does when it tries to keep its balance. I recognized Penti, silly little thing, by the distinctive white daub on her tail.

Reba recognized her too. With a rare sardonic tone in her voice, she remarked, "That adolescent female's been hanging around quite often...we must interest her."

I knew what Reba meant by "We." It wasn't too long ago, just after we found our strength in the thin air of this new planet, that Reba and I had been playing Adam and Eve for real in the thicket. We'd been in there a long time, and when we finally looked around us, there was Penti watching us intently. No telling how long she'd been there. I thought it'd been funny, but Reba never saw the humor in that kind of thing.

Resting a hand on her waist, I said, "You must've been curious when you were a kid. Most of the 'lopes we see are young...Heidi, Baby Boy, Penti, Lucy, Mister...maybe the older ones know better, or just don't care. Remember the autopsy you did on the one...."

"It was dead for who knows how long when Neil entered the thicket and saw it—"

"Next to the hole they'd *dug* for it?"

Reba's cheeks colored deeply; I'd hit a nerve. She waited until the others drifted away from the circle, heading back for the ship, before saying, "We don't *know* that they'd 'dug' a grave. They bury their excrement. No proof at all they're capable of human-style burial. The size of their posterior fossa doesn't bear it out. True, their cerebellum is fairly large, but their neuron count is way too low." Reba's eyes were glistening, and her breath was coming in short sharp gasps, as she concluded, "And the evidence of possible structural thought processes was minimal, at *best*...in other words, they can't be intelligent enough to even *want* to bury their dead. Wanting would mean thinking—"

(Anger can make Reba so beautiful....)

Once more into the breech, into the breech again! Boredom led to the most pointless arguments, and boredom is something we have in ton lots. I chuckled, "What's there to think about here? 'Sides, you're using human physiological standards to judge alien mental abilities. I was there when you ran those samples through the 'scope. Neuron density seemed sufficient—"

"You just aren't seeing it!" she replied with a sudden burst of fervor. "I've *watched* them, daily. They just-don't-have-it. They haven't displayed any skills beyond those of animals. You *prove* it to me that the 'lopes have even the slightest trace of intelligence!"

I love Reba when she gets flustered. "Let's forget it," I said, pulling her closer to me.

"Don't patronize *me*, Scott Renay!" she shouted, then tore

herself away from me and dashed off toward the ship. Sighing, I went over to the nearest husk-fruited tree and pulled off another brown pod, breaking it in half with a clean jerking motion (the dry rustling sound it made seemed startlingly loud) before sucking out the pulp, letting the sticky juices splatter my uniform front. When Jimmie and Elizabeth emerged from the ship, speaking aloud, I moved closer to the hidden place where the 'lopes had been grouped, staring at the deep ruts they'd left in their wake.

Behind me, Jimmie whispered, just loud enough for me to clearly hear, "Lovebirds have another fight?"

"Do 'lopes plow up dirt when they leap?" Elizabeth asked around a slurpy mouthful of fruit pulp. "Betcha I know who the fight was about—"

"What's the matter? Never seen two redheads go head to head before?" the black-haired Irish doctor teased.

"Not 'less they're both human."

"Does he have any choice?"

"Well...Reba had a choice, when she asked him along," Jimmie replied, as the two of them continued sucking pulp out of the husks the slurping sound somehow obscene; I barely heard Elizabeth's reply over the sucking noises: "If he wasn't here, the 'slop would've held out longer...not that this stuff *isn't* good—"

It seems like she said something more to him, around her mouthful of food, but I just made out as if I hadn't heard the conversation at all, as I watched the far horizon, looking for the 'lopes, and told myself, *You two aren't the only ones who wish I was somewhere else. But don't blame me...ask the ship's biologist why I'm here. If you even need to ask...you're the readers, not me. You never had to say a word out loud.*

Not when they were capable of *thinking* the entire conversation I'd just happened to overhear to each other....

No more right now, no more writing. I hear Reba knocking on the cabin door. Time to put this journal away. I think she wants to apologize....

Day 100:

It's been long, so long; I hardly know how to use these words anymore. So long since I started this log. So much has gone on, so much. Have to pull myself out. Day 100...it's an anniversary, isn't it? Can't forget...what was it?

Day 111:

I remember now.

"Ten months is just too *long*," Reba had said to me, when we were still Earthside nearly seven months before the day our food ran out on the 'lope's planet; wrapping her arms around me, she rubbed her forehead against my chest, murmuring, "Really, Scotty, I can't face not seeing you, not being with you, for that long. The trip alone will take two months, with those jumps through hyperspace. I just don't know how I'll—"

"How you'll stand it?" I asked, finishing Reba's sentence for her, as if I were one of her kind, one of the new *übermen*, with a brain full of super-saturated neurons and sub-neurons, that tiny bit of extra structure that made her capable of esper communication. Angry, Reba walked away from me, and than threw herself onto the gold-flecked tweed couch near my apartment's only decent-sized window, her freckled face strained, and her blue eyes darkened.

Reba knew why I was still wary of going; even for an esper such as her, traveling t-space was flat out terrifying. For a non-esper like me, it would be a nightmare. T-space didn't care who you were, and it wasn't about to change to suit the psychology of a few human travelers. It was simply a universe none of us ever grew up in. Perceptions were shifted in a subtle, disturbing way. The first travelers weren't aware of what was happening as they spent solid months in t-space—they just didn't know. When they came back, their minds were gone, lost in a maze of schizophrenic misperception. Then, for ever-after, they saw blues that were not blue, heard conversations that only happened in their heads, saw into places only they could see.

Espers gained a certain immunity to the effects when they had other espers along to back them—a strength in numbers, as it were, a cushion against madness. They became the explorers of this new realm. The rest of us non-espers had to be content to follow the trails they blazed in great ships where a drugged sleep hid our minds from the dangers of consciousness.

It didn't help me that I was an astrophysicist. Not only did I have madness to fear; I knew what was waiting for me out there in t-space. Does this sound crazy now? I thought so then, and so I kept those petty fears buried. What's the point now, what's the point in hiding these things from myself? It's not like anyone will ever be able to hold this diary against me.

But just to think...quantum gravity, eleven-dimensional space, black holes...these were only curious theories back in the days when man considered interstellar voyages wistful thinking. Then those same curious theories became reality, thanks to a lot of hard work and foresighted thinking; new words for mankind's travel vocabulary came into common use—four dimensional space, graviton drives, time and space similarities, and those ubiquitous wormholes. Not that many travelers understand the inherent dangers—did frequent flyers truly understand the never-to-be-quite-overcome dangers of jet flight? Even the *Challenger* screw-up only put a temporary damper on NASA...

And who cared what happened to the drone crews of the test ships that made those first ship-sized incongruities caused by their engines-and flipped into a virtual void? Astrophysicists like me—I was one of the people who helped turn the theory of interstellar travel via wormholes *into* a reality, as part of my dissertation, in fact—cared, but we were relatively few in number, and the bulk of our work was not known to the public. All that mattered was that mankind was able to finally use wormholes as a means of getting from *here to there* with almost as much punctuality and accuracy (depending largely on angular velocity and correct alignment of gravitational vectors) as the airplane travel of my grandparent's generation.

Only, in *their* time, the aftermath of an air disaster was something easily discovered, and dealt with, no matter how horrible the remains of the aircraft, no matter how much time it might take to discover the cause of the crash. There was pain, and suffering, but there was also the promise of healing, afterwards.

The shortsighted fools, with their secret drone ships, and "acceptable margin of loss." If only they had known about the madness waiting for them out there.

Day 113:

Our new home had no name, and, as if in denial of the fact that it was in all probability to be our permanent home, no one bothered to suggest a name for it. Bad enough that the air was thin, high, *high* altitude thin, and took nearly a month to get used to. Nearly a month wasted while our bodies acclimated enough for us to venture more than ten yards away from the ship without feeling like our lungs were being crushed from within. Well, perhaps the first month wasn't a total waste; we dug up samples of the soil, picked the available flora, and tested the water. The soil was crumbly and acidic, too much so to support earth plant life without the addition of alkaline fertilizers which just weren't available to us. But the plant life was carbon based; right-handed sugars, and it didn't kill the lab rats or reptiles. With boiling, the water was drinkable.

And in that first month, we saw the 'lopes. Jimmie named them; he was the crewmember who initially found them, or was found by them, whichever one chooses to believe.

"Out...out there, in...the trees...dozens...maybe, maybe more," Jimmie had panted, as we led him into the ship after finding him lying in a gasping, sprawled heap near the hatch. The others clustered around Jimmie, heads bent toward him, shutting me out completely.

He had always struck me as over-excitable, ever since I met him. So, what if there were animals out there? Anyone with guts would have taken the time for a good observation. Disgruntled, I left the ship, walking slowly toward the dense cluster of "trees" twenty meters distant. They never noticed me leaving the ship; damned espers all wrapped up in their own heads. I walked along cautiously, hating Jimmie and Reba and all the other damned espers, feeling like the ultimate rejected too-big-to-be-graceful kid on the playground, the kid too big to even trick or treat anymore, the one shut out of every game, confidence, or *clique*. I approached the trees, my vision uncertain in the hazy sunset light of the bright umber Class K star which served as our new "sun."

But ruddy light or not, after a couple of minutes it became apparent that something was moving, just beyond the outcropping of short, meaty-fleshed trees. I made out long shapes, upright forms with thinner, lashing body parts. Tails. Beasts. Skin or short fur dappled in shades of brown, dull orange, and pale tan. Smallish heads, with huge, vaguely feline ears. Light shone through the tips of those ears, turning the skin radiant. Large slanted eyes, with the hint of vertical pupils. Short arms, in proportion to the slender elongated torsos. Thick legs, short femur, with near-human knees, merging into narrow fibula-tibia sections, which met elongated tarsals. Or whatever kind of bones they actually had; that they had bones was apparent, muscles, too. Strong, thick muscles. As I stepped closer, my chest growing tight with nervous tension, I saw the ripple of muscles under their finely furred skin.

The creatures reminded me of begging cats, dancing on their stubby metatarsals. No, meercats, stretching their spindly bodies to catch every ray from the rising sun in the cold desert dawn.

Still, they lacked feline whiskers, and the shape of the arm wasn't quite cat-like—and they had hands, not paws. Hands! Long metacarpals between carpals and the fingers—and their opposing thumbs were unmistakable.

Not animals then...but not people as *I* knew them, either. Their lack of clothing may have been intentional, but there was something about these creatures which suggested that even the thought of clothing was alien to them. The things seemed nervous, but only about my presence, not their own light-furred nakedness. I could see the rounded furry sex of the ones I figured to be males, and as I edged closer, peering through the trees, I made out a distinct furlessness and flatness on what had to be the females.

I think it was then that I noticed Penti, the one with the white patch on her tail. Not that she was Penti then, Jimmie didn't get around to bestowing names on the most distinctive of them until a week or so later—two names for each, an everyday name and a fancy name, plus the name only they knew—he'd read his T. S. Eliot! In retrospect, I suppose it was strange of me to dub the white-patched female and her kind *beautiful*, considering that I'd just laid eyes upon them only moments earlier, and knew of no standard by which to judge their appearance. But they had an appealing grace, all of them: Pentilope (she of the white daub tail) with her fancy name of Penti-Lope-Lope, little Heidi (known to Eliot and herself as Schmighty-Heidi), and Lucy (Lucy-Goosie). The oldest of the young males became Pere (Pere Ubu). Then there was Alfy (Alf-Alfred Jarry), Mister (Mister-fister), Baby Boy, Wildcat, and Slim....

The creatures' eyes were canted, with an almost Oriental tilt to them, spaced rather wide apart. Their irises ran from a muddy blend of greenish-tan to more orange hues. Their pupils were small in relation to their eyes; they seemed to float in bright pools of color, not unlike human eyes. That seemed the most shocking part of them, those too-human eyes as a part of a very alien species.

Then I realized that they were looking at *me*, their stares intense yet somehow blank, unreadable. By that time all of them were becoming agitated, leaning in to rub heads or bump long, flattened noses, all the while making a rumbling, grunting sound, talking could it be? I only half noticed them; my eyes were focused on the small daub-tailed female, as were hers on mine, like a cat and its prey, or a mongoose and a cobra.

When her pack took off in a simultaneous powerful leap up and forward, she held her stare. Just long enough for me to realize that I, too, had been closely scrutinized that afternoon, as if being studied.

"I think that one likes you, the spot-tailed one—"

I hadn't heard the others come up behind me. When Huoy spoke, I nearly screamed aloud. I think my cheek jumped; at any rate, Reba came up beside me and took my hand, saying "Sorry, Scott...didn't realize we scared you. Jimmie calls them 'lopes. After jackalopes, something he *swears* really existed—" Her voice ended on a teasing note, but Jimmie cut in from behind me, "Just because they're extinct doesn't mean they weren't—"

"Sure, Jimmie, tell us another—"

"No, no, it's true—" and then they were all laughing, sharing their private joke, and after a while, I laughed too, as I watched the horizon for long loping bodies....

Day 114:

The writing is getting easier now. This is the second lucid day I've had in a row. Don't know how long it will last. I've got to get as much written before the end comes. Before the end of consciousness drops like a heavy velvet curtain between my body and my mind....

The *Sagittarius IV* was a Class Five star transport/exploration craft, with a crew capacity of up to nine people, plus lab animals, soil and plant samples, the works. And there was no law against carrying one-way passengers for a single segment of a ship's total round trip passage. Reba wasn't even required to obtain formal permission for me to join the crew. And with Reba being Reba, she didn't bother to tell her crewmates that I was coming along for the first part of the ride until the crew assembled for takeoff.

Oh, true, none of them *openly* objected to my unexpected presence, but I wasn't blind; I saw the reflexive tensing of their neck tendons, and the quick darting eye movements which were a give away to esper communication. The commander, Neil Aaron, did feel compelled to let me in on a small fraction of the conversation; pulling me aside while the others (Reba Griffith, Elizabeth Hewson, Jimmie Beecham, and Huoy Veng) silently argued, he smiled as he told me, "We can't stop you, Mr. Renay, but the others are only thinking of the *contingencies*...should something happen during the voyage. We only have long-term provisions for five—"

Reba heard him; turning on one heel, she snapped, "Oh Neil, if *that*'s the problem he can bring his own supply of extra 'slop. But he's coming whether you like it or not. *My* guest," she finished, in a tone of voice which brooked no further argument—verbal or esper.

Day 127:

Reba crossed her arms—

Wait, where was I? Wait, look, I need to...my God. Thirteen days have gone since I last wrote; where ever did they go?

Running through the polefruit trees, 'lopes scattering every which way, tumbling on the grass when fatigue came. 'Lopes gathering around while I slept, conserving warmth and scattering like cottonseed when I stirred. I'm here in the ship now and all that seems so far away, like someone else's life. Got to get my bearings. Back then I wanted to run. Right now I want to write. Back to the beginning. It's easier to remember emotions right now. I don't think I ever finished the story of that early morning, when Reba asked me to come along on the *Sagittarius*....

Reba crossed her arms; while she stared at the spindly towers of Bismark beyond my fifteenth story window, she coaxed, "I could help you through it. I could lend you my strength in t-space and the drugs could do the rest...and it's not as if you weren't trained. You've jumped before—"

"Only on a two-week voyage—"

"But we won't be *in* hyperspace the whole time...it's those times *in-between* that will make the whole trip worth it," she finished in a pleading voice; the sound of her voice brought the memory of her voice, her touch, her smell, to my mind, my fingertips, to my tongue. Shyly, she turned her head my way, adding, "And you'll have to make the trip anyhow, Scotty...I checked your assignment before I came here. Your new job is within the same solar system; you'll be taking the same route as the *Sagittarius* for a month. *Through* hyperspace.

Reba had me there; no doubt she'd already learned that I had to report to my job at the Escondido Linear Accelerator on Harcourt's planet within six months; if I accepted her invitation to ride along on the *Sagittarius*, I'd shave a few weeks off my Earthside time, but also finish my workshop on elementary particles and their interactions a couple of weeks early. Which meant I'd have plenty of time on my hands, extra time to do the job at *my* pace, not that of my boss....

But even before I could tell Reba my answer, she began crooking her right index finger at me, inviting me to sit with her, while unfastening her tunic top with the other hand....

Day 129:

I think I'm doing better. I only lost one day this spell, and I was still dimly aware. The blackouts seem to go in cycles, a converging series of alternate mad and lucid spells. I think the convergence is the most reassuring thing of all. Yesterday's spell of madness was nothing like the fifty-seven days that passed without knowing between that day we ran out of food, and the day I began this log a second time.

As it turned out, I did go along, as *Reba*'s guest, but I never did get around to faxing an order for a month's supply of Nurtaform to my bosses at the Escondido Linear Accelerator; not that there wasn't the time to do so, but Reba insisted on hurrying me onto the ship before the others settled in, as if my long-term presence prior to lift-off would assure me future acceptance during my ride on the government-sponsored trip. At least that's what

I thought, initially; but after we'd been through the first of our hyperjumps; I got to wondering if Reba didn't want me along for the thrill of it. She could stay in esper contact with her crew-mates; mentally holding everyone's hand—while she had *me* wrapped up in her, surrounded by her enveloping soft body. Like doing something dirty under the table during a formal, tablecloths and best-china luncheon. A typical Reba trick, but God help me, I loved it. Even though I had to rely on my training to prevent my mind from crumbling under the weight of the crushing claustrophobia that ensued during a nightmare run through a wormhole, everything shifting from blue to red as we thumbed our noses at Einstein and his contemporaries.

And when we weren't making jumps (too many of them spaced too close together put a strain on the ship), Reba spent every available free moment with me, telling me about the mission—the ship would stop off at five different planets, in a total of three systems, studying each of the test planets (all close to earth-type, with similar geophysical make-up) to deter-mine how best to adapt earth-type plants and animals to them, with an eye toward future human colonization. "Something like Johnny Appleseed," Reba had gushed on the morning of the day that everything went wrong, "only instead of apple seeds we'll be leaving seedlings of dozens of kinds of foodstuffs, and also leave behind pairs of small animals—"

"We don't qualify?" I asked her with a straight face; Reba and I were both under five foot five, and redheaded, with freckles. One of our professors at the university used to call us the Bobbsey Twins, whoever *they* were. (The professor *was* old; he remembered a childhood when television was almost non-existent....)

Reba started to punch me lightly on the forearm, saying, "You non-espers are *all* alike—" when the ship shuddered, and the pseudo-gravity a shade over half that of earth's under the best of conditions became non-gravity. Luckily, Reba and I were still dressed; we lurched out of my cabin and into the circular hallway, alternately grabbing and releasing the flap-like hand-

holds positioned around the walls for times of weightlessness—
a few times I almost missed grabbing the next hand-hold, and
almost went spinning off into the air.

The others were likewise making their way to the centrally
located navigation hub, launching with their hands to keep from
hitting the walls, bypassing the flaps all together, in their haste
to discover the source of the problem.

What was so eerie for me was that no one spoke; all I saw
were wrinkled brows and darting eyes. I asked Reba what was
wrong; she only shook her head as she propelled herself into
the control area. After a few seconds, as I watched Neil and
his navigator Jimmie (he was a double-duty crewman) franti-
cally—albeit silently—trying to regain manual control of the
engines, I noticed something so obvious apparently no one had
seen it, something very wrong—the engine console was dark.
Then, the first sound I'd heard since the ship lost gravity:

"I think...we came too close to something." That was Neil,
his voice tight and strained. Immediately, Jimmie countered
from behind his controls, "No way...structure probably gave
way enough for the engines to disconnect, 'sides, the alarms
didn't go off—"

"I believe Neil may be right...." Elizabeth's voice trailed off
ominously, her brogue a lilting whisper of doom as she keyed
up the rear viewer. "Alarm or no alarms, there's the evidence."
We floated toward her, hair and arms waving gently in the non-
gravity, as we took a look at what she'd keyed up: The strangely
enveloping blackness of hyperspace was gone. And in its place,
the normality of a sky filled with a thick dusting of stars—and
the startling strangeness of a rapidly receding, dangerous pure
black spot blotting out the stars to the rear.

"What is it, Elizabeth?" Reba whispered.

"Look in the viewer," she replied, her lips brushing against
the dark hair swimming slowly in front of her face, "The gravitational vectors...." I now realized what she was implying, but
it was almost inconceivable, so slight was the possibility of
coming so close to the gravitational field of a super-dense star.

I spoke through lips almost glued shut with fear, "Our vectors must've grazed a black hole, knocking us into normal space-time." All of us must've realized that the collision avoidance system didn't have the range to avoid those freak fields—the simplest of classical mechanics made it so. The gravitational pull increased only as the mass of the star, but its strength fell off as the square of the distance. The result was a gravitational vector that shot up frighteningly fast. By the time the system had time to react, vectors had already collapsed our field.

My legs were shaking in mid-float. If only we'd passed a little closer to the black hole, if only we'd lost a little more velocity, it would've already swallowed us, and we wouldn't be having this conversation.

"It's impossible," Huoy frowned, "The chances of passing something like that in all this emptiness...."

"You fool!" Elizabeth hissed, "Look at the *screen*, woman! Improbable doesn't mean 'impossible'—there it *is*."

"Look, let's check out what we can, all right?" I asked, hoping to avoid one of those eye-bulging, throat-straining esper fights; apparently, the others were anxious to avoid one too, for we broke into teams, and began looking for every possible reason for the engines to have failed, starting with the in-ship circuits, and finally finishing with my offer to suit up and help Jimmie check the engines from outside the ship.

But what we found out there made me immediately regret my efforts to prevent Huoy and Elizabeth from engaging in another esper-argument...and for once, I didn't mind being the odd-man out when Jimmie opted not to say anything as we neared the ship's engine...and saw that the field antennae, the gravitation generators, conversion units and the radioactive ports were gone. Sliced clean off the ship, as if God himself had just reached out and snatched them off, leaving a void in the ship's warp drive nacelles.

The only sound I could hear over the two-way radio connecting Jimmie and myself was his sob-like breathing, each breath coming in a painful hitch, only to be expelled in a mournful rush of air....

And because Jimmie's esper abilities linked him with his fellow crewmen, he felt no need to speak to me, either...as it was, I had to humble myself and ask Neil what he thought might have happened once Jimmie and I re-entered the ship...not that I hadn't had the time to consider the options myself. But actually *hearing* them from Neil's lips did give me some small measure of cold comfort:

"I think in-homogeneities in the collapsing graviton field took our engines, or most of 'em, I guess. The theory predicted it could happen, but it's never been done, as far as I know. But then, I suppose the test engineers didn't have enough black holes nearby to test those particular conditions, did they?" I appreciated his slight attempt at humor, even if some of the others frowned. He went on, "In normal gravitational gradients, fields have always dropped evenly when the power was cut...but as far as we're concerned, at least we have considerable normal velocity left in the sub-light engines from the hole encounter. Jimmie—" he turned to look over at the still-shaken navigator, "Is there any way to determine where we *are*?"

Biting his lower lip, until the pinkish flesh turned almost red, Jimmie shook his head, before answering, "No way, Neil... can't even raise a signal on the network. Could be anywhere or anywhen...with no way to find out for sure. Nothing looks familiar on the star-charts and considering that we've lost most of the engines, there's no way we can try getting our bearings by changing course...might as well let 'er stay on this course, see what we drift into—"

The navigator said more, to both Neil and the others, but it was a silent conversation...and even Reba was too distracted to fill me in on things.

And even after tasks were delegated, distress signals sent out, stock taken of our remaining rations, and the like, Reba still found herself unable to share the mutual horror she and her fellow espers had experienced after the accident—thus leaving me to wallow in *my* own unexpressed fear.

Day 136:

Been a long time, where have I been? Can't think straight, like gun-cotton stuffed in my head ready to explode if I think. What am I supposed to be *doing* here? Writing, yeah, I'm doing that. But writing *what*?

All I can remember now are the last days—how many? It hurts to think. Wandering in the rain, yeah, looking for shelter. Many images, feelings, just emotions. Scared I wouldn't find a safe place to rest. Wandering along looking for something, anything alive. I found and I lost the 'lopes, or they lost me. I don't know if they like me....

I remember finding a 'loper nest, empty, but the signs of habitation were unmistakable...as was their scent. During the lucid (or what passed for lucid) times, when I wasn't smelling phantom odors which originated in my brain, I realized that the 'lopes, especially the females—had a piquant, musky odor not unlike the husk fruits on which they constantly dined.

I'd previously dismissed the slight rises in the ground, tiny hillocks, as simply part of the environment, until I was walking past one and simultaneously saw and smelled something. There was a hole leading into the hillock, shored up with stones placed so artfully, in so ostensibly a careless pattern, that a casual glance might not reveal anything but a tumbling of stones near a dark spot on a hillock. But I saw how light shone partway into the hole, revealing depth. And the smell of the female 'lopes was strong, almost cloying in its richness. No wonder I never found a sleeping 'lope. They never slept above ground.

Curious, not wanting to simply barge in should there be some trap set—the 'lopes had reason to fear me, since some of my kind stole their dead—I climbed the hillock, searching for an air-hole. That, too, was artfully constructed as to appear *un*constructed. Just an irregular hole in the Earth, shadowed by a tuber tree and artless tumbles of loose pebbles. But it was a deliberate hole, nonetheless. I stretched prone, my ear to the hole. No sound. I looked in, but there was no light visible...not until the sun set a little more, sending a narrow beam into the hole at the base of the hillock. *There*. Packed dirt, and a barely visible rough bed of dried and matted-down limp-grass.

My desperation got the best of my fears and I crawled inside the dry, debris-lined chamber and fell asleep on the soft floor. I woke up once or twice; thinking Reba was in there with me, warming herself at my side, her wet clothes strewn about us. I don't think she really was. I seem to remember, Reba's dead....

Day 139:

Things are going better today! The headache is nearly gone! Well, not *gone*, but at least subsided to the point that I can ignore it. I'm still getting those extra twinges I think. But I'd better take advantage of this time to think of the harder, intellectual things I still need to get down....

By the end of our third month on the planet of the burnt-umber sun and the pulp-fruit trees, we were all more active; our lungs now used to the thin air. And our potbellies vanished, as we explored our new, albeit reluctant, home. Aside from some cooler areas to the north, where the dull tan-green flat-grass grew stubby and coarse, and the tuber trees were stunted, and a slightly warmer band along the middle that Neil guessed was the equator, the 'lope's planet was remarkably uniform. Irregular ponds—home of the only other native life-form we found—creatures we dubbed "crushers," which were easily as big as ancient double-decker busses, and vaguely resembled earth rhinos—and a few languid rivulets...but no oceans. Just lots of arid land, and pulpy trees that drew deeply on the hidden groundwater. Occasional warm rains and weak winds. And every damned seed or sprouting plant Reba and Huoy planted withered and drooped, finally curling into themselves in dry spirals of death.

It didn't help to mix fertilizers (including human waste) with the plant's soil; it simply couldn't sustain the samples which were brought along on the ship, right-handed sugars or not. And as every sample died, a little bit of hope died in each of us. Reba said that she and the espers felt it worst; the pain of one was the pain of all. It didn't faze her that *my* anguish was un-shareable, private. The only bright spot was that none of the lab animals died when they were fed little bits of the indigenous plant life. I don't know if it was in the back of the minds of the others, but I know that I often thought about the inevitable—what will we do when our food is gone?

I suppose it might've been magical thinking on the part of the others: If we don't make ourselves too much at home, this will never *be* home. Surely the loss of the ship had been noticed. *I* certainly didn't show up on Harcourt's Planet on time. And even though radio messages had been sent out, there was no guarantee that they'd be received in time to save us—if whoever received them could find us at all. It's a *damned* big universe....

But even though Reba and her crewmates were trained scientists, it was pathetic how they whimpered like children when we found ourselves opening up the last box of spacer 'slop. Perhaps their distress was sensed by the 'lopers, and that was why they massed in the trees that afternoon. To watch us, and maybe wonder at us. Not much else brought them all so close to us, in such numbers; in all the months we'd been here, none of us had found the places where they slept. No 'loper villages, no 'loper buildings. Just buried 'lope dung, and discarded husks close to the trunks of the fruit trees.

Once we started eating their food, though, the 'lopers made themselves less scarce; seeing one or two of them each hour wasn't uncommon. As always, they kept a screen of foliage between themselves and us, not enough to actually hide behind, but something *there*, nonetheless. For Reba, the 'lopes weren't hidden enough.

A few days after we began eating husk-fruit, and the bulbous, pale yellow things that resembled apples but tasted more like a blend of carob and mushrooms (morels, to be precise), with a hint of bitter coffee thrown in, Reba and I were walking down the gentle slope that led away from the ship down to the pond. When we arrived, Reba edged into the scummy water; her feet and legs were submerged to the middle of her calves. I moved closer, my feet sucking mud with each labored step. I almost had my hand on her arm when she began moaning, and dropped to her knees in the tangle of limp-vines and mucky water. Her face crumpled, the freckles darkening and clumping together, and her eyes were scrunched tight, as if even this diffuse light hurt them.

And when I came closer, I could see the trigeminal artery in her left temple throbbing, a delicate pulsing under the fine skin. *Migraine*, I thought, bending over and almost losing my footing in the muddy waters as I scooped her up and carried her away from the pond. But before I turned around, and faced away from the pond, I caught a glimpse of Heidi and Baby Boy—they were watching us intently, no longer moving and grunting, as if what I was doing was terribly important—

Or Reba's illness was.

Reba vomited on me as I carried her back to the ship; the sight, and the sickly-sweet odor sickened me, made me dizzy, but I kept on walking. The others were waiting for us, and I noticed that Huoy was holding her head, eyes half shut, and her skin even paler than usual. None of them looked very good. When Jimmie came forward to take Reba from me, I noticed that his hands were icy. Migraines, classic ones...and when I entered the ship, the dull white lights made my eyes burn and throb, but the pain was still bearable....

For once, the esper crew of the *Sagittarius IV* was too sick to indulge in esper-speak; I heard their stories of sudden pain and blinding insensitivity to sounds and light first hand:

"It came so fast...then I sicked up on everything, right on the scope—"

"Something...anything...please cut my head off, *anything*—"

"Just want to crawl where it's dark—"

"Scott, what happened? All of a sudden I felt so...oh not *again*—"

"Oh, jeezus, what's that *smell*! I—I can *see* it—"

Elizabeth was having olfactory hallucinations; Neil held onto her while she tried to savagely paw at her face with her long-nailed fingers. Huoy had her fingers on either side of her head, covering the branches of her trigeminal nerves, as she gasped, "Classic migraine. Need...vasoconstrictors...now. Hurry, Scott...make...useful...." right before she collapsed, her left arm and leg twitching spasmodically. Neil fell after that, a heap of limp flesh, then Jimmie, and Reba, and finally Elizabeth, and I remember heading for the storeroom where the unneeded medical supplies were kept, but I don't remember falling down on the floor, even though that's where I woke up hours later....

I came to experiencing simultaneous hunger pangs and dizziness; by my watch, it took me a good five minutes to get to my feet and stand upright, for the hallway kept looping and un-looping, now curled tightly, now infinitely straight. And sometimes the voices of the crew were loud, clear, while other times they'd fade into echoing dimness. But I made it to where I'd left them. The others hadn't had the strength to make it out of the entry dock; they lay next to puddles of their own pulpy vomit, unable to crawl away from the mess and the stink. Reba opened her eyes first, and tried to reach for my leg, but kept missing, as if I had a third, invisible leg that stood next to my left one. Hallucinations, persistent ones, for when I bent down to grasp her cold hand in mine, Reba's eyes widened and she ducked her head, as if unable to look at me.

Pulling her to her feet, then looping her vomit-encrusted uniform arm around my shoulder, I led her to the supply room, where I lay her down on a plastiform case, and began pawing through the color-coded boxes, looking for codeine, steroids, vasoconstrictors, even plain old aspirin, anything to ease her pain. Reba kept moaning, and her entire body shook with fine tremors, as I began to look for some pneumatic syringes to inject the codeine I'd just found.

"Scotty...so sick...so *siiick*—"

"Not in here, okay?" I asked weakly, as the lights haloed

around the box I was looking in (damn those multipurpose storage containers and their hard-to-differentiate colors!), creating rings of rainbows around the pastel plastic. Reba slumped forward, feet first, until she almost slid off the plastiform case onto the floor, making gagging sounds deep in her throat. I caught her by the armpits before she landed on the floor, and dragged her up into a sitting position again. Tearing off her uniform sleeve at the shoulder, I fed the codeine insert into the syringe, and worked the handle of the syringe against her arm.

It took another five minutes, but Reba was finally able to sit up unassisted, and within ten minutes, I was able to walk her down the curving hallway, codeine inserts and pneumosyringe in hand, to where the others lay incapacitated....

Day 168:

It's been a long time—
Just like before, the last long blackout. Thinking hurts so much now—bombs going off in my head. But I have to write. Helps me focus. Helps me—

Day 169:

Write about emotions. I can do that at least. Emotions. Write about the last days before the blackout. I can remember parts of those days, dimly glowing patterns of a campfire, like I remember instincts, like the way your eye holds the after-image of a campfire.

I remember the woods. No, further back. I remember loneliness, wishing, crying out for someone, anyone. Huoy. Jimmie. Reba!

Our lab held a collection of cobbled together genetic engineering equipment, from those days so long ago when Reba was trying so hard to find out what was hurting us. I began the tests again in those days of lucidity, searching madly for something, anything that would kill off the virus. Something that would stop the pain, stop the blackouts, *anything*. What happened next? The transition is hard to recall, like in a dream. You're walking down the street one night in a dream when suddenly you realize the street is a river. It was like that. The next I recall, I was engaged in some project to create my own companion.

Somehow I was going to try and alter the chromosomes of my own tissue, changing my XY chromosomes, but I didn't really know how. Could I split the chromosome into its autosomes and duplicate just the x-half? I didn't know how.

In this dream of mine I thought, no, *knew* that I only had to get other chromosome samples. Would it matter that they weren't human? Still hard to think, I'm not sure. Well, Jimmie and Reba had killed off the lab animals, so I had nothing with which to test out my theory. Catching a 'lope was beyond me; I never knew when a blackout would overtake me. But if I could somehow manage to get a hold of a sample of crusher flesh, just a tiny piece...

It was pure madness on my part to think that I could saunter up to a crusher and casually slice off a sample of living tissue; but living day after day with an A-bomb going off and off again in one's skull doesn't make for a healthy state of mind, or rational, coherent thinking. Hell, maybe I was trying to impress the 'lopes, show them who was the superior specimen on this planet. But I didn't *really* need them, I'd make my own society...all I clearly remember is that the sun was looking like a moldy hard-boiled egg in the sky, all soft and mossy-green and luminescent, as the scummy pond waters scintillated underfoot, divided into sparkling waves by the limp-vines, and the crusher wasn't all *that* big or awful-looking, why its horns were just tiny *needles*—

The sharp *splash* of something fast-thrown and heavy hitting the water brought me back to a semblance of painful reality. I'd waded out into the middle of the pond, up to my armpits, with my extended toes barely touching the muddy bottom—and there was a crusher no more than a foot away from me, head down, twin horns aimed for my skinny, pale-skinned chest, only when the second splash occurred, the crusher turned its head away from me, to stare at the ripples in the murky water.

Before the third splash, I heard a keening mewl, one I'd never heard a 'lope utter before, with the sound coming from behind me. I turned my head and upper body to look in that direction...and saw Penti, standing there on the limp-vines, making a gesture I'd seen before, in a slightly different social context:

Get over here, or near as dammit...

I *went,* dog-paddling through the turgid water, until her brown-toed feet were within arm's reach, while she kept throwing stones into the water, until the crusher forgot about me and glided over to the opposite side of the pond, ripping up great mouthfuls of limp-vines with thunderous churnings of water.

Pulling myself weakly through the mud, I crawled to Penti's feet. Without thinking, I wrapped my right arm around her ankles and slumped into the mud.

Grunting, I got to my feet and began shambling. I walked aimlessly, without thought, like a masterless puppet. The crazed notion of remaking the human race for my own benefit was gone. I don't know how long I went, before my consciousness raised itself again, and I found myself on the ship. I looked around myself to get my bearings. Behind me stood Penti, in the hatch none of her kind had breached before, even when left open in invitation. I turned away, and she followed.

Penti let out a yelp when a dangling handgrip smacked her in the head (I avoided them almost unconsciously), but remained silent as I led her on a tour of the ship, jabbering all the while. I don't recall what I said, and I rarely looked back to see if she still followed.

I do remember a feeling of foolish futility registering in my aching brain. Why was I talking to this animal, this alien who had no way of understanding my words? I stopped talking. And when I turned around, Penti-Lope-Lope had gone.

Day 171:

Yesterday I kept my consciousness, but I didn't write. I didn't think, I didn't analyze, I didn't plan. I simply *was*—a conscious *was*, like in battle or stress, where you simply do what you need to and you don't know what you're doing or know what you're feeling. But you make no choices. But today I need to work; I must write while I can.

Yeah, I left off after the first attack, just about two weeks after we started eating the native food. The remembrance hurts. Oh, it hurts! Reba! As I think of the past, my head begins to ache again, like before. Wait a minute....

It's beginning to recede. The vasoconstrictors I took are kicking in now. There aren't many pills left these days. Where was I?

We were scrambling madly, to find what disease suddenly ailed us. Reba could only work the 'scope if she held her hand over her right eye, the one which hurt her the most, but I helped her prep the sample for the electron 'scope in the ship's lab. I was the only person lucid enough to kill one of the lab rats, without trying to end the life of a phantom rat standing off to one side....

I half-suspected what Reba was looking for, but I didn't ask her any questions; I simply did as she asked, following her terse, pain-punctuated orders:

"Tubers...husk fruits...fat fruits...sam-samples...flat-grass...limp-vines...'lope if you can find one...no, no, forget it...dirt, bring dirt. Anything...and samples. Of the crew...blood. Everyone, blood—"

I almost blacked out near the pond—one of the 'lopes, I was too sick to tell who it was, was watching me in my agonies—but I found Reba's samples. And I stood behind her, exposing the sample slides to ever-increasing magnification in millimeters, until:

"Finally...thought it was a virus...wrong...so *stupid*," and she tried to pull her reddish curls in anger before I stayed her trembling icy hand.

It was a prion. Pleated, sticky sheets of deviant protein that had managed to change the proteins of every damn thing on the planet-foodstuffs, dirt, water. Almost invulnerable to enzymes, unlike normal proteins. And, inevitably fatal to whatever cells it invaded.

When our lab animals were exposed to foodstuffs contaminated by the prions, they initially showed no symptoms, but their autopsies revealed the damage wrought by the invading prions. These prions acted much like the Earth ones that contributed to the 1990s mad cow epidemic in Britain—once they were introduced via foodstuffs, the host animal was infected—with a slight difference: These rogue proteins, aberrations of a harmless protein usually found on the surface of mammalian cells (including brain cells), replicated at a somewhat slower pace than Earth-prions. Which meant, in turn, that we'd been unknowingly ingesting more and more prions, while they slowly migrated to our temporal arteries...and then began their work.

It took Reba over a week to learn all of this; a week of drinking only water, a week spent dizzy and cold-handed (even biofeedback, using temperature sensors attached to her fingertips didn't help)...a week in which she obtained her first human for dissection.

I was the one who found Huoy. She'd broken into Elizabeth's previous collection of antique surgical instruments, the ones Elizabeth couldn't bear to leave behind, for fear of theft or mishandling back Earthside. Her great-great-great-grandfather had been a brain surgeon; those instruments had been purchased by him when the first wave of truly sophisticated lasers came into widespread use, and they'd been passed down from surgeon father to gynecologist daughter to osteopath son to....

And Huoy had used them to kill herself. She left a note, little more than a polite memo. She blamed herself for not preventing this, seeing that she'd predicted that the food was bad. I don't know how she did it without anesthesia, but she'd tried to laser out the pain, the pain she'd somehow perceived as being *inside* her brain. Perhaps burning through her cheeks with the hand-held laser, until her face was as richly veined as a budding leaf had not dulled her pain, or the agony had entered her mind by then. Once she'd eliminated the trigeminal nerves and sections of the temporal artery, she'd picked up Elizabeth's ancient but effective Smith-Peterson power drill, once used to drill burr holes in bone, and...and then she'd picked up the CO_2 laser once more, somehow managed to rig the power supply to up the wattage, set the impact zone to wide dispersion, and then pointed that pair of carbon dioxide and helium lasers into her exposed brain....

The autopsy showed Huoy's neurons clogged with prions. By that time, Reba was a wraith; deprived of even infected food, her stores of fat went quickly, faster than even I'd dreamed possible. And when she discovered, with my help when it came to reading the 'scope—her vision was filled with hallucinations she haltingly referred to as "exploding floaters"—that the alien prions bound up neurotransmitters (an enzyme) that only intelligent beings have. So, while the prions infected all living things that ingested them via foodstuffs, non-intelligent beings were least affected.

And, as the neurotransmitters were affected in each of us, we developed the crippling headaches...and the espers lost their ability to communicate. Which equaled the loss of self, an esper removed from esper contact was suddenly less than half a person, a more-than-emotional cripple. Cut off from their word-less communication, they lost their souls. And as the disease progressed in the others, and they lost esper contact with their fellows—which had apparently happened to Huoy, since no one knew what she was planning—it was worse for them than enduring the head pains. *I* had the migraines, too, which meant it was a shared thing, but losing their advantage over me was unthinkable, even for Reba....

Within the next week or so—by then, my blackouts came more frequently, and I lost track of time, since black-out prone

Reba was no help when it came to figuring out how long I'd been out—we had another subject for the laser-scalpel. Elizabeth, having had her most obvious method of suicide deprived her by Huoy, chose an end worthy of Sir Walter Scott, or Shakespeare's mad Ophelia. Jimmie and Neil discovered her floating in the same pond where Reba first took sick; that they hadn't sensed what she was about to do pained both of them most.

I think that's what made Neil pack it in, impaled himself on that crusher's horns. None of us knew whether he'd thrown himself at the crusher, or it had charged him. It didn't matter....

And Jimmie never smiled anymore; never tried to move past his own agony to brighten our days anymore, as he'd attempted to do in the previous few weeks. He helped Reba and me in the lab, and backed me up in convincing Reba that trying to capture a crusher, and killing it was no good, that it was impossible to try. The thing's hide was too thick, its horns too deadly.

I remember him telling Reba, his voice distorted by the mixture of steroids and codeine he'd injected himself with on his own. "What good is it, Reba? They eat limp-vines; the limp-vines are full of prions. It's a given—"

"'Lopes," Reba slurred, her head lolling in an aimless pattern, "Why not...the 'lopes?"

"Killing them would only be cruel," I began, but Reba tried to shake her head, mumbling, "'ozen brain...dead 'lope—"

"We did slides on what was left—remember the prions in there? You'd missed it earlier, but—"

Reba shook her head again; for the first time, I noticed that her eyes looked like dry spheres of discolored bone, set in nets of wrinkled mesh, and I remembered Elizabeth's comment about the brown leathery heart—

"Noooo...why not the *pain*! Their brain...like ours. Nerves... the 'lope had...something like trigeminal nerve...why not this pain?"

The look on Reba's face told me that admitting that the 'lopes she hated were like us, intelligent beings who might have been our near equals, was too much for her overstressed mind to handle. I was able to calm her more than I could've hoped for, stroking her matted hair and repeating the joke I made when she first lost her esper ability, saying, "Now we're alike, babe...no more brain-juice getting in the way."

She smiled weakly. "Now we're going to be like the 'lopers, aren't we?" She slumped over from the effort of talking so much.

The way I felt then, it wouldn't have been so bad to be a 'lope, not so bad at all. No pain, anguish or jealousy, just primitive animal thoughts and a simple animal life. 'Lopes consumed husk-fruit and the yellow bitter-fruit without the slightest evidence of discomfort even though creatures with such brain capacity should've had headaches. The three of us doubted that the 'lopes had simply learned to live with the pain; after however many weeks we'd been ill, we'd yet to accustom ourselves to the cold hands, the tremors, the hypersensitivity to sound, light and odors, and never mind the pain—nor were they plagued with the hallucinations which affected our own ability to function (watching walls melt into writhing puddles, or seeing the sky flame with rotating patterns that defied geometry, symmetry, or logic...).

Reba stirred then, and asked to be carried to our room. After I'd laid her gently on the bed, I asked if she was all right, and volunteered to stay. She smiled again, and said no, she'd be fine.

Reba was lying, and how could I be so stupid not to see? I woke three hours later in the corridor nearby, and I remembered a particularly bad attack, my leg and arm growing numb on the left side, suddenly collapsing in a senseless heap.

Reba...Reba had ended it all. Put the CO_2 laser to use again, bypassing the temporal artery, which hadn't stopped throbbing on her temple for weeks, and going straight for the jugular— Better not to write of this, to let my poor Reba keep as much dignity as she could have. Oh, it hurts! The thinking is so easy for these strong emotions, but oh, Reba....

When I stumbled into the lab an hour later, the flood level of my grief subsided from a hurricane-shipped frenzy to a churning flood. I saw...I saw her blood, lacework on the walls, the floor, even on the ceiling of the lab, dried to a black-red starchy stiffness, like a bloody mantilla. I never learned when she did it, or even if she'd done it alone or with Jimmie's help; he was too engaged in his work over her when I came to and dragged myself into the lab. He'd already shorn off most of her limp red curls, and had her skull open, exposed to the grey cerebellum and the cranial nerves, five through twelve...the ones which controlled facial sensation, eye movement, taste, balance, hearing, swallowing, involuntary muscles of the heart, stomach, chest and intestines—as he proudly began to explain in that steroid-thickened voice, as I swayed in place next to the table, with her glistening brain exposed, *naked*, in front of me, until I noticed that her scalp had bled freely where he'd sliced it open....

I wondered when she'd grabbed the laser from him, how she'd slit her own throat with most of her head opened like that, before I placed my hand on the laser console and surreptitiously upped the wattage from one to eighty...before I snatched the small hand-held laser from Jimmie and—

His blood slid down his brown skin like sap pouring down rough bark. He didn't fight me; whether *he* knew he'd done wrong or not was immaterial. Death by his own hand may've been too abhorrent a prospect—better to whip me into a frenzy, let me do it.

When a CO_2 laser slices through flesh, it leaves a delicate smoking line...a most scientific way to describe something that resembles the devil's own handwriting. And, God help me, I wrote every word of fury I knew on his body, not stopping until the wounds quit bleeding freely when drawn on his skin....

Spent, panting, my head feeling as if it was cracking from within from rage, not just pain, I dropped the laser wand, and— it crushed easily under my booted foot—

I...no more of this. No more.

Day 172:

Here I am once again. Two days of clarity now. I must finish this soon. Soon....

Jimmie was dead. Reba was dead. Huoy, Elizabeth, Neil. Everyone except me. And all I felt was a rage, a hot rage quickly turning into frosty anger that felt as though it would always be with me.

Jimmie had *killed* Reba. Sure, it looked as though she'd done it to herself; maybe she had made that final jugular swipe with the laser, but it couldn't *be*. Reba wouldn't initiate anything like that, no matter what pain she had to endure. No, it was Jimmie. It had to be him. Please, it had to be him....

I kicked pieces of the smashed laser away then knelt down at Jimmie's side, when my attention was caught by a set of curious, semi-healed scars on one of his forearms, intentional-seeming marks which ran from wrist to just above the elbow. The last of my rage cooled to whiteness, and I looked closer for a moment.

As I traced the pale scars against his dark flesh, I remembered how Jimmie had blacked out once when he was outside of the ship; he hadn't come back for over a day. Reba had been alive then, but not the others. In fact, Jimmie had been outside in order to bury Neil. (Despite Neil's loss of weight, his body was still too big for me to handle...) It had been long enough ago for the scars to just about heal, though. I wondered if Jimmie had fallen against something, raked his flesh that way, but none of the plants were spiny, and no one could fall on the flat-grass in such a way that it would pierce skin. But the 'lopes...their hands and feet ended in nails—nails perhaps sharp enough to rake skin.

But the 'lopes were peaceful, ostensibly harmless...yet, if they weren't, now *I* would be fair game, especially in my dazed condition. I never knew when the numbness in my limbs would strike, nor could I predict the severity of my headaches, but I had to go outside. My food, blighted and tainted as it was, was out there. Plus my water, and sunlight. And the soil to bury my companions in.

I dragged Jimmie to the hatch first, left him in a red-scored heap, then went back to get Reba. I scooped up what shorn hair I could find and taped it to her head, wrapping the sticky whiteness around her skull like a headband. But I didn't open her torso to see if her heart was brown or not. She was lucky if she weighed fifty pounds.

If that. But realizing that brought back my anger and rage, and I began to mutter, "*No*," my voice hollow in the viscera-latticed lab. "Nuts....Jimmie was nuts...loco...clawed himself... like coke bugs...tried to get them out...killed Reba...dug up his own skin...yes...crazy black *bastard*, Reba, *why*? Should've said no, leave you alone...sorry, Reeb, let you down...nuts, left you with a *crazy*...my fault...oh jeezus, Reba, didn't you *know*?"

I folded her bloodied form in my arms and staggered out of the lab, down the corridor toward the open spaces, the open spaces where I could bury her. My head spun from the effort, but I pressed onwards....

After returning to the hatch, I kicked Jimmie's body out until my boots were red-sticky. He rolled with a flat, peculiar motion, a flip and then nothing until I kicked him again. Heaving him out of the ship occupied most of my attention; I didn't realize that the ship was surrounded by 'lopes until I heard them kicking off, and smelled the acrid dust left in their wake. But when I was outside the ship, far enough away to see the exposed hull, I realized that the 'lopes had been busy indeed...and that they'd been the ones who scarred Jimmie. For in marks a foot high, reddish mud daubs—identical to the small ones on Jimmie's arm—read:

The 'lopes respected my mourning period. I didn't see them for a week, maybe more—damn blackouts—during the time after I buried Jimmie and Reba, and when they did make themselves visible, it was at a distance tempered by respect, or so I chose to think.

I needed to think of the 'lopes as being capable of respect, consideration...anything to dispel the thought that I was the last thinking being left on this planet. Only then did I realize why Huoy and Elizabeth and (maybe) Neil had done what they did to themselves. Having been born a non-esper, never having known the deep communication of the esper community, the closeness Reba could only describe it to me second-hand by saying, "It's like...the glove being *part* of the hand, not just protecting it, but *being* it, but shit, Scotty, that's only the *surface* of it...."

I hadn't realized it, but Reba, Huoy, Neil, Jimmie, and Elizabeth were the fingers of my glove. We weren't all that close but they still protected me from this place, shielded me from having to think too much about my situation, our situation. Lost. Stranded. For *good*. No other people. No *hope*, no Goddamned frigging hope at all. And the food made us, made *me* sick.

But I had no choice; it was either eat the food and be sick, or not eat the food and be sick *and* devouring myself muscle by muscle. I thought about the brown heart a lot, and Reba's pitiful bare, bloody scalp. With the curls pasted on, with gummy drying blood and surgical tape. One of the last things I remember her telling me, before I blacked out for that fatal time, was, "Don't blame the...others. Don't know...can't em-empathize, Scotty—"

And the ironic thing was, I couldn't blame the others anymore, even though they'd stranded me more thoroughly than I'd been stranded, in all my isolated-by-virtue-by-birth time here. I mean, I'd been alone all along here in a sense, by virtue of being a non-esper, by lacking those killer sub-neurons, but that was a different aloneness. I was alone, with *company*.

But once I found myself truly, *utterly* alone, with no one to hate or envy or love, I realized what had driven Huoy to drill those holes in her skull, or what had compelled Elizabeth to dive into the scummy depths, never to surface alive. To be a sudden captive in one's own mind, without the succor of one's fellow espers, had to have been as profound a shock as my reluctant monopoly of the planet was later on. But yet...they'd had me, at least. And to know that my presence wasn't enough to cut it against the loss of their precious, elitist esper capabilities, even though I could at least try and share their anguish, their aloneness...well, once I got over the initial shock and hurt over their deaths, I got to thinking, *You selfish, childish boors...for people who supposedly shared so much, you couldn't share the fact that I needed you too.*

Around that time, I stopped visiting their graves each day, quit laying symbolic bunches of dried-out limp-vines on Reba's mound next to the fruit-bearing tuber trees whose fruit she'd sampled first. *Damn you all*, my mind pouted, between throbs of limb-twitching pain. They didn't need me, I didn't need them. Tit for tat, all that childish nonsense we repeat when the hurt runs too deep for adult rationalization.

I scoured the lab and the storage compartments, looking for the gene-splicing equipment Reba had once told me was secreted somewhere on the ship, the equipment no one had had reason to use after the crash. For when I wasn't gripped by migraines, in those times between the pain when my body dared to relax, to *hope*, before being assaulted once again, I'd hatched a plan. Reba said there was simple cloning equipment, suitable for small-scale flora and fauna projects. But if I cobbled here and jury-rigged there, there was a chance I could make it work with my own tissue, to grow my own company. I didn't even care if they grew up mutated, or deformed. I needed company, beings like myself, to talk to, rant at, rule and hurt like *I'd* been hurt...and what better whipping boy than one's own self?—

Once I found the equipment, plus the odds and ends I'd need to adapt the splicer and other things to fill my needs, I decided to lay in a store of food, so I could work non-stop until the equipment had been modified. The husk-fruit in particular didn't spoil once picked, not for days....

A light rain had washed off most of the odd symbols the 'lopes had painted on the ship; symbols that matched the ones that scarred Jimmie's arm. As I gathered fruit into an empty storage container, I cursed myself for not encouraging the 'lopes to write again. *Should've written something of my own, tried to establish a rapport. Something. Anything. Encourage the fuzzy buggers.* Jimmie had been too sick to notice what they'd done to him, as he lay comatose outdoors, and I'd been too wrapped up in self-pity to bother with them....

Setting my nearly full container of husk-fruit on the almost bare ground, I decided to gather a handful of pond mud, try my hand at communication. Not that they'd understand, but they'd see that I, too, could manipulate symbols, that we were at least trying to move in the same direction. I made it down to the pond all right, minimal dizziness, only mild haloes of wavering multi-hued light danced around the sun-dappled limp-vines, so when I awoke covered in cold mud, I wasn't just shocked—I was furious; at the prions, at myself for trying to do something as silly as communicating with long-tailed *creatures*, at the planet itself—

Turning my head gingerly, slightly, against the stabbing pain, I saw a pair of wet-furred feet next to my head. Looking up, I saw Penti-Lope-Lope staring down at me, her oval black pupils narrowed and small against slanted amber-orange backgrounds. She was scrutinizing me, her softly furred face unreadable. I'd never been this close to a breathing 'lope before. I now saw that what we'd all called fur was actually a thick, even covering of body hair, not too unlike my own. Downy hair, less than a quarter of an inch in length, with variations in color much like the differences in human hair color—

As I struggled to rise, my hand brushed Penti's leg. She started, but held her ground. Instead of running, she hunkered down—her spine curved in a huge "C" as she bent her head my way—and patted my face with one hairy hand. Or at least the upper surface of her hand was hairy; the palm was smooth and slippery, the flesh dry and warm. I froze, not wanting to frighten her away. I felt her breath, warm and puffing evenly, as she got down on her knees and peered into my nose, my eyes, as if seeking something. I thought of the old, old films about the great apes preening each other, looking for tasty lice. But Penti's actions were more *specific*, methodical....

First my nose, looking into the nostrils, then each eye was scrutinized. After that, she shifted my head, looking in each ear. Examining me, as if she was worried that I'd been injured. At that point, I realized that I'd been dragged to a place of higher ground, away from the lapping water that tugged on the limp-vines like a shower spray streaming through wet hair. I'd been standing knee-deep in the water, searching for mud—

And Penti had been watching me, hidden somewhere close enough to yank me out of the water when I keeled over, before I drowned. That realization made me too bold; I reached up and grasped her downy wrist, and she let out a grunt before getting to her feet and leaping away. I was splattered with a muddy mist as her powerful feet left the soggy ground. Weakly, I propped myself up on one elbow, my fingers still tingling from the surface of her skin.

And something else connected in my mind just then. Penti's arm. It was scarred. Tiny pairs of oddly-canted short lines, like Jimmie, like our worthless ship....

Day 173:

This clear spell can't go on much longer, I just know it. One day soon, I'll black out and only come back, the next day or the next week or the next year. The time will be gone, I'll be older, and be no closer to a solution to the puzzle that keeps me going now. The puzzle of the 'lopers. What drives them? Do they think? Do they write? Do they dream?

I went down to the electronics lab today, looking for something that could help. I need a way of recording the events through which I drift unknowingly in blackout. It's the only way I'll ever know.

The place was a shambles. Neil had ransacked it in his last days, trying to fill his days with a purpose that could hold him through the spasms of pain. That purpose was building a hyper-space radio. No matter that the best physicists on earth hadn't made that discovery, Neil tried....He left instruments all over the floor, radio parts on the benches and crushed underfoot. I dug through the heaps he left for an intact lab recorder. Nearly passed out twice...my head hurts more and more as the day goes on. But I found one, a little coin-sized button meant for remote observation in confined areas. They were good for 500 hours of vid and sound recording before their superconducting squid memories had to be downloaded. I taped it carefully to my fore-head like a third eye and turned it on. I was set. The question I avoided asking myself was whether I really wanted to solve the puzzle of the 'lopes. My plans for cloning my own company were revealed as Fairy dust. Did I want to lose the question which took their place?

Day 174:

I'm almost it for this log. The chronometer says this is the 174th day on this planet. My head hurts more today. I think this might be the last before I black out again

I left off after the time Penti came up to me, passed out in the mud, to see who or what I was. Sometime between the sixtieth and hundredth day, I'm not sure right now. How should I be? After I woke up in the mud while I was trying to collect enough food, I was in a daze. In the days after passing out, I came lucid from time to time, wandering aimlessly. The fevered idea of the splicer was barred for the moment, or any kind of thinking for that matter. I found my head hurt much less if I didn't think. So I wandered, caring neither where I went nor where I came from.

Still, those human habits of observation, the old, old ones we get from the monkeys, aren't so easily banished. Now that I'd spotted the ten hash-marks on Penti's arm, I began seeing them everywhere. Maybe I was blind to them before, or if the 'lopes had played dumb when we arrived, hiding their light under a bushel, as the ancient saying goes, but the *sign* was everywhere. Scratched in the dirt by buried dung. Incised on the trees using either their nails or some tool I hadn't observed them using yet. Even the discarded peels of the husk-fruit were now arranged in a specific, ten-paired pattern on the crumbling soil.

And when I finally decided to pay a visit to some of the further-out graves, those of Huoy and Neil, I found the sign on their graves, laid out in neat, careful rows of speckled pebbles. Like the markers we'd neglected to give them. I cried when I saw that; would we have done the same for a 'lope? I didn't even remember where we'd planted the dead 'lope; no one kept a record of it, and I hadn't been along, I think I was off some-where with Reba when Neil and Jimmie buried it—no, *her*. The 'loper was a female, a *mater*, perhaps....

Yet the 'lopes had honored the graves of my people.

I tried marking the outside of the ship; I scrawled the "pi" symbol, a model of Sol's solar system, even "Kilroy Was Here," but all the 'lopes did in return was repeat their set of ten paired lines, as if that was all they had to say. Or all they knew. But I did learn something interesting; they didn't use their fingers to make the symbols. I saw Wildcat and Lucy apply the mud to the ship with a crude brush, made of stiffened, dried limp-vines lashed to a dried tuber-tree branch, which Wildcat dipped into a *bowl*, a crude one, made of sun-dried mud and limp-vine fibers, but a *utensil* nonetheless, held by Lucy in her cupped hands. No earth animal ever progressed to the point of using two self-made objects in tandem. I wished Reba could've seen the 'lopes, even though I knew she wouldn't have been able to admit their accomplishments to herself....

My interest in the gene-splicing equipment faltered as I began to observe the 'lopes. I took to following them, when I wasn't too sick to walk in the sunlight, and after the first week of that, I realized that my boots were a hindrance, not a help, when it came to switching to different terrains. Barefoot, I was less likely to slip in the mud my toes could dig in for purchase. And the mud contained more pebbles deeper down, which felt pleasant against my skin. Soon afterward, my uniform pants revealed themselves to be a hindrance, they flapped wetly against my calves when I waded out of ponds, so one morning I sliced them off. Using a regular scalpel, not a laser. I couldn't *look* at those things yet....

Barefoot, almost bare-legged, I found that I blended in better in the surrounding foliage, allowing me to study the 'lopes as I never had before...or perhaps they found me fit to be nearer to them. Regardless of the reason for my newfound acceptability I took every advantage of it.

The 'lopes never let me follow them to where ever it was they slept; come sunset, they'd split up, scattering like blown chaff, so that trying to track them was futile, since I had no way of knowing who was heading to the real sleeping place, and who was a decoy. But I learned something more significant than the location of their main nest—I gradually realized that the 'lopes had a language. Not a simple one, either, like that of the whales or porpoises on earth: theirs was a subtle, yet complex system of communication. Aside from the grunts and half-mewls the crew and I had observed—and summarily discounted—the 'lopes communicated by touch, gesture and limited facial expression, with all the discrete forms combining in a language which had what I suspected to be grammar, syntax, the works. All the signs of Reba's elusive sense of self.... They even had names for each other; certain combinations of sound/gesture/special-ized touch in a specific spot which were repeated frequently enough in greeting/departure situations for me to recognize them after repeat witnessing. For example, Baby Boy's "name" was a two-beat grunt, uttered simultaneously with a cupping of the listener's chin with the *left* hand, and a gentle nudge with the right knee. What the name meant, I had no idea; there was no Rosetta Stone or its equivalent for me to use, for names are utterly unlike "words" for common things, and even then, the language of the 'lopes was marked with subtle nuances which differentiated words and meanings according to the time of the day, the size of things, the oldness or youngness of a thing, and so on to infinity.

It was like trying to partition a three-digit integer; the possible combinations were almost incalculable, yet finite. Every time I thought I had this or that "word" and all its permutations in the bag, I saw/heard another variant—and realized just how little I really understood the 'lopes. And what was maddening was how *easy* it was for the 'lopes to learn and understand their language—the mature females had had young not too long before, perhaps six or seven months before Jimmie killed Reba and I killed him, yet the baby 'lopes were already attempting crude speech....

But I understood just enough to get a *taste* of the 'loper language and/or "philosophy," if one could call it that. This planet was everything to them—mother, father, friend, lover— as if they needed any *more* sexual activity. From what I could tell of the ones I recognized, they were *always* eager to make love, as if in a near-constant state of rut....

One drawback to running around *sans* shirt and long pants was that whenever I blacked out, I'd wind up with short grass burns on either my chest or back. Once, I spent a full day in unconsciousness, out in the open. My head began to spin, and I went down before I could get myself to cover. The sun was just past the "noon" mark then, and I awoke when the sun was again approaching the "noon" mark. One of my legs was asleep, twisted in an odd position under the other one. I think I dreamed of Reba, and not remembering then that she was dead, I found myself disappointed that she wasn't standing next to me. I also woke up with burns that stung for hours....

After that day it became harder and harder to hold myself in this world. Mixed in with periods of outright blackouts, I began to have short periods where my mind simply went away. I kept moving, continued to act, but held no recollections of those times. I simply found myself in places far removed from where I remembered being. Shortly thereafter the mania for cloning returned and I had that episode with the crusher. Then came the spell before I began this log once again. Twenty-four days, gone without a trace.

The log is up to date. What can I do now to hold on to this conscious world?

Day 183:

I've been out eight days. I started to come to a couple days ago, but I really wasn't all there yet. It was like I was; yet I wasn't, that unthinking state I mentioned before. I knew I was, but I didn't know why or how or what *for*. Anything more than a minimum level of consciousness just hurt too much. Is that to be my fate?

Time to download the recorder and see what I did.

I'm back. There was a little trouble getting things going. It seems like I can't even remember how to do the simplest things these days. If they ever find me and put me back to work on physics, I doubt I'd be of much use.

What I saw was astonishing! I don't know what it means yet. I'll just have to put the tape in the archive and hope a better mind than mine can figure it all out....

Much of it was garbage, of course. There was one thirteen-hour section where my head didn't move at all. I was just staring out onto the plain, fixed on, the same tree all day long. Maybe I was just unconscious. Then there were times when it was obvious I was sleeping, face down on the ground or face up along a tree trunk. Lots of those, but day or night, none of them were longer than two hours, so I really don't think I was asleep during that long spell....

Thinking! It's not only hard to do now, but I even wince at spelling it out on this log! I'm being conditioned, conditioned by pain, like one of Pavlov's dogs.

The astonishing things were the episodes when I ran with the 'lopes. It seems like they really accept me now, at least, when I'm semi-sentient. We ran, we cavorted, we rolled in the flat-grass and dug for tubers. I sat around and played with the young ones while 'lopers all around me were having sex. It was their favorite activity. As I turn my head, the recorder turns with me, and I see that it's the local pack I'm running with. There's Penti, now Baby Boy, Slim, Heidi, and Mister. Plus the younger pups, and a whole crew of older 'lopers I'd never seen before. The tribe was *big*—there must've been close to a hundred. Many of those nightly encampments occurred in a dark grove we'd never found, shelters piled against trees in spots. It was obviously permanent; many of the shelters centered around a neatly maintained cave entrance marked with the ten-slash symbol.

I wandered off with a few chittering pups in tow, one time when the 'lopers were all occupied with each other. Wandered off down the cave. I wasn't exactly exploring, not in the normal sense of having direction and a goal. What I did was wander in and out of the cave entrance with no obvious purpose. Then it started raining—splashes all over the recorder lens—and I wandered deeper into the cave.

What the recorder caught was amazing. The light level fluttered as we went deeper in, until the recorder reached its limits. Must have been really dark, because I piled into the wall a few times, and the picture went dim. Then as I went down, things brightened as though we were nearing some source of light. Baby 'lopes cavorted happily around me. Cute little things, really.

The "cavern"—it was now apparent that the tunnel was dug by hand—widened out to abut a crusted metal wall relieved with a single open door. I wandered into a maze of narrow, round-walled metal corridors. They were all nearly clean of dirt and debris, as if some messy housekeeper lived here, but a housekeeper nonetheless. The technology I saw before me was baroque, surreal, with instrumentation set into the walls, and hanging down every where from the curved ceiling. The interior of this metal cavern reminded me of a spaceship's gangways, but one which made our own seem ludicrously simple. Corridors meandered off in bizarre angles, totally unlike anything on-board the *Sagittarius IV* or any earth ship. But the alien design pleased me in ways I could never describe, leaving me full of a sense of wonder, for only creatures with a consistent and thorough aesthetic vision could've created this ship, with all of its mysteries intact.

Was it a buried ship or an old, very, *very* old building? If it was a building, then why hadn't any other traces of civilization been found? There were the hillocks, but those were little more than hollowed earthen mounds, artificial caves. This was *much* more....

I remembered Reba going on about the "degeneration" of the 'lopers brain structure. Were they the builders of this ship, or fortress, or whatever it was? Or were they merely squatters?

I ran around touching everything and pressing keypads, until the little 'lopes dragged on my arms and legs, apparently to stop me. They seemed deadly serious for baby 'lopes. Even the ones not attached to my limbs were standing motionless. Then when I dropped my arms and backed away, they let go to begin playing again. There was something about this place that spooked them. Not a "child" among them went anywhere near the instrumentation, as though it were something...holy.

I wandered a while longer, sitting against a column. The room must've begun darkening then, because I caught the telltale flutter of the exposure control on the recording. New sounds began, rhythmic sounds, sounds other than the chittering of the children. Then the sounds changed, to become something like 'lope-speak, yet faster....

There was a screen up there on the wall. Not that I watched it much. I seemed no more aware of it than anything else, looking that way for a moment, and turning the next. But something was going on up there. The color was washed out, sometimes wavering hazy rainbow splotches, sometimes bleeding into black and white. Pictures of creatures like 'lopes facing out from the screen like news commentators, but with sharper eyes and none of the 'lopes' fidgety habits. Different enough as to almost seem a different species, its image fuzzy, divided into crude horizontal lines like the earliest television images broad-cast back in the first half of the twentieth century, a hundred lines or less, with only minimal definition.

The recorder tape doesn't really carry many views of the screen. Like I say, I wasn't paying attention. I had none to give to the screen. But I did look that way often enough that I can get the picture now. The creatures on the screen were similar in ways to the 'lopers, but smoother, with less hairy skin on the exposed face and gesturing hands. Large eyes, a sort of muddy green-tan, with the distinctive oval 'loper pupils. Longer hair on the head, like *Homo sapiens*, but much finer and flatter than my own. A more defined nose and lips on the mouth, thin lips, but not the furry slit of the current 'lopes. Teeth much more like these 'lopes, the canines even more pronounced, perhaps....A narrow, shallow-ribbed torso, a longer neck, and a bigger jaw-line.

For maybe five minutes the thing spoke into whatever device was used to record the footage. Then it was over.

What did it all mean? How long had all this *been* here?

Day 184:

Just what is there to *do* on this planet? I'm totally alone when I'm conscious. The 'lopes seem to know when I'm conscious, and they avoid me. All except Penti, who came up within a few meters yesterday while I was resting under a tree, nursing an agonizing headache and trying not to think.

Do the headaches come when I'm out and roaming? If they do, I don't know about it, so it doesn't matter, does it?

There's none coming to save me....

Day 198:

It's been a long spell this time. I came out two days ago, and I've been fast-forwarding through the recorder tapes ever since.

Do you know, I think the 'lopes have been looking out for me, like a pet or a feeble child?

The last thing I remember back on the 184th day was sitting out under my favorite tree when suddenly the darkness reached out for me like oil gushing from a well. I dug until I found that spot on the tape. Suddenly the ground rushed up to meet the recorder, well, that was it. Forty minutes passed until I roused. The recorder flashed past Penti and another 'lope, each patiently looking my way. I don't think I was aware of them even in the blackout state, because the recorder didn't linger. They were still there, the next time I looked up.

What in the world did I mean to the 'lopers? I wasn't one of them. Yet...they trusted me. And that time I was in danger of doing myself in, Penti saved me. Was life that sacred to them, like some kind of religion without the subtle rules? Was the ten-slash some kind of symbol of faith? Not that *they* could tell me.

Didn't I see the ten-slash on the recording in the subterranean chamber? Quickly as I could, I scanned back to my last set of recordings. Yes! There it was, on the wall behind the 'loper gesturing on the screen. I'm going to call him a 'lope, if only because he almost looks like one.

I scanned back to the last recent set of recordings. There Penti stood, chittering softly to the other 'lope, stroking his arm. Her arm bore the sign as well. The same set of symbols one of them had once incised upon Jimmie's arm....

Day 212:

I saw Reba today! It's been *so* long! I woke up out in the Open an hour ago. My head was nearly splitting, but in my joy I hardly noticed. She stood there resplendent in a green dress, her red hair floating in the still air, a slight glow surrounding her whole body. I think the glow might've been just an illusion of tired eyes, though.

She *was* acting kind of odd; every time the 'lopes standing beside her moved, Reba would move the same way. When she opened her mouth to speak, she spoke to me in 'lope-speak, I wonder when she had the time to learn 'lope-speak? Maybe it was something espers could learn. *I* sure didn't understand it....

I passed out for a few minutes more, and when I woke up, both Reba and the 'lopes were gone.

Day 245:

This is my third lucid day in a row. I've finished moving a record/playback system into the 'loper cavern. Oddly, the 'lopes don't seem to mind—in fact, it really seemed like they were trying to help in their clumsy way. Every time I turned my back, a 'loper rushed in to mark the equipment with a ten-slash.

This is a landmark time, really. After I decided to do it, I retraced the old recording to find the cavern. When I burst in on the clearing suddenly, the 'lopes panicked. But they made some tentative attempts to retake their clearing soon enough. The place must be really important to them, for them to overcome their fear. They're still skittish, but they seem to accept me again.

Anyhow, the equipment is set up and ready. If any humans come by this way in a late rescue attempt, they'll find the *Sagittarius IV* and play back our logs. That is, if they come by in the next century or so. I've noticed that the *Sagittarius* is starting to settle into the ground just a bit. If it continues, she'll eventually fade from view in the soft soil. I certainly won't be here to maintain passage to the airlock....

But the 'lopes will be sure to keep the tunnel open to *their* fortress or ship or whatever. It seems like a religion to them. And maybe the rescuers will find the 'loper tunnel while 'loper pontiffs introduce the newcomers to their greatest Mysteries. They'll play this log back and learn. The power supply should last indefinitely, if the 'lopes don't play it too often. They really like watching.

I can't help wondering what will happen if another unlucky crew finds itself stranded here. What if they're not human?

If they're lucky, they'll metabolize left-handed sugars and starve.

If not, and if they're slow to go insane, they may find this cavern, and they may just be able to get more clues to a cure.

Or they might not. They might become the 'lopers, creatures of low intelligence who *were* great, remembering what they once were by scratching that reminder on their own flesh, by wearing their past as their present selves.

"For God so loved the world, He gave His only begotten Son...."

The words of my childhood religion, the ones I'd eschewed in favor of the hard sciences and Darwin, came back to me, before they devolved into a different, yet intrinsically similar message:

The 'lopes had so loved themselves, they gave up their sentience, their selves...they devolved or even aided in their own devolution. I've watched the 'loper commentator again on the big screen. There's a lot more to that recording. Rapid jumbles of images, some squeezed onto vertically or horizontally split screens. A downed ship. 'Lopes studying the indigenous crushers. 'Lopes taking samples, running tests within the ship. The early 'lopes eating the husk-fruit—

—while they still had their own supply of food. For the shot of their mess table showed foodstuffs totally unfamiliar to me, resting on the same oblong, shallow bowl-plates as the foods native to this planet. There were young ones, too, infants and toddler-sized proto-'lopes, seated alongside their elders, all of whom were eating meals of mixed foodstuffs. The next images weren't unexpected, 'lopes in obvious distress, holding their hands over their cheeks, their temples, mouths twisted in rictuses of pain not unlike the ones on the faces of my crewmates at the onset of prion infestation, eyes either closed or rolled up into their skulls.

The children crying hurt me the worst, I think.

The first piece fell into place for me. The screen was split horizontally, the top showing that familiar set of ten pairs of seemingly random-length lines...while the bottom showed a slightly blurred picture, taken through the lens of some powerful microscope.

Genetic material. Pairs of chromosomes. The basic units of life. If the ten-slash was the sign of their religion, the early 'lopes worshipped life itself, without apparent need for any intervening godhead. Their descendants continued the tradition, albeit devoid of meaning....

The images that followed showed 'lopers working complex equipment while the chromosomes on the other half of the split-screen broke, changed, rejoined. The 'loper infants shown after that were placid, happy little things, furrier and more active. None of the crying bouts that afflicted their older brothers and sisters bothered the new children. Pre-landfall images of school-rooms showed children performing complex pattern-matching tasks. The other half of the screen showed these altered children tossing blocks back and forth....

In the face of almost un-faceable contingencies, the 'lopes lived on, despite the loss of their greater surface intellect, their mastery over incredibly advanced technology. I think it may have been worth it....

Day 276:

It's going to be all right. Reba was with me today, walking along with Alf Jarry and me down a streamside path. I just wish she'd hang around until I was really awake, so we could talk....

Funny, how the 'lopes watch out for me. They still tend to avoid me when I'm conscious. But when my mind shuts down, blinded by the pain, they're looking out for me. They always show up in the recordings, two or sometimes three 'lopes trailing along, watching over me when I sleep, pulling me out of danger. I don't think I mean much to them, not for *who* I am. If they're anything like their ancestors, they watch out for me only out of reverence for life, *any* life, whether intelligent or not. For God gave His only begotten Son to live amongst the foolish, the stupid, and the devolved, that He may keep them from all harm.

It is a good feeling, to worship and be worshipped. Just as it is a good feeling to see friendly faces, to hear the voices of my friends. And the sun feels good on my bare body, if I am lucky, maybe my skin will toughen like the soles of my feet have, to shield against the short-grass....

Nothing is truly given up without something else coming up to fill the void. It didn't seem so hard for the 'lopes to lose their intelligence, not when happy survival was at stake. Not such a hard thing to lose when tenderness remains and grows to fill the gaps....

When I die, I sense that I will be missed by the 'lopers for just as long as it is proper, and forgotten when it is the right time to do so. 'Lopers are excellent philosophers on living if nothing else.

Day 312:

Whenever will my mind die? Flee intelligence, and leave my body in peace!

Afterword for "Contingencies and Penti-Lope-Lope"

Writing this novelette took several years, and selling it took even longer; initially it was a solo work, but I decided that my grasp of the science elements in this were too poor, so I let my long-time pen-pal, and sometimes co-writer, John S. Postovit (who does have a degree in physics/math, as well as an art degree), see the story, and add in whatever he felt was lacking—another aspect of the work which needed rewriting was the relationship between the narrator and his girlfriend Reba, something which John was able to fix up as well—so the piece soon bloomed into a very long novelette. As a rule, novelettes and novellas aren't all that easy to sell, especially for mid- and low-list writers (why else did even Stephen King feel the need to put out collections of novellas, rather than get them printed in magazines?); they take up too much space in a magazine, and many publications don't even use them. But this tale did need the extra wiggle room, and so it bounced around from *'zine* to shining *'zine*, until it seemed as if it had found a home at a short-lived digest-sized *'zine* called *LC-39* (which had already published a very long piece of mine called "Guardsmen Fed to the Tigers"—it isn't here in this collection, though, due to the use of visual/graphic devices in the work which make it impossible to scan into an e-file), but then the editor pulled the plug on the *'zine* a few issues in, right before the novelette was to appear. It languished for a while then I managed to get it into an *e-zine* called *The Fifth Dimension* in 2001, and was grateful to get it out to the public after so many years.

The character of Penti-Lope-Lope was based on one of my cats, Penny, who lived into her mid-teens (old age for a cat); she was a beautiful, smart and feisty little creature, a former stray kitten who grew into a sleek tiger-stripe cat. (In 1992, she thanked me for taking her in by batting my face when the house was filling up with carbon monoxide, startling me out of my stupor; luckily, none of my cats died in that incident!) She was a cool little critter, something like the female alien in *Avatar*, all lean muscle and big wide green eyes, just an exquisite little female.

I know the whole concept of sub-neurons is pretty much junk science, but then again, who really knows just how the brain actually works? Seems to me we're still trying to work out all the nuances of human thought/brain function even in the age of CAT scans and what-not....

For me, the real meat of the story is the aspect of situational ethics—what the 'lopes choose to do in order to stay alive on their new planet may not appeal to human sensibilities, but it is a viable option. Their take of what a worthwhile life means might not be what humans would consider a life worth living, but it's an option, nonetheless. At any rate, I am fond of this novelette, if only because it keeps my memories of Penny, aka Penny-Lope-Lope, alive....

CINÉ RIMETTATO

"All those kinds of neat special-effects-type things will become standard features of PCs over the next five years. Our whole thing has been to take technology and not have it be a barrier. So anybody who has got the creativity doesn't have to learn the bites and bytes."

—Bill Gates,
"The Emperor Strikes Back,"
Entertainment Weekly, January 7, 2000

(In 1995) [Dusty Springfield] had just won a round in her battle with cancer and seemed to be in no hurry to get back to the recording studio. "Although if someone let me record an album of every cover I've ever dreamed of singing, I might think about it," she coolly intoned.

Sadly she never got to make that album. But here's what it might have sounded like...

—Rob Hoerburger
"The Sound of...Pop" from "The Lives They Lived,"
The New York Times Magazine, January 2, 2000.

Roger Ebert had nothing to do with the creation of *Ciné Rimettato per se,* but that essay he wrote about the *CR* "remakes" for his "Questions for the Movie Answer Man" column sure as hell made things a lot harder for guys like me and Keith, and never mind the intellectual property attorneys representing all those film makers *Ciné Rimettato* had (take your pick here) ripped off, venerated, or just plain perplexed, befuddled, and baffled.

Not that a person could blame Ebert. He'd been inundated with so many e-mails and letters asking about the films *Ciné Rimettato*...reworked, that he felt obligated to download them for himself, just as thousands of web-heads had already done for the past five or six years.

And, like most of the others who'd logged on out of curiosity or boredom, or just plain stumbled on the sites after following random links associated with someone or something they'd wanted to know more about, Ebert was hooked.

Because *Ciné Rimettato* wasn't the typical micro-cinema site of short films, featuring *Blair Witch Project* spoofs or anything like those wonderful Billy Crystal Oscar-night movie send-ups. Parody had nothing to do with it; not one word of dialogue was changed, and each *CR* "film" was—where applicable—shot-by-shot true to the original. Even as they were wildly, wondrously, and wholly changed, by virtue of the smallest of alterations to the cinematic fabric of the whole.

And while Ebert was as lavish with his praise as he was with the tacit warnings that *Cine Rimettato*'s films broke just about every copyright, fair trade, and intellectual property law known, his message was unmistakable:

These films are the best thing you'll never see at your local multiplex or rent from Blockbuster.

He didn't need to tell anyone to seek them out—people simply *did.*

Which is why I was sitting through my third viewing of *Ciné Rimettato*'s *The Terminator* (all of *CR*'s "remakes" were clearly labeled as such), watching Lance Henriksen's Terminator blast all the unfortunate patrons of club Tech Noir who stood between him and Linda Hamilton's Sarah Connor, waiting for my partner Keith to come back from his interview with one of the actors from another *CR* remake of a classic, the former *Stand by Me*, now *CR*-dubbed *The Body*.

Even though I'd already seen it twice, I still reflexively jumped in my chair when Henriksen crashed through that club window—I don't know if it was the actor's quietly determined expression, or his smaller-than-the-original-Terminator's frame flying through that glass, but I was spooked. Me, a twelve-year veteran of the FBI's Profiling and Behaviorial Analysis Unit, who'd sat across too-small wooden tables in more than one maximum security prison spending quality time with serial killers who'd told me with smiles in their eyes that they'd be able to unscrew my head from my neck easier than I could open up a jar of olives...if they felt like it. I suppose the whole effect of this particular remake was the small-threat factor; how something seemingly innocuous and gentle can become so fearsome when it attacks. James Cameron had basically said as much years before this "film" emerged bit-by-byte on the Web, he'd wanted to cast Henriksen in the role, but the special effects technology back in the mid-1980s was insufficient to allow for a lean, compact "Terminator"—a situation remedied by the time *T-2* was made, but apparently the initial casting glitch niggled at the mind/minds behind *Ciné Rimettato*...or more correctly, "Cinema Put-Right."

Not feeling up to a continued adrenalin surge so late in the afternoon, I shut off the video, and, in anticipation of Keith's arrival, I turned my chair around to face the VCR on Keith's desk, the one with the tape the lab guys had created from our download of *The Body*.

Out of all the re-creations, this one had us stumped. Until it appeared a couple of years ago, we'd been working under the assumption that *CR* was something of a would-be casting director's wet dream. Except for putting Harris Glenn Milstead (the actor known as Divine) in the Sydney Greenstreet role of Ferrari in *Casablanca* (along with the better-known almost-cast Ann Sheridan as Ilse Lund and Ronald Reagan as Rick Blane), which in turn may have been attributable to Mr. Ebert's 1985 review of *Trouble in Mind,* in which the good critic actually compared Divine's performance as Hilly Blue to Mr. Greenstreet, the recasting of each *CR* "production" was based on Hollywood lore regarding actual screen tests or offers turned down. Hence, "Ten Scenes from *GWTW*" consisted of the epic's ten best, most memorable scenes redone with women like Paulette Goddard and Bette Davis (who, in my opinion, did a far superior "reading" of the "As God is my witness, I'll never go hungry again" speech in that backlit field), while the revamped *The Cable Guy* gave the world what might have been Chris Farley's most unique and—ironically—just about funniest performance since the airplane bathroom sequence in *Tommy Boy.* Putting Farley's two-time film partner David Spade into the Matthew Broderick role was a bit of a departure, since no one could be sure he would've gotten the role even had Farley decided to take it. But even Keith (who normally isn't into comedies) had to admit the result was eerily hysterical.

Figuring out the *how* of these films had been the job of the guys down in the FBI's tech department, and they'd filed their jargon-filled reports over a year ago with the newest Attorney General. But the *why* continued to stump everyone brought in on the case...which is why one of the Assistant Directors up High had the last-ditch idea of having a profiler or two try to get into the head of this particularly elusive Unknown Subject. Even Keith had to admit it beat the hell out of looking at crime scene photos and delving into the psyches of human mutants who killed, raped, or blew up people for what basically amounted to sport and/or what they considered a basic need.

Before I leaned over to turn on *The Body*, I glanced over my shoulder at the green board where Keith had started our list of personality traits for the *CR* UNSUB which, despite the immeasurably vast difference in each criminal's crime, wasn't all that different—so far—from that of the majority of serial killers we'd dealt with over the years:

white male
middle-aged (35-45)
college education/tech school/self-schooled (??)
cinema buff
single
lives alone/self-employed
owns large house/loft/converted warehouse
needs storage space for multiple computers
no criminal record/possible legal background/aspirations
peripheral film/theater ties/aspirations
speaks/understands Italian (possible B.A.?)

That was about it. Five exquisitely re-mastered, re-thought, and re-conceptualized movies later, each done with artistic thoroughness and imagination despite the self-imposed constraint of remaining as true to possible to the original work, and we'd come up with a profile that added up to three-quarters Unabomber and one-quarter D. W. Griffiths, with a trace of computer geek thrown in for seasoning.

But *The Body* challenged our profile. Before it appeared (and was brought to the attention of millions of Web surfers, thanks to all the links—the crucial one to Stephen King's own site, or because of the original cast's subsequent careers—we'd considered our UNSUB to be someone who felt slighted in his own life, and who sympathized with actors who'd been passed over for or who'd not taken roles which might have changed their careers. The type of guy who'd been passed over for promotions, or whose previous programming efforts had been co-opted by his employers. (That the software which made *Ciné Rimettato* possible wasn't owned by any of the Big Names in the biz was a given; if it was it would've been selling for $1K a pop in every computer supplies store and catalogue around.)

Yet there it was. *The Body* as no one had ever imagined it back when it was known and loved by moviegoers as *Stand by Me*. Although the original casting had never been in doubt, the makers of *Ciné Rimettato* had, decided to put something right that no one had previously considered to be wrong.

I've been a fan of Richard Dreyfuss since *American Graffiti* came out when I was a senior in high school, and I adored his narration of *Stand by Me*...but when I saw *The Body,* I was first dumbfounded, then exhilarated, as much as I'd been when I first read the novella upon which the movie was based.

And the irony is Kevin Spacey wasn't a major player in Hollywood when the film was cast in 1985; hell, he was only twenty-six, much too young to play The Writer, and way too old to play any of Ace's gang. But matters of age and time meant nothing to the genius who created the digital miracles of *Ciné Rimettato.*

So, there he was, parked on the back road, newspaper in hand. As genuine-looking and as character-specific as anyone might want, playing a role wholly unlike Verbal Kint or *Seven*'s John Doe or Buddy Ackerman in *Swimming with Sharks,* or even the suburban love-slave Lester Burnham in *American Beauty.* About the only thing Keith and I could ascribe to another movie Spacey *had* been in was his hairdo, which was straight out of his smallish role as the editor Osborn in *Henry and June,* a sort of modified bangs over the forehead thing, very mid-eighties in this particular context. And the voice *was* Spacey, voice analysis proved it (as our tech guys had likewise proved was the case in every *CR* revamp; no impressionists or imitations were utilized, *a la* Humphrey Bogart's voice in the "You, Murderer" episode of *Tales from the Crypt,* back in 1995—a scant five years before Bogart's *Casablanca* role was itself *CR* recast), but he'd never, ever uttered any of those lines in any of his movies or filmed stage performances to date.

The verbal cadence, the dry inflections, the explicit subtext, it was all there...only Spacey had never stepped into a recording studio to dub those lines. I don't know why, considering that other *CR* "actors" had turned in posthumous "performances," but this particular movie, out of the whole *CR* "catalogue," gripped me. Maybe it was the way the actor's performance changed the entire subtext of the movie—what was only slightly dark, tempered by Dreyfuss's innate deft touch with words and subtext, was now far more edgy, intense, with undercurrents of unshakable mourning. Definitely more in tune with the performance of the young Writer, Gordie La Chance. Oh, I'd noticed earlier (who hadn't, really?) that Richard Dreyfuss and Wil Wheaton didn't look all that much alike, what with their different hair and eye color, and body types, and their voices weren't that similar either (although when it comes to a twelve-year-old boy, who knows what he will sound like at forty or so), but it wasn't a major issue in the film, and given the strength of the movie as a whole, it didn't actually matter...until *Ciné Rimettato* came along.

And the irony was, a person could appreciate both films for what they were and for what they weren't; I think Keith was right when he said the titles said it all. One film was King's *The Body,* and the other was what it was, period. Another irony was that of all the *CR* "movies" this one was changed the least...and actually improved upon in a few scenes—the small technical problems concerning the infamous train-on-the-bridge scene and the subsequent swamp-crossing/leech sequence had been cleaned up, not in a flashy manner, but as if to say, As long as I'm doing one change, I'll just fix these small glitches—More of an afterthought, really; I didn't catch them myself until Keith and I ran the original film side by side with the remake, with the sound turned off, just to catalogue the actual differences. Which is when we came across the UNSUB's signature...a detail that simultaneously brought our profile closer to that of what I now considered a "real" criminal even as it made out elusive quarry far more quirky and human than either Keith or I had dared to hope for, given the virtually-reflective firewall of graphic mastery he possessed....

"Thought you'd be sitting on your can, Rune." Keith's voice echoed warmly in the small confines of our temporary office space; I'd been so engrossed in Spacey's piquant line-reading of how his younger self had become the "lost boy" that summer of 1959 that I hadn't heard Keith open the door or come in. And given Keith's hefty 250-plus weight, stretched over a six-four frame, said frame not known for being light on his oxfords, his voice made me start visibly in my chair.

I thumbed "pause" on the remote, and turned around to face him. Luckily for my neck, he sat down so that we were almost eye to eye before he added, "You were right, my man, the guy didn't have much more to say than the tech guys upstairs already told us. But it's a shame you lost the coin toss...they were filming when I arrived. Could've used an extra—"

Keith's teasing aside, he was right about it being a shame that I'd lost the coin flip. Not that either of us expected that interviewing the lone person from all the *CR* remakes who'd actually worked in computer programming in the early 1990s would lead anywhere, but I had seen more of Wil Wheaton's film work than Keith had, and I knew that Keith would never have thought to ask him for an autograph.

Leaning back in my chair until it made that metallic screech I knew Keith hated, I asked, "So, what did he think of *The Body*? I'm assuming he hadn't seen it—"

"You're one for one on that account. Said he'd been too busy. Not that he wanted to. I got the impression it wasn't his all-time favorite role—"

I shook my head. For a profiler, Keith could be so pitifully obtuse. Of course, he didn't have subscriptions to *Premiere*, *Movieline*, and half a dozen other movie- and TV-related magazines like I did, or he'd have known that Wheaton was probably the last actor who'd want to watch his younger self on screen over and over. We knew he'd been too busy to have done the *CR* transformations himself; aside from his two-year stint in computers, he'd been visibly busy acting, with almost all of his downtime accounted for. But still, he was the only actor who'd both been part of a *Ciné Rimettato* and had the knowledge necessary to create one...plus he'd worked with one of the other *CR* replacement "stars," Henriksen, in one of those historical films Ted Turner made a few years back. It wasn't enough to make Keith or me change our profile (which excluded the actor on over half the points), but we'd been working on this case for over two years already, hitting dead end after blind alley after firewall, so we'd hoped that a fresh perspective might help. And when we'd gotten word that he was doing another historical for Turner, down in Virginia, there didn't seem to be much to lose by heading over there to talk to the man.

"—but he did admit to having seen parts of some of the others. 'Just browsing,' naturally," Keith smiled; we both knew that Keith Athmore isn't the typical FBI agent...apart from being tall, big, and black, he happens to look like a hirsute version of the actor who played John Coffey in *The Green Mile*, so there is an inherent intimidation factor which would prevent anyone, no matter how innocent they knew they were, from actually admitting they'd downloaded or even looked at a *Ciné Rimettato* film, no matter *how* enticing Roger Ebert's essay made them.

"But he'd heard of it, no?" I rocked back and forth, filling the room with those "screes" until Keith planted his shoe sole on the armrest of my chair. Satisfied that I was pinned down, he smiled and said, "Oh, yeah, he seemed to know what I'd come for—made the whole movie-computer connection without my having to bring it up. Had a hell of a time getting him to watch the thing was all—"

"I would've loved to have seen that." Glad that Keith has a B.S. in Psychology in addition to experience as a detective in the Chicago police department, I asked, "His reaction tell you anything?"

"I only got him to watch the parts that were changed...he was on lunch break, and the director told me I could have him for an hour or so...man, it was strange, watching this guy wearing a Civil War uniform, sitting there in a director's chair with a bottle of fancy spring water in one hand and a remote in the other, watching himself from half a lifetime ago...the *look* on his face, while he was shakin' his head. I knew right off he hadn't seen it before; he was obviously shocked. The parts with Spacey affected him, but now that he was seeing it...he felt bad about the substitution, said the other actor was a friend and all, but he *was* drawn in by the thing. And those parts where they changed stuff? Adding the image of the oncoming train during the shot where he and the *Sliders* guy are running on the bridge, and when they fixed the color values so the shot of him and the other kid blended in better with the rest of the frame? He was impressed with that, and the way they added bruises to the arms and shoulders of him and the other kid who fell off that bridge...he said he'd wondered about that, since the characters did supposedly fall a hundred feet off a bridge onto *rocks* and all. He said whoever did this has an exceptional eye for detail, same stuff our tech eyes and the people over at Pixar, DreamQuest, and everywhere else said. And he agreed with us about the cat; he admitted to seeing it when he was 'browsing' the other films...although he could've found out about it from Ebert's article. Ebert did mention that, didn't he?"

I craned my neck backwards, until I heard some of the bones pop; closing my eyes against the glare of the overhead light, I said, "Yeah, Ebert mentioned the cat. I suppose because he has one. I missed it when I read the article, I suppose because I *don't* have one."

"The thing's never in the frame long enough to register the first time through," Keith tried to mollify me, but I still hated it when he brought up the whole subject of the cat and the article, and how we'd missed the mention of the former in the latter. Trying to work the conversation back to the interview, I asked, "And you asked him if there was a cat anywhere on the set, I suppose?"

"Oh yeah, right off. He was adamant there were two animals in the film, the dog in the junkyard, and the deer on the railroad tracks. No cat. But he was sure the cat in the *CR* version was a real one, and not an animation. Said it looked like it was smaller in the *Casablanca CR*, and obviously bigger in his movie. He did have a suggestion...not that it would be viable—"

"What wouldn't be 'viable'?"

"He said that since whoever did these films probably lives on the west coast, like you and I think, and since the cat obviously ages from picture to picture, chances are it might be the pet of whoever's doing this...and a vet might recognize it from a picture. Not that dark long-haired tiger cats are uncommon, but he thought it might be worth a shot. Something we could cross-reference in our databases...I asked him if he knew how many people in the U.S. own cats—"

"Still, it might be an option...we've pursued stranger leads. You didn't insult the guy, did you—"

"No, no he was cool. More shocked that anyone would do what they did to the movie than anything else. Man sure doesn't like to live in the past, though. Just zapped through what he didn't need to see. None of that ego-tripping crap like you see on TV with a lot of actors. 'Course *you're* the expert on that, eh? How is that satellite dish workin' out?"

Keith had yet to stop ribbing me about that extras-added dish system I'd bought last year; in addition to HBO, Showtime, Cinemax and Encore!, and more eclectic options like The Independent Film Channel, Sundance, and Turner Classic Movies, I had the new AllFilm, EuroFlix, and AlTerNate channels to savor at will. I'd told myself that the dish was purely for research; the *CR* UNSUB seemed to have wide-ranging tastes, and clearly he'd had to download visual and aural data from almost every film or TV show his virtual "actors" appeared in prior to the creation of each "performance"...but no profiler can or should live 24/7 in the mind of his UNSUB.

And even Keith didn't know about Birkita; she was someone wholly untouched and un-sampled by the UNSUB, given the fact that the type of indy films she appeared in were in and of themselves so close to the results of the *CR* UNSUB's labors—quirky, seemingly oddly-cast movies whose subject matter was geared to a mindset totally at odds with multiplex tastes. Typical hardcore indy fare, the kind of movies that showed up—in much shorter form—on those micro-cinema sites like AtomFilms, Short BUZZ or Bijou Café. The kind of stuff our UNSUB steered clear of, films that couldn't take additional tampering, lest they become parodies of pastiches of recreations.

Besides, Birkita had only been a regular in indies since 1999 or so (she'd done one film in the late eighties). That meant that she'd never have been under consideration for any roles in major Hollywood productions filmed between the 1980s and the first five years of the century, the kind of movie our UNSUB claimed as his own personal playground between 2000 and 2005, when his films first and last appeared on the Web. And aside from the surreal *tour de force GWTW* mini-epic (which clocked in at a trim forty-six minutes, opposed to the original 231-minute running time) and Ilsa in *Casablanca,* the *CR* UNSUB had devoted his efforts to replacing male actors with male actors... even if Keith had thought that Divine *was* a woman, which I suppose was something of a tribute to the talent of the late female impersonator.

(I kept telling Keith that he really did need to go find himself a life outside law enforcement, but he'd go, "Then why is Court TV on basic cable?")

Reluctantly putting Birkita and her filmography out of my mind, I rubbed my closed eyes before lowering my head and facing Keith. "The dish is fine. What else did he have to say? Any thoughts on how the UNSUB did this?"

Keith wagged one finger at me while feeling around in his breast pocket with the other hand, saying, "It's *déjà vu* time— you will observe that I took notes, even though this was nothing new to me...merely so as not to make him think I was wasting his time, which ultimately I was...here goes, Rune, and don't blame me for rehashing this shit—

"He figured our suspect used at least one thousand processors or around four hundred ordinary computers, mostly without monitors, Macs most likely, for parallel processing, that is. Sorting data: video samples of all the actors used for the substitutions; the entire original movie, meaning, oh, about five to twenty gigabytes per computer. And all that hardware means a whole lot more power. So we were right about the UNSUB living in a single-owner dwelling. A power bill like that would stand out in an apartment complex. And he agreed with the guys upstairs about the UNSUB breaking into Web servers or individual computers through cable services. Servers are always going down, so no one would've noticed if someone broke in, stole some power and got out again. As long as data wasn't taken, who's to link a power loss with something like the *Ciné* thing? And breaking into home computers would be more time-consuming for less power, but less likely to attract attention.

"He thought the process would take more power during the image-storing stage, but after that—provided whoever was doing this made the films one after another before sending them out over the Web piecemeal—the break-ins wouldn't have been as frequent.

"But he said that the UNSUB would need to use additional computers to create those wireframe pre-visualization whatsits, those things the guys at Pixar and so on told us about—"

I nodded; we'd spoken to the graphic artists at over a dozen special effects places up and down the coast, who'd said typically, in order to animate a figure in CG—computer graphics, to laymen like me and Keith—a *maquette*, or sculpture-like figure usually made of clay, is sculpted, then marked with a digitizing pen, in order to make grids on its surfaces which can be "read" by a laser device and scanned digitally into a computer, where a 3-D wireframe is created. Once a person has this wireframe figure, the next step is to create "pre-visualizations," or a moving, computerized version of a storyboard, upon which one can manipulate the figures. Not a difficult concept to grasp, especially when animators showed it to us on a computer. They even showed us digitalized skeletons of people and animals, used for motion studies, and stripped-down-to-muscles wireframe images, like the mouse in *Stuart Little* six years ago. (The guys responsible for that told us that the mouse had 600 *thousand* individual hairs....)

Next, we learned how background plates for an animation are shot, leaving a clear field for the figure to be layered in later. The same principle holds true for special-effects shots using humans; if you want someone running around with a hole in their middle, like Goldie Hawn in *Death Becomes Her*, you film the scene twice, once without her and once with her, making sure the two match up perfectly, then take out the blue-screening over her middle, and there you go, a woman with a donut middle. I'd seen rudimentary examples of this on cable; shows about movie special effects are big—

"—but he thought what the UNSUB did was easier than what's being done in regular special effects studios, since the guy didn't have to figure out blocking for the pre-visualizations—all he needs to do is mimic exactly the same movements the actor he's taken out made, and redo the costumes on a different size frame."

"What about creating movements the replacements never made? Wouldn't that take up a lot of power? And time?"

"He didn't think so. Remember the software that guy from MIT came up with a decade or so ago, the program that makes photo mosaics out of stored images? Like the one they used for that poster for *The Truman Show?* It's basically a single software program that automatically sorts out the images in the file to match the photo you want replicated. Wheaton thought that this *Ciné* guy developed similar but more sophisticated software, which automatically scans through a catalogue of digitalized images and motions, and matches the replacement's face and body type to the new movements. He thought it would be a database of textures, skin tones, hair, whatever. The only thing he wasn't too sure about was how the program got around the need for a digitalized wireframe for each actor—he said he was guessing, but he thought that what this person did was measure each actor's body according to found objects in scenes; things like brand-name cans of pop, whatever, that you can buy and measure, then cross-reference them against the body parts of the person to get a numerical idea of that person's body size in relation to the rest of the actors and things already in the individual frames of the movie. Plus he did notice that the early

CR films, the *Gone with the Wind* and *Casablanca* ones—only what he'd browsed on the Web, mind—looked something like that commercial from Superbowl XXXIV, with Christopher Reeve's head on another body, so it looked like he was walking. Shortcuts, which makes sense if you consider that that cat in the movies was probably a kitten when the *Casablanca* one was made in the 1990s. The actors were wearing so much clothing in those two movies, who'd notice if the body didn't change from one person to another. Probably refining his art as he went along. But the other two films—not counting *The Body*—needed people running around with nothing or next to nothing on, so their real bodies had to be used *as* a template."

I elbowed Keith's foot off my armrest, and turned my attention back to the movie I'd put on pause, keeping the sound muted so I could just watch the images while Keith continued to read from his interview notes.

The scene with the cat was coming up, but you had to watch closely—literally without blinking—to catch it; right after Gordie and Chris Chambers fire a gun in the alley behind the diner, while the two boys run off, but just before the waitress comes outside to see what's happened, a cat darts across the screen, running low from right to left, on enough of an angle that all you catch is a streak of grey-black fur, and an upright, puffed-out tail. Less than a second of screen time, far less than the other four films, where the cat is more visible, and full-face to the "camera." But the motion blur was too realistic for it not to be a real cat. I made a mental note to try and get a few good blow-ups to send to veterinarians on the West Coast, especially those in major cities—another theory of ours, since the tech guys told us the UNSUB would need a T-1 line to download the *CR* data to all his Web sites—on the off chance someone might recognize it.

It certainly couldn't be a worse dead end than the Bureau's attempts to find out who'd paid for all the Web sites (each with a different variation of the phrase *Ciné Rimettato* surrounded by portions of the revamped films' titles, the directors' names, and so on) used by the UNSUB over the last six years; each site had been set up by an anonymous account, initiated by letters sent from over a dozen different addresses in California, with money orders enclosed bearing as many different phony addresses and signatures. So the sites went up...and remained, untended, not updated, just waiting, connected to the rest of the Web link by link as various search engines and fans slowly discovered the sites, and linked them to other, related sites.

No matter how much it pained the Department of Justice to admit it, there simply wasn't any way to track down who really set up any of the sites. By resisting the urge to "return to the scene of the crime," the UNSUB had achieved the necessary distance needed to sever his links with his creation. Once the films were out there, and people found them, they mushroomed across the Web; some showing up in whole or in part on fan sites, home pages, or even converted to screen-savers. But then a bunch of people from Keith's hometown of Chicago thought it a good idea to ask the city's resident film guru, Roger Ebert, about them...which is when things got *totally* out of hand.

Not long after that, the original sites were removed by order of the DoJ and the FBI, but who could trace all the *other* sites that had appropriated them? Or do anything about all the downloads made before the sites were taken down? And how to stop people from sharing what they'd downloaded?

And the rub was, whoever created *Ciné Rimettato* wasn't profiting from it. Mixed in with the end credits (or opening ones, in the case of the two older films) were reminders to the viewer that actors do depend on residuals, that copyrights had been extended as of 1998, and that it might not be a bad idea to check out the work of those actors whose work had been excised from these *CR* films. And every *Ciné* remake had an attached file, listing the titles and distributors of every *other* film the affected actors and actresses had appeared in, as well as filmographies of the rest of the actors, directors, screenwriters, and so on, plus additional pleas for the person downloading the movies to go and rent as many of these titles as possible, so that the rental fees might trickle down to the persons affected—or to the studios involved, at the absolute least. There was also the address for the Screen Actors Guild, along with instructions for making an untraceable donation—

When Keith stopped talking behind me, I tapped the "mute" button, just in time for both of us to hear Spacey wryly comment that finding ways to insult one's mother was held in high regard back in those days. Without turning to look at him, I asked my partner, "What did Wheaton say about the voices?"

"Well, *after* he rehashed the synthesizer bit, which he figured involved sound cards, JAZ drives, and a keyboard, like the other guys already told us, he said he could name at least one actress who'd never appear in any future *Ciné* things—"

"If any more do appear," I couldn't help but interject, before Keith went on.

"'Meryl Streep.' I went, 'Why not?' and he goes, 'Her accent is never the same.' That's when it hit me...everybody this UNSUB's sampled has a distinctive, repetitive way of talking— not monotone, but they don't do accents very often—"

"Spacey did a southern one for *Midnight in the Garden of Good and Evil*," I reminded him, while the junkyard dog Chopper tried to bite a chunk out of Teddy Duchamp's wagging fanny through the wire fence.

"Was he in that?"

"Yeah. Remember, his hair was grey—"

"You *sure*?"

"Very. Remember, the guy who played Gordie's big brother was in it—"

"Ohhh...Cusack. Oh, yeah. Him I remember—you sure about Spacey, though?"

"Extremely. I can bring the video tomorrow. But *aside* from that one, I don't recall Spacey doing many accents, either. Some of the *CR* re-vamp actors' voices changed over time, but the technology to age voices existed back in '91, when they re-dubbed *Spartacus*—"

Behind me, Keith rocked backwards on his chair; I could

hear it hitting the wall. "Uh-huh, when they made an old Tony Curtis sound like a young buck—but they had to use Anthony Hopkins for Olivier's voice, no?"

"Considering Sir Laurence had been gone for a while, yes, they did have to use Hannibal the Cannibal's pipes...too bad whoever did this—" I jerked one thumb in the direction of the screen "—wasn't around then. Or didn't have the software up and running...."

"Know what else Wheaton suggested? He thought that whoever did the films was working on them for at least a good five years or longer before they dumped the first one on the Web in '00—weird how the CG pros we spoke to didn't want to admit the UNSUB was way, way ahead of their own technology, eh? He said whoever did this had to digitally erase the original players from each frame, fill in the missing background with parts cobbled from other shots, then go back and put in the new people—once he got *them* guys animated, and digitally dressed in costumes, whatever—where the old ones were. He said it's picky, time-consuming work, no matter how much the software is programmed to do for you. Then there's the matter of making the mouths move in sync to the dialogue, which he reminded me had to be 'spoken' by the new actors with more or less the same speed and cadence as the originals...he was amazed that someone would go through all that trouble, and for no pay, no recognition. I think the no recognition part bothered him the most...know what he said before I left?"

"'Goodbye and good riddance'?" I ventured, finally cocking my head in his direction.

"Nah, I said the man was cool...he told me how proud he was of the computer work he'd done over a decade ago, and said he couldn't imagine how whoever did this could keep it all in—knowing he'd done something so incredible, so far ahead of the pack, with such potential for the industry, and not saying word one about it in public. That's when he reminded me again that this had to be a one-person gig...if someone developed it while working for a company, using the company's equipment, it wouldn't be the property of the designer. And any software or computer firm that knew about this kind of technology would've sold it, without the designer being able to make stuff like this—"

"So Bill Gates is officially off the hook now?" I smiled, while the Barf-O-Rama movie-within-a-movie flickered across the screen.

"Didn't we eliminate him the first day we got this case?" The smile in Keith's voice made me grin; watching the remainder of the storytelling scene by the campfire in silence, I waited until the part where the boys started to take turns watching the campfire, gun in hand, before muting the movie and saying, "In a way it's a shame Gates *didn't* invent this...if the technology was legal, and in use now, can you imagine how it would change movies? Insurance fees would go down, as long as there was a way for someone who died in mid-filming to 'finish' the performance...no one would need to haul ass back to the redub booth to make 'R' movies 'TV-14,' little mistakes could be fixed in postproduction without the need to bring the actors back or rebuild sets—production costs would go down, and ticket costs would be lower—"

"Which brings to mind the *other* thing Wheaton told me, when I was leaving," Keith said softly. "As much as he admired what our UNSUB had done, he said it was frightening, too— he wondered when the time might come in an actor's career when he or she wasn't needed any more. He wanted to know when a producer could say, 'Hey, we don't need So-and-So after all...we have what we *do* need right here in the database.' Or what would happen when casting directors could pick and choose from every actor who'd ever been on film, be they dead or alive? What he said got me thinking...ever notice that most casting directors are women?"

"So?" On screen, Wheaton's much younger cinematic alter ego was having that bad dream about his brother Denny's funeral, as Keith said simply, "So...what if we've been limiting our own profile?"

"As in—?"

"I know all them programmers we talked to were men, or most of 'em, but why couldn't a woman be doing this? We've kicked around the possibility of someone involved in the business—"

"Casting directors are busy people," I reminded him, "They have to look at a lot of people for a lot of roles...anyhow, women are more social; they need more interaction. Our UNSUB has to be a loner, probably a webhead whose social circle *is* movies—"

"But my theory would explain the requests to reimburse the affected parties by video-rental and SAG-donation proxy... this person has ties right *now* to the industry. Probably rubs shoulders with some of the people he or she's been messing with digitally. And you gotta admit, our UNSUB is awfully verbose...here, gimmie the remote—" Quitting his chair and striding over to me in a couple of easy steps, Keith slid the remote out of my hand and fast-forwarded to the last couple of minutes of *The Body,* right when Spacey's Writer is looking at the words he's just typed into his computer, while his kid and the kid's buddy are talking about him. The part where the new adult Gordie stopped outside to play with the boys zipped past in a squiggle of sugary horizontal lines, until Keith found the end credits. Aside from the insert for Spacey (now dubbed "The Replacement Writer"), everything looked like the original's film credits, until just before the part where the copyright information should've appeared.

"This motion picture is not the original made in 1985 and released in 1986. You know and I know that it violates the Sonny Bono Copyright Term Extension Act of 1998, the fair use laws, general copyright law, and just about every other film-related law there is. So, what to do about it? The people who really acted in this and those who didn't do so originally don't normally do what they do for free. Normally these people get residuals for the repeat showings of their work on TV, and sometimes a cut of the rental fees, depending on their original contracts. So what can you do about it? Go out and rent the videos featuring these people. If any of them have a movie out now, go buy a ticket. Buy more Stephen King books and e-books, even if you have the whole library already. Buy/rent copies of *Star Trek: The Next Generation* and *Sliders*. Especially go rent/buy Richard Dreyfuss's work, since he was removed without his permission. Go make out a money order to the Screen Actor's Guild or the Director's Guild of America. The addresses are listed below. Just remember, what you've seen is not a licensed, legal movie. What you want to do next is your business."

The Unabomber may have been more prolix, but he was never that direct and colloquial...I tried to imagine a woman saying those words to herself as she added them to the finished creation, and it didn't sound as strange as it should have.

I suppose my constant contact with mostly male UNSUBs had tainted my perceptions after all...not that I'd let Keith know that.

"The UNSUB could be a lawyer," I ventured, but Keith snorted in disagreement.

"Uh-uh...oh, he or she knows the ins and outs of the law as it applies to the film industry, but this ain't no lawyer. Their syntax is worse than the Unabomber's, and they don't care if they're not making any sense. This person, this UNSUB does care, and wants to make sure the message is understood and acted upon. Been working so far...last I checked with the SAG folks, they've raked in over seventy-four K in small-denomination donations. Most of that's gone into the fund for retiring actors...the families of the deceased *Ciné* 'performers' wanted it that way. And rentals of movies featuring just about every actor in the *CR* remakes are way, way up. You can't say the same for all those *Blair Witch* and *Star Wars* parodies out there."

"But it still doesn't answer the *why* question...I suppose you found time to ask Wheaton about *that*—"

"Yes I did, and he had an answer...sort of. I could tell he was kind of freaked by *The Body,* so I didn't ask until he was done watching it—what he did see of it—and at first he didn't answer, changed the subject to the *how* of it all, but I asked him again, and he said whoever did this must have a specific agenda, something that has meaning to that person, or else we'd be seeing remakes of every film out there whose roles were known to be offered to someone else, or films where people had to turn down roles for some reason...you know, like Tom Selleck almost playing Indiana Jones. He thought that whoever did this had the time to do more movies, but didn't want to. I asked him if he knew what the word *rimettato* meant, and he admitted he didn't. Once I said it meant 'put right' he mulled it over, then said he thought this way beyond casting...more like creative *intent*."

I nodded; we knew Wheaton had helped create a video editing system, one which Keith and I had decided quite a while back probably hadn't been used to create the *Ciné Rimettato* revamps.

"—I think he meant a movie as a bigger picture. Total sum of all the parts. He seemed to be pretty affected by the movie, so he didn't want to discuss it beyond that."

"Keith...where's the copy of the film you took with you?" I noticed for the first time that he hadn't been carrying the cassette case when he walked into the office.

"Left it there...I thought he might want to watch it in private. And yes, I know it's government property, but hell, I'd wasted his lunch break already...it's not like he's going to toss it back on the Web with scene-by-scene commentary. Guy knows better than *that* —"

"I wasn't thinking about that...it just struck me how we're doing what everyone else has been doing with these movies. Passing them on...funny, how I used to blame Ebert for that essay of his, when we're doing the same thing. I mean, how many copies of the films did we leave with the other animators we've talked to? One, two dozen? We're just as guilty as whoever did this in the first place...and besides, if someone was just browsing these on the Web, how can you take away the memory of what you've seen? That's something copyright laws can't control...trying to squash creative freedom to borrow from the culture is one thing, but how do you police the imagination?"

There was a beat of silence between us before Keith exhaled loudly and said, "I dunno know about you, but I'm going start revising the profile based on what Wheaton had to say...personally, I think the most useful thing he said was how proud he was of the program he worked on, 'cause I can't see someone as verbal as this UNSUB staying wholly silent about it. A person would have to be proud...I don't care who he or she is, I don't think someone can keep a secret like that for this many years without blowing apart from the strain. No matter how much of a loner he/she is. Tellin' it to your teddy bear at night won't do it. As it *is*, I can't believe that the UNSUB never went back to check on the original sites—"

Something Keith had said earlier, about dumping *The Body* back on the Web with behind-the-scenes commentary, niggled at the back of my mind. The UNSUB could've kept going back to that particular *Body,* just as some serial killers do...as long as no one knew that *was* the person who'd been responsible for the thing in the first place....

And as long as the UNSUB never altered what was there, visiting the site without downloading, s/he could've been lurking on the net like a serial strangler hiding behind a tree in the woods, watching his victim bloat and decompose. Hell, the UNSUB could've been checking to see how many individual users visited each site—we'd determined that the sites didn't leave any cookies, so we hadn't been able to track who'd visited them, or when.

Monitoring each site's traffic would be as satisfying as reading newspaper accounts of victims found in a river; the effect may have been radically different, but the basic psychology of this criminal wasn't terribly far from that of all the shackled prisoners I'd talked to. There was even a signature—the inclusion of that admittedly cute kitten/cat in each movie, the sort of mental quirk common to serial killers whose urge to kill isn't totally satisfied by the act itself, or even the basic mechanics of the crime. Hence, the *need* to do something idiosyncratic, something meaningful only to the criminal, which is not an intrinsic part of the crime *per se.* Adding the cat was pure artistic embellishment to an already complete digital canvas.

"Y'know, it might not be a bad idea to send out pictures of that cat...target the biggest cities, and the most expensive veterinarians. If the UNSUB wants the kitty in the picture, I'll bet he—or she—would want the best care for it—"

"Which means *I* gotta do it, right?" Keith tried to affect a frown, but his eyes were twinkling. It may have been a remote lead, at best, but it beat the hell out of sitting in a cramped makeshift office, watching the same five *CR* remakes day after day. Although Keith had had his field trip....

"Want to flip for it?"

"What's the loser get to do instead?" Keith dug around in his pants pocket for the same nickel we'd tossed that morning.

"I've another idea...based on that whole being-proud thing. Where can a person brag without saying a word? Out loud, I mean? And without anyone knowing who you really are?"

Keith pocketed the nickel, smiling down at me as he stood up. "If I sit behind a computer all day, dropping in on chat rooms, my ass'll meld with the chair cushion. I'm outta here, my man...have to make sure the boys in the lab pull a clear image off the films. Good luck with the surfers, Rune. Don't let the netcronyms make your eyes go crossed, ok?"

The original *Ciné Rimettato* Web sites had long fallen prey to hordes of angry intellectual property attorneys and copyright holders, not to mention Ted Turner's lawyers, and were nothing more than a wistful, flickering memory of pixel dust, but there was no legal way to shut down sites devoted to their appreciation—especially if the webmasters were canny enough to forgo showing clips or stills from the banned releases. As it turned out, during the first hour of following the most obvious links (most, URLs containing the words *ciné* or *cinéma*...like "Ciné Rinascimento.com" "La Cinéma de Fantasia.com" or "Cinéma

Immaginazione.com"), I came across over twenty sites, some comprised completely of text (like the fellow who'd not only reprinted Ebert's essay, but almost every other review of the *CR* films from everyone else's Web sites), others a combination of commentary and message boards ("AFAIK, Kevin Spacey hasn't been approached to _do_ a Stephen King movie—you're thinking of Tom Hanks." "YYSSW, but I still think he was up for the James Caan part in MISERY—" "Wasn't he doing Mel Profitt on WISEGUY then?"); but some offered genius chatrooms, where chatspeak sputtered across the monitor and everyone had an opinion about the *Ciné...oeuvre*:

Shadow: UGTBK...you actually rented all the videos suggested after THE BODY?

MassGuy: Every one. Including KRIPPENDORF'S TRIBE. Which is actually pretty good. Course I already had all the ST:TNGs on tape.

Shadow: Bought or taped?

MassGuy: Both. My local station stopped showing it midway thru season four.

Akkadian: ICCL about renting/taping stuff—what about THE BODY? What do u think of it?

Shadow: DIKU?

MassGuy: The same —?

Akkadian: DTS, but again, what's your opinions?

Shadow: Floored. I'd seen the original 5-6-7 times, but this one IS "The Body" I'd read. Too bad they didn't add the part where Gordie's story from his teenage years was excerpted from —

MassGuy: No, couldn't be done. *CR* films redo, they don't add.

Shadow: Yeah, but it's a thought. Couldn't the real director do that later on? How old's the real Gordie going to be for the 30-year anniversary of the original? Do the words _Director's Cut_ mean anything? ;-S

Akkadian: Q-l, Who Knows? Q-2, 44, and Q-3, They could

mean More $$$ for all involved.

Shadow: Didn't the director go to high school with Dreyfuss?

MassGuy: Yeah. Hollywood High. But not in the same class.

Akkadian: What about the other *CR* films? Seen all of them?

MassGuy: BTDT - I transferred mine to DVD.

Shadow: Seen them all, wasn't too nuts about the GWTW one but THE CABLE GUY was awesome. A bit morbid if you think on it for too long, but the original was _so_ dark, and this was just funny. At least now there's three Farley-Spade films, so it's a real duo now—

MassGuy: What about CONEHEADS?

Akkadian: They weren't in the same scenes except for one in that film. So it barely counted. Q?: was this CABLE GUY as good as TOMMY BOY or BLACK SHEEP?

Shadow: As good. Not better, but as good. I missed the part from the original where Chip was singing the Jefferson Airplane song. What was put in there was from SNL I think, and not a whole song. But using a Meat Loaf song was ok, tho.

Akkadian: I don't think *CR* films can redo songs like they can re-create dialogue. Spoken words are different from sung words.

MassGuy: The scene in the jail, when Chip smashes his chest up against the glass barrier was wild.

Akkadian: Thank SNL's Chippendales sketch for that one.

Whoever Akkadian was, s/he was obviously older, and more thoughtful than Shadow and MassGuy—not too many of the other postings on the message boards or chatters brought up the *SNL* connection in regard to *The Cable Guy*...the hard-core *SNL* crowd tended to be older, and less likely to rely so heavily on e-mail argot. I'd printed out the conversation, and looking it over, noticed that this Akkadian had addressed one of the problems with the *Ciné* films, something quite a few *CR* fans seemed to miss...aside from the karaoke scene in *The Cable Guy,* the *CR* substitutions avoided singing. Duplicating an actor's spoken words via a synthesizer or sampler was difficult, especially when nuances and inflections were taken into account, but singing was staggeringly formidable. And another thing Akkadian said made so much of the *CR* process abruptly clear—that infamous "Chippendales" skit, with Farley and Patrick Swayze stripping down, brought me into the mind of the *CR artiste*...and solved the basic problem of getting around a wireframe for each digitized character. Apart from the people in the two earliest *CR* films, all the other actors used for substitutions had either done nearly-nude scenes, or partly disrobed at least one film or TV performance. Before anyone knew of a fifth *Ciné Rimettato* film, Keith and I had studiously watched every video of every movie the substitute actors and actresses had made...and I'd been struck by *Light Sleeper*, which featured a brief but uncannily gripping appearance by David Spade as a strung-out cokehead searching for God. He'd been sitting with Willem Dafoe's pusher, dressed in socks and briefs, and I remembered thinking at the time that Spade could've very well been a straight dramatic actor if he'd wanted to go that route—he was that convincing—but what he was wearing, or more rightly wasn't wearing, should've been more important to me. Thinking back on his filmography, I realized that he'd been a living wire-frame in just about everything, both in film and on TV—he was out of his clothes as often as he was in them. All the *CR* creator had to do was figure out his measurements as based on surrounding items, and there it was, a ready-to-use element, available to render into an existing movie.

And the other actors had done their share of undressed-scenes; it took the memory of that Chippendales sketch to bring it all back, but suddenly I could picture the UNSUB's hands, as s/he fed this data into the computers, and I could feel that sense of accomplishment which comes after approaching a seemingly unsolvable problem and coming up with an unexpectedly simple, accessible solution. Add in the existing movements of each person's mouth as s/he produced individual sounds and words, redub the synth-scrambled voices (sweetened or roughened as necessary), and there they were. Animations from real flesh, propelled by original skeletons, and not mere digital-wire armatures. Filling in old backgrounds, then covering them up again, was just computer busywork after that.

By the time *The Body* was loaded onto the Web, the UNSUB had his/her act down patter than pat. Which accounted for why Spacey's narration was so exquisitely on target, each line reading as succinct and as deeply felt as Dreyfuss's original... albeit much darker. And the limited amount of time his character was on camera made for a more perfect "performance"... so perfect that the UNSUB couldn't resist adding touches to the later scenes, blending in the oncoming cowcatcher of the steam engine between the running legs of the two kids on the track, or overlaying bruises on their shoulders during the leech scene. Even if someone wanted to remove the new narration and Spacey's two scenes from this *CR* remake, what was left would still be more fine-tuned than the original...although as Shadow had pointed out in his/her roundabout way, the best Writer possible was shooting another historical drama for Ted Turner just a few miles away from where I was now sitting.

But Wheaton wasn't in his forties yet—he was barely into his thirties. Half a lifetime away from his childhood performance, but still another eleven-twelve years from being the right age to play The Writer. Just as Spacey (who'd actually been born in 1959, the same year the film took place) was then too young to play The Writer, but was now currently a couple of years too old—

Which was the basic trouble with finding the ideal cast to populate any movie—what you might *want* wasn't necessarily what you'd need at that time in order to make such a film. Even if Rob Reiner and Richard Dreyfuss went to school together, if Reiner had had someone like Spacey available, *and* if Spacey had been fortysomething *at that time*, there was a strong chance he might've been cast *as* The Writer. That later King film, *Dolores Claiborne*, featured two actresses who looked astonishingly alike playing a young and an older Selena...even Keith, who hadn't been to a theater since Clint Eastwood stopped making Dirty Harry pictures, was impressed by how much the two girls looked alike. Said it made the movie all the better for him.

Leaning away from the keyboard, I muttered into my cupped palms, "I'm missing *something* here...are you a perfectionist, a die-hard movie buff, or...*what?* You aren't in it for the money, you don't want the fame...if you love movies so much, why love just *five* films?"

Thinking, Maybe the Ebert article scared him/her off...maybe the torrent of hits on *The Body* sites was too intimidating, I began rereading the chatroom conversation...and noticed that despite Akkadian's keen interest in what others thought of the *CR* films, s/he didn't offer any opinion on them...something the other two chatters didn't notice. After all, they didn't know this person, if "DIKU" meant "Do I know you"...which meant that Akkadian was someone new to *CR* chatrooms.

Which in turn brought up that whole *pride* thing again—

Exiting the room (where Akkadian had left a "POOF" shortly after I'd looked away from the screen, according to my print-out) I backed up to the Yahoo! portal and checked for links to an Akkadian Web page....

All I got was the Web site for some small press magazine. I was about to check out the remainder of the *Ciné*-related sites when I found myself typing in "Birkita Saleen Newman" and clicked "search" with my mouse.

I'd never thought to see if she had any Web sites, be they fan-made or official; this *Ciné* case had been so time-consuming, I was lucky to have caught the late-night airings of her films on the Independent Film Channel. But no matter how culturally pervasive the *CR* films had become, other movies continued to be made, with real people telling new stories...and as the URLs for five Birkita Web sites appeared on my screen, I told myself, so *I am not the only person who'd discovered her*, though the slightest twinge of apprehension plucked my nerves. Hoping that none of the sites were anti-fan postings, I tried the first one, hoping that the simple "www.birkita.com" indicated that it was her official site.

Apparently, her domain had been co-opted early in her career; fortunately, though, the person who'd created this page loved her work as much—or maybe even more—than I did. Good-quality stills taken from press kits, short downloadable clips from her early films (*Custom Kind*, *Rhymes with Thyme*, and the one that won the award at Sundance, *G2G*), including that memorable sequence from *Rhymes* when she's walking away from her boyfriend, out into rush hour traffic, only to have each car stop precisely a finger's width before her, as she seemingly meanders through the slow-moving cars—until the camera does this amazing crane-pan of the street below, to reveal the open spaces between the stopped cars, as they form a lopsided heart.

But mostly, there were pictures of her, especially those eyes...that between-shades mix of tan around the pupil and bluish-aqua beyond, which some people called hazel, while others found themselves unable to describe them as anything but beautiful. Slightly cat's-eyes, with subtly upturned outer corners and one pupil that veered off by half a degree or so...so no matter where she directed her gaze in any of her films, she could almost be looking your way as you sat there in the darkness below her flickering image.

Oh, the rest of the pictures were of her, too, but they were full-body shots that diminished her remarkable, wistfully ageless eyes. True, seeing her entire body may've been enticing for a lot of other men out there (especially in the low-cut waitress uniform she wore at the beginning of *G2G*, before the diner was bombed), especially men sick and tired of stick-figure fashion slaves with T-square collarbones and sunken abdomens, but I kept moving my mouse up to the head shots, to enlarge them....

After a few minutes of this, my conscience (and the realization that my bosses might be monitoring what I was doing) warned me that I wasn't likely to find any links to the *CR* UNSUB in some young indy-film queen's retinas, so I reluctantly left the site—even as I tried the following URL, www.

G2GBirkita.com, with my next heartbeat.

An official site, apparently one to which she contributed original material, judging by the photos of her pre-film stage work, back when she was in her teens or early twenties (I'd never learned exactly how old she really was; apart from having been dipped in the waters of the Dick Clark gene pool, even her voice was ageless—girlishly light, with a smoky, burr-like undertone that echoed like a distant purr). All the productions were period pieces, and she herself was so unchanged (apart from her now-blonde hair being a shade closer to honey-tan), that I couldn't even begin to tell when she'd appeared in those plays...Helena in "A Midsummer Night's Dream," a rather chesty Laura from "The Glass Menagerie," Mrs. Zero in the 1920s play "The Adding Machine," a makeup-aged Mrs. Antrobus to a black Mr. Antrobus in Wilder's "The Skin of Our Teeth," and, in the only modern-dress role shown, the teen seductress Patsy June Johnson from Lanford Wilson's "The Rimers of Eldritch." But even there, her outfit was timeless...a flared pink skirt and what had to have been a knit bodysuit, grey with a deep V-neck. By enlarging the photo, I did notice that she seemed to be wearing those god-awful Earth shoes from the late 1970s, the ones with the backwards-sloping heels, but that could've been a strange whim of whoever costumed the play....

I'd saved and printed out the enlargement without realizing until the freshly printed page rolled out of the printer.

The guys upstairs would love to know why I did that, I found myself thinking as I quickly plucked it from the printer and tossed it into a drawer. Deciding that the folks who hit the *CR* sites had to have felt the same compulsion to download what they saw, I told myself that the FBI may pay my rent, that finding criminals was my vocation, but there was no damn way anyone was going to put handcuffs on *my* needs.

The rest of the site was as photo-oriented as the fan site; interspersed with stills and downloadable clips were statements from Birkita:

"Acting hasn't been a passion for me—it's Passion, period."

"When other actors were kids, they pretended they were accepting their Oscars while holding a hairbrush in front of the bathroom mirror...for me, my rattle was my 'Oscar' when I was still in my crib."

"My only regret about doing pictures back to back is missing out on the face-to-face with my fans..."

The only biographical material on the site mentioned that she'd been born in Chicago, was "still" single, and adored cats.

She'd contributed pictures of her "boys," Baby Brutis, Quinn-Quinn (apparently she'd seen *Sliders,* and was aware of the whole "two Quinns" subplot in the last season of the show), and Woody, "a.k.a Woody-Wumpus."

"Baby" Brutis had long ago outgrown his name—he was a huge black-mitted cat with a swollen, strangely serene face, while Quinn-Quinn was a semi-harlequin white cat with splotchy black markings. And then there was Woody—

I don't know how long I sat there, staring at the image. I *do* recall thinking that I really *ought* to call the lab, and tell Keith to take a look...until I told myself, cats like that are as common as dander. You don't know how many people out there own cats exactly like him.

True, the pose was different, but Woody looked so much like the cat in the *CR* remakes he could've been that phantom feline's littermate. The same creamy white rings around the eyes, the same slanted oval green eyes, the same eager expression....

Without bothering to print out Woody's image, I clicked out of the site. Cats *are* the most common house pet in the country, and every year some cat food company puts out a calendar of famous people and their felines, plus the other pet food giant has one with cats owned by everyday people...many of whom are interchangeable with those belonging to the celebrities.

Reflexively, I typed in the commands for another search of *CR*-related sites, and within minutes I was watching a chat about the altered *Terminator*:

SueB: Has anyone considered that all the person who made this did with the final skeletal Terminator was squeeze the image, so that it looked thinner? Too bad they couldn't have done that in the first place, so Henriksen could've really played the Terminator.

Wiley: But Cameron couldn't have sold the picture if Arnold S. was only playing one of the cops who gets killed midway thru.

Jean-P: The irony is, Arnold is so funny playing the cop— when he drops that cigarette into the black cop's coffee —

Wiley: Reminded me of what he did in KINDERGARTEN COP. But the switch between the actors was cool.

SueB: I'm surprised Harlan Ellison hasn't claimed this *CR* version was his idea, too.

Jean-P: The whole Terminator plotline is straight from 20 MASTERPLOTS. I can download the pages to prove it—

Sensing that this conversation was about to go off on a more literary than visual tangent, I exited, and was about to click onto another when the phone rang.

"Rune, you ain't gonna believe this—"

"'Aren't,' and you know better, Keith—"

"Aren't-smaren't. *This* man's gone got himself a lead."

His voice cut through the monitor haze in my brain, and made me aware that not only was my butt sore but I was also hungry and thirsty—a sensation undercut with dismay when I glanced at my watch and realized I'd been surfing the net for over seven *hours.*

"The photos of the cat?" I heard myself whispering, as the need to empty my bladder insinuated itself in my consciousness.

"I'm gonna send that actor an application for the Bureau— you won't believe it. The eleventh vet we tried. In Oakland. Not only did the vet recognize the cat, but he faxed us back that the owner works in the computer field—housebound on top of *that.* And rich as all get-out—brings in the cat so damn often, the vet bought himself a second X-ray machine from the profits."

"Is the cat named Woody?" I asked.

"You psychic, man? Yeah, he named the cat after a damn cartoon character of all things—"

The sound of that one gender pronoun almost made me relieve myself behind my desk; crossing my legs, I asked, "Does this person have other cats?"

"Uhm...lemme see...no, just this one. Guy brings it in every month, for a tune-up. Check for worms—"

"I'll take your word for it," I smiled into the receiver, before picking up a pen and asking, "Ok, what's the name—and no damn coin toss this time, I'm due for a break from this playpen of ours."

According to the fax, our suspect's name was Michael Tillich. Keith and I cross-checked for priors, not so much as a parking ticket. Which was in keeping with our profile. California driver's license showed us that he was white, and looked like an extra from that old TNT movie about Steve Jobs and Bill Gates. A Silicon Valley boy, with a cat named after one of the characters in a Disney movie. Thirty-seven, single, just a profiler's dream. He'd been a software designer for almost half his life. He even belonged to those vintage-TV video clubs, buying mostly science fiction and fantasy shows. Man had the whole *Xena: Warrior Princess* collection.

He didn't have any overt connection to the movie industry, a factoid I found troubling, but Keith thought the purchase of old episodes of *The Twilight Zone* and *Kolchak: The Night Stalker* indicated at least an oblique interest in Tinseltown.

It wasn't until I was putting in a requisition for a round-trip ticket to California (coach, alas) and Keith was arranging for an agent from the local field office to accompany me that we came upon the major discrepancy between Tillich's driver's license and the stuff the veterinarian sent us—either Tillich needed a whole lot of room to house his multiple computers/processors *plus* his collection of vintage TV shows, as in two houses' worth, or he was a closet polygamist whose wives loathed each other. One address (next to his laminated photo) was in Oakland proper, the other in a suburb a few miles outside the city limits. Both were single-unit dwellings, which—based on what information we could glean from the realtors who'd handled both properties—fit our profile precisely (large rooms, huge basements, close to a major T-l line). And Tillich owned both of them.

Not that a good software designer couldn't earn enough to afford two houses, *but —*

"Ok, so which house do I visit first?"

Keith spoke without hesitation. "The one where the cat lives. He'd need to have it close while he works. I'll bet the other one's full of damn *Xena* tapes...."

I'd brought my laptop to Oakland; it sure beat the hell out of the Adam Sandler film they were showing on the flight. I'd downloaded the entire *Ciné Rimettato* file (minus the actual movies) and all of the notes Keith and I had made...but it was going to be a long, long flight, and the download from Birkita's personal Web site fit nicely on my hard drive. I'd even included the clips....

Between bites of my dinner (which bore a dismaying resemblance to the fare Steve Martin ended up with in *Planes, Trains and Automobiles*), I pulled up the file photos of Woody the cat—both of them—from Birkita's site and the *CR* remakes. The two could've been related; picked up from the same shelter, perhaps. The name was easier to explain; Keith told me he'd found thirty-eight Woodys and eighteen Buzzes or Buzz Lightyears in the Los Angeles and San Francisco areas alone— at the first ten vets. Not all of them were cats, but for some reason the names were popular.

Next, I lined up Tillich's photo next to that of his cat...but somehow the *connection*, my first real look at the person behind the whole mess, continued to elude me. No matter how bland-looking the average serial killer, or bomber, or kidnapper, typically there's...something, in the eyes, or in the demeanor, or in the person's *soul*, that tells me, Yes, this is the man.

True, Tillich actually wasn't in front of me, but the eyes in the photograph just didn't *grab* me. I suppose it's a residual effect from my days as a cop, the gut feeling that simply *tells* you things without the need for words, or even concrete thought.

Driver's license pictures are always bad, I soothed myself as I sipped my coffee...half the time they don't resemble the subject. But something I'd thought I'd trained myself to suppress in the name of psychology and criminal theory, told me that no picture is ever *that* bad....

The special agent who was supposed to accompany me to Tillich's suburban address was out sick; one of those Asian flu bugs making the rounds on the West Coast. I was offered another agent, but demurred—the field office was half-staffed, and I needed the time alone in the rental car to collect my thoughts. No matter what I found or didn't find that day, I was merely going to pay Mr. Tillich a neutral visit—a routine background check, concerning one of his software-design buyers.

The house was unchanged from the photos the realtor in Oakland had faxed us, save for one detail—a redwood ramp leading from the three-car garage to the single-story-dwelling's double-wide front doors. The realtor had sold Tillich the house in the past four years, but the ramp was weathered to the silvery-grey shade of his cat Woody's fur—

I'd looked at his license so many times in the past two and a half weeks that I could recite all of Tillich's personal data by rote: DOB 2-25-68, Ht: 5' 10", Wt: 152, Hair: Brown, Eyes: Blue. And he needed corrective lenses in order to drive. But he wasn't handicapped—no indication that he'd need a ramp— telling myself that he might've had two warring wives—one in a chair—after all, I walked up to the door and thumbed the bell, listening to the muted chiming tones behind the Spanish-style oak doors.

I hadn't noticed the speaker grill beside the door until the voice crackled close to my left ear: "Yes, may I help you?"

A female voice, distorted like an answering machine left unchanged for too long.

"Hello, I'm looking for a Mr. Michael Tillich...I'm Special Agent Rune Volney with the FBI.... Could you please tell me if he's in?" Speaking to blank, *faux*-carved wood was unnerving.

I couldn't tell if there was a security camera hidden by the stuccoed door-surround, but I suspected I was being watched.

"Could you please hold up your badge and ID to the right-hand door? Middle of the panel?"

The voice was as glitchy and as scratchy as before, but it obviously wasn't a recording. Obediently, I opened my badge holder before the door panel—where I finally made out a small convex lens, hidden among the bold Spanish-style ca7rvings—and continued to wait in the wan, watery sunlight. The neighborhood beyond me was quiet, but I could make out a distinct humming noise to my left, close to where a marionette's worth of long wires snaked down from a power pole to somewhere off to the side of the house. It was quiet enough for me to hear a car revving up, but no sound came from the attached garage.

The sonofabitch is checking out my badge number, I realized, as the wait continued...then, that static-spiked voice again:

"Please, come in, Agent Volney—"

The doors slid aside—I hadn't realized they were pocket doors before—and a granular wedge of blackness yawned before me. As if realizing that I couldn't see, remote-controlled ambient lights winked into a trail of brightness, like the rows of lights in some old movie theaters—

The connection, that sense of *knowing* I was close to my prey, came on me in a knee-melting rush. Tillich had to know what those lights looked like—Once my eyes adjusted, I saw that I was in your basic California ranch-style house: wide open doorways, low ceilings, tile floors...and not much in the way of furnishings, save for a massive HD-TV and banks of top-of-the-line stereo equipment. And movie posters on the walls... framed in matte chrome, covered with non-reflective glass. Real poster-posters, not the ones video rental guys put in a barrel and either sell for a buck a pop or give away with a rental.

I found myself in what passed for the living room, although

there was little of a lived-in look about the space. Not even a place to sit down—There were three doorways leading to other rooms, all of them darkened...until I heard that voice again, still marred with hissing pops and electronic burrs, coming from behind me:

"I'm sorry to have kept you waiting outside, Agent Volney—I assume you've guessed that I was looking up your badge number....I trust you're here on official business, no? Although I thought they only sent out profilers in Thomas Harris novels—"

Although it had only been a movie, I suddenly knew exactly how Jodie Foster's Clarice Starling had felt when she'd realized that she was standing in the same room with Buffalo Bill in *The Silence of the Lambs* —strange, how the lexicon of cultural references tends to be so closely linked with the cinematic after all. And I wasn't even a fan of Foster or the movie itself. I liked Ted Levine's Jame Gumb, but the whole film was simply too pat and coincidental for my tastes—

But all I could think of was being small and fragile and alone with a killer who skinned women—even though I myself was six-one, hefty, and presumably alone with a software programmer who didn't look strong enough to depress his keypad—Only, the voice wasn't male, and I hadn't heard any footsteps.

"You can turn around—I couldn't shoot you if I wanted to...."

Another drinker from the creative well; the tacit reference to the basement shoot-out at the end of the movie made me smile despite my unease. And I made sure the smile stayed on my face as I turned around, for realization was sinking in as to the reason for that rasp on the speaker, and lest I display that most politically-incorrect reaction of all toward an ostensible cripple—Michael Tillich hadn't spoken those words. He may have owned the house, probably by proxy, but it was with a great inner gasp of relief that I realized that he wasn't the *Ciné Rimettato* creator—

—even as another part of me, a more primitive, feeling part, died a slow, sad, withering death.

She was already assuming the near-fetal position of the advanced stages of what appeared to be either ALS or MS; her hands were supported by leather- and shoelace-like bound braces, although she clearly had movement in her fingers. The twin trays of keyboards jutting out like folded-in wings before her were level with her hand. Her legs were thin, the calves under the straight-leg jeans were broom-handle straight beneath the webbing which helped to hold her onto her chair. There was a microphone device held over her larynx with pink-edged surgical tape, half-hidden by her hair. Which was back to its original honey-tan shade....

Of course, her eyes were the same; only they'd glittered with tears on screen....

"Come, there's a chair in the back room," she finally said, with that metallic simplicity, and with a trembling pass of her left hand over the keyboard below, she was off, moving silently in her chair. I followed in her wake of soft-rushing air, down a sloping hallway which led to the rear of the house, into what I now realized was a basement converted for wheelchair access. The sensation was like being in a movie theater; while the air was filtered clean, I could almost imagine a whiff of popcorn.

As promised, there were chairs—director's chairs, one even bearing her name stenciled across the back—downstairs. And, as Keith and I had surmised, there were hundreds of monitor-free computers, Macs by the look of them (not those candy-colored Ju-Ju-Be home units but serious workhorse models) sitting on banks of wire shelving, much like the workings of a cable TV system, only with JAZ drives added. Power cables shone like so much licorice, black, red, and even yellow, thick candy-like ropes squiggling across the tile floor and up along the rows of utilitarian racks. There was a humming sound in the room, far more intense than the minimal noise her electric chair made.

And there were monitors near the chairs...one showing her earliest movie, *Los Gatos Express* from 1989. The one I'd kept missing, save for the last few minutes caught periodically on IFC.

"It's on video," she said suddenly, as if gleaning my thought. "I've a copy somewhere upstairs. Not DVD, though, But that one *is* me."

"'Is' as in...you were in it."

Up close, I realized that Birkita Saleen Newman may very well have been wearing her own Earth shoes in that long-ago college production of "The Rimers of Eldritch"—her skin was supple, slightly oily even, but the fine wrinkles on her forehead and around her eyes were enough to tell me she was pushing fifty, or damn close to it.

For two years, I'd been pouring over those five remakes she'd made, trying to figure out the *why* behind them, trying to get into the UNSUB's head...when it was the *body* that was the motive all along.

I had to smile as I thought of the films she'd chosen to spring on an unsuspecting, unprepared, but ultimately delighted (save for the legal types) world—all of them connected with bodies, in one way or another. Scarlett O'Hara, the character whose body was part and parcel of *who* she was. Divine in *Casablanca*, a man who used a *faux* woman's body to achieve fame...a smaller, leaner, unobtrusive Terminator in exchange for a hugely muscled, obtrusive killing machine...and the changes in body sizes and types in *The Cable Guy* were beyond obvious. Which left *The Body*....

Where the young, would-be-some-day Writer could visually "grow": into a more visually-matched adult Writer. Without making the viewer wonder what the teenage Gordie might've done to himself in the wild 1960s to make his brown eyes blue....

And I remembered what she'd said to me just now, "But that one *is* me"...which meant—

She must've seen the spark of recognition—of connection, in my eyes, for she said, "Yes, the *Ciné Rimettato* films were practice. I had to know if what I was planning to do, once I found out what was going to happen to me physically, would actually work. I'd switched gears in my early thirties, given acting a try and got a role after my first audition. Made me realize that I'd lost a lifetime of opportunity working behind one of those—" she jerked her head in the direction of the computers racked for parallel processing "—tap-tapping away half my life...but my mid-life crisis wasn't precipitated by poor job performance. I designed a lot of software, probably some of it used by your employers. I managed to make a *great* deal of money...and I invested it. And I was lucky with those investments. So...when I decided to go to one of those open indy auditions, and got the part...I thought I was set. I found out just before that picture wrapped that I'd soon be like this. Once I got over my anger, I remembered an old movie, that one Michael Crichton did in the '70s, *Looker*...all about these evil corporate types who digitally scanned beautiful women in order to create their commercials. Or something like that. The plot wasn't important, but the idea...came back to me, pulled me out of my self-pity."

(Mentally, I kicked myself for overlooking that movie—it might've helped us create a better profile much sooner....)

"And I could still move well enough for motion capture, so I had myself digitally mapped. Recorded my voice, enough for a hundred films' worth of sampling. Just like in *The Stepford Wives*." She smiled at me. "But that wasn't enough...I knew money would buy me screen time in virtually any newbie director's indy film, that enough money up front to make extra prints and buy real advertising time would guarantee me a role in any movie I wanted 'in' on...but I didn't know for sure if I could take out some other actress, and put me in. So...I practiced with previously made films. To see if the finished product would look right—I had to make sure a replacement actor would look really *real,* using sampled images and voices. After the first four films I redid, I was satisfied that my idea was sound, and I got my software past the beta stage—

"Oh, please don't look so pained about me replacing someone else—it happens more than you'd want to know about. And I made sure that every woman I ended up replacing was well paid, and that they got roles in the next film I starred in...I don't think I've permanently damaged anyone's career."

"But...don't people talk?"

"In Hollywood? Or outside it, on the fringes? Not if you want to work again...no need to frown, only the surface of this business is beautiful. But I don't kill careers. Only...delay them, one picture at a time. Disappointment is a fixture of the profession... but being paid to be let down is rare. Only a handful of people know...know what I've done...but they don't know about *Ciné*, *I* did that by myself, although I had some friends make out the money orders. Like Mike...he's getting this house in my will. He's earned it. Woody's going to live with him, eventually. Like Brutus and Quinn-Quinn will stay with the people who take them to the vet for me....I'm dying," she added without rancor. "I've been this way for some time now, and the doctors say I'm very lucky to be able to still breathe on my own, and talk after a fashion. I still have my vocal cords. That Hawking fellow didn't, after a time."

I could tell that her voice was failing, from fatigue. Just as I knew there was no way, no way at all, no matter how many lawyers and television station moguls and people back at the Bureau and the DoJ were tugging at me, that I'd be able to let anyone string her up from the nearest movie marquee and leave her to dangle in the wind. Even if a judge and jury convicted her, how long might she live once she was incarcerated? Fining her would amount to a death sentence—she needed the money to maintain herself, even on a most basic, no-frills level. And to merely expose her to the world would've been the cruelest punishment of all—She lifted both arms at the elbow, shaking hands held out with their palms parallel, and said, "Don't make the cuffs too tight, ok?"

I had to laugh. "You've pissed off a lot of people, you do realize that? But...you haven't killed any careers, let alone any people, which as far as I'm concerned would be my only motivation to turn you in—"

"I'm still very much a threat...I've read about me in the

papers, seen the articles on the Web. I'm a danger to Copyright Land—"

I thought about the nearly $75K sitting in the SAG retirement accounts, and all those videos that had been sold or rented, and all the money those actors and actresses she'd chosen to digitally manipulate had earned...not fortunes, but money nonetheless paid for their "work."

And I also thought about the sheer creativity of her efforts, and how she'd made my partner back at the BAU laugh at *The Cable Guy*—Keith, who never watched comedies. And all those people in the chat rooms, actually *thinking* about what they'd seen both in her versions and in the original films she'd altered for such an overtly mundane purpose—

"Why not replace actresses with your image...why did you pick those other people—"

"For the software, actually...to make it applicable for anyone, not just my image. And because there were people who didn't make movies they should have, or who passed them up for one reason or another...I didn't want to grow bored working with my own image too quickly. And I suppose my intellectual curiosity needed to be sated—"

"How long did it take you to do them? The first remakes, I mean—"

"Depended...some took nearly a year, others six months. I write good software," she added simply. "But *The Body* only took three months. And I did that one long after I'd put myself into my own pictures. And most of that time was spent fixing the glitches they couldn't do back then."

"So...why do that one at all? You knew how to dub in dialogue, you could manipulate images—I can see putting the casting right in the other movies, but that one...I mean, everyone knows that Tom Cruise was supposed to star in *The Shawshank Redemption*, Brad Pitt too—and that River Phoenix died before he could appear in *Interview with the Vampire*—"

For the first time, I saw a spark of anger in those bi-colored eyes. When she spoke, her voice quavered with distortion:

"Don't mention people who squander their lives in mid-project. Phoenix was working on some other film before *Vampire,* some small movie. And he partied too hard right in the middle of shooting, when he was still obligated to the people he was working for. I can understand Farley—he admitted his problems, tacitly. And he wasn't making a film when he died. But even if I could've finished the thing Phoenix was working on, or replaced him in *Vampire* —and I could've written the software to do either film, as long as the other actors resumed their roles...I knew how to do it then—I wouldn't do it after such a display of irresponsible rudeness. Understand?" Her eyes softened, as she continued, "As for *Shawshank*, it's all but achieved religious significance with the public. I wouldn't have dared touch it. Not that I couldn't have done it. But *The Body...*I just wanted to see what it would've looked like. With two actors who matched physically...I made another version of it, one I never put up—I paid for some domains but never used them. I made it, I watched it, and then I erased it. Because I didn't want it to surface, and prevent it from possibly being made for real someday. I don't take away roles from people who might age into them, should someone get the idea to do an ultimate anniversary edition—"

—Knowing that I *had* linked up with my UNSUB's motivations, without realizing it, made me smile again, despite the moist tightness I felt behind my soft palate and nose.

"Too bad you destroyed it...I would've liked to have seen it. Although maybe I will see it, eventually. I don't think that particular actor is going to quit the business anytime soon—"

"Or OD," Birkita added with a ringing metallic finality, followed by a smile which looked almost as beautiful as the ones she'd worn in all those photos I'd downloaded.

Sensing that her strength was ebbing, I knelt down close to her chair, and said, "I trust that no more of these...'put-rights' of yours will be appearing anytime soon. No one cares—no one minds about your films, but the others—"

"I've made what I wanted made...and what I wanted people

to see. Apart from the one film I did purely for myself, I just couldn't bear for the others not to be seen...and people *do* enjoy them, don't they?"

"As long as they're the only ones like that, they will. The FBI doesn't have the manpower to seek and destroy every last copy...even if we say we do. I guess we're like Hollywood in that regard—"

"I guess you are," she agreed. "I promise, I won't make any more."

Realizing that our time was limited, I did ask quietly, "I need to know—why add in your cat? My partner, he's stumped—"

"I wanted to. Sly Stallone put in his dog, once he got the *Rocky* films.... Woody is just too cute. And he'd sit on my monitor while I was working...so one of my helpers filmed him with the digital camera one day...nothing more than that. He was there, and, then he was in the films. He's my favorite cat, and...what else can I say?"

"I can't think of anything," I said, patting her hands, and wanting more than anything to be able to ask her for an auto-graph, or something....

Keith and the others believed me when I said that Michael Tillich was a dead-end; the cat was the same, but nothing else checked out. Just a home entertainment junkie with too much stuff for one house.

Once new "product" stopped showing up on the Web, and the people who'd downloaded what they wanted finally talked themselves dry about it, the matter died away...until about a year later, when the codes for Birkita's software showed up on several Web sites. No explanation, just a lot of code...which someone eventually turned into a *CR* program. Then told his friends, who e-mailed their friends, who....

Keith actually thinks that our old UNSUB is back at it; what with that version of *Titanic* "starring" Gwyneth Paltrow and Billy Crudup, all three *Star Wars* movies featuring a young Christopher Walken as Han Solo, and even the inevitable Tom Cruise version of Andy Dufrane in *Rita Hayworth and*

Shawshank Redemption (which lit up the Web like the proverbial Christmas tree, inspiring Web pages and protests alike) all floating around on the Internet, I can't blame his assumption, and I haven't done anything to hinder his continued efforts to profile the *CR* UNSUB. The software is available, after all, shared freely on the net, so anyone with a yen to put some real or self-ascribed "wrong" casting "right" is now free to do so—and just as free to become a target of the combined strength of the Feds, the legal suits, and whoever else might decide to come between creativity and copyright....

I could tell Keith, I suppose, but the point is moot. She is dead, after all. I saw the notice about it scrolled across the bottom of the screen during CNN's *ShowBiz Today,* under a clip from one of her latest films. *E!* likewise devoted only a few seconds to her demise. Ostensibly from a "sudden illness"—both channels claimed she was in her thirties. But she happened to die on a big news day; not only were there SAG nominations to report, but there was a major opening on Broadway. Wil Wheaton and Kevin Spacey were starring as Biff and Willie Loman in yet another revival of Arthur Miller's *Death of a Salesman.*

There was already Tony buzz about the production.

I suppose Birkita was lucky to get her ten seconds' worth of air time that day.

Special thanks to Jayge Carr for her help in researching this novelette. Italian translations were provided by John S. Postovit. Thanks also to the filmmakers and actors mentioned in this novelette.

Afterword for *"Ciné Rimettato"*

Where to begin with this one? The genesis of this novelette was a sad one, actually—literally the moment when I heard on my local rock music radio station (which never aired news after drive time, yet broke into the late afternoon show with a bulletin) that Chris Farley had been found dead in a Chicago apartment that morning. I was born in Chicago, and although I never did encounter Mr. Farley, back in 1976 I had spent a week at his childhood/teen alma mater, the Edgewood School, which is a twelve-year Catholic school down in Madison, Wisconsin, attending a writer's workshop for high school students, so I'd spent some time at his old stomping grounds, as it were, so I felt some (albeit slight) attachment to him as an entertainer. The guy made me (and a lot of other people) laugh, and he wasn't such a total hypocrite that he kept all his addiction problems hidden and denied, so...I felt terrible when he died. He was too damn young to go like that. No matter what sort of behaviors he indulged in. What was especially sad was that he'd made so few movies and what saddened me was that he'd had a chance to be in *The Cable Guy*, but passed, which might have been a far different picture with him it, maybe even a hit picture (since I was sure his approach would have been less dark/unsettling). But he was gone. Yet the thought of what *his Cable Guy* might have been like persisted, until it became the germ of a storyline, specifically, What if there was a way to insert one actor into another's role, digitally, and have it look real, not all CGI-weird/zombie-like?

Once I came to that mental question, the bulk of the story fell into place: the terminally-ill inventor/performer (for the record, Birkita suffers from ALS), the beta-films, and the whole copyright/FBI angle. Around then, I realized I had to come up with other altered films, which had to be, 1) well-known to even the least avid movie-fan, 2) of some interest to an sf audience, 3) easily available to the person doing the changes, and 4) one of them just had to be based on a Stephen King film—just because so damned many films have been made from his work in the past 30 years—which meant that everyone would at least be familiar with whatever title I eventually chose, even if they hadn't seen the film in question. Lots of air time on cable was also a consideration, thus ensuring that most readers would have seen at least one or more of the films mentioned/altered, even if they didn't have a VCR/DVD player.

The old films, *Gone with the Wind* and *Casablanca*, were easy picks—virtually everyone knows about them. Plus the alternate casting possibilities for both films were fairly well known, and could be easily visualized by the reader. (And I had to pick something I could put Divine in—his death also hit me quite hard. The man was a unique talent, on the verge of mainstream success when he passed on.)

The Terminator was an obvious pick—not only because it is one of the best sf films made in the 1980s, but because of the vastly different sizes of the men considered for the lead role, which played a major part in my rationale behind the beta films Birkita creates—she was planning to insert herself into pre-made indy films, and thus might need to replace a physically bigger/wider actress, or vice versa, and the replacement of Arnold S. with the much shorter/leaner Lance H. was perfect (much as changing the tall, thin Jim Carrey—who despite the oddness of the character in his film was quite brilliant—with the shorter, wider Farley accomplished in the other "beta" effort) to showcase the hypothetical substitution programming the main character developed. Which left me with the King film—and originally, what I had in mind was something far different than I wound up with. What I had planned was leaving the bulk of the film I settled on, *Stand by Me*, intact, save for the narration/appearance of the adult Gordy, which I was planning to turn into a use of the software programming's ability to physically *age* an actor, specifically the person who played Gordy as a child (and who was only in his late twenties when the story was being planned). I was going to have the character take his young adult image and age it to forty-something, thus having one person play the role throughout the movie. But there was a problem... the same actor was also an adept computer-programmer, who really had left acting to pursue a career in computers/software, which in turn meant that the reader might deduce that he was the person behind the whole string of *Ciné Rimettato* films (which, given that most actors want to work more, wouldn't be that much of a stretch to assume that an actor might plug himself into a movie for the exposure), or worse yet, had simply recorded his own narration for the movie, and videotaped himself wearing make-up in the scenes featuring Richard Dreyfuss. But by then, I had my heart set on that specific film (that the original novella was entitled "The Body" made it all the more irresistible to me; plus there was the distracting [make that glaring] lack of resemblance in any way, shape or form between the two actors playing that particular character, which to me was just *begging* for some sort of re-do, do-over, whathaveyou!) so I kept trying to mentally iron out that problem of making a real person not be the obvious culprit behind the (albeit make-believe) illegal remakes. Personally, I don't really like using real people *in* a story, yet it was looking like I'd need to come up with some way to make it clear in the story that this (actual) person wasn't "behind" the fictional action in the story. During this time, the same actor appeared with Lance Henriksen in some TNT telefilm about Lincoln, which messed up *another* part of the story (as in "hey, he was doing his former co-worker a favor by putting him in—"), so by that time, I had to ditch the whole aging concept behind the alteration of *Stand By Me*, and just concentrate on replacing the adult Gordy with someone who looked more like the young Gordy. I decided to pick an actor who was in his 40s at the time these adapted/altered movies were being made, which would have made him an actor in his twenties (thus too young to have played The Writer and too old to have been cast as any other character in the movie) back in 1986. With brown hair, brown eyes, and an adult height of 5-10 to 5-11 or so, and a slim body build. Trouble is, I had a hell of a time coming up with anyone who fit the bill, aside from Kevin Spacey and Billy Bob Thornton, and the latter's accent was a problem for my purposes (Southern accents and New England accents aren't interchangeable!), so...Keyser Soze, it had to be. I still had two actors involved in one role who still didn't look all that much alike, but the coloring and general size were more compatible. Plus both actors have this sort of mannered way of speaking, somewhat stagey if you think about it, but in the same general range/pitch. And Spacey's previous characters sure do a hell of a lot of talking in every film he's been in, which was a plus. It would be easy to cobble together a narration out of his past performances, so I felt I almost had the whole problem solved, until I remembered that the film Gordy grew up to be computer-programmer/actor...so I was faced with what I still consider to be a rather creepy/weird/just-plain-sucks option: I had to insert a real person into my fictional universe, in order to establish that he didn't have anything to do with these (again) fictional films, which didn't even exist in the first damn place! Otherwise, I'd be risking insinuating that a real person might have committed a copyright crime (albeit in a fictional setting), which is offensive to me. I made up my mind that he was *not* going to appear "on stage" as it were, so once I decided on that, the work went from Stalled to Drive, and I was able to actually start writing the damn thing, about three years after I first came up with the idea.

However, I now realize that I was thinking *waaaay* inside the box in regard to the whole real-person-with-the-necessary-skills-to-be-the-film-re-maker mess...I should've just re-cast the two primary roles in the movie, Gordy and Chris, with actors I happened to like, just to please me, and in turn create something mentally startling for the reader. Some pairings which immediately come to mind (now, though, not when I was working on the thing!) are Matt Damon and Ben Affleck (which would've gone back to my original plan, for that film to be an exercise in aging an actor), Ethan Hawke and the sublime Jude Law (who, for my money, isn't in enough movies...take that, Chris Rock!!), who were so magnificent together in *Gattaca*, or possibly a weird but fun re-casting of Owen and Luke Wilson, with their big brother Andrew tossed in as Gordy's older brother (can anyone get enough of those guys, I wonder? Yes, I am obviously a fan of them and their buddy Wes Anderson!)...or Christian Bale and who knows who else, just any actors who weren't strongly into computer programming, but who were possibly child actors.

So that aspect of the novelette, the whole real-people bit, is sort of a bummer for me now, re-reading the work. (Plus when you use real people, there's that attendant will-they-be-alive-when-the-action-in-the-story-takes-place [in this case, roughly 2005-06] question, which is what usually makes me wary of using real people in my fiction.) I think it worked out ok (but just ok), but I'm not thrilled with what I did, either.

What I do find amusing is that not long after my novelette came out, the film *Simone* (which dealt with a similar subject, specifically a virtual actress) came out, and tanked, but at least "my" version came out before the film did. It is cool to see more and more commercials coming out which utilize the whole concept of actor substitution within movie clips—I feel like I was on the right track, at least! (My favorite was the one for that cola which used a clip from *Easy Rider* with another guy taking Jack Nicholson's place on the bike....)

Regarding the actress/software designer who comes up with the films, she's more or less a version of me (a "me" who isn't computer illiterate!) especially when it comes to physical appearance, and actual acting "résumé" (the college plays, not the movies!), plus her full name (Birkita Saleen Newman) is a basic IBM/HAL letter transposition from my given name. I did minor in theatre arts in college, and I was in all the plays mentioned in Birkita's website, and yes, I even wore what she wore in that production of "The Rimers of Eldritch" back in the late 1970s. I just wasn't all that good as an actress, so I didn't pursue it (and not being able to drive didn't help me any, since acting is not a viable option out in the northwest Wisconsin sticks!), but yes, I still think about it, and wish I had been able to at least attend the open auditions The Guthrie Playhouse was holding back in 1977 or '78, which my drama instructor refused to give me a ride to (he was going there himself to audition, and no, he didn't make it), since he told me I wasn't good enough, and that someone like me had no chance, so just forget about it. I realize that I wouldn't have made it in, but it would've been cool to simply have been able to say, "Hey, I auditioned for the Guthrie once..." whether I made it in or not. It's the missed chance to actually try which still niggles at me.

But I still watch movies avidly (see my own top thirteen lists of the best films of the '90s and '00s below), and I do have my favorite directors whose work I idolize (Quentin Tarantino, Wes Anderson, the Cohen Brothers, David Fincher, etc.), plus I even speak fairly fluent *Caddyshack*, so it was fulfilling for me to write this piece, the whole real-actor-lurking-in-the-background thing aside. I only wish I was actually smart enough to run a computer, let alone program it, like my fictional alter-ego....

Just to let you, the reader, know what sort of films I'm into as a viewer, here are my personal top thirteen lists (because ten just isn't enough) for the two decades affected by this tale: 1990s:

The Usual Suspects: As close to a perfect film as humanly possible—tied with *Fight Club* : A brutal, bloody master-piece.

Pulp Fiction: The ultimate rule-changer/non-linear master-piece.

American Beauty: Exquisite work by all, but Chris Cooper's garage scene with Kevin Spacey is breathtakingly nuanced and devastating.

Slingblade: Billy Bob Thornton's Karl Childers is the ultimate angel in human form.

Fargo: Oh, yea, you betcha I loved this one....

Se7en: David Fincher's *other* brutal, bloody masterwork.

The Shawshank Redemption: What can I say that hasn't already been said?

L.A. Confidential: Big, brash, mind-blowingly good.

The Green Mile: Exquisitely heart-rending.

Toy Story: Pixar took animation into the future with this one.

Jackie Brown: An underrated masterpiece; Robert Forester is superb.

Kung Fu Hustle: A cross-cultural/genre mash-up, Stephen Chow's love letter to American and Chinese-cinema. Irresistible.

2000s

Kill Bill: Volumes 1 and 2: Face it, it's *one* big movie. Easily the best revenge flick I've seen; a woman's movie for those of us who hate chick flicks.

(tie) *Shaun of the Dead*: it's a zombie pastiche, it's a wry romance, it's a tender romance, it's amazing—and worth repeat viewings.

(tie) *District 9.* Aside from having a brilliant script and mind-blowing special effects, Sharlto Copley's performance as an alien immigration bureau paper pusher promoted above his abilities is one of *the* most perfect performances of the decade—this is literally a must-see film, and performance, period. As in, go rent or stream or whatever this film *now* if you haven't seen it yet! Trust me, you'll understand once you view it.

The Royal Tenenbaums: Deliciously perfect; dry wit and droll performance abound. As Royal T. put it, "I want to be a Tenenbaum, too."

Frailty; Bill Paxton's directorial triumph, a bone-dry chiller.

Idiocracy: A Mike Judge gem, set 500 years in the future, about a dumbed-down dystopia which is coming into existence starting now. Not given a wide release, which was a huge mistake.

Little Miss Sunshine: Never has the dysfunctional been so wickedly entertaining

Confessions of a Dangerous Mind: Actually made me care about Chuck Barris...the guy who invented *The Gong Show*. Who would've thunk it?

Minority Report: One of the best Philip K. Dick-based films, and one of Tom Cruise's best performances since *Rain Man*. Peter Stromaare's creepy surgeon is a killer cameo.

A.I. (Artificial Intelligence): Heartbreakingly unforgettable.

Toy Story 2: A rare sequel which surpassed the original in scope.

Hot Fuzz: The other UK import proving that Simon Pegg is a comic genius.

The Incredibles: A script that puts most live-action films to shame, superb voice casting, and a lush, exotic score, plus Edna Mode!

Granted, I missed a lot of other films I also loved from those two decades (*Avatar, The Talented Mr. Ripley, Gran Torino, Shaiolin Soccer, Lone Star, The Sixth Sense, Bottle Rocket, Wall-E, No Country for Old Men, Signs, Monsters, Inc., Unbreakable, Up, Charlie and the Chocolate Factory*) but this is basically What I Like when it comes to films (What Do I Hate? Romances, chick flicks, most modern musicals, most kiddie films, superhero comic strip adaptations, anything based on an Oprah! Book Club selection, etc); as far as this new decade goes, I know that *Toy Story 3* and *Rise of the Planet of the Apes* will be somewhere on the list....

Aside from watching movies since I've written this piece, I've also become quite addicted to the CBS/ABC Studios join effort, *Criminal Minds*, about a somewhat fictionalized FBI Behavioral Analysis Unit (ironically, one of the characters is a black former Chicago cop!)—and wouldn't you know it, in the fourth-season episode entitled "Paradise," my literary thorn-in-the creative side showed up playing an UNSUB. And now with AutoTune, the whole "problem" of having substitute characters sing is a moot one....

BOOG'/4 AND THE
ENDICARAN KLUGE

I.

déjà vécu ("already lived through")

"Yes, I know you! You know me, too!"
—Bernann McKinney, owner of cloned pit bull "Booger"
upon seeing the five puppies cloned from his cells, 8-5-08

"Panta rhei, ouden menei" ("Everything flows, nothing stands still")
—attributed to Heraclitus (c. 540-480 B.C.)

Turning over onto his left side, so that he could nudge the
back of his newly Emerge-ated partner with his bare abdomen, Duncan/Badru Tearlach whispered into Annemie/Rabiah
Egidius' freshly pierced ear, "Let's go down to Deck Six, see
how they're growing.... I need to see how Duncan/Anum's doing." Without moving, or acknowledging his persistent body-
slams against her buttocks, Annemie/Rabiah thought, You said
exactly the same thing when *you* were still 'woomed on Deck
Six...of course, you were Duncan/Mensah then, and wanted to
stare at Duncan/Badru, just as *I* was Annemie/Ottah. And in
a few years, once we've gone through Dissolution, and we're
Duncan/Anum and Annemie/Layl, we will have this same

conversation yet again, as you use my behind like the wall of a racquet-ball court....

Funny, how each of their successive cloned incarnations felt the same; each time Duncan pushed his abdomen against her bare skin, it never felt different. The texture of his skin was a constant, as much so as his predictable post-lovemaking prattle. Always just slightly rough, richly textured, as if he were still deeply tanned and wind-chapped from rock climbing shirtless, or windsurfing for hours on end, while she'd sat waiting patiently on the beach, watching him with that first rush of pure, undiluted longing she'd felt during their Alpha existence, four Boog' lifetimes ago. No, not really life*times*, more like life *segments* ago. Out here, far between planets, far between major star systems, the lifetime of a Boog' was less than a decade, depending on how much prolonged weightlessness and cosmic radiation a particular Boog' could stand.

In the case of each of the Annemie's, starting with /Alula, and going through /Pili and most lately /Ottah, her Boog's could stand about nine years' worth of the worst the galaxy had to offer a human (or cloned-human) body, before bone degeneration and widespread cancers weakened each installment of her never-ending young adulthood, and her lifepartner Duncan/ Whatever, who'd been Emerge-ated (Boog' slang for Emerged/ Reintegrated) between two to three years before her latest version, would stay by her bedside while she was Rested (more Boog' slang, for Terminated, Killed, Put to Clone Pasture), then greet her during the post-Emergence stage, when her previously blank mind was absorbing the engrams and biochemical datadump from not only her Alpha memory, but each successive set of memories. Just as she would do the same for each new Duncan/Whoever, during their Overlap periods.

As much as Duncan/Et Al. seemed to relish their Overlaps, for the renewed opportunity each one gave him to literally start their relationship exactly where it left off the last time, down to him ordering each version of Veronica Lea to make sure that the newly de-woomed Annemie had exactly the same piercings and tattoos in precisely the same spots on each new body, plus her hair had to be cut and styled exactly the way it was when her Alpha was placed in Cryo-Storage, deep within the bowels of their spacecraft. And since Duncan's Alpha had had an inkling that his little soulmate, his once-student/now lifemate/forever partner might not be so concerned about making sure that each and every new Duncan resembled Him-As-He-Began, he'd left explicit, specific, and do-it-or-freaking-else instructions as to how his latest clone was to be prepared for Emergence: all head and body hair trimmed to a precise quarter-inch in length; left ear lobe pierced twice, right once; *"Gra anois agus go deo"* tattooed in Midnight Black 4-Ever ink across his heart, and "Annemie Always" along the crease of his left thigh, where it met his pelvis; and three scars, of unvarying length, placed on his right knee, left forearm, and right underside of his chin, in honor of significant sporting accidents.

So every time when her latest clone bade farewell to the space-aged Duncan in the Dissolution Chamber, she knew that the next Duncan to occupy the Parthenogenesis Chamber (the official name of what they soon dubbed the Emergence Chamber) would be absolutely, undeniably, mind-numbingly the same as the old one whose carcass was slowly being absorbed in the Deck Ten Fertilization Pit, turning into food for the worms used in the Bio-fuel lab. Which rendered their initial meetings *déjà-vu*-like in their sameness—

Just as he had done before, and *before* and be-freaking-*fore*, Duncan pulled her close to his body, forcibly spooning, as he whispered more loudly into her ear, "Let's go, OK? See the new kids? They won't know—"

"—we're looking at them," Annemie/Rabiah finished for him, as she wiggled out of his encircling grasp, and sat up on their bed, staring down at Duncan/Badru's clearly puzzled face, trying to remember just what it was about him that had made her decide to *do* this in the first place. In the Alpha time, when they were originals back on Earth, he her former professor of Applied Quantum Physics, and she his TA/turned lover turned lifemate, when the twenty-year age difference between them was a real thing, and not merely a trick of the memory arbitrarily imposed through successive cognitive downloads in his now-younger body.

He placed a hand on her left thigh, the one with the newly-applied tattoo of a white rose over his first name (this latest tat was by far the closest to the one her Alpha had received months before they found out that they'd both passed the endless medical tests, physical, psychological, and most importantly, genetic, prior to being cloned; clearly, this latest Veronica Lea was improving as a tattoo artist), but she gently pushed it away, saying, "Why do you always ask the same question? It's been less than a week since I was 'woomed, and you want me to go look at the next 'woomed me. In all her uncomprehending glory...untouched by Veronica's artistic ministrations—"

Duncan pulled his legs under himself, Lotus-style, and began fingering the small hoops in each ear-lobe with both hands while he cocked his head to the left (a sure sign he was genuinely puzzled), and said, "Why wouldn't you want to see her? I never get tired of seeing my successors...all of them lined up, each in a different stage of growth...I can't think of anything more beautiful to behold. Remember Heraclitus? We flow from one form to another, yet always end up the same—"

"I seriously doubt that *that*'s what the good Greek meant at all. I took it to mean that life constantly changes, which enables our eventual growth and transformation...not an endless cycle of growth, culminating in a repeat of what was before—a deliberate repetition of our former selves, I must add—"

"Is this about your hair? It is, isn't it? Before we left, you loved it, and I distinctly remember, after four neuro-transfers, that you adored the way mine looked, too—"

She pulled her legs up close to her body, hiding her intimate parts from him, and covered the sides of her head with both hands, before closing her eyes. He would think it was just about their hair, of all the trivial things. Four neuro-transfers later, she did recall that uninhibited evening when they'd gotten the news that both of them had made the cut, been accepted for the colony ship mission, out of hundreds of applicants across the country, when they'd eaten at that Eastern Chinese restaurant, ordering all the extra spicy things on the menu, then wandered off to a neighboring bar to cool down with a few beers, and during the walk back to their apartment, they'd passed that barber shop, the slightly punk one which stayed open until ten, and Duncan had suddenly remarked that between his growing bald spot and the increase in gray hairs along his temples, perhaps it was time to do something permanent about it, even though he'd soon be in cryo suspension once the clones were harvested from his body, and the condition of his hair would be a moot point. Looking at the sun-blued posters of various hair styles (or hair removals, depending on one's point of view) a drunken Annemie had teased, "Why not get rid of it?" Ever the literalist, Duncan had pushed open the door, and told the lone stylist in the shop, "Take off everything above the Adam's apple but the eyebrows," before plopping clumsily into the nearest chair.

She remembered exactly what she'd thought that evening, sitting there across from Duncan, seeing him free of professor-foliage for literally the first time since they'd met five years before—he looks so much younger, and so sexy. Like a student, not a teacher....

Which, in quadruple retrospect, should've been a warning sign, but she was young, buzzed on MSG and good German beer, and when Duncan suggested that she get what he dubbed a "Pixie-cut"—something he'd had to explain to the Mohawked barber who'd just shorn him—Annemie had willingly hopped into the chair, and allowed herself to be draped, but she did recall how she'd flinched and kept on flinching when the clippers peeled away layer after layer of her honey-amber hair, until she was left with close-cropped sides and a short-banged thatch of barely-enough-to-comb hair on the top and back of her head. Closer to a Fauxhawk than what Duncan called a Pixie, but once she saw it in the mirror, she'd told herself she loved it, because of the way Duncan was beaming at *her*. But another thing she remembered, when they were being officially cloned in that lab a week later, their cells harvested by tyvek-clothed labtechs, was that she kept telling herself it would all grow back once they were on the colony planet....

She'd never said as much to Duncan, but when Annemie/ Alula finally wore out, eight years into the first leg of the voyage, the last thing she had thought before closing her eyes was When I'm Annemie/Pili, the Pixie's *gone*...only to awaken, and groggily reach up and feel close-cropped hair, under Duncan/Manu's approving stare. To keep peace with him while both of them were active, she'd kept the hairdo he claimed to love so much, at least during the first cloning period, but once she awoke pre-clipped, she realized that Duncan and change were incompatible concepts....

"You never griped about seeing them before," Duncan/ Badru pouted, as he quitted the bed, and began pulling on his tee shirt and pants, while she continued to sit curled up on the bed, silently watching him. Easing on the slipper-like shoes all the Boog's wore (once they were outside any cabins or work areas, where near-Earth gravity was maintained, it was pretty much free-float and grab onto whatever hand grips were available, a situation which made wearing hard-soled shoes inadvisable, least someone float into another person feet-first), he continued "I'm surprised they don't fascinate you anymore. What was it you said the last time? 'It's like watching myself grow up all over again.' And once we'd watched them for awhile, we came back here and—"

"Annemie/Pili said that. Not Annemie/Ottah. By the third time, seeing myself enter puberty, again, was more depressing than stimulating."

"Puberty depressing? I never thought I'd hear you say that... how old did you say you were when you first—?"

"Not me, *Alpha* Annemie. Ever since her, I've lost my virginity at the relatively ripe age of twenty-five. What she did when she was thirteen is a moot point, now. *She's* still twenty-five and holding, and *she's* the one who lost it less than half her life ago. I don't remember my puberty...I don't remember anything, because *I* was only half-alive. Same as your clones—"

For a few minutes, Duncan/Badru stood near the pocket doorway, arms folded, lower lip pushed out, eyes narrowed, watching her, as she remembered how all of the colonist/crew members visited their Next Bodies at least once or twice in the years following their most recent Emerge-ation, either singly or in groups; but to keep visiting one's own Next long before it was to be needed was a sign of almost unforgivable vanity and hubris, a form of mirror-gazing that would've bored even Narcissus after a while. Damn Duncan and his insatiable self-love, she found herself thinking, as the object of her growing bitterness abruptly shrugged and said, "Stay here if you wish, I just have to see Duncan/Anum. I'm going to stay long enough to see if his eyes move under his eyelids. That's a sign he might be dreaming.... I read once that babies and even chicks in the shell dream. I wonder what he might dream of...." Duncan/Badru let his voice trail off in a false show of Hey-everything-will-be-OK-*fine*-if-I-keep-filling-her-silences-with-happy-prattle. Something Duncan/Manu had started, of that she was sure.

Once he'd quitted their cabin, she got up and pulled on her own tee shirt and pants; all of the Boog's had stopped wearing underwear two body changes ago—living in space, one's sweat and body oils tended to cling to one's body, and the officially-issued coveralls they'd been given to wear were like body-soil traps which didn't let their skin breathe properly, and underwear only exacerbated the problem. Thankfully, Jansur Lea Alpha had crammed dozens of tee shirts into his allotment of personal items (whatever fit in a standard, ten-gallon plastic tote), so once the second clones decided that not only were their uniforms uncomfortable, but that they never did rinse out well in what little non-drinking/non-bathing water they had available, they all began wearing whatever tees each subsequent Jansur grew tired of, along with his surgical scrub bottoms. Glancing down at what was written on her shirt, Annemie/Rabiah had to laugh:

If you knew what I was thinking,
you'd be very disappointed.

It might even be worth following Duncan/Anum down to Deck
Six just to see his face when he emerged from the Gestation
Chamber and saw what her shirt had to say to him during her
tense silence.

As she bent down to toe on her slipper-shoes, Annemie/
Rabiah unexpectedly found herself on her palms and knees on
the grubby, low-napped felted "carpet," her slipper shoes inches
away from her nose, as the ship shook and rolled around her;
and then she was on her back, her right side slammed against the
side of the bed, and her stomach felt as if it had actually parted
company with the rest of her body, and was free-floating somewhere in the walkway beyond the cabin she and the Duncans
shared. The ship's usual smooth gliding motion (less nause-
ating than a multiple-story Earth elevator ride, thanks to the
craft's combination of nuclear engines and solar-sail propul-
sion) was now erratic, wrenching, but the lack of any unusual
sound was disconcerting. The ship's hull was well-insulated,
but surely one of the other Boog's had to have been walking
from one deck or another, or out in the corridor, or found him
or herself out away from their cabin, caught up in the rolling
motion—she knew that if she weren't in her cabin, she'd be
screaming and yelling, and every one of the Veronicas were
noisy as hell under any circumstances, so not hearing anyone
say anything was disconcerting....

(Oh god, please don't let them be dead, she thought,
beseeching a non-specific deity, since she and all her crewmate
Boog's were nonbelievers by happenstance, not by selection...
no deeply religious sorts had passed the would-be-colonist
psych exams, but in this instance, she unconsciously proved the
atheists-in-foxholes adage to be more or less true.)

Then, as unexpectedly as it had begun, the rocking, jarring
motion stopped. Wondering how many minutes the ship had
been in rough flight, she pulled herself up onto the bed, and

inched her way across it lengthwise, so that her still bare feet were hanging off one side. Let Duncan/Badru waste his time taking navel-gazing to new extremes. She doubted that he'd even bother to read her tee shirt's inscription—none of the Duncans, from the Alpha on down to his fourth clone, could look at her for more than a few seconds without his eyes wandering down level with her nipples....

She didn't realize that she'd dozed off until she heard the muffled pounding on the cabin door, something unusual in that no one ever bothered to actually knock—the walls within the ship had poor soundproofing on the corridor end, and all anyone had to do was speak loudly with their mouth close to the door to be heard—so initially Annemie/Rabiah thought she was dreaming after waking, until she heard Mila/Rabiah Demkakova, the Med-Tech who worked in the Clone Gestation Chamber yelling, "Annemie? You in there? Open up, *now*...I've got...some news for you," only there was something in the way she said "news" that made Annemie/Rabiah realize that she wasn't asleep anymore—nor would she be able to sleep for what might be a long, terrible time.

II.

jamais vu ("never seen")

"Few people have the imagination for reality."
—Goethe

All the while Jansur/Badru Lea was speaking to her, after she'd warily left her cabin arm-in-arm with Mila/Rabiah (at the latter's insistence; despite years spent together in various incarnations of the same body, the two women barely knew each other), who brought her to the cabin shared by the married Leas, all Annemie/Rabiah could think about was the lecture on Paradigm shifts she'd heard while still an Alpha, once she and the first Duncan had arrived at the space center for their cloning. It was then that she'd learned for the first time that none of the Alphas would be awake during take-off—thanks to some Nobel prize winner earning his award for figuring out how to cure a rare but horrifying childhood genetic illness called progeria, the genetic team who'd be doing their series of clones could create a first round of clones which would mature to the physical equivalent of early adulthood within less than one calendar year—the main problem with these clones would be an extremely short, intense life span—within a decade, they'd literally wear out, due to the genetic acceleration brought about by a combination of deliberate genetic mutations which mimicked certain elements of progeria, plus changes in the teleomeres within each cell of the clones' bodies. Thus, a clone would mature at a hyper-fast rate, only to physically peak for a double handful of years, then rapidly age and expire.

At the time, sitting in that almost empty lecture hall, along with the other seven people whose bodies would soon be imperfectly duplicated for what amounted to built-in obsolescence, Annemie Alpha had reached over to give Duncan's hand an apprehensive squeeze, as if to say, Hey, they haven't done this to us *yet*...we can leave; but he'd merely brushed her hand away, as he'd leaned forward in his hard plastic chair, his eyes glittering with excitement. Midway through the lecture, the balding, slightly plump doctor stopped speaking about the group's minimal number of naturally occurring single nucleotide polymorphisms, or SNPs (which he pronounced in his crisply over-enunciated Midwestern accent as "snips") within their genomes, which was one of the reasons why the eight of them had been selected for the trip, due to the low incidence of possible diseases, medical conditions, and other genetic screwups within their three billion base pair sequences, something most desirable for long-term space travel; not to mention their eventual roles as colonists on some still-unnamed Earth-type planet billions of miles and decades away...and addressed a problem specific to them as both a group, and as individuals:

How does a person, or a group, adjust to going through several deaths and rebirths within a century? The need to make sure that not only the memories would be passed on, but the person's actual identity *as* that specific person, and not merely fungible clones filling in the gap between Here and There. The question of how best to maintain the delicate internal balance between knowing that one was a physical continuation of an Alpha original, yet also a vital part *of* the Alpha's eventual reawakening had been (supposedly) solved by a group of consulting psychiatrists, psychologists, therapists, behavioral profilers, and even concerned lay people who'd offered their input on-line to the other members of the group...and at the time, sitting in that echoing lecturer hall, Annemie had thought, All those degrees, all those hours spent rebuilding shattered psyches, and this, *this* is the best they can come up with? while the lecturing doctor had brought up a chart on the graphic-screen behind him. A paired list of twelve India-Indian names, in columns marked

"Male" and "Female":

"Mosi"	"Alula"
"Manu"	"Hili"
"Mensah"	"Ottah"
"Badru"	"Rabiah"
"Anum"	"Layla"
"Msrah"	"Nura"
"Quaashie"	"Sabah"
"Haji"	"Neema"
"Nkrumah"	"Masika"
"Chenzira"	"Mukantagara"
"Mukhwana"	"Kahra"
"Adeben"	"Akila"

"Does this mean my wife won't need to tattoo 'Boog' One' through 'Boog' Twelve' on everyone's asses?" Jansur Lea had deadpanned from where and his wife sat in the row behind

Annemie and Duncan; turning her head, she'd seen the couple for the first time that day, and found herself wondering how she could stand either seeing or listening to either of them for the duration of their training, let alone the next century or so. He had one of those blatty, slightly nasal voices, like a teenager whose voice had just begun to break upon hitting puberty; only considering that the man was a medical doctor, he had to be in his early thirties, or possibly more. His lack of any discernible beard stubble on his bony face didn't help much in guessing his age. Both he and his equally scrawny wife had nondescript blondish-brownish lank hair, worn straight and limp around their pasty faces. But he wasn't kidding about the tattoo part—each of the Leas had numerous tats on their exposed skin (both their arms were sleeved from what showed under their short-sleeved shirts to their wrists), plus she had piercings in her nostril, lower lip, eyebrow, and ears. Annemie started to wonder if more than a few of the couple's three billion base pairs might not be damn near identical as Veronica added, "Did whoever thought this up have a fixation on India, or were they just flexing their creative muscles?"

"Considering that most of the people responsible for bringing cloning to this current level came from India or Pakistan, the focus group felt it best to utilize pre-existing names which indicated, for the most part, birth order...although the first clone names are both female, while the second set are male, due to there being—"

"So...lemme get this straight. By giving all the clones within a series the same middle names by gender, that makes them... what? Like a family? Or a caste? Members of the same scouting troop? *This* will help my future clones avoid a mind-altering paradigm shift when they wake up in age-reversed bodies every eight to ten years? Having the same middle name as all the rest of the Boog's around them?"

"Dr. Lea, the term 'Boog's' is more than a *bit* derogatory, and certainly politically incorrect—"

"So how *are* my clones going to be different from the clones of that woman's pit bull, Booger? They all looked like the original, and I'm assuming that all *my* clones will look just like me...and he was the first pet cloned *en masse*, same as we'll all be—"

"Dr. Lea, I assure you, there is a major difference between five cloned pit bull puppies and twelve clones each from eight highly talented, individualistic people—"

"What, volume?"

Things went on like that all during their training (which was more for the benefit of their first "Mosi" and "Alula" clones, who began their accelerated lives within hours of that first chaotic lecture than for the Alphas themselves); the Leas continually questioned and mocked their handlers, until that weekend prior to the eight of them being put into cryo-sleep, when they were all shown their Nexts, lying in their womb-like nurturing liquid murk, where only parts of their developing bodies were visible—a floating hand there, a bobbing big toe, a swirling nimbus of kelp-like hair. The tanks which held the first clones were different from those on the ship; thanks to their highly engineered genetics, their gestation chambers had to be unique, and thus less viewable. But the sight of the eight blank bodies in those clear chambers was sobering for all of them, and even shut up the ever-gibbering Leas. This time, Duncan had squeezed her hand back as they stood side by side, looking down at themselves; they'd been told that the first clones would exactly resemble their Alphas, down to expertly applied matching tattoos, piercings, and other assorted cosmetic enhancements (plus barely visible vasectomies and tubal ligations, for zero population growth within the crew), all designed to avoid any emotional shock for the clones upon awakening with their freshly implanted memories just prior to lift-off; but none of that work had been done yet, so each couple saw themselves in a primitive state, with long hair and nails, and eerily bland, unmarked body parts.

Right before cryo-sleep came an entire morning and afternoon of lying on padded tables, with a myriad of electrodes and sensors attached to their scalps, while needles were eased into their necks and temples for biochemical extraction—of all the eight people in the group, perhaps only the gratingly obnoxious Dr. Lea fully understood the entire process of memory extraction/duplication, but once they were all injected with a drug cocktail designed to stimulate all areas of the brain's memory centers, the last thing she clearly remembered as her Alpha self was fast-forwarding through every damn memory, of every second of every minute of every hour of every day/week/month/year/decade in a dizzying rush of images, pseudo sensations, emotional twinges, and physical sensations...and then they were all quiet, as the needles and sensors and electrodes were removed, and the realization of what was going to happen to them, or more rightly the other Thems, finally hit each of them. Next to her on the right, Mila Demkakova started sobbing, while her life partner Colin Garbhach groggily whispered, "Shut *up*...my head's splitting!," and the Leas sighed in unison, while the other couples, the ones Annemie barely knew, had hardly spoken to, Ophelie Jivanta and Koenraad Dehaan, and Giulano and Rafela Aefre-Sheppard, leaned over to face each other, and whispered soft, reassuring words to one another... but Duncan was different from all the others. He'd lifted up his hands, fingers tented, and placed them on his chest, and began smiling into the flesh-surrounded triangle of space before him, as if deep in one of his Yoga meditations. Not once did he look at Annemie, or acknowledge any of the others around him. But she could tell from the calm look on his face, even in profile, that Duncan had somehow achieved a personal Nirvana—and that he alone was actually looking forward to this process....

While Annemie/Alula didn't physically recall the events which transpired in that memory extraction room when she awoke, she did read the brief journal entry which her Alpha had left for her, and which the lab techs who de-wombed her gave to her a couple of days after she'd mentally and physically integrated to the point where she was actually capable of reading the lines which Annemie had scrawled minutes before she was tubed and injected and sedated, on paper still wavery with immersion-fluid stains....

Neither of them had spoken about the events of the memory-extraction process that night, their last night as regular, single-issue people; after a final exam, and the indignity of requisite intestinal voiding prior to a last night of sleeping in a real bed together, Duncan had maintained that Zen-like calm, so much so that Annemie was afraid to break his envious serenity. After a fitful, sleepless night listening to his even, fluttery breathing, they'd been placed in the chambers which would be their literal "home" for the next century or so, shielded from as much cosmic radiation as humanly possible, due to a combination of structural design (their cryochamber was located deep within the ship, surrounded by multiple work stations and outer walls well-padded with insulating tiles plus Kapton thermal blankets of coppery hue) and bio-engineering (the fluid in which their naked save for skin-tight waste-extraction/removal lower briefs bodies rested was filled with antioxidant chemicals and non-organic substances specifically created to avoid radiation poisoning, should any manage to seep into their individual chambers), and the last thing Annemie Alpha had to say to her Next was a barely legible "love, now and forever."

The translation of Duncan's tattoo, the Gaelic phrase they'd planned to have engraved in their wedding bands, before the whole colony/cloning project came to their attention....

Those words had proved inspirational for her /Alula and /Pili selves, but by the time /Ottah was 'woomed, they'd become something of a burden, considering how Duncan's /Mosi, /Manu, and /Mensah selves became increasingly possessive, and deliberately unchanging throughout each cycle of their young-to-very-early-middle-age existence...when not working (he in navigation/bio-fuel lab/air purification, while she maintained the botanical lab, and also worked the "day" shift monitoring the passing cosmic dust for stray particles of Brownleeite, a rare, mineral less than 0.0001 in width which the ship encountered perhaps once a decade—what little of it they'd managed to collect was stored for later use as a natural semi-conductor on their destination planet), the two of them holed up in their cabin, rereading cherished books on their personal datapads, or rewatching favorite movies from the cultural database, or listening to the same music over and over on their personal music systems. Always personal, though, always shared...just as they always looked the same upon 'wooming, and stayed the same while in each cycle. Which made all the days and weeks and months and years somehow bleed into each other... until today, until an hour ago. When everything changed, all at once, but all Annemie could do was mentally go through the list of successive clone names as both of the Leas (although mainly Jansur) tried to explain to her What Had Happened to Duncan/Badru *and* Duncan/Anum: "It was a freak accident, nothing anyone could've foreseen, or prevented—the vectran straps holding Duncan/Anum's 'woom snug against the inner support columns were weakened, like they'd been rubbing on the corners of the support, which is crazy, I'll admit, that stuff is two times stronger than *Kevlar*, but you know how strong the Duncans are—"

Anum means "born fifth" but Layla means "born at night." I guess people in India didn't count on having more than two girls...Ottah is a male name, too, Duncan/Manu looked it up once—

"—the nearest thing I can figure is, Duncan/Badru kept hanging on the tank itself, maybe lying *on* it, and all that moving around made one of the straps rub against the support, which wouldn't have happened if they'd put *round* supports in the gravity-enhanced sections of—"

"Like I've said through the last two Emerge-ations, those squared-off supports are insane in *any* section of a ship, zero-grav or not," Veronica/Rabiah cut in, leaning against her mate's fully tat sleeved left arm, and stroking the top of his hand, which rested on his seated thigh.

"Rabiah"—another one of those birth names which had nothing to do with any particular birth order. It meant "born during spring," but who knew when spring *was* on this damned ship?

"Yeah, but who's gonna rebuild the supports now? And with what? All the building materials are in the aft cargo hold, the sealed one—anyhow, when that meteroid shower hit the solar sails this time, it tore one of them loose, and that's what made the ship rock—Giulano's been outside, repairing the sail, and Rafela's working on a way to better secure all the rest of the tanks, just in case the next time the ship takes a hit nothing will come loose—"

It's funny, how the names for the boys skip from "born third" to "born fifth"...maybe four is an unlucky number for Indians, like it is for the Chinese...my roommate in college, her parents changed her birthday from May 4 to May 1st, because her Mom was Chinese, and it was an unlucky number—

"—which is something we'll have to think about after we figure out what to do about the Duncans...actually, I *know* what to do with Duncan/Anum, it's the other one that's the—I mean, you are going to have to make the final decision, you being his partner and all, and there being no next of kin around—"

"You sound like an intern, Jas," his wife sighed, before leaning over and grasping Annemie/Rabiah's interlocked-fingers-hands with both of her tattooed hands. Glancing down at them, Annemie/Rabiah found herself confused to the point of feeling queasy; for awhile those same hands had tiny stars on the knuckles only, then they were covered with henna-red Indian bridal style decorations, and just a short time ago, they were covered with the words "Boog'" and "Three"; but now Veronica/Rabiah's hands bore Sailor Jerry-style brightly hued tats, the outlines clear, thick black around blobs of color she couldn't quite make out as specific figures, because of the liquid pooling in each eye. Wrapping her palms and fingers tightly over those of Annemie/Rabiah, Mrs. Lea explained, "Jas has several options available for you, but some take too much time, which Duncan doesn't really have in his condition, while others are...sorta *out* there."

"Yeah, and Ronnie means that literally...like from *out-there*—*" he indicated the vast emptiness beyond the surrounding confines of the ship with one large hand extended toward the nearest bulkhead.

All she could do was echo "*Out there*'?" while the couple sat staring at her intently, probably watching for signs of impending shock. They'd already told her the extent of Duncan/Badru's injuries—the ripped-off-its-moorings 'woom had landed directly on top of him, and the weight of the clone within coupled with another hundred pounds of chemical-rich nutrient-laden pseudo amniotic fluid, plus the added pounds generated by the life support/waste removal equipment inside the tank, plus the artificial womb itself had created sheering/crushing injuries severe enough to damage his right leg from the thigh on down, his abdomen (including some of his intestinal tract), his right arm from the shoulder to fingertips, and his right ear was severed when the remaining half of the broken vectran strap whipped past it before hitting the floor. Nerves, blood vessels, and bone were crushed beyond even the ministrations of the Da Vinci robotic surgical arm, so for the time being, Dr. Lea had cauterized the wounds at the trunk, leaving on the damaged limbs prior to obtaining Annemie/Rabiah's consent to amputate, but he had repaired the internal damage to the intestines by removing the affected section and attaching the free ends together—a simple procedure, one the Alpha internist Dr. Lea could've performed on Earth in even the worst of conditions. The missing ear was actually the simplest thing to fix, once Veronica/Rabiah carved a new scaffolding ear-form out of inert sterile cartilage, and her husband grafted on some induced pluipotent stem cells derived from Duncan/Bardu's skin cells, But even with the sophisticated-but-limited medical instruments and computers on board their ship, there was nothing either Lea could do about the missing limbs. If the Next had been more severely damaged, *and* much, much younger than the still 'woomed Duncan/Anum happened to be, a transplant of the damaged clone's limbs might have been a possibility, but—and this was a massive, insurmountable *but*—Duncan/Anum had only received minor injuries, mostly deep tissue bruises and a couple of easily-splinted broken bones in his tumble from the unmoored 'woom, and given his closeness in age to the more badly injured fourth Duncan, Dr. Lea told Annemie that the best option would be to keep her mate alive for as long as possible, until the Next was at least a couple of years older/more mature, so that the gap between Duncans would be lessened...he'd been up and around for a couple of years longer than *her* fourth version, which meant that given the usual rate of cellular degradation of the Annemie clones, even under the best of circumstances, the usual order of Duncan/Annemie deaths/births would be reversed, probably for the entire remainder of the journey. Which was enough of a paradigm shift in itself, but there was also the matter of Duncan being the dominant member of their partnership, something Jasnur/Badru explained would "create an entirely new relationship between you...I don't know if your partnership will last through this. And given the importance all of the Duncans place on their physical selves, I don't think prosthetics will work in this situation, especially in zero grav...he needs some sort of actual, physical replacements, if he has any hope of regaining his sense of self—"

"Wait-wait-wait," she mumbled, shaking Mrs. Lea's hand off of hers, and waving one forefinger in Jasnur/Badru's pasty-pale face, "I heard you when you said the clone is out for a transplant. And I know this equipment which will let you regrow fingers and small...stuff like that is locked in the cargo section. Hey, we're just Boog's, so what's a missing finger? Wait a few years, and it'll be back next time, right? So which one of us donates a limb, huh?"

"None of us. But I think we have something on board which... might work. For a while, at least. In form, if not in function—"

"You sound like a freaking intern, again, Jas—listen, Annemie, did Duncan tell you about what Ophile and Koenraad found when they took the shuttle to that planet in the Delta Pavonis system, the fourth one from the star, a heavy-g, dense planet with a minimal axial tilt, and a 79% nitrogen/20% oxygen, 2 % mixed argon/carbon dioxide/nitrous oxide atmosphere? The one with the ocean, and carbon-binding life forms—"

"Now *you're* sounding like a Teaching Assistant—listen, Annemie, they found life forms there. And brought some back—Duncan never told you? I'm not surprised, it was something *new* for a change—where Ophelie/Rabiah's been keeping them alive in her lab—"

"Sentient beings?"

"No, love, no wise tribal types who can magically cure Duncan, but it is a carbon-based life form, which—"

"—naturally binds with the hydrogen, nitrogen, oxygen, phosphorus, and sulfur in any living organism," Jasnur/Badru continued, his words merging effortlessly with those of his wife, "regardless of the host organism's inherent suspension medium, until a bond forms between the two organisms...a form of symbiosis, which lasts indefinitely—or at...least until Ophelie/Rabiah peeled the life form off a sheet of cloned skin cells in a tray. Anyhow, this creature is part of the chordate phylum, or something damn close to it, with a notochord—" noticing her open-mouthed confusion, he backtracked, "—which means a flexible rod-like 'spine' in its back. Anyhow, it has a radial shape naturally, somewhat like a starfish back home, and it's cephalized...all the sensory organs, such as they are, are in one location. But in terms of physical structure, it's an endicara, too...on Earth, such creatures were sort of...quilted beings, consisting of layers of cells in long ribbons, flat cakes, or sheets. So this...thing can mold itself into a variety of basic five-limbed configurations. Plus physically bond to a host-being—"

"—and as it bonds, and...feeds, it can grow. And change shape, in a semblance of aggressive mimicry, to more closely match the appearance of the host organism. Once Ophelie laid one of them on that sheet of her own cloned skin cells, it started to look like her—"

Gradually, what the Leas were describing began to become real in Annemie/Rabiah's mind...while she'd had no idea the others had an alien organism on board, thanks to Duncan/ Badru's choke-hold on her every waking free moment, what they were telling her about stirred memories of all the biology courses she'd taken while an Alpha, and suddenly she blurted out, "Are you suggesting I allow this...endicara—whatever to... to *bond* with my Duncan? How can that be of any help to—?"

"Annemie, listen, you know Duncan better than any of us, perhaps as well as he knows himself. Now do you honestly believe that he will be able to actually *live* as either a double amputee, or as someone with no real feeling in whatever limbs we are able to give him down the line? You know yourself, even transplanted limbs take months, sometimes years, to generate feeling. This organism responds to stimuli, so we suspect it has a sense of touch. Which may well transfer to the host organism. In time, it will begin to look like his flesh. We can develop armatures which will take the place of his bones, and this organism will surround them, if they're organic-based cartilage. In zero grav, the ability to make the leg weight-bearing will be moot. And the arm will function well enough for him to continue with his share of the workload. The creatures have no real brains; they're not advanced enough for that. And they seem to need to attach themselves to something, anything, on a primal level. Ophelie/Rabiah has ten of them in her lab...more than enough to mimic the muscle/flesh ratio on his limbs, to keep him roughly symmetrical. Don't look away, this is crucial—before I amputate, I'd like to have everything in place, to begin reconstruction or augmentation or whatever you want to call it to make yourself comfortable with this decision; so...will you allow me to do this? Or would you rather I bring him out of sedation so he can make the decision? I have him on the same type of cooling catheter as our Alphas, to minimize further damage, and he's on massive doses of painkillers...which I'll have to stop for awhile before he can give any consent. I won't operate on a doped Boog's say-so...but you can decide for him, spare him the pain, and shock—"

"Do I have to look at him? Before I decide?"

"Not...if you don't want to have that memory passed from Boog' to Boog'. And not if you want to remember him as he was this morning. As he will be, again, in a few years...what's in the lab is not the same Duncan you've known. You can if you want to—I can't stop you. But personally...I wouldn't. Bad enough his paradigm's gonna be shifted around at least 180° when he finally does come to. This will blow his /Mosi awakening out of the freaking water...."

Overlapping memories of each Duncan's unchanging form filled her mind; from the plushy bristle-haircut, to the unvarying tattoos and piercings, to the habitual poses he'd strike after uttering the changeless platitudes and rote words of carbon-copy affection, all of them virtually indistinguishable from Duncan Alpha all the way down to Duncan/Badru (the number four must be so, so unlucky—); but all that mental symmetry was gone, ripped asunder and patched together just a tad off center, like trying to tape together a piece of paper torn across the jagged, against-the-grain center. There was no way to reconnect the edges cleanly. Her Duncan, her Duncans, were gone.

For this segment of her stop-and-start-over life, at any rate.

She felt the Leas watching her, waiting, and before the thought actually registered in her mind, she heard herself say, "Do whatever you have to do. As long as those...things won't be harmed. Or torn apart. If they'll stay on him, put them there. Just...leave me alone until he heals, if he heals. Don't tell him I gave permission until I can tell him myself..." and then propelled herself along the corridor for a few feet, until she thought of something and worked her way back to the waiting Leas.

"Don't cut his hair while he's recuperating, OK? Just tell him—just tell—oh, the hell with it. Don't tell him anything. Just don't do it, OK?"

If the paradigm is going to shift, let it be a *huge* shift, she found herself thinking, as she grabbed jutting handstrap after handstrap along the corridor, moving in a slow bobbing motion, like hair floating in a cryo tank....

III.

presque vu ("almost seen")

PESSIMIST: The Glass Is Half Empty
OPTIMIST: The Glass Is Half Full
ACCOUNTANT: Does the Glass Really Need All That Water?
PHILOSOPHER: If No One looks at the Glass, Who's To Say
    How Full or Empty It Is?
ENGINEER: The Glass Is Twice As Big As It Needs To Be
QUANTUM PHYSICIST: The Glass Has a 50% Probability of
    Holding Water
CLONE: No Matter If The Glass Is Full or Empty—It Was My
    Alpha's Glass, Not Mine
    —Augmented inscription on a tee-shirt belonging to Dr.
            Jansur Lea (Alpha)

During the twenty-four hours it took for Dr. Lea and the fourth Mila Demkakova to work on Duncan/Badru (doing what amounted to experimental surgery no doctor back on Earth would have even begun to consider...but Alpha human doctors and fourth generation Boog' doctors were not at all the same animal, Annemie/Rabiah began to realize), Veronica/Rabiah and Colin/Badru took turns sitting with her, attempting to explain what the creatures found on that fourth planet looked like, since she adamantly refused to go to Ophelie/Rabiah's lab to see them for herself:

"Remember starfish? Imagine one that's soft, tender to the touch, like sun-burned skin, and longer, tapering limbs, only flatter, with a darkish vein or cord running just under the dermis on one limb...sort of an off-golden russet color—"

"But the cord, could it be a brain? Are you sure it isn't sentient?"

"No, we're not sticking something onto him which doesn't want to be there...there's no neural tissue in it, anywhere—

Ophelie cut up one that was already dead on the planet, not any of the living ones. They simply have this way of adapting, physically, to whatever they attach themselves to. Like an inchoate need to merge with another organism. They feed by exposure to sunlight plus submersion in whatever chemically nutrient-loaded liquid they could find on the planet, which included puddles of the planet's precipitation. They don't actually crawl from place to place, but sort of...ooze is the best way I can describe it. Really, you should come see them...they're sort of beautiful, in a...slippery sort of way—"

But what Veronica/Rabiah, she of the artistic hobbies and throw-back hippy-Earth-Mother-free-love aesthetics, thought was weirdly beautiful, Colin/Bardu merely considered a means to a somewhat dubious end:

"Once these things are bonded to Duncan's stumps, they'll be self-sufficient. Along the terminus, cellular bonding will occur. These things latch onto virtually *anything* organic. Once they're on, my mate and the doctor will secure them with temporary braces and bindings, until they adhere to the artificial bone armatures. If we had the equipment in storage, they could attempt to re-grow the remainder of both limbs, but there's no use taking things our Alphas will need on the colony planet out for use on a fungible clone. Besides, this is mostly a cosmetic surgery—I'm sure Duncan could do most of his duties with no prosthesis at all...all he does is push buttons, and he can learn to do that left-handed...personally, and I must add, this is just *my* opinion, what I'd do if Mila were in Duncan's predicament would be to amputate, rehabilitate, and do the same thing to her Next that was done to the Manu/Pili clones...accelerate them just enough to fill in the age gap between our first sets of fully age-accelerated clones, and the natural maturation of the Mensah/Ottah series. Considering that the last three sets of clones haven't even been started out yet from their embryonic states, all Dr. Lea would need to do is change the clone-gestation schedules—"

Listening to him, Annemie/Rabiah recalled the discussion

she'd had with Duncan while they were both Alpha, back when they'd first signed up for the government-sponsored colony-ship program, while Duncan was still teaching, and she was working toward the graduate degree she never quite finished on Earth...prospective candidates were initially screened, much like prospects for those computer dating services which had been around for over a century...when they got the e-mails saying they'd made the first round (that round consisting of over fifty couples from all over the country), her Alpha had wondered aloud, "Why are they planning to narrow this down to only four couples? That can't provide enough genetic diver-sity once the colonists arrive, and start makin' babies—"

"You didn't read your Heinlein, did you? That's why it pays to take more electives, whether you need them or not... Professor Moussaieff's Science Fiction 405 should've been a must for you last semester. I've audited it five times over the years...anyhow, in *Stranger in a Strange Land*, the fictional Mars mission included four couples, since that was the number of people best thought to be able to stand being with each other on a long space journey, without ending up killing each other along the way. Less or more than that was deemed unsuitable. Of course, fiction *being* fiction, complications are needed, and all eight people end up dead anyhow, but I suspect this mission's crew compliment has more to do with storage of food and fuel for a rotating eight-man crew than anything else. Besides, I heard that they'll be taking along a sperm and donor-egg bank's worth of genetic material. Which will take care of the genetic diversity aspects of the project. I just don't know if I can stand playing day-care operator for at least eighteen years once we get there—"

"*If* we get there...and I thought you said you wanted kids? My kids—"

The discussion had petered out that rainy afternoon back in Boston, mainly because Duncan had started taking her clothes off, but partly because Annemie hadn't wanted to somehow jinx their chances of making it into the final four couples. Of getting the opportunity to be with Duncan for over a century without actually aging herself...at the time, it had seemed so wondrously magical, an almost endless time to get to know each other like few couples had the opportunity to really *know* each other, and all without having to actually grow old along with that person.

What she hadn't counted on was the discovery that knowing Duncan meant merely that...*knowing*, not understanding. Like never being able to progress beyond nodding at a passing neighbor in the apartment house hallway day after day, without advancing to exchanged pleasantries or an exchange of names....And the most annoying thing under these genetically-contrived circumstances was the fact that all four couples had been specifically chosen for a single factor above and beyond great genes—they were hopelessly, inherently, unshakably hard-wired as a couple to *stay* a couple. None of them were philanderers by nature, and in four lifetimes of cloned "life" none of them had swapped mates. So there would be no chance of them cheating (the very thing which caused the deaths of the crew in that Heinlein novel, which all of her clones eventually did get around to reading), no infighting, and no leaving one's soul-mate. Even if one's current mate was a being whose status as a being with a soul was in philosophical doubt....

"Colin/Badru, how long do you think Duncan/Badru will be able to live with his injuries? Long enough to prevent his Next from being accelerated?"

"Uhmmm...the doc would know for sure, but from what Mila's told me...this might knock a few years off due to the ongoing stress, and of course, the missing four feet of his intestine might play hell with his ability to absorb nutrients, no one knows for sure, but he should hold out for probably most of his projected lifespan. But I'd prepare myself for lasting longer than he does this time around, definitely. I'm thinking depression alone will subtract more than a year or two—"

"Just how old *are* our Nexts? Chronologically, to the year?"

"Jansur/Badru keeps track of that, but I'd guess around

twelve-thirteen for yours, and about fourteen-fifteen for—"

Age of consent was usually sixteen in most states, back on Earth. Give him another year, and make it a safer seventeen. Given that she now realized that Duncan's emotional age was somewhere just shy of post-adolescence, that somehow seemed right. And from what she recalled of previous /Alula-/Pili-/Ottah visits to the tanks with Duncan, he'd been a gorgeous teen, less buff but somehow more physically vulnerable than he'd trained himself to become as an adult. Every Duncan who'd stood beside every Annemie had commented on how he loved seeing the "raw potential" of his younger selves, before going on to subtly criticize his pre-Emerge-ation self...gradually, after repeated visits, and the quadruple reiteration of the Duncans' unguarded, spontaneous utterances upon seeing his latest Next, she'd figured out what Duncan found so appealing, yet so repellant, about his pre-birthed yet fully-formed future replacements: they were free of a lifetime's worth of rigorous self-improvement, body modification, and protective layers of emotional and intellectual self-defense. Their bodies weren't scarred due to years of risk-taking, dare-devil physical abuse, nor were they decorated with artificial colors and holes in the most unscholarly places. They were pure potential, unmarred by his layers of past life unwaveringly pre-repeated. They were Change incarnate, albeit destined to be turned into Continuations of a life now put on cold, century-long Hold.

"Thanks, Colin," she mumbled, before getting to her feet and heading for the corridor access point, and it wasn't until she'd almost made it to her cabin that she remembered forgetting to add the appropriate Clone-name to his given one. He hadn't corrected her, so perhaps it didn't really matter to him? Duncan was always so stringent on that point, drilling it into her about the importance of always, always, identifying the others by their proper nomenclature. True, Colin/Badru had used the name when speaking about Jansur/Badru, but was that for his or her benefit? An attempt to make her feel comfortable in the temporary loss of her by-the-book mate?

Regardless of what Colin/Badru did or didn't have in mind, the fourth clone of twelve projected clones fell asleep the second her aching head hit the pillow which still faintly smelled of her damaged lover's sweat....

* * * * * * *

"He's still under the influences of the drugs we pumped into him during the surgery, so if he says anything, it probably won't make much sense...or it'll be off the top of his head, and lacking...forethought or restraint—"

Which was Dr. Lea's way of saying Duncan/Badru might blame her for his current kluged state of being, especially if the full implications of being a hybrid, chimera-like clone were to have hit him already.

He'd been conscious for over a day, long enough to have been told what happened (at her insistence), but not long enough to have regained the ability to move around, or utilize the brace-like devices the Leas cobbled together during the month he'd been in a medically-induced coma. A month in which the ship actually ran as relatively smoothly as it did while he was up and about; everyone had had to take on odd shifts doing his work, sometimes after studying computer-stored texts to catch up on his skill-set, but his presence wasn't so much missed as accounted for. They'd moved him from the medical ward to the Emergence Chamber, and removed his coverings, so Annemie/Rabiah could see him (again, at her AMA insistence) as he now was, and would be until his time to surrender his presence on the ship to his Next. Doped or not, he seemed to be aware that he was uncovered, vulnerable, for the first thing she noticed when she entered the chamber was that he was trying to pull covers which weren't on the mattress over his body with his left hand, while his bleary, half-open eyes kept darting down to look at himself, then darted up to stare at the low ceiling, then rolled slowly down to stare at himself, or what was left of Himself—

The grafts had taken with surprising smoothness along the terminator points on his shoulder and mid-thigh; the slightly slick/shiny flesh of the endicaraian beings did resemble sun-burned human skin, albeit a child's skin in its lack of fine-grained texture, while the basic shape of the augment-limbs more or less mimicked those now removed.

The main difference was in the hand and foot portions—while there was a definite indentation where the wrist and ankle would be, the "hand" and "foot" were flatter, less defined, and digitless, of course. The Leas swore that the new limbs had something akin to muscle tone, based on their daily manipu-lations of the limbs while he was in the coma, so with proper bracing, he might well be able to walk, after a fashion. And he could probably push buttons and flip levers with the new "hand," too...if he could bring himself to learn how to do so.

The scarring on his abdomen was visible, but minor, and the new cosmetic ear scaffolding had been covered with new skin, and attached to his head...and the slightly longer hair on his scalp covered the faint scar where the new ear adhered to the rest of his head.

Suddenly, he noticed that she was in the room, and stopped his jerky efforts to pull the absent covers over his body. His head bobbed slightly on his neck as he turned to look her way, and began muttering, "The first litter of Boog's, they were born to be service dogs, like their Alpha...he was a service dog, saved his owner...pushed her wheelchair, pulled off her shoes and socks... so his clones, they were predetermined to be service dogs the second they popped out of the host dogs' behinds...only, the first dog, the Alpha, he had cancer, so all his clones, they got it too...good dog, bad genes. My Alpha...good genes, good body. Not 'sposed to...not 'sposed to be a...science project—"

"We're all science projects. We have been since the first set of clones were augmented with that mutation of the progeria SNP...all of us are experiments. No exceptions, Duncan...just variations. You're just a little more unique. Think of it this way, you're spec—"

"Freak." Spat out with a coldly conscious emphasis. Even his eyes looked clearer, as they glared at her from the high-resting mattress top.

"I wouldn't say that. Kluge sounds better...and this has proved to be effective, under the circum—"

"Back in...1862, they called a 'kluge' an 'ill-assorted collection of poorly matched parts, forming a distressing whole'...or a.k.a. *freak*—"

Not knowing for sure which text from 1862 contained that definition, Annemie decided to let it go, and instead approached her lover, hands out, and try as he might, he couldn't wiggle far enough away from her to prevent Annemie from gently stroking his new symbiotic flesh, each hand extended palm-down against his kluged arm and leg.

Under her own flesh, the new skin rippled slightly, before smoothing down against the underlying sculpted bone armature beneath. And Duncan felt it—clearly, some sort of permanent bond had been created between his remaining stumps and the limbs grafted onto them, one which included active nerves and sense of touch.

After a few minutes of silence, he cocked his head to one side and asked flatly, "How does it feel?"

"Like skin...your skin, but younger. *Not* freakish. Different, but...not unappealing."

"And this?" He tried to hold up his right hand, moving it slightly at the pseudo-wrist to approximate an open palm facing upwards.

"A *little* more kluge, but it looks good. Simple, streamlined."

"Embryo flipper...first trimester clone hand. Paddle-hand—"

"If you insist on considering it that. If you insist on playing the freak, the cripple. If you really *want* it, *be* it—"

"Want...same. As before—"

"Our sameness is an illusion. An accident of creation in some lab. The Leas, they have the right attitude, enjoy what we are, for the time we're here. Change, mix it up if they feel like it. Screw the paradigm—"

"You let your hair grow out. Is mine—" he limply raised his left arm up, and let his hand flop down on his scalp "—need to have Veronica/Rabiah cut it...or you do it—"

Shaking her head, she mouthed *Nope*, before rolling up the bottom of her tee shirt, the faded black one with the phrase— "What part of the quantum theory don't you understand?"— printed in flaking electric blue letters across the front, and exposing her taut midriff, which now bore the inch-high lettered inked inscription:

SI HOC LEGERE
SIC NIMIUM
ERUDITIONIS
HABES

He blearily stared at her new tattoo, mouthing the Latin silently, until he was able to translate in a breathy whisper, "'If you can read this, you're overeducated'...I never thought it was funny when the Jansurs still had the tee shirt it was printed on—"

"I did."

"But you said you didn't—"

"I guess I said a lot of things to make you happy...no, make that made me want to make you happy. At the time, I believed I had to."

Duncan/Badru's eyes left her bared midriff, and rolled down in their sockets, as he peered at his altered body yet again. He said something which was too soft for her to hear, so she leaned closer, placing one hand on his abdomen (mindful not to touch his long scar), and the other on his left thigh, just above the "Annemia Always" tattoo, the one the tattoo artist had screwed up, misspelling her name, which meant Duncan argued his way out of paying full price for it, since the original drawing he'd handed to the guy did have an "e" at the end.

"You said?"

"Did you mean what you said now, about my...body? The...

new parts? Or was that something you thought I wanted to hear, too."

Love, now and forever, that was what her Alpha told her, just before she went into that long, cold sleep, and allowed her Next to continue not only her life, but her dreams...with Duncan. As he was, and as he would always be. Physically imperfect now, emotionally imperfect for perhaps always.

Leaning down, she lifted up his right hand in both of hers, and gently pressed her pursed lips against the new flesh, before whispering, "I'd lie about a tee shirt, but about *this*...it's not who I am, who any of the Annemies are."

Duncan/Badru nodded, and said, "Tell Veronica/Rab—Veronica, that she should get out her tattoo gun. I want a new one, too. The one Jansur Alpha suggested we all get, back in that lecture hall—"

"*Not* 'Boog' Four'—"

"Why not? You got the tee-shirt one—"

A sense of *presque vu* rippled through Annemie/Rabiah's body as they verbally sparred...the rhythm and pacing of the banter was familiar, something almost-seen before, but the subject was utterly new. Which when it came to any of the Duncans, was nothing short of a true paradigm shift....

* * * * * * *

During the months he did live with his kluged limbs, Duncan/Badru never did get fully back into the swing of his former daily routine on the ship; he never quite learned to walk *per se*, but he always managed to drag himself down to Deck Six, to stare down at Duncan/Anum's slow but natural progress toward late adolescence. And perhaps it was his own memory of *exactly* what he looked like at the age of sixteen that triggered what he managed to do before he then limp-crawl-surged into the Dissolution Chamber on his own, and strapped himself down one-handed, and affixed the electrodes and needles in his own neck and scalp, before beginning his anagram process minutes before Dr. Lea found him in the chamber. There was nothing he could do but allow the process to finish, before calling Annemie/Rabiah—still relatively healthy, still vigorously untouched by the insidious effects of cosmic radiation which surrounded them—to his bedside. Perhaps he willed himself to go, or maybe the symbiotic beings were tired of their host body, for as he wordlessly died before her, the limbs shuddered in place, then physically detached from their host body, and curled tightly around the artificial bones beneath them. Reflexively getting to her feet as she backed away from the body of her Fourth Clone mate, Annemie/Rabiah dimly heard a commotion in the corridor beyond, and as the voices became clearer, a frantic exchange between the Leas, she slowly began to smile as she made out their words:

"—damaged Duncan/Anum—"

"He didn't destroy the—"

"No, but they're badly broken—he'll need at least a month of 'woom time to heal properly before he can be Emerge-ated—"

"Don't tell me, Jas—the right limbs—"

"Hey, we're talking *Duncan*, so—"

Looking down at the body of her mate, she shook her head and said softly to herself, "You knew the memories of what happened to you would transfer no matter what, so you made sure your Next would be able to continue the same sort of new beginning you had after the kluge...so utterly *Duncan* of you. Prevent change any way you can, maintain that status quo no matter what...but I've learned how to out-think you, love. I can stand being mateless for a couple of years, and while you were incapacitated, we *all* learned how to compensate for your absence.

"I hope you can stand Emerge-ation with fuzzy short-term memories...Jansur once told me that the longer memories are stored between Dissolution and Emerge-ation, the less distinct the most recent ones tend to become. So you'll be waking up with crippled memories in a perfectly sturdy body...a slightly younger-than-usual body, and a much more hirsute, tattoo-

and-piercing-free body than anytime before. Most definitely different than the one you left behind—or tried to re-enter...."

As she walked out of the Dissolution Chamber after taking one last look at Duncan/Badru, one which would have to last her for quite some time, she mentally added, And this time, one of us *will* be older, mentally as well as chronologically, only a different one will be the more confident, experienced partner. Something I do hope *both* of us will remember, in *all* the subsequent bodies together....

* * * * * * *

In memory of Baby Biscuit (August, 2004-August 4, 2008) and Max (?-2007-August 5, 2008); your lives fell far short of the mythical nine promised to your kind, far too short to be either fair or just, but they generated beautiful memories which will live on long after your brief time in this particular life. Two precious lives never to be again, but never to be forgotten.

Afterword for "Boog'/4 and the Endicaran Kluge

I don't know if a lot of my readers are aware of this or not, but during the latter half of the 1990s and up until 2005, I mainly wrote erotica, under my own name (occasionally), and two pen names, one female and one male. I managed to get into far more erotica anthologies and magazines during that period than horror or science fiction markets; thanks to an early appearance in one of Susie Bright's *Best Erotica* volumes in '96, I was able to place many, many stories due in part to having that credit on my cover sheet—while I'm not going to reveal the two pen names here, since 1) if you, the reader, aren't specifically into erotica to begin with, you probably won't like those works, and 2) I used the names for a reason, specifically because those works were so radically different from my usual output that I felt that they literally *were* the work of two "other" writers, rather than something I'd put my name on. Not that I don't like those stories—I actually think some of my best work as a writer *per se* appeared under those two pen names. It just wasn't work I felt that fans of A. R. Morlan might like.

I think I sold about three-quarters or possibly four-fifths of my erotica output during those ten years, far better than my ability to sell my trunk stories in the horror/fantasy/sf genres, with only a handful of outright rejects in that field; I have a small cache of trunk stories, far smaller than my other work under my own name, but one of them, a piece I'd done for one of Cecilia Tan's Circlet Press trade paperback anthos—a gay sf one, by the way—kept niggling at the back of my mind, whispering to me, "Try rewriting me as straight sf...." It took almost nine years of mental nagging on the part of that plotline, but I finally rewrote the thing, changing the cast of characters from an all-(gay)-male crew to a mixed-sex cast of shipmates, plus I updated the storyline as based on the current trend of cloning house pets (including the infamous five-puppy cloning effort back in '08), plus some additional space-travel-related information I'd read about.

I think the reworking from erotica to more or less straight space opera style sf turned out fairly well; this is not my best sf story by any means, but those editors who saw it did like it well enough to share positive comments on it. I eventually sent a copy of it to a sometimes co-writer/pen pal of mine, James B. Johnson (a really fine writer in his own right), and he and I tossed ideas between us about turning this into a novel, with each chapter dealing with the successive batches of clone crewmen; but I eventually shelved that idea, since I've had a hard enough time trying to sell hard-copy-only manuscripts in an increasingly online-only field, and trying to sell a non-electronic version novel would be impossible. Jim didn't want to take it on as a novel on his own, and I know I don't have enough of a hard science background to be able to expand this into a proper hard sf novel, taking all possible space/science/medical ramifications into account, so *that* particular version of this story will *not* be coming to a bookstore near you anytime....

But for what it is, an exploration of science vs. human nature, I think it is entertaining enough, not bad for one of my rare sf-erotica rejects....

Postscript

When I wrote the above Afterword for this novelette, I had yet to have experienced my own utterly life-altering paradigm shift—in the spring of this year (currently 2011, as I write this in November of that year), I received a letter from what I initially thought was possibly a fan of mine, since the letter came from a city and state I didn't recognize, but it was addressed using my full given name, which none of my fans have ever used before. So I opened it with a great deal of trepidation, not knowing what to expect.

It turns out that the writer was my aunt, my father's youngest sister, and in the letter she explained that my father had used an online people-finder company to find out my current address. She said he and the rest of the family were so thrilled to have found me (*if* I was the same person they were looking for), and as proof of who she was, she enclosed copies of some specific family photos showing both me and my mother, as well as included specific names and dates which only I'd know.

I was slightly puzzled by the letter; ever since I was small, I was told by my mother and her mother that my father knew where they'd taken me after their divorce; and furthermore, that he didn't want me, or (most especially) didn't want another girl, since he already had two daughters from his first wife. I was also told many other things, which are much too unsettling for me to even relate to his side of the family; but, basically, these things I was repeatedly told made me frightened to contact anyone from that side of my family—plus, as I was warned many times when I was younger, my mother and her mother would literally kill me if I tried to contact my "other" family.

I wrote back to her, rather cautiously, and didn't hear from her for a while, during which time my relationship with my mother ended (for personal, family reasons, I'm not going into the details here), and she left my house...and just over a week or so after that happened, I heard back from my aunt. Turns out she'd been waiting on some material from my father before writing to me again; and she enclosed some very old photocopies of the documents surrounding my disposition after the divorce—specifically, that my mother's custody of me had been terminated, and that he had been awarded custody of me.

There was a two-week window between her being officially notified of this matter by the courts, and him coming to pick me up—and during that time, the two of them kidnapped me and flew to California, leaving no forwarding address, or anything to let him know what had happened to me. For the last fifty years, he's been looking for me. And—in a major irony—even though I've had my name on many magazine and anthology covers over the years, plus had two novels published under my pen name, which isn't all that different from my given name, no one in the family saw them, because they're not into horror or science fiction...they *are* avid readers, but prefer other genres. So they simply weren't aware of me or my work over the last twenty-five-plus years. Just as I was under the assumption that I was not only not wanted, but actively disliked because I was a girl, and somehow not worthy of anyone's affection in that family. I had been lied to countless times over literally half a century...and when I found out that virtually my entire life as I knew it was founded on a complete lie (a self-serving, cover-their-asses-from-criminal prosecution lie!)...well, it was a really good thing that I happened to be sitting down when I opened that second letter from my aunt. I couldn't get up out of that chair for a long, long time that morning; my entire world had shifted one hundred eighty degrees, and absolutely nothing would ever be the same again....

Since then, I've seen my father again for the first time in fifty years. It was an emotional meeting, but a good one. The rest of what's been happening to me is still too new for me to adequately voice my multitude of emotions about the matter; but...when I was re-reading this novelette again, which proof-reading it, I was struck not only by the irony of it all, but by my realization that I'd actually captured the main character's feelings over *her* fictional paradigm shift quite realistically....

ROBIN WILLIAMS, SPEAKING SPANISH

"Amazing...that's amazing. He should work for NASA, or something like that."
"So much for NASA...."

Ronald Bas and Barry Morrow,
Rainman, 1988

Case #290727DD/I-R
03-01-58/T. Kenward, caseworker

Day 1: Contact

"The Jones' cabin's down past Storage Module Four...don't bother to knock. Ain't like he's gonna get up to greet ya—"

"Throw some cheese balls in first, he'll never notice you're in there—"

Sabriah put one hand on my shoulder and pressed her dark fingers into the soft hollow between my collarbone and the top of my upper arm, as she told the to asteroid engineers, "Dalton wouldn't appreciate that...he's lactose intolerant." Turning her scarf-wrapped head my way, as she steered me down the diffusely-lit corridor, away from Broga Hastings and Moire Payne, Sabriah continued, her voice loud enough for the man and woman behind us to hear easily, "I also have Dalton on a yeast and gluten-free diet. I'm not all that sure that it's helping him, but between that and his meds, he does seem to be content."

I guessed that the last part was strictly for my benefit: every ships' nutritionist on every asteroid-tracking or asteroid-mining vessel I'd visited in the last eighteen months inevitably managed to toss off some sort of comment about how "happy" or "content" or "integrated" his or her Savvy happened to be. Even when the rest of the crew was attacking their Savvy, taunting him, teasing him, or calling him names like "Rain Man" or "Equipment" or (on the last vessel I'd been on before boarding the *Isen-Rodor* a few hours ago) "Ballast."

Nodding my own head, I said, "That *is* the goal here... although, I have to admit—" twisting my neck as far to the left as it would go comfortably, I made sure that the pair of engineers were out of hearing range "—it doesn't look like the rest of the crew is all that content with Mr. Durwin's presence on this ship. Not that that's uncommon," I added quickly, when I saw what seemed to be a *moue* of consternation pucker the nutritionist's mouth. "The presence of a Savant-Contingent usually does create some interpersonal difficulties...which is why I'm here—"

"Listen, Ms. Kenward. You can cut the socio-worker babble with me. You're here for pretty much the same reason Dalton's here...there's a big damn glut of social workers running around on Earth and the Moon, tending to all the Savvy-babies who've grown up to be a bigger damn burden on the economy than anyone could've guessed when they were all born some thirty-odd years ago. Only thing is, at least someone got creative when it came time to find all those Savvies jobs....I don't see much of anything creative or useful in your job. Especially when it comes to the Savvies."

"Well, I do think what I'm doing *is* 'useful' when it comes to Savant-Contingents. Have you *been* on some of those other ships—"

"Do you think things actually change once you've been on *any* of those other ships? I doubt anything you can do will make asteroid monkeys like Moire and Broga change when it comes to how 'content' they are with a Savvy like Dalton. As long as all *he* does all day and all night is sit around, doing however little he does, while *they're* floating around a damned asteroid out in the middle of nothing, with just a few cables attached to glorified harpoons keeping them from really floating away for good and—" here she deliberately stared at me, her dark hazel eyes boring into mine "—they're getting paid the same as *he* is, I'd say that it isn't too likely that they'll ever be 'content' with a Savvy taking up space on their ship."

"If by 'space' you mean room, I don't think that's the problem...this vessel was assembled over the moon, so keeping it streamlined or even small wasn't a consideration. There's plenty of room for—"

"Do they have a course in Obtuse down in Social Worker School?"

"No, there's no course in—"

The nutritionist let out an open-mouthed sigh and backed away from me, until the top of her scarf-wrapped head was resting on the slightly curved corridor wall behind her. Finally looking my way after letting her chin sink low against her neck, she said, "I was being facetious. I'm sorry, I know you were sent here, and I know I should co-operate. Dalton's room is just ahead. One with the picture of a cat pasted on the door. Not that he did that...I don't know if it was Moire or Broga who's responsible for that. But the guys in navigation and astrometrics aren't into *Alien* movies, and I know the Captain's strictly a reader. Go on...Broga was right about the knocking part. Dalton won't notice, and I don't think he'll care."

As I watched the woman walk away from me, back toward those "asteroid monkeys" who'd been so quick to ingratiate themselves with me from almost the minute I'd boarded the *Isen-Rodor*, I finally made the connection between Hastings' "Jones" reference and the typical Savvy nicknames—Jones, that "ship's cat" from the first two *Aliens* films. The orange tabby who was ultimately the only survivor of that mining ship's original crew, since that woman (Ripley?) left him back on Earth before heading back to the Alien's planet. I'd have to make a note of that one in my report—calling a Savvy a "Jones" would have to be added to the official list of non-PC phrases included in asteroid-mining training classes. Not that it had helped so far when it came to the words "Rain Man."

Sabriah was right about the picture pasted on the door. An old shot of the cat food spokes-cat, Morris, crudely clipped from a calendar. Orange cats—anything orange, for that matter— mostly look alike to me, but there was a bit of lettering from the calendar cover slanting across this cat's front paws. Wondering if Dalton was a redhead (and hoping he wasn't—bad enough Moire had dark red hair, so dark-yet-bright it hurt my eyes), I nonetheless did knock first, before pressing the palm-pad to the left of the sliding pocket-style door, and letting myself into the Savant-Contingent's room. As the door slid into the bifid side- wall, the cut-out of Morris rasped against the narrow opening, and tore a bit more along the cat's right side. A few more trips back and forth, and that picture would be decapitated. I'd have to remember to rip it off the door before that happened.

For a second, I was mentally torn—shut the door behind me, risking a possible panic attack on the Savvy's part, or allow those asteroid monkeys to listen in, in case they happened to follow me down the corridor? While my eyes acclimated to the darkness, I slid my hand along the smooth surface of the inte- rior wall until I found the palm-pad, then reflexively pushed it in. As the door emerged from the recesses of the bifid wall, I turned around, taking in the Savvy's quarters.

Personal quarters on asteroid ships tended to be large by Terran or Lunar standards, thanks to the vessels being constructed in space—the need to streamline was gone, since the ship wasn't designed to land, let alone move through an atmosphere. The design of the *Isen-Rodor* was common to all the other asteroid miner/trackers I'd visited. Navigation, astro- metrics/main computers/locking springs for asteroid-landings and launches were lumped on one end, with a short, thick axial connector (giving each ship its gravitational spin) between, surrounded by a series of smaller, well-shielded walkways which allowed the crew to enter the assemblage of prefabricated units which made up the other end of the "dumbbell," including storage units, crew cabins, and reserve air/fuel/food/water units. From the outside, the *Isen-Rodor* was lumpy, asymmetrical, and studded with solar panels and un-deployed space-sails (another contingency measure, this one less subject to crew-member ire than the Savvies). But on the inside...there was an astonishing amount of personal space.

Personality clashes might have been inevitable, but every crew member could retreat to a twelve by fourteen private room, complete with a personal bathroom—no shower, but their own sink and toilet—whatever sound/movie system he or she desired (within reason; each person could consume a limited amount of power for their own entertainment devices), plus enough space for whatever tchotkies each crew member deemed necessary for his or her continued sanity while trapped in what some miners called intergalactic trailer parks. (The "intergalactic" part made no sense to me, since none of the asteroid ships ever left this galaxy, but the "trailer park" part made sense, especially since the assembled units which made up each end of the rotating "dumb-bell" did tend to be rectangular in shape.)

Dalton Durwin's cabin—once my eyes grew acclimated to the dim interior—seemed little different than that of any of the Savvy cabins I'd seen so far during this assignment. Lots of MDVD's, tall thin stacks of them like upended packages of soda crackers. And just as big as a square cracker—they looked like the old DVD's but held more information per disk, for less mass. Virtually all the Savvies watched movies; while they'd been unlucky enough to be born during such a severe economic recession that even the Individuals with Disabilities Education Act—not to mention the already failing SSI benefits—couldn't guarantee the children of the Savant-Syndrome catastrophe previously standard treatments like music therapy, Lovass-type behavior programs, augmentation devices, facilitated communication, sensory integration, social skills programming, or auditory training, it was soon discovered that selecting the proper movies for these children could be of limited (i.e., cheap) benefit. At the very least, it kept them occupied while their parents and educators tried to figure out what to do with a second baby boom comprised largely of severely autistic, mathematically inclined savants. That this Savant-Syndrome was the result of a drug company foul-up of the highest order was of little help to either the children or their parents. After the manufacturer realized that a mix-up between what was supposed to be several batches of a common antacid and a newly-designated over-the-counter testosterone supplement for men was what had triggered an epidemic of autism, said drug company promptly filed for Chapter One bankruptcy. So even the lawyers were shafted some thirty years ago.

Before the Savant-Syndrome mess, perhaps one in ten autistic persons (most commonly a boy) was also a savant, but within a single generation, over 100 thousand expensive-to-educate savants were born. All of these children had no left/right brain division, but instead had one combined brain which was a full one third larger than the average human brain. The Social Security safety net was frayed to breaking by an ever-diminishing birth rate, and the whole SSI system was virtually cleaned out. True, the old system of reimbursing companies to hire the handicapped was still in place, but how many companies actually *needed* a worker whose lone talent is remembering long strings of numbers, or calculating square roots?

As I slowly looked around the cabin, with its stalagmite-like deposits of MDVD's sprouting from every horizontal surface, I tried to find Dalton amid the clutter. I had to smile when I remembered how the bulk of the Savant-Syndrome babies managed to find their way into the astro-mining sector...The phrase "Rain Man" was now considered to be both un-PC and possible grounds for job termination after at least five written complaints within one year for any miner or tracker stupid enough to keep calling the ship's Savvy by that name. But none of the children of the '20s Savvy-Boom would've ever been *on* an asteroid ship if it hadn't of been for that movie.

I'd seen the film so many times myself, I knew the whole sequence by heart—after the autistic savant, Raymond Babbitt, gets on his brother Charlie's nerves once too often, the younger man takes his older, autistic brother to a small-town doctor. And the doctor just has to try something he's read about, specifically asking Raymond some difficult calculating questions, which Raymond answers easily. And is his brother ever amazed...he immediately thinks his older sibling is ready to work for NASA. Only, after doing those amazing feats of calculation, Raymond quickly reveals that he has no concept of numbers as they apply to money...to him, a candy bar and a car cost the same amount of money. So, so much for NASA.

But Charlie Babbitt forgot something...NASA-style calculations have nothing whatsoever to do with the cost of either candy bars or automobiles. For them, numbers are numbers, to be crunched, calculated, and compiled. So one day, someone at NASA who also happened to have a neighbor whose wife had given birth to a Savant-Syndrome son a few years earlier suddenly remembered a forty-some year old film, and a short scene within said film—and within a couple of years, when the oldest of the Syndrome boys were close to their teens, first NASA, then the private mining companies, began their Savant-Contingent training programs.

Which, in a few more turns, had brought me to this particular ship, where I now stood in this specific Savvy's cave of a cabin, trying to figure out exactly where he was—then I noticed the reflected light on his face and body, as he sat with his legs crossed in a semi-Lotus position on the far corner of the bunk attached to the one narrow end of his cabin, with a portable MDVD player resting on his knees. The rectangular back of the unit—which resembled a standard laptop—hid most of his chest, but the suddenly brighter light illuminated his arms and face rather clearly.

I must have walked into the room when he was loading the movie into the player; the first few seconds of play time usually showed a black screen with a white inset ratings symbol. He must have been wearing a private earphone—I couldn't hear any sound at all, save for his slow, steady breathing. Wondering if he could see me, I cautiously made my way toward his bunk, saying loudly-but-evenly, "Hello, Dalton. Can you hear me? I've been assigned to work with you during this run, by Social Services—hello?"

I wasn't expecting him to do anything specific—when it comes to dealing with minimally socialized savants, no set reaction can be anticipated, or expected—but what happened next did surprise me. He looked at me. Directly eye-to-eye. Then... smiled. Not that his behavior was *impossible*; after all, the Rain Man character was something of an extreme case, in that he virtually never made eye contact. Autistic people, even savants, could make eye contact and sometimes did so without previous social skills training.

Aside from the asteroid-monkey twins, and the nutritionist, I'd also I spoken to Gremian Penn, the bored, deeply wrinkled captain, as well as Kevan Lawler, the navigator, and Sloan Garrick, head of astrometrics—one as mild as the other was openly aggressive. Judging from the brief conversations I'd had with all of them, Dalton Durwin was not only not welcome in the rest of the ship, but he had never expressed any inclination to venture out past his own cabin, regardless of the feelings (or more properly the lack thereof) his crewmates had for him. Kevan and Sloan couldn't recall saying more than each asteroid-run's successive approximations to him over the intercom. And I don't think the captain even knew what Dalton looked like; he was so utterly disinterested in talking about him after I'd given the man my orders that the most I could get out of him was that Sabriah was more or less responsible for the man's care and feeding.

So he wasn't in the habit of holding extended conversations with anyone, save perhaps for the nutritionist, and I already gathered that she wasn't the most gifted person when it came to give-and-take conversations.

I smiled back at him, thinking that his smile may have merely been a reflexive action, something he'd learned from watching all those movies. Anyone can learn a lot about a nation's culture from watching its films, and considering that his brain literally had no barriers to information, that just about everything which went in stayed there, ready to be accessed, perhaps he simply picked up the notion of smiling-as-a-greeting from what he'd seen.

But he kept on looking at me. None of the other Savvies on any of the other ships had done that. A couple of them barely spoke to me after I'd spent days working with them.

Telling myself, Don't become overeager, he hasn't said anything yet, I kept on smiling, before coming a few steps closer, and asking, "May I see what you're watching?"

Standing about three feet from him, I could see the thin wires snaking from the back of the player up along his chest, where they puffed out to form two dark foam rounds over his ears. Simultaneously yanking the small earphones off his head with his left hand, and pushing the screen around toward me with his right, he said, "Standard Model's scattered in the names," as I slowly began to hunker down so that my eyes were level with the screen. One look toward that flat rectangular image, and I immediately knew what he was talking about—although hearing that unmistakable Danny Elfman score helped, too. The Savvy was watching that old Disney remake of *The Absent-Minded Professor, Flubber.* The Robin Williams vehicle, with the opening credits that mixed physics symbols, including the unique letters which comprised the Standard Model, along with the remaining letters in each cast and crew-member's name. I'd loved that film when I was a child; my grandpa had one of those original DVD players, and he also had a small toy made for one of the fast-food places which featured a translucent bright green man-shaped blob of flubber dancing on an even older VHS videotape box. He'd bring out the toy whenever he played the film for me...but it wasn't until I was much older that I figured out what all those "funny" letters in among the people's names really stood for.

When the credits were over, just before the film itself began, Dalton suddenly said, "Still looking for the one for the Higgs boson."

Physics was one of the subjects I almost didn't pass in college, but I remembered that it was a tiny particle, something still theoretical after being proposed in the 1960s, which had something to do with mass. I think. I did remember that there was no sign for it in the Standard Model. Just as I remembered that most of the Savant-Syndrome children were lucky if they received the equivalent of a high school education...and subjects like physics were definitely considered unnecessary for them. But there was no way he could have learned about Higgs bosons by watching a family-oriented comedy film...even if the main character was a physics professor, let alone understood that they were something to be searched for, be it in the film's admittedly imaginative credits, or elsewhere. Maybe he'd seen a Standard Model chart somewhere, but to connect that with movie credits—

I was about to assure him that he wasn't the only one looking for the Higgs boson when I noticed something was off-kilter in the movie: Everyone, even the professor's cute little yellow flying robot, was speaking Spanish. I dimly recalled that Grandpa's DVD had some alternate language tracks, Spanish and I think even French, so I found myself asking him instead, "Do you speak Spanish?"

No answer at first, so I tilted my head just enough to be able to watch the Savvy instead of the film. He was trimmer than most of the other Savvies I'd seen in the past year and a half; considering that he seemed to spend his time watching movies on his bed, he looked to be the right weight for his height. No roll of fat pushing out the middle of his standard-issue tan cover-alls, no tell-tale creases over the thighs. Sabriah's special diets did seem to be doing him some good.

And thankfully (for me) he didn't have red hair; it looked dark, either black or brown. Like his eyes; those were definitely brown, with long, thick lashes. A little soft around the jaw-line, but not excessively so. No laugh or frown lines to speak of anywhere on his face. Not unexpected, there. He wasn't bad looking by any standards, either savant or average male. If his mouth hadn't been so immobile, with the lips pulled in a virtually straight horizontal line, he most certainly would have been considered "cute" by any standards. Not handsome—his features were a bit too slack—but unequivocally attractive.

I'd noticed how Moire was all over every man she happened to be within close proximity to, regardless of who he was (including the obviously gay navigator Lawler, who not-so-tactfully slid away from her), so I realized that there was no way she'd ever been in Dalton's room. She would not have been able to leave him alone, regardless of his emotional deficiencies. So there was no possibility that he'd been doing any socializing on his own—

"Robin Williams, speaking Spanish."

Five minutes or more had to have passed since I'd spoken to him. But it was more or less an answer to my question—

"So you don't speak Spanish yourself?"

"He is."

I took that to mean No, as far as Dalton went.

"Umm...I don't think that's the *actor* on the *screen* speaking Spanish...most actors can't speak too many languages and I know they sometimes dub these films into more than one language. Do you know what dubbing is?"

Silence from Dalton, more unintelligible Spanish from the speakers.

"The studio hires someone who does speak Spanish, or whatever, and they record another audio track for the film. Then, when you make the selection, you hear *that person* speaking Spanish. Or whatever. Like French. There's a French track on this, isn't there—"

"French sounds wormy."

I had to agree with him there. I had no facility for languages myself so all I could do was nod, then say, "Yes, it does sound...'wormy.' But I can't understand Spanish, either. Can *you* understand it?" Considering that he'd somehow picked up more than a rudimentary understanding of physics seemingly by watching the opening credits of a Disney film, I thought it worth a try to ask him about languages again.

And again, I got the same answer:

"Robin Williams speaking Spanish."

No pause this time, no verbal comma. I supposed that he felt that Robin Williams' body with a different-sounding Spanish voice equaled *that* actor speaking *that* language. Deciding that this Savvy's linguistic skills were both unknowable and unimportant at the time, I decided to try a new approach.

Turning away from the view-screen, I strained my eyes in the sugary haze and looked for the nearest stack of MDVD's, before I began counting them softly, from the bottom to the top of the thin square tower. "—Eighteen, nineteen...twenty. One, two, three...four, five—" Gradually, Dalton turned down the volume on his player, and I let my voice grow louder as I began counting the last stack of films resting on the low stool near his bunk, "—Seventeen, eighteen, nineteen. That's twenty, nineteen and...twenty on the stool—"

"No. Twenty, twenty *and* nineteen. Nineteen's twenty is in the machine."

Hoping that he couldn't see me smile in the darkness, I said, "You got me. I never was any good with numbers...but you are, aren't you?"

"Very good." He went back to watching the gelatinous leafy-green dancing blobs of flubber on the viewscreen.

Resting my crossed arms on his bunk, I asked him, "Do you like that color?"

"Nice color."

"But do *you* like it?"

"It's nice."

I hated to make assumptions, but that seemed to be a yes.

"You like this movie, though. In Spanish and English?"

"Nice movie."

"Are your other movies just as nice?"

He watched the fluorescent green goop hop across the Professor's floor, replicating bounce by bounce for a few seconds, before I noticed a thin vertical frown line appear between his dark eyebrows. A change in expression could mean just about anything with a Savvy, and I subtly shifted my body away from him, just in case he started hitting himself, like the Savvy on the *Ignance-Roche* did five months ago. But he remained in his Lotus position, moving only his left hand as he began pointing at the various narrow piles of MDVD's around the room, while speaking in that low, slightly strident but still basically pleasant-sounding voice of his, "'Twenty-two, twenty and twenty are good. Eighteen, eighteen and twenty...ok. Twenty, twenty and nineteen, nice. Twenty-one, twenty-one, twenty-one...don't watch much. Sixteen, sixteen, sixteen...ok."

He went through every stack of films in the room (odd, how I'd not noticed how he had them in sets of three before), rating them by his own system of "don't watch much" to "nice" which—judging by the ever-so-slight emphasis in his voice— seemed to be his version of thumbs up, four stars, or "highly recommended." For some reason, to Dalton, "nice" was better than "good"—whether that was a strictly personal, idiosyn- cratic determination, or a deeper insight into what qualities made up that which was merely *good* as opposed to that which was intentionally *nice,* I had no way of knowing. And I doubted that he could tell me.

"Dalton, did you choose these movies, or were they given to you? By the mining company." I knew that everything Dalton owned was courtesy of the multi-national mining conglomerate which owned and operated the fleet of asteroid miner/tracker ships now scattered between the Earth, the Moon and Mars like so much debris in the heavens, the same company which was forced to seek out ore-rich asteroids once the majority of the Terran and Lunar mines were depleted of their mineral riches. But it was important to the people I worked for to determine whether or not the Savvies understood where they fit into the mining conglomerate's personnel structure. In short, did they think of themselves as employees, or as equipment?

"Given." A pause, then, unexpectedly, "I choose among them."

"I'm glad to hear that," I found myself blurting out, before I refocused, and continued, "So you did watch them all. Before you chose." (I had to know if he was selecting his "favorites" by content, or by some more intangible system, like how he reacted to the jewel-box artwork. It was something my employers felt was important.)

"All of them. Once or more. Nice ones most."

For once, I regretted my habit of not reading a Savvy's personnel file before speaking to him—usually, those first, unbiased opinions were far more useful than static clinical assessments stored in a data file—since Dalton was just so *different* from every other Savvy I'd spoken to so far. Despite the darkness in that cabin, I had this feeling that he was studying *me*

"Dalton...may I ask you a favor?"

That thin vertical furrow reappeared between his brows, then: "Oh...kay...."

"I have trouble seeing in the dark...everything looks really grainy. I can barely see your stacks of movies over there...once the movie is over, could you please turn up your lights?"

From his silence, I realized that I may've overloaded him with too many requests, but as soon as the end credits of the movie were over—he obviously watched every disk from beginning to end—he reached over to the light panel above his bunk and flicked it on with his left hand. His action took me by surprise; I had to steady myself against the side of the bunk when I realized that his bunk had a red blanket on it. The intense color made my eyes ache, as the hue filled my range of vision.

"You ok?"

Narrowing my eyelids over my throbbing eyes until I was peering through a rainbow haze of eyelashes, I looked up into Dalton's face. Limited as my view was, I could see that he was a rather good-looking young man. And I'd been right, his eyes were brown, a deep mahogany, like his hair. He'd put the player on his bunk, and had shifted around so that he was facing me, albeit with his legs still crossed. His hands were resting palms up on his thighs, the fingers loosely splayed. I didn't expect him to put his hand on my shoulder, anything like that, but his voice did have a distinct note of concern.

Nodding, I shakily got to my feet, then—as I patted the nubby surface of his painfully cochineal blanket with my right hand—asked, "May I sit down?"

I wasn't offended when he simultaneously nodded even as he edged closer to the cabin wall. Personal space was more than an issue with the majority of autistics, especially savants.

Positioning myself at the far end of the bunk, barely resting my weight on the mattress itself, I smiled at him, saying, "Red hurts my eyes. Just something I was born with...it's not your fault. You know how it is, to be born a certain way. You're good with numbers, I'm bad with red. Yours is useful, mine isn't. But it's the way my brain is—" I was about to say "wired" but I still wasn't sure if he thought of himself as employee or equipment, and a simple word like "wired" could so easily be misinterpreted by a Savvy, so I finally ended with "—structured. Genetically."

"GATC."

He said it so quickly, I wasn't sure if he'd said it at all.

"Pardon me, I didn't hear—"

"*Geee. Aaay. Teee. Ceee.* Genetics. Like *Gattaca.* Good movie."

One mystery solved. At least he was paying attention to the dialogue in the films. Then, he continued:

"VIP...CGRP, BDNF...NT four. Proteins. In the brain. My brain."

He was right. Autistic people tended to have high levels of those four proteins in their blood samples, which indicated that non-normal brain processes were in play before birth. Did he hear that when he was a child, perhaps when some doctor spoke around him, as if he were an inanimate object in the examining room?

I was making too much of what he'd been saying. Dalton was simply plugging in accurate responses following general observations I'd made.

He had to be of at least normal intelligence; every Savant-Contingent had to have an IQ of at least 99-100 in order to be employed by the mining company, which just happened to be a subsidiary of the remains of NASA in the United States. So of course he could link up random nuggets of information with my comments. Just as he could input, store and recite the successive approximations for figuring out where and when to launch radio-transmitter-tagged asteroids toward the nearest mining ship, or toward the Moon itself, once Lawler and Garrick used their computers to calculate those approximations, then transmitted the figures to him in his cabin. Which was literally all he was expected to do on board the vessel; he and his fellow Savvies were nothing more than computer backups, riding each vessel for months at a time, simply waiting for their laptops to spew forth rows of figures which they'd remember, on the *off-off-off* chance that something unforeseen might happen to the ship's main computer. A random solar flare, or an on-board fire. Something statistically unlikely to happen in the first place, but—just in case—the Savant-Contingents were there, ready and waiting, with the necessary information right when it might (i.e., when icicles formed in hell) happen.

Thanks to the effect of various gravities working on both the target site—be it another ship, the Moon, or wherever—and the ship launching the asteroid toward the target site, elliptical orbits and ever-changing flight times, successive approximations were the backbone of the asteroid-mining industry. Those figures had to be there, when needed, and if for whatever unforeseen reason they *weren't* there, ready to be inputted from the main computer to the navigational console, things could go wrong. Not life-threatening things, but money-wasting things. Things which might necessitate changes in schedules, which in turn affect the timing of each ship's other mining-operations...

miss one mining ship, and a radio-tagged asteroid might keep on going, to interfere with the orbit of yet another ship, or asteroid or—

—or the mining company could take advantage of the existing government programs set up to encourage firms to hire the handi-capable.

A simple extension of supply and demand...over 100,000 savants ready to be the flesh and blood back-up for silicon and gold computer chips. The company gets a truly nice tax break for hiring them, the government doesn't have to shell out SSI payments, and the Savvies get pensions after age sixty. All for remembering a few numbers (which they'll never be called upon to actually recite) with complete and unwavering accuracy—an accuracy so precise, it eliminates the ever-so-slight possibility of a crew member in navigation or astrometrics inputting the figures off their own laptop, or from jotted down notes, and making a mistake. The basic detachment of the Savvy is another prized factor...since they don't understand the gravity of their gift, or of the information entrusted to them, they can coolly rattle off the missing successive approximations without nervous hesitation.

Or without the possibility of making a mistake, or transposing any numbers out of panic.

Granted, some Savvies occasionally hit themselves, or flailed out, but things other crew members found catastrophic never fazed them. On the *Ignacio-Silvio,* a fire once broke out in a fuel storage unit, and that Savvy didn't so much as turn his head in the direction of his running crewmates, or seem to notice anything unusual when the corridor beyond his room was sundown bright with reflected flames, let alone covered with slippery billows of extinguisher foam.

But, considering that it sometimes took hours, even days for the crew to calculate said successive approximations, then more days might pass between the time when the calculations were made, then relayed to the Savant, followed by even more days before the figures would be needed there was precious little happening on any mining/tracking ship which directly concerned the Savant-Contingent. So, there was virtually no reason for them to consider themselves a part of the crew *per se*, which in turn was the reason I was now sitting on Dalton Durwin's red blanket, listening to him blurt out tidbits of genetic information.

Information I hadn't specifically requested, though, which was interesting. And unique. Not that getting to the essence of what any Savant was thinking or feeling was ever easy, but in this particular case, I suspected that the study of science itself actually interested him. For the time being, I pushed aside all those rote questions I'd been hired to attempt to ask in the interest of making sure that the Savvies were treated humanely by their fellow crewmates, and instead leaned forward ever so slightly, not an overt invasion of his space, but a gentle sign of interest, and asked, "Do you ever talk to Sabriah, when she brings you your food—talk about science?"

"We talk...not science. About food. What I eat. No lactose. No yeast, no gluten. But the food is good. She makes it."

"How about the other people in the crew? Do you talk to them? About science?"

"They talk about science...with each other. I...listen."

That furrow appeared between his eyes again, and he was definitely looking away from me, at his open palms. Which, finger by finger, became cupped palms. I had suspected as much. Dalton's door wasn't locked in any way, and he had to know the layout of the ship, after having spent months at a time on each asteroid-seeking trip.

But I couldn't come out and accuse him of eavesdropping on the other crew-members; I knew from experience what open denunciations might do to an autistic person. Gradually, his gaze rose to about the level of my jaw-line—not quite eye contact, but for him, it was close enough.

"The things the others say...they're interesting to you?"

"Like the movies...only different every time. No pause. No fast forward."

"For whatever bores you?"

Those round dark eyes were now level with my nose.

"Bores me...like Moire and Broga. Always saying the same things. Putting...things on my door."

"Like...the picture of the cat?"

"Jones."

"From *Alien*...yes, Jones was the ship's cat. But you aren't a cat, are you?"

"Leo...that's a big cat."

His birthday. Late July. Why wouldn't he know Zodiac signs, too? They were more common than Higgs bosons.

"Do Moire and Broga know that? Do you think they might?"

"Dunno...they climb on the asteroids. Attach the radio transmitters."

"Does that make them smart? Smart enough to know your birth sign?"

"They're engineers, too. Sabriah calls them asteroid monkeys."

"That's because they climb on things with very strange surfaces...they have to be agile," I soothed, thinking of that wiry twerp Broga and that harpy Moire and wanting to strand both of them on an asteroid *sans* life support, "and most monkeys are agile."

"Monkeys sound wormy."

I wondered if Dalton had placed any *Planet of the Apes* movies or anything else with chimps in it in one of his "don't watch much" piles.

Not really wanting to pursue the subject of those backbiting idiots much longer, I awkwardly crossed my own legs as I tried, "But Kevan and Sloane are more interesting?"

This time those eyes met mine, and didn't waver as he said, "Yes. Listen to them...talk about science, space...everything. Not boring. Make fun of Moire and Broga. Make the Captain yell sometimes."

I'd only spoken to Gremain Penn for perhaps a minute or so after boarding the ship, but I'd sensed that he had little patience for anything but staying in his small command room just off navigation, with his nose illuminated by his e-book. I could almost feel the cursor blinking on the last page he'd been reading before I interrupted him, beckoning to him like a lighthouse beacon.

"The Captain's not very friendly, is he?"

"I dunno."

He'd finally said it. There *was* an "I" in there.

Hoping he hadn't noticed my excitement, I continued smoothly, "Do you know what his name is?"

"Gremain Penn. He's old. Wrinkled. Up and down on his cheeks."

Penn did have deep vertical creases on his cheeks, amid dozens of other wrinkles.

"Does he know you've seen him?" This question might be dangerous, but I was willing to risk it.

"I don't think so. He never looks up from his reading. Unless someone making noise."

"Do you know what Kevan and Sloan look like?"

"Kevan's dark-haired, like my hair. Young. This tall—" here, Dalton uncrossed his legs in a fluid motion, and stood about three feet from me.

He was about the same height as the navigator, roughly five ten or eleven.

I just nodded, and he continued, standing there with his arms dangling limply by his sides, "Sloan is smaller. Skinny. Blond hair, big forehead. Narrow face," and he used his left hand to indicate a pinched, small face in front of his own, before dropping his arm again.

"And Sabriah has a scarf around her head," I added, hoping Dalton would take the bait. He did.

"She's a Muslim. She doesn't like dogs. She likes cats."

"And Leo is a big cat, isn't he?" I smiled, resisting the temptation to get up and stand near him.

"A very big cat...more hair, though." He wore his hair short, like Kevan and the Captain did.

"Hair grows," I said, not expecting any answer, and not getting one. "But Sabriah does have hair under her scarf, I'm sure. She does like you, takes good care of you. But...I think Kevan and Sloan might also like you, might want to talk science with you. GATC, Higgs bosons. Standard Models, too. Do you think you'd like that?"

His hands pressed down hard on the loose rough fabric of his jumpsuit but his eyes stayed level with mine.

"I...don't know. Maybe. Just Kevan and Sloan. About science."

This wasn't part of my job description; my heart was lopping in my ribcage as I uncrossed my legs, and let my feet drop slowly to the floor of the cabin, before I got up, and stood perhaps four feet or so away from Dalton, hands placed on my own thighs, making myself into a small, unthreatening presence before him. No, socialization wasn't a goal during my stay on this ship, nothing was ever specifically said about it during the training courses—I was supposed to make sure the Savvy felt reasonably good about himself and his job, that he didn't feel like an inanimate object, and I was also to make sure that the rest of the crew treated him like a human being...albeit a very unique, very special human being, and not a living calculator.

I wasn't supposed to be a social coordinator...but none of the other Savvies were anything like Dalton, either. Sabriah had told me that I couldn't change anything on the ship, that nothing I might do would make any difference once I was gone.

But Dalton was interested in science. *Interested.* Like Kevan and Sloan were. The situation with the asteroid monkeys might not change, but Lawler and Garrick seemed reasonably polite, at the least.

And as long as I was there, supervising the conversation—

"I'll ask them, about you talking with them. Would that be all right with you?"

A pause, then, "All right. Kevan and Sloan. Science. Talk about science?"

Nodding, I assured him, "Science. With Kevan and Sloan.

I'll let you get back to your movies now, Dalton—"

"Who are you?"

I stopped so quickly I almost fell over from the forward momentum of my body. I'd started to tell him who I worked for, then completely forgot to give him my name. Feeling my face flush, I turned around and said. "My name is Temple Kenward. I'm a social worker. I go from ship to—"

"Temple. Like Temple Grandin?" he asked, naming one of the most famous autistic scientists and authors from the late twentieth century.

Pausing to pull a bit of dead skin off one lip, I nodded and said, "Yes, Temple is my first name, and hers too."

Obviously, he'd been exposed to either her work, or someone who followed her physical-closeness theories. While she'd been primarily involved with livestock science, some educators had utilized therapies based on her experiments with close, steady physical contact to calm animals.

"Temple-not-Grandin." Was he looking at me expectantly?

"Temple, period, is okay. No 'not-Grandin,'" I said patiently.

"Temple, per—"

"*Temple.*"

Behind me, the pocket door swooshed open, and Sabriah was framed in the empty doorway, a tray of food in her dark hands. "Dalton, time for lunch," she said softly, before motioning for me to leave with a couple of quick jerks of her cloth-swathed head.

"Dalton, it was a pleasure talking to you. I'll see you soon, okay?"

"Talk science later?" Sabriah kept staring at me as she walked into the cabin, and placed the Savvy's tray on the end of his bed.

"Later. Enjoy your meal," I said over my shoulder, before hurrying into the corridor. I wasn't fast enough; within ten strides I could feel the vibration of the nutritionist's footsteps behind me.

"Ms. Kenward, what was *that* about? 'Talk science'? With

whom?"

"That's a privileged conversation...client confidentiality," I said over my shoulder.

"Clichés won't cut it with me—" she began, but I slapped my open hand against the palm-pad next to my cabin door, and slid through the door before it was half-open—and immediately pressed my palm against the interior pad before she could say anything else I didn't want to hear.

Dalton Darwin's case files didn't tell me much more than I'd already been able to surmise from merely talking to him: Diagnosed shortly after birth via blood tests for the proteins VIP, CGRP, BDNF and NT4 and neural-imaging tests which revealed small, densely packed cells in the limbic region of his brain, he was immediately given up for adoption by his unwed, college-student mother. Raised in foster care until he was fourteen, at which time he was enrolled in the Savant-Contingency training program. Prior to that time, he had not received much more than drug therapy—mostly mild antide-pressants to control some moderate compulsive behaviors. No Applied Behavioral Analysis, no treatment for what the mining corporation discovered to be a mild-to-moderate case of sensory integrative dysfunction involving certain sounds (the "wormy" French he'd mentioned), no one-on-one Lovass therapy...he was moderately verbal from an early age, so no Facilitated Communication therapy was deemed necessary. True, most of the treatments he never received were simply too expensive; unless an autistic child was lucky enough to be born into a well-to-do family nowadays, most of the long-standing therapies developed in the latter half of the twentieth century were simply out of reach. And foster-care homes—forget it.

Nothing was mentioned in his case files concerning his diet, so apparently Sabriah had taken it upon herself to try the still-disputed diet-therapy approach.

Since he was fairly articulate for his condition, an IQ test had been administered shortly before he joined his first asteroid-tracking flight, shortly before his eighteenth birthday. It was listed as a "probable" 111—and, according to my fraying and flaking copy of George I. Thomas and Joseph Crescimbeni's *Guiding the Gifted Child*, that meant Dalton's IQ ("probable" IQ) placed him in the high average/bright/fast learner category. Or, at worst, if the estimate was a bit high, he was still likely to be an average learner.

Average or above-average enough to have a passing knowledge of physics—and to be able to make what may well have been a joke about finding the Higgs boson in the opening credits of an old Disney film.

I wondered if Sabriah was jealous of my progress with Dalton—she may have taken it upon herself to adjust his diet, but healing the body should also mean healing the mind. She may have read up enough on the subject of autism therapy to attempt a yeast/gluten free diet, but there was so much more she hadn't tried. Simple things, really, like inclusion therapy. Dalton wouldn't get that as long as someone brought him his food tray three times a day.

Case # 290727DD/I-R
07-01-58/T. Kenward, caseworker

Day 5: Initial inclusion

It took me a few days to figure out exactly when Sabriah took her five breaks for daily prayer, days spent watching movies with Dalton (a daily screening of *Flubber*, but also other "nice" films like *Cast Away*, *Raising Arizona* and what seemed to be his second-favorite film, *Con Air*—he liked the part when the one cop's sports car was attached to the wheel of the airplane, and "flew" through the air), but once I knew when she'd be occupied, I waited until Dalton's latest disk had finished the final line of on-screen credits, then gently suggested, "How about if we go talk science now? With Kevan and Sloan?"

It had only taken me a couple of days to work on them; initially, Sloan was annoyed to learn that the ship's Savvy had been listening in while he and Kevan were discussing their work, but Kevan seemed to be mildly bemused by the prospect of anyone finding shop-talk so interesting. The day before, they'd agreed to "talk science" with Dalton, provided the Captain was holed up in his quarters—Penn was close to retirement age, and considering that most of the ship's basic navigation was on a form of gloried auto-pilot, he seemed eager to begin practicing for a remaining lifetime of doing virtually nothing—and Moire and Brogan were off doing whatever it was they did when not planting radio transmitters on the asteroids...which, judging from the sounds which alternately could be heard through either of their cabin doors, was unabashedly carnal.

"Talk science in the daytime?" Figuring out when Dalton had been roaming the ship hadn't been difficult—like many autistic people, he had sleep disorders which often kept him awake well into the post-midnight hours, or he'd intermittently wake up during the night. I heard him myself the first night I'd spent on the *Isen-Rodor*, walking with that stop-start gait down the corridor, occasionally patting the walls as he walked. And since Sloan and Kevan sometimes visited each other's cabins, talking shop, or occasionally stayed in the other part of the ship, working on their approximations after the ship's sensors picked up an ore-rich asteroid in the distance, Dalton had had many opportunities to listen to them.

"In the daytime...that's right," I said, getting up off his bunk and motioning for him to follow me out of the cabin. According to my watch, Sabriah should be on her cabin floor, praying, head pointed toward wherever Mecca (or, less specifically, Earth) happened to be. And she usually stayed in her cabin for a half hour or more afterwards.

Not able to physically steer him in the right direction, I was forced to keep on motioning for Dalton to follow me. I didn't dare say anything, lest Sabriah hear me. He did pause for a moment in front of the navigator's cabin door, but quickly picked up on my forward-pointed finger, and followed me.

I hated walking the connecting corridors between the cabin/

storage units and the ship's main navigation section; while the ship's artificial rotation was moderately noticeable else-where, here it was a physical impossibility to *not* notice it. The walls were well-rounded here, with only a narrow "floor" and "ceiling" whose surfaces were level and flat. I'd had a mild inner-ear imbalance since childhood, one which I'd been trained to virtually ignore, but in this twenty-yard stretch of unvarying straight closeness, I'd began to feel disoriented. But Dalton didn't mind—in fact, his hesitant gait actually improved the closer we came to the cluster of console-filled rooms.

Kevan noticed us first.

"Welcome to Navigation, Dalton...want to see what it looks like in the daytime?" Consistently the most openly polite of the crew members, even if he did tend to slip into what might be deemed (in most un-PC terms) as "gushing" gestures and vocal flourishes, he stepped up to Dalton—I had been right, they were the same height—and, mindful of the latter's need for physical space, extended one hand in what could either be construed as an impending handshake, or a simple welcoming gesture. A few steps behind him, Sloan leaned against a wall largely given over to luminescent star charts, his narrow face twisted into a bemused smirk. Glancing away from Sloan after his eyes suddenly grew wide, I turned to see Dalton tentatively extend his right hand, and briefly align it just under Kevan's hand, their palms almost touching, before Kevan smiled, and led Dalton into the Navigation section, with its myriad of blinking lights, computer screens, and small windows revealing a thick swath of grainy stars against blackest-black. Too many of the lights in there were just too red for my comfort, so I hung back, only half-listening as Kevan began showing Dalton the various pieces of equipment within.

Kevan was saying something about how fast the Earth and Moon rotate, and how fast the ship could accelerate when Sloan reached out to grab me by the upper arm, saying, "How did you sneak him past Our Lady of the Scarf?" Gently shaking off his fingers without trying to appear openly offended that he'd touched me, I leaned against the opposite wall of the short corridor and said softly, "You must've been dozing during Tolerance Training in high school...she's busy in her cabin. Tell me, Sloan...has Sabriah always shown that much interest in Dalton's welfare?"

He shrugged against the wall, the rough fabric of his uniform rasping against the textured metal behind him. "Yeah, I guess... she's been bringing him his meals ever since I've been here. That's five years come March. Kevan would know, he's worked this ship longer. Probably since the Sav—Dalton was instal—assigned here."

"Installed" was a common term for Savant-Contingent placement on asteroid ships. But I was grateful that Sloan was making an effort for my sake, at least.

"So Kevan's around Dalton's age?" I had to move a few steps into the corridor proper—and a bit closer to Sloan—to see what Dalton and Kevan were doing in Navigation. Kevan was showing him a computer screen, saying, "—you have to figure how long it'll take the asteroid to reach the mining ship, which can be a problem because there's no standard amount of time for—" while Dalton leaned forward, peering at the screen. Sloan crossed his arms, before replying, "A few years older. Thirty-four, thirty-five...a year or two younger than I am. Not that the bastard looks it," he added, "Must be a hormone thing."

I knew and he knew that homosexuals didn't have excess estrogen, so I let the gibe pass.

A few beats of silence, then: "Is this some new thing the government's cooked up for Sav's? Take Our Savant to Work day? Every other ship I've been on, they've just holed up in their cabins."

"Can you blame them?" I whispered. "I've been on other ships, too. Nobody's actually welcomed the Savants into their cliques—"

"Lady, how can you—oh, screw it." He slumped against the wall.

"Screw what? I mean, they're *crew* members, same employer,

same damned uniforms, same missions....I realize that they're unique, but every person I've ever met has been unique in his or—"

"You got a talent for understatement, I'll give you that. Christ, how do you talk to someone like him? If they do say something back, it doesn't make sense...believe me, I have tried, and eventually, after blank stares and *non-sequiturs*, you get god-damned tired of trying. Like *they* did," he added tersely, motioning with his head of lank blonde hair toward the connecting corridor...where the monkey twins, Moire and Brogan, were walking side by side toward us. Wincing at the sight of her sleep (or whatever) tousled hair, I started to make a move toward the room where Kevan and Dalton were talking, but Sloan shook his head, saying, "Stick around...see for yourself. It's *not* us—"

"I thought it was intermission time...come up this way for some popcorn?" I felt as if I'd known Brogan Hastings—or someone all too much like him—my entire life: the eternal smart-ass with the witty jibe, too wiry and short and not-too-good-looking to impress anyone otherwise. I'd even met a few men like him while earning my degree in social work. One or two of them were working the same job I was—the wave of pity I felt for *their* Savvies was interrupted by Moire's "No, I think he ran out of toothpicks...the butter on the popcorn's hell on the wood."

They were worse than Dalton was when it came to thinking in movie.

I tried staring them down; aside from being roughly the same height (tall for a woman, short for a man), and wiry-but-muscular, they were so utterly ill-matched—she had that thick, waving mass of painfully bright hair, framing a face that might have been pretty if she'd done anything besides pull her small lips forward in a pout, while he was runty-faced, with greasy, thinning salt-and-pepper hair, with an equally sparse mustache—that their status as a couple was solely based on their joint job titles. On Earth, the Moon, or virtually any other floating body with a minimum of gravity, her kind would never look once at his kind, let alone a second time.

But they sensed that the ship's cat was out of his cage, and both of them elbowed past Sloan and me to see what Kevan and the Savvy were doing in Navigation.

"Hi, stranger...how long has it been?"

"Look who's learning how to fly this junk-heap—"

"God, he'll never understand what they're jabbering about," I started to say, as I went to follow them, but Sloan shook his head, and held up one hand in front of me, palm out. "No, don't... they won't hurt him, for Chrissakes. They're teasing him, not taunting him. If you'd have spent some time with them, you'd know what they're like. Damned 'stroid monkeys, that's all. Goof-balls. What they do, on the rocks...the pressure is intense. It's that way for every monkey...we sit in here, they get to do the real hands-on work. So when they aren't risking their lives, they make the rest of ours miserable." I couldn't figure out why he said "miserable" in such a light tone, but I kept my silence as he went on, talking so fast I couldn't make out what the others were saying: "You spend so much time with Savvies, you forget what the rest of us are going through on these junk-heaps. We could use some social work, too.

"Something better than the movies and playthings they send up here with us on every run. Something—" here he leaned in uncomfortably close to my face "—to help us deal with all the waiting we have to do before we reach those damned flying chunks of minerals. I've requested transfers from six different ships—including two mining vessels—because I couldn't *stand* my crewmates. You think this bunch is bad—"

"I've seen plenty of other crews. I've witnessed their group dynamics. I know there's as many assholes as asteroids out here in space, but my job is to just make sure the Savvies are well-treated. And respected for being the crew members they are—"

"Who here has said different about him? You're freaked 'bout the 'Jones' poster on his door? Moire did that. When she and Brogan were playing out some weird *Aliens* sex-game scenario.

Her Ripley, him...whoever Ripley had the 'jones' for in one of the sequels, the one where she's got no hair. The doctor dude, I think. Those two, they get weird, play their games, and the rest of us ignore them until they're actually on the rocks out there. But remember how everyone on the first mining ship ended up dying, while Ripley was out looking for the cat? That ball of fur *was* crew to them. Like he—" Sloan jerked one thumb in the direction of the Navigation room "—is to us. We act stupid, but we aren't retards—everyone here is aware of what he 'does' on the ship. You might drive your car for a hundred thousand miles and never blow a tire, but you'd be nuts not to have a spare in the trunk. He's a spare that watches a lot of movies. In his cabin. Which is what every Savvy I've ever known has *wanted* to do. I think they make out like they don't understand people 'cause they don't want to. What's up in their heads is a lot better than what's running around the corridors.

"Hell, I was pissed when I found out he was eavesdropping on me, but mainly 'cause I don't like it when anyone sneaks up on me. Has it occurred to you that he had all damn day and night to wander around? He can watch movies whenever he wants. And there's no lock on the—"

First Sabriah, now Sloan. God, I was getting so tired of being harangued by these people I wanted to hole up in my own cabin and cover my ears with earphones, too. I'd dealt with some obnoxious crews before, but these people seemed to have issues with me as a person. Everyone else had tried to steer clear of me, considering my status as a government-sent social worker, but *these* people—

"—an accelerator...one loop is larger, the other...one third as big. Put together like a snowman—"

Dalton's voice was far less hesitant than normal, while Kevan's was gushier than before as he said, "*That's* the Tevatron accelerator...and the spot where the protons and antiprotons are produced sticks out from where the 'neck' would be like—" I entered the room just in time to see Kevan miming what looked like a necktie against his neck, while the monkey twins watched in bemusement as Dalton puzzled out Kevan's charade, then said, "Like a scarf, only with a small circle on the end."

Moire actually smiled when he said that, and side-stepped closer to where Dalton was standing. As if he were attached to her at the hip Brogan inched over a couple of feet, too.

Obviously uncomfortable, Dalton in turn stepped away from Moire, and, as he noticed me, said, "We're talking science. Accelerators."

"We're listening science. Atomic drag races." I wondered if Brogan realized how funny he wasn't.

But everyone was laughing at that...and Dalton was smiling. So I decided to keep my peace, and wait to see if Brogan would move on to ridiculing Dalton himself, and not just his speech patterns.

Making sure that he moved slowly, Kevan placed one hand lightly on Dalton's forearm, before saying, "I hate to run you out of here, but I think our friend Sabriah will be coming around soon...I'd hate to have her bring a meal to an empty room; wouldn't you?"

"No one to eat it." Dalton didn't seem offended, and as he walked out of the room, and back down the connecting corridor toward his cabin his face was unlined and placid. The same way he looked after watching one of his "nice" movies. Once he'd gone, I found myself saying, "I appreciate that you all put up with him...I think it went well. He might not want to come out again, but he did seem interested in science."

"No need to apologize," Kevan smiled, even as he didn't bother to try laying a hand on my arm, "He is fairly knowl-edgeable about physics...high school level, but considering...his circumstances, that's not bad at all. For him, excellent, actually. Too bad he's been holed up in there so long," he added, and Moire cut in too quickly, "'*Too* bad'...he can be funny, once he gets going."

It wasn't until I'd gone back to my own cabin that I real-ized that Kevan had subtly put me down, stressing that Dalton was interested in *physics,* not science *per se.* But any residual feelings of inadequacy I felt over that were brushed aside by my surprise over how well Dalton had done—even with the monkey twins. And he'd been reluctant to talk to them at all just a few days earlier.

I was just glad that the Captain, not to mention Sabriah, hadn't seen Dalton roaming outside his cabin.

Case #290727DD/I-R
11-01-58/T. Kenward, caseworker

Day 9: Personal Interface

For the first time since he'd been assigned to the *Isen-Rodor,* Dalton received the successive approximations for the upcoming asteroid boost directly from Kevan and Sloan, rather than via a message on his in-cabin laptop. It was also the first time he'd watched exactly what the monkey twins did once they were jettisoned from the ship in their two-person-sized landing craft. The craft utilized a locking spring due to the near-zero surface gravity of this particular asteroid, which was perhaps the size of a domed football stadium. As Kevan explained to him (and to me, since I was perhaps less knowledgeable about asteroid mining than even Dalton was), the surface gravity of this asteroid was less than one-ten-thousandth of Lunar gravity which in turn meant that "—escape velocity is oh, around 0.3 kilometers per hour, or 0.1 meters per second. Not very fast... which means they have to descend to the planet differently than ship-to-ground shuttles do. Once they've landed—see, they've turned on their helmet-cams, they're getting out of the lander now—they'll need to use those power anchors, those harpoon-like things...see, Moire's shot hers into those rocks. If it wasn't powered, it'd take minutes to hit the ground."

Dalton watched the live feed from the monkeys' cameras with the same rapt, unblinking attention usually reserved for his "nice" movies in his cabin. I wondered if he realized that what he was watching was happening in the now, as opposed to something which was filmed, edited, then recorded decades earlier.

"—now Brogan is spiking in the transmitter, that's what the mining ship uses to track the asteroid after we boost it into the proper orbit...which is where your successive approximations come in. Every orbit is different—"

"Different by x-number of days and x-number of hours," Dalton said.

"Exactly. Once the mining ship gets the asteroid, they de-spin it, then erect the solar-powered mining equipment. Or blow off sections, depending on the asteroid's size. Then again, there's tunneling, and sometimes strip mining is necessary, but none of that can happen unless we get that tagged asteroid into the right orbit."

"So the mining ship can catch it." On the screen before us, the pair split up, each moving with surreal slowness against the multi-faceted, scabrous asteroid's greatly foreshortened horizon, until one of them was standing directly in the sight-lines of the other's helmet-cam, resulting in full-body views of both engineers. After fumbling with the main bib-like "pocket" which covered the chest area of their exploration suits, each of them slowly withdrew a sheet of that thin, Mylar-like "netting" the engineers on the mining ships usually carried while doing surface work (in zero or near-zero gravity, small chunks of chipped-away rock tended to float unless covered with a canopy, then netted prior to the engineer's return to the ship), and unfurled the sheets to a reasonable facsimile of "flatness," revealing the messages darkly scrawled on their individual squares of Mylar:

Camera One: "Hello—"
Camera Two: "Dalton!"

As soon as I read that, I turned to look at him: Dalton was smiling, not showing his teeth, but his mouth was unmistakably turned up at the corners. Beside him, Kevan—very gently—patted his shoulder, and said, "See that? They knew you'd be watching...what do you think they'd like to hear when they get back to the ship?"

(Next to me, Sloan leaned over to whisper in my ear, "'Up yours' might be interesting—")

"Hello Moire and Brogan?" Dalton seemed to have completely missed being touched unexpectedly, he was so excited about what he'd seen on the screen. On the screens, each of the engineers let go of their hand-made signs, and the Mylar continued to flutter in space, even as the two asteroid monkeys made their way next to each other, so they could continue to watch the ever-so-slowly falling glittering squares of metallic fabric against the inky backdrop of star-dusted deep-space "sky."

I wondered if Dalton realized just how beautiful the sight was; his dark eyes were focused on the screens, darting from one camera's viewpoint to the other, but I'd seen him stare like that at CGI green goo doing the mambo, too. He'd come so far in the last few days, but there was no way to measure just how much emotional distance "far" *meant* for him—

"Is this what my god-damn taxes are going for now?"

I hadn't spoken to Captain Penn in so many days, his voice was virtually unfamiliar to me. Kevan, Sloan and I all turned around as one when we heard that obviously pissed-off snarl behind us; Penn was standing, arms crossed (invariably a bad physical sign), pale eyes glaring like sunlight sheeting across ice, furrowed face a craggy twin to the convoluted surface of the asteroid which still filled the screens on the console.

Dalton turned around a few beats after the rest of us; he wasn't smiling this time.

"Since when—what the hell is this? Ms. Ken...whatever, is this your doing? I take it you brought him—" the captain pointed at Dalton with his e-book-holding hand "—up here? Were you aware that this is a working ship? All you're supposed to do is check on the status of our Savant. Which I assume you did. What's he doing up here?"

"He wanted to come out...he's not causing any problems," Kevan quickly soothed, "I already gave him the figures, so that part of his job is done...Ms. Kenward was just supervising him. Sloan and I are fine with him being here—" Sloan let out something between a grunt and a snort, then turned his attention back to the engineers, typing in something on his keyboard "—so we didn't want to bother you. The transmitter's in place, and working—we'll be in boosting position in a few hours. Milk run. No problems with having him up here...." Kevan punctuated his short speech with a smile, one that showed virtually all his front and side teeth.

"So what was that on the screens?"

"Moira and Brogan being themselves," Kevan schmoozed; obviously, he had some sway over the Captain, for the older man uncrossed his arms, and merely warned before quitting the room, "Just as long as everything works...."

Down on the asteroid, the monkeys had finished climbing the surface leading up to the lender; once they got in, and removed their helmets, voice contact resumed: *"Isen-Rodor*, this is the *I-R One--"* Brogan's voice.

"I-R One, copy. Guys, your half-time show reached a larger audience than anticipated," Kevan teased, while punching in something on his own keyboard.

"Male or female demographics?" Moire asked, her voice brittle over the receivers.

"Male...but he's switched channels. Didn't like what he saw—"

Kevan let the tip of his tongue extend past his front teeth while shaking his head at the unseen engineers.

"No frigging kiddin'. He didn't send the Sav—Dalton back, did he?" It may have been the slight static, but I thought Brogan sounded concerned.

"Nope...the man's here. Come over here and speak into this mike—"

"Hi Brogan...hi Moire—"

"Hi, kid...did the Captain chew you out?"

"No...Moire. He went away."

"That's nothing new—"

"I'm surprised he came out of his cave in the first place... Sloan, everything a go up there?"

"Yeah, Brog, lander doors are open—"

Something Brogan said about the Captain leaving his cave made my eyes grow hotly moist: it had all been so obvious, Dalton and the whole Plato's cave-shadows-on-the-wall analogy. Only in this Savvy's case, it was more like voices beyond the walls—

Now that Dalton had come this far out of his cave, I didn't think he needed me to stand next to him, out here in the place where voices and shadows became flesh. Quietly backing out of the navigation bay, while the men sitting near Dalton continued to bring him into their conversation with the returning engineers, I went as far out into the semi-circular corridor as I could while still able to see and hear what was going on in Navigation without actually being a presence in the room.

"Congratulations. You must've aced Obtuse 101." Sabriah's voice wasn't bitter, just...resigned? Under the over-hanging folds of her scarf, her smooth dark face was almost as expressionless as Dalton's used to be, mere days before. Glancing away from those staring dark eyes, I noticed for the first time that she wore the skirt version of the standard-issue mining company cover-alls.

Finally, I admitted, "I'm sorry...I don't understand what you're talking about. I'm just doing what I was sent here to—"

"Oh, stuff it, would you? You weren't listening at all a few days ago, were you? Didn't I tell you he was content? You're acting as if I wasn't doing my job—"

Not wanting the others to hear us, I motioned for her to walk a few yards down the corridor with me. Judging by the sharp *swicks* her uniform skirt made as she walked, she was still upset, as I tried to explain, "I never said or assumed anything about the way you were doing your job—Dalton's in excellent physical shape, he seems healthy...I'm just doing what I was sent here to do, as I tried to tell you before. I'm improving communications between one crew member and the other crew members. They're treating him better, and he's responding to them in a positive manner. Things are going much better than they have on any other ship so far...they've stopped calling him names, and he's interacting with them. Dalton has progressed so much in such a short time," I stressed, hoping she'd understand that my efforts were in no way contradictory to hers...but I realized she wasn't open to my ideas as she deliberately crossed her arms over her breasts, and just shook her head slowly, the ends of her scarf making that same slightly mocking snicking sound as they slid over her uniformed shoulders.

"Ms. Kenward...how old are you? If I may be so impolite as to ask?"

"Forty-three, as of a week ago. It took me...a while to finish my degree, but that should be beside the point—"

"I wouldn't have guessed you were that old," she mused, her voice somehow softer, less condescending. "You don't look it at all...before you received your degree, you were—?"

"A student...I've more than one degree," I added, trying not to sound as defensive as I felt. Then, figuring that she'd ask me anyhow, I added, "Yes, my family was able to send me to more than one college and university. They value education—"

"So they're educated themselves?" Her voice was still soft.

"I'd say so...they both have Master's degrees. But that has nothing to do with Dalton. I've made a genuine difference in his life, here on this ship. Which impacts everyone here...even you. Eventually, he won't rely on you to bring him his food, like a servant...he'll be eating with the others. Like a real crew member—" I stressed, but she cut me off with an upward-raised palm in the air between us.

"Truce...truce. I won't interfere...my faith urges me to be tolerant, so tolerant of your actions I will remain," she said in a strangely light tone, which contrasted with the intricate formality of her words, before turning away from me and walking toward the corridor which led to her quarters in the other half of the ship.

Behind me, I actually thought I heard Dalton laughing, as he greeted Brogan and Moire from their expedition on the asteroid.

Case #290727DD/I-R
15-01-58/T. Kenward, caseworker

Day 13: Solo

I'd only fallen asleep a short time earlier, after what seemed like hours of flipping from side to side under my covers, when I felt the jarring impact of movement, shuddering me awake. Not a floor-vibrating motion, such as I'd felt when the *Isen-Rodor* had maneuvered itself to a position behind the asteroid, and forced it from its orbit with a powerful explosive charge aimed opposite the radio-transmitter-imbedded end of the massive rock, but something more specific, localized...and intermittently repeating.

Then, I heard the indistinct, wall-muffled sound of voices, male, in the corridor beyond, followed by another *whump* against the outer wall of my cabin. Silently cursing the obviousness of pocket doors as I padded over to the source of the sound, I slowly moved along the wall, trying to make out what was being said beyond in the corridor.

They were speaking too softly to be plainly heard, but one of the men was doing most of the talking, an undulating, continuous vibration punctuated only sporadically by the other, lower voice. Only when the voices and the minute vibrations ceased did I dare to palm open my door, and then only part-way. During the "evening" time, the already nebulous corridor lights were further dimmed, so all I could make out in the distance were two men, of identical height and dark coloring, walking closely side-by-side toward the forward half of the ship. From the rear, I couldn't tell which was which, even as I realized who they were. Releasing my palm from the pad near the door, I shuffled back to my bunk, and slid between the enveloping covers.

I tried to tell myself that Dalton had to have done this many times, leaving his room at night, to go eavesdrop on the others while they worked late, but I'd been on enough ships following enough asteroid boosts to know that once the target asteroid had been located, tagged and sent orbiting toward a waiting miner ship, or planetary body, no one spent much time at all in the forward compartments of the ships come evening time. And nothing I'd experienced so far explained the sounds against my wall, the resonating *whumps* which had woken me. Telling myself, One of them must've tripped, fallen against the wall, I tossed myself back to sleep.

That morning, there were no sounds coming from Dalton's cabin, no daily morning *matinee* (a part of his routine he'd never missed before), but I forced myself not to palm-open his door to check on him. I'd be leaving the ship once the *Isen-Rodor*'s path intersected with that of the *Berde-Pedar,* a comet-mining vessel with a rare female Savvy on board, so I realized that the time was drawing near for Dalton to start learning to function as a solo Savvy—he'd have to continue living with these people, his crewmates, once I was gone, and I wouldn't be around to serve as a personal facilitator, he'd be on his own—completely.

That brief, noisy interlude from last night only came back to mind when I found Dalton and Kevan sitting together at the main console in Navigation, their swivel chairs positioned facing each other, each with a cup of something dark and steaming in their hands. At least one of them had chocolate; I could smell it as I stepped into their space, and asked, "You two have a good night?"

Kevan turned to face me, but his glittering eyes seemed to move everywhere but in alignment with my own eyes. Balancing his half-full cup on his crossed knee, he said, smiling, "Excellent. We were going to be passing through the tail of a small comet, and I wanted Dalton to see it. What did you think of it?"

Dalton started nodding before he spoke, "Excellent...I enjoyed it. It was...excellent." But he never did look my way, instead glancing at Kevan between sips of his chocolate. I felt a twinge of sadness that he no longer felt it necessary to address me specifically, even as I knew his conduct was utterly within the parameters of autistic-savant behavior.

It was good to observe that Dalton and Kevan were maintaining eye contact; feeling somehow that I was intruding on them, I said my farewell for the moment, then left them to their talk of comets and Standard Models. As I quitted that end of the ship, I saw Brogan and Moire coming toward me, both of them far less friendly-looking than they'd been after tagging that asteroid a few days earlier. I tried to merely squeeze past them, but Moire grabbed my upper arm just as I was about to walk past her.

"Temple, where's Kevan? And Dalton?" She leaned in toward me as she spoke, her mouth a tight puckered moue, her eyes dark. As she spoke, Brogan slid in front of me, so our three bodies formed a tight triangle.

"In Navigation...sitting at the console. Talking—" I began, and the engineers glanced at each other, as Brogan echoed, "'Talking'...ohhh-*kay*." Moire's grip on my arm tightened, as she asked, "Did you hear anything strange last night? An argument, in the corridor?"

"Something hit my wall a couple of times, but—"

"Did you hear voices? Someone fighting?"

"No...talking, but I wouldn't call it—"

Brogan began striding toward Navigation, and motioned for Moire to join him; as she let go of my arm, the engineer said, "And you didn't go out there to see what was...*jeeesus*—" before running off to join Brogan.

Wanting to tell her, What kept *you* from seeing what was happening? I debated what to do—if this was something between Kevan and the navigators, it was none of my business, but if Dalton was involved....

The uncertainty was paralyzing. Wondering if I should go find the Captain, I started to walk in the direction of his cabin, until I heard a powerful echoing voltaic *snap*! Back in

Navigation, a sharp, hot burst of sound that left a full, rubbery feeling in my mouth. A series of brief, sizzling snaps followed, tiny percussive fizzles of noise, then the human sounds took over—concussive thuds of flesh hitting unyielding surfaces, flesh-sheathed bone hitting thick skin, and the shuffling squidge and squeak of rubbery-soled boots moving fast and sloppy against hard flooring. And the voices...mewling animal sounds of pain, angry whispered hisses, and over everything else, the inarticulate keening of someone rendered near mute with fear—

Behind me, footfalls pounded closer, closer, then Sloan and Sabriah pushed me aside, as they ran forward toward Navigation—

That keening. *Dalton*—

Apparently Brogan had grabbed him and held him just outside the room before Moire and Kevan went at each other; he was still holding Dalton around his midsection, pinning both arms down, the muscles in his own thin forearms taut from the effort of restraining the larger, younger man. For his part, Dalton strained to release himself from the engineer's grasp, trying to kick his way free, but Brogan was faster and more agile than Dalton, and adroitly avoided the younger man's jerking legs. Still making that horrible shrill moaning sound, while unshed tears turned his eyes a dark shimmering copper hue, Dalton kept trying to look into Navigation, but every time his head was parallel to the doorway, Brogan jerked his body back into the corridor.

Moving past Dalton and Brogan, I saw why the engineer refused to allow the Savvy out of his grip. Kevan was slumped on the floor, his arms and legs jerking spasmodically, his fingers spread wide in clawed cages of twitching flesh. His eyes were glazed, as he stared up past Sabriah, as she knelt next to him, murmuring, "It was just a shock, it's over, you're all right," even as the console above him kept on sputtering and sizzling where someone (Moire?) had doused it with coffee, prior to throwing something heavy (Kevan, I realized) against the panel, which not only broke the keyboard, but shattered most of the underlying structure of the console surface.

Thanks to the navigation computers and the ship's main power being controlled by separate electrical systems, it was painfully easy to see all the damage done by the battling crewmen. At least one entire bank of computers was fried, probably down to the hard drives. And from the way the lights on the surrounding banks were flickering, the damage might be more widespread. Glancing away from the ruined console, I noticed Moire leaning against the far wall of the room, hands pressed flat in back of her against the smooth wall, her chest rising and falling as she hyperventilated through slack, open lips.

Finally, she began talking, her voice wheezy, but still strident in its intensity: "Your...your fault. Had—had to bring him out, didn't you? Didn't you realize what...what'd happen? Are you that *stupid*!

"I'm not the one who trashed the—" I began, but Moire kept on, "Couldn't you figure things out? I can't believe a social worker would be so utterly blind to this sort of thing...what the hell do they *teach* you people, anyhow?"

On the floor, Kevan protested, "I didn't do anything wrong... or illegal. He's a goddamn *adult*...he's thirty damn years old—"

"And he's a *Savant*, you prick! His brain isn't wired like yours or mine—emotionally he's a damned baby! I don't care how old he is, he's just *not like us*. He doesn't *think* the same! You took advantage of him you horny son of a bitch! He didn't understand—"

"I'm not retarded—" Dalton's voice cut through the throb of angry voices and sparking components, as he pulled himself— and Brogan—into the threshold of the small room. "No, not a baby...I'm not retarded—"

"No one said you were, Dalton," I tried to soothe, but I knew he'd heard everything we'd said, all the insults Moire had thrown Kevan's way,

"Like you...like...Kevan. Brain's wired all right. Understand. Not a baby. Am like you. Not a retard...." He'd stopped fighting, so Brogan released his hold on the Savant. I wondered if he'd go over to Kevan, but Dalton simply stood there, staring at the ruined console just above the navigator's head, until he muttered, "Gone for no good" to no one in particular.

"That's right, Dalton, the console's gone. I'll have to fix it," Sloan said; until he'd spoken, I hadn't noticed him there in the room, but he walked away from the wall where he'd been standing quietly, and approached the damaged console, a small fire extinguisher in hand. Motioning to Sabriah to move Kevan out of the way, he aimed the nozzle at the ruined plastic and freshly exposed circuits, and sprayed a layer of foul-smelling foam over the sparking mess. Sabriah pulled Kevan to his feet, while Moire went to take Dalton by one arm, to lead him out of the room while Sloan worked, only he shook off her offered hand, and left the area on his own. I started to follow him, but Brogan blocked my way with one arm, asking, "Don't you think you've done enough today? For the past few days?"

That was it. I couldn't stand the way these people kept on attacking me, verbally, for things I hadn't *done*—

"What is this about 'done enough'? I didn't do any of that—" I motioned to the spot where Sloan was already starting to dismantle the ruined portion of the console "—and I had nothing to do with whatever happened between Kevan and Dalton. All I did was try to get this crew into something resembling a working *unit*—a *whole* crew, not six people and something everyone treated like a freak—"

"Who is 'everyone'? Moire asked, as she came over to stand next to Brogan, "Nobody was treating Dalton like a 'freak'—like a Savant, yes, because that's what he is. He's not like us in that way. Which affects everything else he does. We weren't trying to force him to be something he wasn't...sure, we made fun of him, but we make fun of each other. No one ever regarded him as something less than a crew member...we just couldn't talk to him. Haven't you noticed? No one talks to the Savvies that much. They stay by themselves, and remember things all day—that's what they're *paid* for. Not to be mascots, but to *work*. Hasn't anyone *told* you—"

"Ohhh...*shit.*" Sloan's voice was oddly buoyant, as he quickly said, "I hear you, *Arianrod.* There's going to be a delay on those approximations—"

An unintelligible gurgle of static, then Sloan went on: "We've had ourselves an accident, with one of the computers—nothing the Savvy can't cover. Lemme get him—"

Turning around, Sloan whispered, "Get him, *now*—"

Brogan sprinted off down the corridor, while Sloan told the crew of the *Arianrod,* the silver-mining ship whom Kevan had told us would be intercepting the asteroid the *Isen-Rodor* had boosted five days ago...only, the *Arianrod* needed to get those successive approximations at least three days before it could in turn estimate its own successive approximations for when the orbits of the ship and the asteroid would meet, but it hadn't been close enough for radio contact all those days ago.

Back when there was nothing wrong with the computers, and back when the Savant-Contingent's input was still theoretical at best.

"Yeah, our Savvy's hard to coax out of his shell, too—" even as Sloan tried to joke with the *Arianrod*'s crew, he kept on motioning with his left hand for us to get Dalton *here, now*—

The pound of several pairs of feet on hard metal behind us, then Brogan pulled Dalton—who obviously didn't like the feel of Brogan's hand clamped down so tightly on his wrist—into the area, where Sloan quickly said to him, "Take this mike and tell the crew of the *Arianrod* the successive approximations Kevan gave you a few days ago. They need those figures."

Nodding his head, Dalton grabbed the mike awkwardly with his right hand, and began repeating a series of numbers, saying them slowly and clearly, just as he'd been taught years before by the mining company, back when the whole Savant-Contingent program began merely as a way for the conglomerate to score a legal tax break for hiring people like him...in all the months I'd spent on mining and tracking ships, no Savant had actually been called upon to recite those successive approximations.

But he sounded something close to confident, as he went

through that long string of figures, then repeated them upon request from the other ship's barely intelligible crewman, millions of miles away. It was impossible to tell that he'd been crying and keening only a few minutes before.

When he was through, Sloan gently took the microphone away from him, and finished speaking to the other crew, telling them, "No, just a couple of circuits got fried...the navigator spilled his coffee on them. No biggie...."

"Ms. Kenward, you're confined to your cabin—" the Captain's voice took me by surprise; I hadn't realized that he'd come forward along with Brogan and Dalton.

Turning around, I began, "Captain Penn, you don't have the authority to do that—the company's orders were—"

"Screw the company, and screw their god-damned orders. You're out of here. And he—" the Captain pointed at Dalton with his free hand "—is back in his cabin. Where he *belongs*," he added, slapping his e-book against one thigh for emphasis as he stalked down the corridor back to his cabin.

Next to me, Moire said, "Which is what I was trying to tell you. Savvies belong in their cabins. Didn't anyone tell you that before? They're not locked in. but they just stay in there anyhow. It's what they do."

Shaking my head I told her, "It's what they do because they don't know any better....Or aren't curious. Dalton...that wasn't enough for him. And as for Kevan...he is right. Whatever was going on wasn't illegal. You might not approve, but they're both of age—"

"That's not the *point*!" Moire started to grab for my upper arms, but I pulled away before she could touch me. "That's not the kind of one-on-one therapy he needs...it isn't *necessary* for his job—"

"But you were willing to talk to him when I brought him out," I protested, to Moire and to all of them, "You all paid attention to him—"

"Because you pushed him on us...because you were acting like that was what the company wanted...the company sends a damned social worker, we try to co-operate with her. Because that seems to be what the company wants...but I can't see the company wanting *this*—" she pointed to the ruined console, and to Sloan as he began taking out circuit boards "—so I can't see them wanting him out, either. Social worker my ass, you're a damned menace," she finally hissed, before quitting the tight circle that she and the others had formed around me.

Kevan was the next to leave, after Brogan told him, "And you stay the hell away from him, understand? I don't care if he did let you—"

Brogan started to say something to me, then closed his mouth and shook his head, before he too walked away. Which left Sabriah.

"Make that an A-plus in Obtuse," she said softly, before taking my arm and leading me back to my cabin.

Case # 290727DD/I-R
19-01-58/T. Kenward, caseworker

Day 17: Status—limbo

Sabriah was the one who told me, when she brought me my noon meal.

"The figures were wrong." She was actually standing in front of the closed door, her hand moving toward the palm-pad, when I asked, "'The figures'...you don't mean the approximations, for the other—"

Turning around, she crossed her arms over her breasts, and nodded her head until the scarf began sliding around on her hair underneath.

"Yes, they were wrong...only two transposed numbers, but guess what? Those two transposed digits were enough for the *Arianrod* to lose the asteroid. The thing orbited right past them, and they couldn't intercept it. So...since it was loaded with silver, they had to break their orbit, and try to catch up with it. Which took them off course for the rest of their run. Because if they didn't go after it, and de-spin it, it would've gone on to crash into the Lunar mines. The orbit was that far off the figures Dalton gave them...Sloan managed to get the original figures off his own laptop, but *that* was back in his cabin, while Dalton was right there with the wrong figures—"

"Brogan got Dalton...he wasn't there in the—"

"I don't care about that. Dalton did what no Savant-Contingent is supposed to do. He messed up. Got the data wrong. Savants usually don't do that...unless they've been socialized for too long. Personally, I'd hoped that what you'd done wouldn't set him too far back, but I guess whatever it was Kevan was doing with him really rewired his brain—too many new emotions, too much stimulus...you do know, don't you, how the autistic brain differs from 'normal' brains...how changes in routine can affect previous function. And you know how that can mostly be a good thing, don't you? It was good for you, when you were young, wasn't it?"

She'd had the time to radio Earth, maybe to even get a response, but I had been assured—no, *promised*—by both the last university I'd attended as well as by the mining company itself that information about my condition would be kept confidential. There were laws about that, after all—

I wasn't obligated to say anything, but I'd been away from the others for so many days, with no stimulus, no interaction, save for Sabriah's brief, virtually wordless intrusions into my cabin three times a day, I simply needed to talk to her.

"Yes, it was 'good'—being autistic can be so *lonely...* especially when a person is affected with sensory integrative dysfunction. Mine was so *bad...*colors seemed to scream and claw at my eyes, red and green especially...certain sounds were all wrong...and no one understood, they just talked around me, or through me.

"You cannot imagine what it was like...or how long it took, now many different teachers my parents had to hire...you can't imagine. And once I could think, more or less like the rest of you, I did not want to ever go back to where I'd been...I wanted the companionship, the interaction, the interface...was that so wrong of me?"

That dark scarf-covered head now moved from side to side. She didn't answer me, but did say as she opened the door, "I'll try and get you some movies, and a player. I don't use mine much," then the door slid out of the bifid wall, and I was alone again.

Case # 290727DD/I-R
23-01-58/T.Kenward, former caseworker

Day 21: Status—missed connection for *Berde-Pedar*.

Sabriah told me that the Captain had contacted Earth, not her. Said he told the company everything, and that they gave him the information they'd promised they wouldn't. She said the Savvy is all right, that he's in his cabin, watching movies. She brought me some of his, the ones from his "don't watch much" pile. Two of them are Robin Williams movies. *Dead Poets Society* and *Awakenings*. I know she put them on top of the stack on purpose. I only watched them once myself. I know she meant for them to show me the error I've committed with Dalton, that I'd done little better than that prep school teacher who set a chain of events into motion which resulted in that one boy killing himself, or that bearded doctor who'd given all those frozen people that drug, so they improved...only for a brief, brief time, before going back into that metaphorical cave of theirs. As if I don't know that already.

Perhaps two of us graduated from Obtuse 101.

She did write me a note, folded up small and square like the MDVD jewel cases, and slipped between some of the movies in the stack.

Lately she hands me the food tray and leaves immediately, so I've had to re-read the letter quite a few times, while waiting for whatever ship is going to pick me up and, I assume, take me back to Earth:

"Temple,

It looks like you won't be playing Anne Sullivan to that female Savant over on the *Berde-Pedar* anytime soon. I heard the Captain requesting an immediate transport back to Earth for you, as soon as we cross orbits with an Earth-bound ship. Which might take a while. Until then, you're off limits to everyone on board. Me included. Dalton. He's about back to normal—*his* normal. Watches his "nice" movies every day. Kevan's behaving himself too—looks like you'll have company on the ship back to Earth.

I realize that you must think me a bitch, or worse, but I have orders to follow, too. We all do, or did, until you came here. But I do realize how tempting, how necessary, it must have seemed to you, to try and bring Dalton out of his isolation. Even as you weren't able to 'read between the lines' so to speak. Perhaps that was one of the hard things for you to overcome—I do suspect you still haven't mastered reading people yet. Not the way you seemed to have misunderstood all of us so thoroughly. Just as I noticed that you still seem to have an aversion to the color red. Perhaps, after you managed to earn all those degrees of yours, you might've considered all of your autism-related difficulties conquered. But there's no way to completely erase autism, even though science has discovered the responsible genes, even after all those therapies have been tried. Not that you should want not to be autistic—from the brief 'conversations' I've had with Dalton. I do realize that he lives in a special, perhaps even beautiful world. A cave, as Plato may've thought of it, but such a warm, cozy, nicely-decorated cave. And a cave he has always been able to leave as he chose. I never had to urge him to exercise—he took walks at night, on his own. And came *back* to his cabin afterward. On his own.

Back when I was a small girl, living in Kentucky with my mother, my grandmother was rear-ended in her car, several times, many years before that whole 9-11, World Trade Center thing made us conspicuous, by the local rednecks. So they did terrible things to her, and to my mother. Because they looked different. Because they prayed differently. I remember asking my Nana, Why don't you take off the scarf in your car? It's like being in a small house, only she told me, Sabriah, honey, I can't live in that car. I gotta come out, too.

I know you're not a Muslim, and I know you don't live in a car. But you are what you are, *everywhere* you are. Hiding it will only cause you grief. Your parents must've known you were autistic right from birth, probably why they named you Temple, after that autistic scientist, Temple Grandin. Only no one's ever forgotten she was autistic. And she always said she was.

It didn't make her accomplishments any less important. But it did put her and her work in context. Lose the context, and the meaning is lost, too. I hope you can understand. Without his context, Dalton's just another cute guy for someone like Kevan to hit on. And maybe hurt—I don't know what did or didn't happen, nor do I really want to know. As you said, they're both of age.

Even if Brogan and Moire don't see it that way. But as good looking and as young as Dalton is, he's *not just* a good looking young man. He's special, and he has a purpose in this world. Even if that purpose is to sit around all day watching movies to escape boredom, and wait for someone to give him a set of numbers to remember and not mess up. It isn't an unbearable life for him.

I do admire your effort to transcend your unique-ness—but I cannot condone someone ignoring that uniqueness in the process. Hope you enjoy the movies.

Sabriah"

I wonder how someone like her ended up working with people. When all she does is try to hold people back, make them bow down low under a yolk they cannot tolerate any more.

But the movies help...just as they helped when I was small, and the colors jumped up at me, tearing at my eyes. Mostly the red and the green. Until Grandfather showed me that movie with the harmless, transparent green goo, and gave me that little burger-place toy, the one with the dancing green blob I could cover over with my hands when the color was too bright, until it didn't hurt my eyes so much after all. I never did get used to the red Thunderbird the professor in the movie drove around, but I liked when it rode up into the sky, and hovered there. Like the sun, only not as painful in the eyes.

I didn't realize how much I'd missed that movie until I saw Dalton watching it. Or remember how much it helped me. Only I'd never seen it with the other language tracks—foreign languages sound so harsh, so bristly to me. Not wormy like Dalton hears French, but still strange.

Sabriah didn't tell me so, but I found out I'm not locked in this cabin. Last night when I couldn't sleep, I opened my door, and walked out into the corridor. The others were asleep, but Dalton wasn't. I heard Robin Williams in there, speaking Spanish.

Special thanks to Jayge Carr for her help on this novelette.

Afterword for
"Robin Williams, Speaking Spanish"

A few years back, I was reading an article about the writer/director/actor M. Night Shyamalan, and in it he revealed how he came up with the "twist" in his Academy-Award-nominated screenplay *The Sixth Sense* (which I won't reveal here, just in case you haven't seen it), which basically involved a lot of rewrites, sitting around and thinking, and finally, an *a-ha* moment, when the missing element fell into place, and he knew he had a special screenplay.

What he experienced was akin to what I went through while writing this novelette—I had all the elements in place save for the fact that the narrator was also autistic. Once I realized that Temple's rigid approach to her work, and her lack of humor/lack of basic people skills, despite her job as a social worker, were all autistic traits, I had my story. But there was an irony lurking behind the work which I didn't fully comprehend until late 2005, when my ever-increasing depression made me seek some professional help...and I discovered that I myself have a form of autism—specifically Asperger's Syndrome. (Actually I found out that a series of tests I'd been given twice in elementary school and once in junior high *were* tests for autism...something the schools in question never saw fit to share with my mother, or me.)

I really can't describe what it's like living with this condition, save that I realized from early on that I don't think, react, or behave like other people, even if I can't quite comprehend why my take on life is so different than theirs. It simply is what it is, and there's nothing that can be done for me, since I was diagnosed so late in life. Being kept isolated during most of my childhood didn't help, either, but that's another story entirely. I don't even know if it is a good thing to be this way, but I suppose it is what led me to be a writer—I live far more in my mind than I do in the physical world. I think in pictures, and have figured out a way to transform what I see in my mind into words on paper. I can't stand physical contact, and I tend to rock back and forth when upset, so physically, at least, my teachers should have known something was wrong with me (the having no friends part was another obvious sign), and I now suspect they did realize something was wrong, hence the tests, but nothing was done about it, nor was my mother ever told what was wrong. All the schools did was yank me out of my third grade class in mid-year, and dump me into another class, where I knew no one at all, in a futile effort to "make (me) more friendly" by forcing me into a new situation, or tell me (when I was much older) to "forget" about dating and whatnot, since, as one teacher put it, "You have no personality."

In a way, I suspect poor Dalton is actually better off with his movies and his futile dreams about physics, locked away from his shipmates. As is Temple, since her job is merely an illusion created by well-meaning parents and teachers. There may be treatments for autism, but there will never be a complete cure. And if you happen to be an adult when the diagnosis is actually made, even treatment isn't an option. From experience I can say that sometimes knowing what is wrong is better than merely enduring without answers or explanations—but it still doesn't help the situation. It merely defines it.

Getting back to the story, the little burger toy Temple mentions was a real Happy Meal toy—since it helped inspired this novelette, the little green guy dancing on the VHS case has a place of honor on my writing table. And Dalton's "wormy" reaction to the sound of French is something I experience, too, only in my case it's specific voices which create that "wormy" auditory sensation. I don't know how else to describe it, save that some things sound...*wormy*. Aural-slipperiness. Just... yukky.

One last observation—when I wrote this, I was under the impression that the guys who were credited with writing *Rain Man* wrote the entire script; but later on, I learned that much of the dialogue was improvised, including the NASA speech at the beginning of the novelette. The credit line should also read Tom Cruise, for what that's worth. (I still love the movie, no matter who came up with the dialogue....)

WHAT FALLS
FROM THE LIFE

WITH JOHN S. POSTOVIT

"Life would be tragic if it weren't funny."

Dr. Stephen Hawking Interview,
New York Times Magazine, Dec. 12, 2004

"...Gleaners were the people that were so poor that they would come to the fields after the fields were picked and they got to pick up what was left behind.

"This comes to mean someone who by watching takes what falls from the life of the culture and puts it into something...that there's a value in what they have lived."

Bill Murray,
"Murray is the Catch of the Day," by Rachel Abromowitz,
The Los Angeles Times, December, 2004

"THEY ARE HERE—MANKIND NO LONGER ALONE"

Headline from *The New York Times*,
February 2 A.A. (After Arrival)

1.

Ugoku Shiro no Tani
(*Moving Castle of Wind*)

Word for Word/freerebubic.com,
The New York Times, Sunday, March 1 A.A.

From Fear to Wonder: Witnesses to the Arrival

The February 1, 2003 *Columbia* shuttle disaster was perhaps the first such event to unfold live on the Internet, prior to being picked up by radio or television, but it was far from being the last. But no earthly event subsequently came close to The Arrival on another February day, exactly one month ago, a day which became known first via the Internet, then in all mediums, as the first day of a new era, the Year One, After Arrival.

Just as they had with the *Columbia*'s impending arrival and subsequent break-up, a group of space enthusiasts first learned of the impending Arrival via NASA TV's Webcast...along with Mission Control, these on-line trackers were the first to learn that an object previously thought to be an on-coming comet had abruptly changed course, and was approaching Earth over the lower half of the North Atlantic Ocean, with an east-west flight path.

The first record of the approaching bogie comes at 6:49 p.m. Eastern Time, a full fifteen minutes before the breaking news announcements hit cable, then network news outlets.

Excerpts from the on-line observations follow. The times are Eastern and Pacific, as noted.

The first observer was "i-land boy" at 6:49 p.m.

If anyone out there has access to NASA TV or nasa.gov, watch—NOW—They're tracking Something coming in over St. Vincent flying toward Miami. Looking out my window, I can see it—God, it is big. Not one of ours. Not the comet they thought it was. It's mostly round, but something is folding in on the sides. Solar sails, perhaps. Self-illuminated. Not Mother-ship big, but it's not a scout ship, either. Bigger than a jumbo jet. It just took a slight turn toward Florida, has to be guided. Better take a look before we nuke it or worse.

From Otaku99 at 6:51 p.m.

It's over Miami now, but the sails or wings or whatever i-land boy saw are tucked against it now. It is bright. Ugoku Shi-ro—Moving Castle. Not aerodynamic, but I can feel the sonic vibrations as it passes. It seems whole—the Red States haven't attacked it. Yet. Probably too freaked to push the button, or too busy praying under their desks.

From i-land boy to Otaku99 at 6:55 p.m.

You think they'd attack it? Doesn't look like it's oozing oil.

From EarthMama at 6:57 p.m.

Whatever it is, it's just passed over Louisiana and is headed west over Chireno, TX. I've lived over eighty years, and have never seen anything this beautiful. A pox on whoever might attack it! BTW, not everyone in the Red States votes Red.

From Tumbleweed at 7:01 p.m.

Awesome!!! Like something from Balloon Days here in Albuquerque, only nothing full of wind moves that fast, and stays in one piece. I have a telescope and there are wings or something like them folded on the sides. It is so freaking huge, but not as fast as a shuttle.

From SlotsBarBarBar to Tumbleweed at 7:03 p.m.

It's over Nevada, and Elvis Has Re-Entered the Building. My bet is, it ain't planning to land in the US of A-Bomb. Not slowing down enough, side bet, it's headed for Japan. Or Russia. Anyone want to cover me?

From landsurfer to SlotsBarBarBar at 7:05 p.m.

No cover, but the house says betting when this will reach the TV news is a sure thing. Still nothing, no breaking—sorry folks, all bets are off. They just broke in with some suit at NASA. Looks like he's gonna lose his salsa and guacamole all over his cowboy boots.

From SlotsBarBarBar to landsurfer at 7:08 p.m

Where are you, landsurfer?

From landsurfer to SlotsBarBarBar at 7:10 p.m.

Eureka CA. The NASA dude just said it changed direction again, but has yet to establish contact. Way it's moving, I'd say it's headed for Japan, over the Aleutian Islands. Just hope they can avoid causing another tsunami if they're planning a soft landing in the North Pacific.

From Otaku99 to landsurfer at 7:15 p.m.

If the Moving Castle can come through our atmosphere without tearing itself apart so far, I'd guess it can land safely. Let's hope so, for the sake of all those people on the islands. Ugoku Shiro no Tani, please—

From landsurfer to Otaku99 at 7:20 p.m.

Me no speak Japanese—lemme see, the Moving Castle of What???

From Otaku99 to landsurfer at 7:22 p.m.

Of wind. Moving Castle of Wind. From a couple of Anime; Kaze no Tani no Nausicaa and Howl no Ugoku Shiro. You got a better name for it?

From landsurfer to Otaku99 at 7:24 p.m.

Nope, and no offense intended. Just don't spend much time surfing toons.

From Miya-5an63 at 7:26 p.m.

I cannot believe you folks! The Earth is being visited by real Aliens, coming in for a landing, and you can sit around and make bets, and argue about Anime? And BTW, I see some Red-State Specials coming in for a fly-by hope it's an escort, and not Abu-Guardians. But the Ugoku Shiro isn't fazed, hope it is a good omen. It is just passing over the Isle of the Four Mountains, slowing down gradually—there! Its sails are coming out, layers of them, like blossoms surrounding the pistil. If I were the betting type, I'd give a soft landing even odds.

From GokuZ at 7:30 p.m.

Let me make it official—at 10:31 (Japan-time) a.m., we are no longer alone in the universe. One of our TV networks has just shown the soft landing, splashdown, what-have-you, of Ugoku Shiro no Tani. The aircraft from the West are circling above it, but so far no shots have been fired by either side. The deployed sails now rest on the waters of the Pacific, glistening like spilled oil on the choppy surface of the ocean, all colors swirling into each other. They fan out around the ship itself, a gleaming freshwater pearl of near-symmetrical oval shape. A shed tear from the heavens. Waiting to open. It bobs lightly on the waters, but causes few ripples. Now helicopters from my country surround it, but it merely waits, silent, serene and—I do hope—benign. But it is not a comet. And it is not one of ours.

From KawaiiKyotoSS at 7:35 p.m./10:35 a.m.

According to information coming across the NASA site, the alien-craft landed at 143° long and 41° lat, just off Japan's eastern coast. It is said to be approximately 150 meters in diameter, not counting the solar sails surrounding it. There is no obvious hatch, or windows visible, but—oh I hope everyone is watching this, I cannot believe it!! It is opening!! They are here!! I think I am going to cry. They are so beautiful! They are here!

From Yuko-san at 7:42 p.m./10:42 a.m.

Please, let no one shoot at them. They have no fear, they keep coming out, and looking up at the helicopters and the planes, just staring up at them, and looking at each other. They are perfect. So peaceful....

Book: Review: The New York Times, August 12, 8

"From *Close Encounters* to *Astroboy*—Shifting Preconceptions of Alien Life: *How It Changed: The Alien in Popular Culture Following 1 A.A.* by Toshio Sato, illustrations/photos, 546 p., Simon & Schuster, $55.95"

By Christian Kuntz

Growing up in the Midwest in the 1980s, I was subjected to the usual cultural touchstones regarding the possibility of Extraterrestrial Life—be it the roly-poly nakedness of E.T., vainly attempting to "phone home," the aethereal, quasi-Christopher-Walken-like spindly alien who emerges from the Mothership in *Close Encounters of the Third Kind*, the everyone-speaks-English-thanks-to-the-Universal-Translators bickering life-forms from the Gene Roddenberry stable, or the oddly-jointed, menacing creatures of the *Alien/Predator/Xtro* series—but after the events of February, Year One, After Arrival, my Westernized mindset was reeling from the Easternization of Alien Reality. Reeling, because that reality turned out to mirror a persistent form of *unreality* courtesy of Japanese Anime.

Never mind that the initial splashdown of their craft occurred in Japanese waters. Or that some Anime fan living in Miami, Florida was the first to dub their craft the Moving Castle of the Wind. Those things were little more than coincidence. But when they emerged, with their exaggerated curves under those clinging, semi-transparent garments, their huge, rectangular-pupiled eyes, and that free-form stiff-spiked hair, all the established Westernized notions of what An Alien Should Look Like were shattered. Even though their mouths were small in proportion to the rest of their faces, they were not Greys, those sexless, spindly-limbed, naked little Roswell-survivors celebrated in Western sf since the 1940s. No fictional starships ever beamed their kind aboard. And they didn't seem to be looking for Richard Dreyfuss, either. Nor were they followed out of their dewdrop-shaped craft by huge Art Deco robots named Gort.

They simply landed, emerged, and stood on their floating craft, quietly waiting for someone to sail out next to them, so they could make it to the shore. No one had to play the five tones. And they didn't seem interested in phoning anyone or anywhere.

Those of us weaned on Western notions of all things Alien were quietly awestruck by their arrival, and never mind their appearance, but those raised in the Far East were openly jubi- lant—not only had the Aliens landed, but they were the living echo of Japanese cultural phenomenon going back to the 1960s. While the Aliens didn't actually look Japanese, or Asian, they did bear an uncanny resemblance to the inhabitants of Manga (Japanese comics), more specifically the characters in Kodansya and Margaret Comics. True, their eyes were more goat-like than humanoid, with their black rectangular pupils (one sf touchstone realized by these beings was the image of the black rectangular form from *2001*), but otherwise, their appear- ance proved to be far more familiar to the average Japanese fan-boy or fan-girl, than to the average western sf geek, and it is this very cultural touch-point which makes Toshio Sato's *How It Changed*...such an illuminating—yet disturbing—read. Recalling his own childhood in Morioka, Japan, close to the eventual touch-down point of the Aliens, Sato draws upon both the initial reactions of his countrymen to the first emergence of the Aliens as well as their subtle first glimmer of the resulting cultural power-shift throughout the world, in his understated, casual style:

From E.T. to Manga, in less than one hour—Culture Shock: 101

"They were here, and they were more like Us than the Oth- ers, more like our dreams, our vision, our preferences. A vindi- cation of our tastes, opposed to outside influences, a testament to the uniqueness—and validity—of our aspirations. And when they came upon our shores, and saw how closely our visions resembled them, there was an immediate connection, despite the lack of a common language. Speech was unimportant, vision was the key to understanding...."

Following his personal observations, gleaned from his first-hand encounters with the Aliens during their maiden visit to Japan, Sato moves into cultural territory more familiar to Western readers, specifically the various Western-origin preconceptions of aliens in the media, then—again, in that same understated fashion—debunks each of these westernized images via examples from Japanese as well as Eastern European (mainly Russian) literature, television and cinema.

...Whether one buys into Sato's viewpoint or not, one thing is unmistakable: Just as Japanese culture changed following their defeat in World War Two, when American tastes gradually became a staple of Japanese life, down to their enthusiastic adoption of purely Western-based holidays like Halloween and Christmas, so Western culture was forever altered by the arrival of the Aliens—but in this case, the adopted cultural norms weren't those of the invader, or the conqueror, or even the winner of a war, but merely those of the predictors of the outward characteristics of the Aliens themselves. That no one was able to glimpse the culture of the Aliens *per se* is a subject left un-discussed by Sato. It is left up to the reader to decide if this omission of the obvious was intentional or unintentional—the case of the latter, one can argue that the Aliens never had the chance (or simply the time) *to* relate their culture to us, but if the former case is true, then one is left wondering if the first host nation to the Aliens was content to allow the visitors to admire *their* culture, and thus negated any reason *for* the Aliens to reciprocate culturally.

2.

Dini-0003 Hawaii!

("Cute Dini-0003")+

+Re: Dini's Surface, Mathematical Form 0003

In Theatres Now—

Chisu Higashiyma and Noriko Kogura—*That Day in February*

From the daily Blog of Capricorn-Eyes-Man, March 11, 2 A.A.

—have to admit it, the aliens are__hot__!!! the way they walk, all jutting angles teetering forward, like a duchamps painting come to life, is mind-blowing, fragile, yet strong, too, like when you see butterflies scissoring through the air, and the wind feels strong enough to knock a person over, but they keep flying into it and the way their pupils narrow down to a thin__sort of like a window-shade being drawn down to just brush the bottom of the windowsill, only you can see a sliver of light—only with them, it's like a slash of darkness, on a bright-lit wall, no eyelashes, so it's just that thin line of black against their pale skin, like brush-strokes of jet against rice paper, when they close their eyes, in profile, they're like dini's surface, twin jutting angles going around in a twist

$$\frac{x = \cos u}{\cosh y}$$

$$\frac{y = \sin u}{\cosh y}$$

$$z - y - \tan y + au$$

$$(0 \leq u < 2\,\pi.\, \text{-}\,\infty < v < \infty)$$

—only the trigonometric formula doesn't do the image justice, you'd have to look at the photos hiroshi sugimoto took of those stereometric models, the ones where he helmut-newtoned simple plaster into something sexy and stark, to me, the photo of form 0003 is like the venus demilo of the alien form—the head and the arms aren't there, but the torso is pure alien, but for me, the best thing about them is that they don't talk, just smile and nod and point at what they want, pure body language, which is why i suppose they hang out where they do, in movie theatres and ice rinks, movies are all action once you strip away the dialogue, and ice skating...pure movement, i've taken to going to ice shows, just in the hope of seeing one of them there— they tend to show up where-ever, and since no one demands that they show a passport or id, they could be there, in the place where the next ice show is. they could be in theatres, too, but since it's dark in there, you can't see them, but ice shows...the audience is always visible. i've heard they like the rink-side seats, close enough to the ice that you can feel the displaced air off the skaters' bodies, sometimes, the skaters lean over the boards to hug them, if they're sitting out there, you can't miss them, not the way they look, they bob back and forth while they're sitting, rocking in place, making their hair undulate; over those huge eyes of theirs, if i were a skater, i'd skate close to them, make sure i'd land all my jumps right in front of them, when they applaud/ their torsos ripple, everything moving up and down, undulating in place, they should make movies, the way they look—black and white movies, stark contrast of light and dark, accentuating shadows, but until they do, i watch anime, mostly the shoujo stuff, no action, just lots of romance, kissing, things like that, or i buy those manga comic books of theirs, not the alien-theirs, but japanese-theirs. which is pretty close, when you come to think of it. they're backwards, though, the front cover is what we'd call the back cover, so you look at them from right to left, i don't know what the text says, but the images are so stark, and so much like them, all you have to do is use a sharpie pen to turn their pupils into those little rectangles, the story you can make up for yourself, sometimes you can get copies of their comic books—which are like little books, hard covers with dust jackets—on ebay with their eyes already re-done, so i know i'm not alone, in what i'm thinking, when i buy one of those, not being the only one who thinks of them this way makes it easier, even if i can't find one of them yet. if not me, then someone else is looking, too.

3.

Comments from a Secret Agent: Preliminary Notes: United States Central Intelligence Agency

Malcome Cooke, Special Agent
(Overseas duty)
April 18, 2

"—physically, the Aliens are bipeds, displaying bilateral symmetry of external organs/limbs. Humanoid features (*i.e.* eyes, nose, mouth, ears, hair). Skin tone is fair to light tan. Internal sexual differences impossible to discover from external (and distant) observation, but there appear to be two distinct sexes, corresponding to human male/female. Females have pronounced breasts (also bi-lateral), larger hips/buttocks, and (again, based solely on observation via their clothing) inverted sexual organs. The males have larger ribcages, but also exhibit wider hips/ buttocks than human males. Based on observation, they seem to have externalized lower torso sexual organs.

Both sexes have four digits per hand (presumably on their feet as well), with one digit opposing the others. Eye color tends to be dark (brown/hazel) while their pupils have a horizontal rectangular shape, similar to Terran goats. As with terrestrial life, the pupils contract in sunlight/bright light.

Based on this agent's expertise in reading human micro expressions, the Aliens do seem to have fewer facial muscles (based on a human norm of 43), since their facial expressions are far more limited than the average *Homo sapiens*, and (again, based strictly on comparisons with humans) they seem incapable, of expressing more than four overt categories of facial expression: Sadness, surprise, fear and happiness. These categories have been assigned according to specific situations during which the reactions of the Aliens have either been observed or recorded. They have yet to be observed making any expressions correlating to anger, contempt, or disgust, which may merely indicate that their experiences so far have not been sufficient to generate those specific responses. While I have been trained to recognize 10,000 human micro-expressions, the general immobility of their faces does not seem to allow for more subtle subconscious expressions. As it has been observed in many public web-blogs and the media in both Japan and the rest of the world, these Aliens do bear a close physical resemblance to *anime* characters—including a corresponding stiffness of expression—which in turn significantly lowers the possibility of reading their facial expressions.

Physically, their musculature seems to be less dense than humanoids, while their seeming lack of bone density (based on their demonstrated physical lack of weight as opposed to their height, which is close to that of Asian adults) can be attributed to their prolonged exposure to zero/low gravity conditions.

They can breathe our air with no difficulty/ need for assistance, again indicating the possibility that their home world is Earth-like. They consume right-handed sugars, and do have teeth/tongues/an apparent digestive system.

The major difference between the Aliens and most humanoids centers around linguistic abilities, specifically the low number of sounds they are capable of producing. While the Japanese language is notable for the relatively low number of different sounds produced by its speakers (and is also highly dependent on an understanding of written Japanese to fill in the inherent gaps in the variety of available sounds associated with spoken Japanese, *e.g.* the practice of speakers sketching Kanji—pictographic characters—into the palms of their hands to augment their spoken language), the native speakers of the language can learn to produce non-Japanese sounds associated with foreign tongues, albeit with varying degrees of difficulty. But the Aliens seem to be completely incapable of producing sounds other than those associated with their particular language—nor can anyone, including their Japanese hosts, understand them. There does seem to be another similarity between the two races in regard to linguistic methodology, *i.e.*, the use of a form of visceral communication akin to the Japanese *haragei* (a "belly language" consisting of pauses, silences, facial expressions and grunting sounds between words/phrases). While the Japanese version of this form of communication is far more complex, the Aliens do seem to be utilizing several consistent non-verbal "cues" interspaced between the "words" spoken between themselves, including a head-tilt (both to the left and to the right), chin thrusts, two-to-three second pauses, and a gutteral "ooomph!" noise quite unlike the "oooh" "uuuung" and "looooah" sounds which make up the remainder of their speech.

It is this tangential similarity to Japanese communication which might explain the rationale behind the Aliens' choice of where to land—if these beings are capable of comprehending human broadcasts *et al.*, they simply might have chosen a race whose native tongue/physical communication are the most similar to their own, in the hopes of establishing contact in the future. Or one which already prized a visual form (*i.e. anime* characters) close to their own.

Galley Review proof, THE NOT-SO-HOLLOW SHIP: *Life After the Aliens*, Ana-Rose Dobrowolski, Chanticlier Press, 34.

...it soon became apparent to both the native Japanese as well as the millions of ancient astronaut believers that the dozen or so aliens who emerged from that smooth round craft on that fateful morning were definitely *not* descendants of the mysterious women who emerged from the *Utsuro Bune* ("hollow ship") just north of Tokyo in 1803; while that woman's image, as shown in various artistic renderings of the period, was similar to the native Japanese, these aliens were nothing like the woman who carried the mysterious box who emerged from that likewise round alien craft. These aliens carried nothing; nor did they resemble the far more ancient *Dogu* (c. 1400-300 B.C.), in that they were not wearing anything which resembled the complex helmeted, goggled, and multi-strapped space-or-diving gear shown on all traditional *Dogu* carved figures. Nor did they show any signs of knowing the Japanese language, writing systems, or any of the other elements of Japanese culture which the ancient *Dogu* allegedly "taught" to the natives of the Japanese islands. While some ancient astronaut theorists maintained that they (or more rightly their ancestors) may have been responsible for the five-layered stepped pyramid underwater structure which was discovered in 1987 off the shores of Yunagoni, Japan, these aliens did not seem to be that industrious or driven enough to have engineered such a massive structure....

The New Yorker, February 14, 15
Photography: Malcome Cooke

A set of fifty-seven evocative duo-tone portraits and group shots of the Aliens, taken while the artist was still a member of the former United States Central Intelligence Agency working undercover in Japan. Several of the photographs capture individual Aliens engaged in otherwise mundane behavior—looking at copies of *Shukan Asahi* and *Yomiuri Shimbun* at a newsstand, buying *Muji* clothes and accessories in a Tokyo outlet, gazing at their karaoke-singing hosts in a Hiroshima Hostess Bar, huddled in the rain outside the *Dan Chi* concrete block apartments lent to them by the Japanese government during their stay—while others, subsequently cropped and embellished with examples of the Aliens' quasi-pictographic writing, resemble *manga* comic books of the last two centuries. Cooke's manipulation of these images (including hand-drawn "thought balloons" filled with excerpts from blogs, overlapping and slanted portions of other photographs, and close-ups of their upper faces) simultaneously brings them firmly into the Japanese *manga* format even as he further distances these enigmatic departed beings from whatever cultural impact they had as Aliens *per se*, apart from the imagined influences of their long-term hosts. Some of the images are eroticized in that Cooke deliberately plays up those qualities of the Aliens which many humans found overtly appealing—in one, he superimposes an Alien female's in-profile whole body shot over one of the plaster models of a mathematical form (#0003), while in another, he gives a full-face image a *noir*-ish treatment using shadows from a window blind to create a sense of sexual mystery. Accompanying the show are recordings of the actual Aliens' spoken words, a soothing jumble of sound often compared to the infamous "Dalai Lama" scene in the 20th Century film *Caddyshack* (a favorite of the Aliens), which in turn inspired the now out-of-favor nickname "Uuuungas" for the Aliens around 4 A.A.

Through March 20th.
(International Center of Photography,
Sixth Avenue, at 43rd St.)

4.

More Fun in the Blogosphere

"Gunga galunga...gunga, gunga-gunga-galunga.... On your deathbed, you will receive total consciousness. So I got that goin' for me...which is nice."

Carl Spackler (Bill Murray)

Caddyshack (1980)

From: Chishu79@Yahoo.com 23-2-4 A.A. 05:06:25:86
To: Saburi-toy@Yahoo.com
Subj: Reassessing Radishes/daikon

Sab-toy:

Just got home from the hostess bar—the Gaijins from Ugoku Shiro no Tani wanted to go there, or so said Haruki, as if he can understand them any better than the rest of us. Me, I think he follows his compass pointer wherever there's warm meat. But our visitors did appear to have a good time. I've never actually sat through one of those karaoke sets, or paid any attention before—a very strange, weird world unto their own. I was told that this bar devolves into the same rotation of four or five regular singers—strange, the allure that being on the karaoke stage seems to give them. No less than two of the visiting females made passes at me while I was up there on stage. I was singing that song from the Sofia Coppola film, the Bill Murray one. Cannot remember the name. Before I was through, both of the females were walking up to the stage, swaying like they do on those thick daikon legs of theirs, only for the first time, they didn't look so radish-like to me. For beings jointed more or less like us, they have an entirely different form of locomotion. Everything sways, when they walk. And their eyes—pupils were more narrow than a knife slash.

I know the standard of beauty here does not include women with daikon legs, but these females are not of us, nor do they try to mimic us, which I suppose is an honor on their part. I do wish I could have spoken to them, I think they would have been as willing as I was. Haruki would have, I am sure, but they did not come up to the stage when he was singing. Maybe it was the song—I plan to find them a copy of that Coppola film, if that was what they liked. Perhaps they will be thankful. The Embassy has asked me to accompany them to the upcoming

Nationals Skating competition, as if they had also indicated that they wanted to see ice skaters! But everything here is new to them, and potentially as good as what they saw yesterday. We have all been instructed to be cautious during the nema-washi period, feel them out as best we can, given the lack of a common haragei. That they use belly language is so obvious, but how many bellies might they have under the skin? It is so impossible, but I do suspect they liked the karaoke. Or at least that song.

eBay listing from June 25; 4 (later deleted by order of the US Central Intelligence Agency)

Own a Piece of World History!!

A genuine example of Alien writing, in their own hand, obtained from their__Dan Chi__ (apartment block) trash. This piece of paper, 8½" x 11", unlined, contains the actual writing of the Aliens. Who knows—this might be page one of "To Serve Man" or whatever they're up to! For a minimum bid of: $10,000, you can own a part of the new millennium!! (Digital photo of item)

o Ooo o/oo.. o//.o/. Oo.OOO/.O/.O oo/oo/oo oOoOoO.oO.o // oO..O//......0.../..0..ooo/. /. o/oo//oo. oo/oo. ///0///0.//O///..oO//ooo/ ooo./0..../oooo/OOoo./.ooO//////././.O/.o////0...oOoOoo. /./. OoO//./ /////././O/.oOo//...

eBay listing from November 3, 18

'Uuuuunga-lovers, rejoice! Check out the actual films they rented and enjoyed during their visit to the western-most province of Canada, Pacifica. This invoice from a Los Angeles Blockbuster® was filled out by a clerk, but contains a list of all the DVD' and mini-DVD's they bought during the week of August 9-15, 9. This item comes with a copy of the in-store surveillance tape made during their visit to the outlet, showing real 'Uuuungas interacting with the astonished and delighted counterman.

Use this list to create your own u'Uuunga film-fest (ice-skates and karaoke machines not included!), for a minimum bid of only: $500.

Los Angeles, Pacifica, New Canada Blockbuster® invoice from August 9, 9 A.A., paid for with cash (signed by the Japanese Ambassador to New Canada), for purchase of ten new DVD's/mini-DVD's:

Caddyshack
Rushmore
Lost in Translation
The Royal Tenenbaums
Death to Smoochy
The Life Aquatic with Steve Zissou
Ice Castles
Duets
Slapshot
Happy Gilmore

5.

Further Secret Agent Observations

From: *Secret 'Uuuunga Man: The Unauthorized Biography of Malcome Cook*,
                          by R. M. Charles, Doubleday, 32 A.A.

Waves lapped against the side of the inflatable raft, rocking it wildly as Cooke stepped down from the rope ladder. Darkness was starting to fall as the Navy crew started up the *Zodiac*'s outboard and swung away from the *Zumwalt*. Once they were clear and Cooke was settled in, the little boat's pilot gunned the engine. They had a long ways to go before the night was over.

Cooke was a year into this assignment, and a handle on the 'Uuuungas still eluded him. He watched them at theatres and skating rinks, boxing matches and bicycle races. He'd been a spectator observing these perpetual spectators, the 'Uuuungas. He watched them aimlessly wandering Japanese cities (always in male-female pairs), trading yen for roasted sugar crabs and other Japanese junk food. He snapped surreptitious photos of the Aliens on their occasional forays outside Japan on commercial flights. He constantly wondered, how could they have come so far from who knows where, without bringing simple machines needed to transport themselves around Earth? It was a mystery. He made countless hours of surreptitious video, and studied the tapes for the slightest clues to their thinking, their reactions, their emotions. Nothing. They were a mystery wrapped in an attractive enigma.

Who was to know what they thought and felt? Could any human ever really know the things that motivated another species? He'd studied a dozen languages in every major linguistic group found among humans, yet the spoken 'Uuuunga language showed no similarities. The only thing he'd found to date was a seeming link to the gestural *haragei* component of Japanese communication.

The 'Uuuungas were no help whatsoever, disdaining any contact with humans at any level more complex than learning the rudiments of human economy. They always paid cash, always the correct amount, even when stunned theatre attendants tried to wave them in for free. 'Uuuunga representatives made the occasional foray to Amsterdam, where they traded ingots for Euros at Schiphol Gouden Handelaar, a nondescript gold traders', Euros which they usually traded for yen at the exchange brokers in the center of Amsterdam. The traders themselves, interviewed by Interpol, contended that no words were exchanged. Ingots were weighed, cash counted out, recounted by the 'Uuuungas themselves, end of story. Surveillance cameras revealed nothing contradictory, revealed nothing other than proof that 'Uuuungas understood the human numeric system.

Interpol induced the traders to take Cooke on as a floor agent. Two weeks into that assignment, a pair of 'Uuuungas came in and gracefully laid two satchels containing a total of fifty-two one-kilo bars of gold on the desk. Cooke had gone through the motions of checking a sample bar, and typed out a receipt. He handed the receipt to the 'Uuuunga male along with a stack of currency that was 3000 Euros short of what it should have been. He watched while the female flipped through the bills. She looked at him with that exaggerated 'Uuuunga "surprise" expression and wagged a graceful finger at his nose.

Did the 'Uuuungas really feel the emotions their expressions would indicate in a human? It seemed so at that moment. Or were they merely "translating" to what they knew of human expression, like a human does when she extends a finger toward a housecat in greeting?

And where did they get so much gold? In the past five years, they'd traded over 2000 kilos of gold.

The *Zodiac* sped on through the moonless night. The clouds overhead were an extra bonus that would keep them unseen from casual observers. Good so far, though if anyone was watching them with IR goggles, their body heat and the heat off the engine would make them stand out like a beacon. Who knew if the 'Uuuunga ship they were scouting could observe them or not? But then, who cared? The 'Uuuunga had never shown any interest/fear or reaction to humans outside of the limited interactions they had in theatres as they "laughed" at Bill Murray. They wouldn't do a thing to harm humans merely passing by.

The Japanese government was another story. They'd been very protective of the Aliens whose ship bobbed in their territorial waters. Requests from the CIA, MI5, Mossad and the Russians' GRU for expeditions to visit the Aliens had all been rebuffed. The CSA had made rumblings about bombing the

"Godless Aliens" until New Canada had issued a quiet counter-threat, sparking rumors of a second Civil War.

For that matter, sources in the Japanese government itself claimed that the Naicho Intelligence Agency had prohibited any attempts at contact. Was the Japanese claim of respect for their visitors' privacy true, or were they simply scared by having a potentially deadly enemy so nearby?

Cooke pulled on his own night vision goggles as the raft throttled down for the last few miles to the giant ship floating silent and dark in the waters ahead. Satellite photos had shown jets of water constantly spouting from a vent in the side of the spherical 'Uuuunga ship. It couldn't be bilge-water. Any craft tight enough to withstand interstellar space wouldn't leak. So why were they pumping so much water? Seawater contained all sorts of trace elements, including gold. So maybe the 'Uuuunga were extracting their spending money from the sea, along with who knows what else. Cooke intended to take a sample of that water and find out.

6.

Capricorn-Eyes-Man Continues to Obsess

ALL NEW SELECTION! INSPIRED BY THE LATEST MANGA-ART! "SAYINGS SOCKS" FOR THE CARTOON CUTIE IN YOU! ALL WOMEN'S AND GIRL'S SIZES, FIVE SHADES OF WHITE—SAYINGS IN SIX COULOURS! "SWEET-TART! "SUGAR" AND MANY OTHER COOL SAYINGS IN ALL SIZES! KNEE-LENGTH, SUPER-FINE COTTON—FOR SUMMER—WINTER WEAR! AVAILABLE AT DAIKON-LEGS-R-U.NET/ALL. CREDIT CARDS WELCOME!

From the daily Blog of Capricorn-Eyes-Man, July 21, 4 A.A.

—keep wondering why the 'uuuungas prefer to stay together as a group, no matter where you see them, they're in pairs or a pack, clustered together like grapes encircling an invisible stem, I've read up on japanese culture, now__they__prefer to be with each other, like in tour groups (anyone able to forget those japanese tourists in the movie the spanish prisoner, or that whole bunch of them watching that crooked italian cop get hanged by dr. lecter in hannibal, snapping pictures as first his cell phone, then his guts, fell on that piazza?) but what i wonder is, are the 'uuungas that way__because__they're that way, or because their hosts are that way? It's like the socks thing—do they really wear the white socks, like the manga chicks and like_every_woman you see in japan, because they want to, or because that's what they saw, and thought would be polite to do? with those thick legs of theirs, the women-'uuuungas are only emphasizing their solidness...not that that's a bad thing, not too long ago, that korean sculptor lee bul's cyborg series was showing here at the field museum, and it was so hard to believe that she made those things years before the 'uuuungas came, one in particular, "cyborg w4," struck me as being totally 'uuuunga—thick smooth curves, angular bust, all shades of white and light grey, and the fact that the statue had no head or left-side limbs only intensified the resemblance to some sort of abstract shape, like one of those old carnival pictures with the space for the head empty, so you could stand behind it and make your head part of that picture of a different body, only if you stuck an 'uuuunga female behind "cyborg w4" you'd have a perfect meld. makes me think that maybe sugimoto and lee bul and all those manga and anime artists were simply waiting, knowing that their visions would be validated from beyond, which is why they kept on creating these not-quite-human people of theirs, only with all those small details which would only make sense in the a.a. time, which in turn makes me wonder—were all those other cultural things, like the white socks, and the wanting to be close to each other, some sort of collective memory of an impending event? sort of a jungian thing? collective unconscious? and for__their__ part, were the 'uuuungas consciously searching for the right time in__our__ collective culture, when we'd be the most open to them? did they land__there__instead of__here__for a reason, or because it was convenient? and did they look the way they did when they emerged from that gigantic bobbing quicksilver sky-drop-let because it was their nature, or because it would provide their best defense against an entire world of aliens-to-them?

i wish i knew what they wanted, just as i wish they'd figure out what it is so many of us want from them, can their coyness be for real, I wonder??? or might they be waiting for us to come up to their standards?

http://www. 'uuuunga-gaijin.com website chatroom 12-16-8:

Haruki67:

How could their choices of films__not__be important? Clearly, they indicate the undue influence of Western culture on their cinematic tastes. As if our cinema was inferior and the contributions of Kurosawa, Ozu and Mizoguchi had no impact on Western cinema. Which I know is a lie—do you Americans believe that The Magnificent Seven had__nothing__to do with Akira Kurosawa? Or that you people generated The Ring and The Grudge, et al.?

Groundhog-exterminator:

Yes, Haruki67, there__is__a Kurosawa. Don't get your kimono stuck in your butt over it. The 'Uuuungas like what they like. Besides, your government traded them the yen or whatever you people use nowadays to go on shopping sprees to Blockbuster and Muji outlets. Do you hear us people here in the CSA griping about how the 'Uuuungas like Muji better than Wal-Mart? Do you realize how many Wal-Marts those...folks put out of business, even here in the Conservative States of

America? Where I guarantee nine-tenths of the everyday people don't give a squirt in a pot what those aliens like to watch on their DVD's. So what if they like crazy groundskeepers blowing up gophers better than some chick reporter trying to find out why this danged videotape is killing people who watch it. I'm not a complete cracker, I know what Japanese cinema is about. Pretty much. And I know if I had my druthers, I'd go for the Seven Brides for Seven Brothers over the Seven Samurai. It's all a matter of taste, H-67. Me, I don't know why all those 'Uuuunga gals would want to wear those white socks. Maybe it doesn't get that hot where you are, but down here in Georgia, socks in the summer time are just plain nuts.

ChokoCartoonCuite.84:

No wonder your people lost that Civil War back in the 19th century, Mr. Groundhog. Does all that heat fry your brains, or is it the humidity? If I can bring the discussion back to the point Haruki-67 was trying to make, I am disturbed by the dichotomy of the 'Uuuunga's choices—while it is clear that they prefer our Japanese way of life, as well as practice haragei in their everyday speech, I am saddened that they have become so consumed with so many things Western...ice skating, Bill Murray films, golf—

Groundhog-exterminator:

And you people don't golf? What the heck was Sean Connery doing with all those Japanese businessmen in Rising Sun? Looking for Easter eggs there on the green? And I remember a couple of Japanese ladies winning the World Skating Championships and an Olympics away from American girls a few years back. True, Bill Murray is all ours, but maybe he was channeling their lingo in Caddyshack? Maybe like "Gunga galunga" was a dialect only they could understand.

Haruki67:

Maybe you weren't aware of it, but Mr. Murray ad-libbed many of his lines in that motion picture. The Dalai Lama scene was scripted, but he embellished it with his own words of wisdom. And he was__not__speaking Tibetan. Or the language of the Aliens.

SanFranMan:

On the behalf of all Canadians, esp. those of us in the New Provinces, I'd like to apologize to Haruki and Choko—hell, the whole country of Japan—and as for you, Mr. Georgia Groundhog, people like you are part of the reason the blue states seceded from the rest of what used to be the US of A. I don't know if you think knowing who made the original version of The Magnificent Seven makes you a Genius of Culture, but consider what's waiting for them in your redneck of the woods, I don't blame the 'Uuuungas for not venturing into your country anymore. I haven't been in the CSA since it was formed, either, and I certainly won't be eagerly awaiting the next backwoods blockbuster any of your film-makers crank out. If anyone in the Bible Belt knows how to load a video camera for something other than a NASCAR race. And as for the popularity of Muji over Wal-Mart, hcy, the 'Uuuungas have simple, elegant tastes. I didn't see any NASCAR stripes on their ship, and none of their women have B52 Big Hair, either. It's their business which cultures they chose to emulate—at least they know culture when they're confronted with it.

ChokoCartoonCutie.84:

Well said! I don't plan on visiting the CSA anytime soon, either—but from what I've heard, the 'Uuuungas weren't__ welcome__there, thanks to all the anti-Alien propaganda their throwback government has been churning out. I hope nobody took my comment about "so many things Western" as an insult—I meant to say that considering how we offered them ambassadorial status upon their arrival, and helped to facilitate their movements outside the country, it would have been nice if they had given our culture a more thorough consideration, before investing all their energies in the pursuit of purely Western entertainment.

Haruki67:

That is true, but if they had been too thorough in their emulation of us, I suspect that you and many other people in our country would have been uneasy. While their taste in movies does leave something to be desired, what I am concerned with is that because of their choices, people—like us, I admit—are spending much too much time discussing__their__choices, as opposed to expanding our personal knowledge of the cinematic art. And I think even Mr. CSA will have to admit, when things like ice skating and golf begin to appear in the movies of otherwise untouched cultures, like the Bollywood films from India, it is time to be concerned. Very, very concerned....

7.

*"Arigato gozai mashita...*for shopping Wal-Mart!"
July 30, 8

Little Rock, AR CSA
"Cupid Club" Sex-Toy Party Webpage advertisement:

LADIES—do your men look with longing at those 'Uuunga gals on the TV? Has your man been comparing your legs with theirs? Or has he ever wondered out loud what they're really "like"? If you can answer "Yes" to any of these questions, here's the thing to put the "'Uuuunga-La-La" back into YOUR relationship!! All you have to do is get our newest product, The 'Uuuunga-Mate®—an enticing latex and silicone garment guaranteed to fit all and best yet, Please All! Guaranteed to make your Alien-watching mate keep his sights on his own little Celestial Hussy-san! All 'Uuuunga-Mates® come with a free 2 oz. bottle of Pleasure Salve® and are guaranteed not to rip or fade for one full year! PRICES/SIZES: Ex-Small (00-0) $100, Small (2-6) $150, Med. (8-12) $175 Lrg. (14-20) $200 XL (22-28) (+ TWO bottles of Pleasure Salve®) $250 XXL/ XXXL/XXXXL—Special Order: Ask for Prices when Ordering (+THREE Pleasure Salves®)

(All Orders Include FREE White Knee-Highs For That "Cartoon Cutie" Look!!)

"Special" of the Week!! Give your man a taste of the 'Uuuunga's favorite flavor—Sake Body Oil! 6 oz bottle, only $10—One Week Only! $50, for a case of six bottles!

Letters to the Editor,
Deer Creek Chronicle, Deer Creek, TN, CSA, June 17, 9:

"Garbled Greetings?:

I don't know if this bothers anyone else who still shops at Wal-Mart instead of those Moojie (*sic.*—the Ed.) department stores which are starting to spring up all over the place lately, but I have a beef with the new policy for Greeters in the Wal-Marts—the way they have to add Japanese greetings to their welcomes. My grandfather and both my husbands *(sic.)* grandfathers fought in WWII, in the Pacific, back when they were the enemy, not the people to copy. I would hate to see the look on those gentlemens *(sic.)* faces if they heard the store Greeter say *'Ah-ree-GAH-toh-Go-zigh-Ma-Hashta'* or however you really spell it, followed by "For shopping Wal-Mart!" What has this world come to? Isn't this the reason, or one of them, that we separated from the old USA, to form a place where American values are held high, and not corrupted by foreign and worse yet, alien 'values'?

What's next, adding the Japanese Rising Sun to the middle of the Starred Bars? It makes no sense, the CSA doesn't allow the aliens to visit here, so why be followers of what *they* follow in Japan, New Canada, and the rest of the Godless world out there? Bring back American Values, for Americans!!

> Mrs. Tuttie Bounds
> Deer Creek"

(All letters to the Editor sent to *The Chronicle* shall be no more than 250 words, and must contain the writer's name, address and phone number. All letters will be printed "as is" and any corrections in spelling, grammar or punctuation will be at the Editor's discretion—otherwise, any errors will be printed, followed by (*sic.*). Any letter over 250 words will be edited. A limit of three (3) rebuttal/answering letters per original letter will be printed. All letters become the property of *The Chronicle* and may be viewed by the public as necessary during business hours.)

Letters to the Editor,
Deer Creek Chronicle, Deer Creek, TN, CSA, June 23, 9:

"Responds to Garbled Greetings:

I read Mrs. Bounds' letter in last week's *Chronicle* with interest, having been a long-time resident of the area prior to moving up to the New Canada Great Lakes Province shortly after the Secession, but I would like to express my disagreement with her argument that the gentle states of the CSA should not fall victim to outside influences—especially those of one of our former war foes. While the CSA's policies may be inherently separatist, with an increased emphasis on the *union* of Church and State, no country in this world can consider itself free of

'Godless' influences (to quote Mrs. Bounds)...unless that nation wishes to set up its own version of the Taliban. Not only do all continents, countries, states and individual villages, towns, and cities share the same world, but they share a co-mingled culture, language, and basic humanity, regardless of differences in faith, specific beliefs, and body language. If the newly formed CSA's citizens (or those who share Mrs. Bounds' specific beliefs) truly believe that they are to be a nation free from outside influences, I'd say it's time to start creating your own language...one without words like 'openness,' 'tolerance' and 'freedom' in its vocabulary. And I'd also suggest that when it comes time to print up new geography text books, that you'll be sure to leave off all the 'Godless' nations. Including New Canada. And especially Japan.

Geoffrey McKeegan
St. Paul, MN
Great Lakes Province, New Canada"

Letters to the Editor,
***Deer Creek Chronicle*, June 30, 9:**

"Clarification for: Garbled Greetings:

It appears that there may be some misunderstanding among the members of the Deer Creek shopping area in regard to the new Wal-Mart Greeters policy of saying '*Arigato gozai mashita*...for Shopping Wal-Mart!'—as it is well known, our company does do a great deal of business with Asian suppliers, more specifically China, but, due to the great demand for Japanese-themed merchandise (brought on in large part by our Alien visitors), an appropriate change in the unofficial store greeting seemed appropriate. The general reaction to this change has been favorable, and over-all, sale in the chain's CSA-based outlets has risen by 15% since the new greeting was added. Since the interest in 'all things Japanese' has skyrocketed all over the world (and not just in the CSA), we at Wal-Mart strive to bring our customers a combination of American friendliness and Japanese 'flavor' in their daily shopping experience. We have no intention of offending any of our loyal customers, and we are sorry if anyone has found these changes to be offensive.

Davis Jackson, Manager
Deer Creek Wal-Mart"

Letters to the Editor,
*Deer Creek Chronicle***, July 7, 9:**

"Garbled Greetings Agreement:

Please add my voice to Tuttie Bounds when it comes to the Asianification of CSA stores and culture. If it wasn't bad enough that I wasn't able to find a single can of black-eyed peas for the New Year's dinner at Wal-Mart last December, now all we get is Asian this and Asian that in our stores, the newspapers, and on TV. Even local channels. I agree with Tuttie—who won that war??? Last Halloween, when I went Trick or Treating with my son and daughter, they got mostly Japanese candies in their pumpkins! No Blow-Pops, but some weird mountain shaped things called 'Botsuki Apollo Choco'! And some white stuff called 'Morniga Hichew Yogurt' instead of good old Starbursts! But what was worst of all were those 'Sweet and Salty Roasted—CRABS'!!! Yes, little bitty real crabs, with sesame seed on them, and the eyes left on! I don't care if that is what those Aliens like—let them keep them in Japan! And now we hear Japanese when we go to what used to be OUR stores! I don't care about those Muji outlets, those were Japanese to begin with, but where can we go to escape this Asian-Alienification? My own church has gotten into the act— they're sponsoring Karaoke Nights and Ice Skating parties for the children's choir! This is not America anymore! When will we wake up?

Julia Le Hayne
Deer Creek"

*Coming This June—From the Acclaimed Novel by Haruki
Murakami—"Hardboiled Wonderland and The End of the
World"—Starring Tatsuo Tida, Shin Niigata and Jude Law—*

A Muramatsu-Pictures/Fox Searchlight Release—Rated R

From the daily Blog of Capricorn-Eyes-Man, February 23, 9 A.A.

—ban on admitting the 'uuuungas really__s+u+c+k+s__as if every woman you see on the streets doesn't already look and act like them, and even the men try and wear their hair like them, too (death to the mullet!). i mean, hellow, they're__here__. what are we, the middle-east? bad enough that i got transferred out of new canada into the buckle of the bible belt, thanks to the n.c. government's efforts to help pull the csa out of its financial hole (which, if you ask me, all goes back to what should've been done after the civil war—pull out the slaves, and force the plantation owners to do all the grunt work!), which used to be the usa's financial hole, before the majority of blue staters got smart and accepted canada's offer to merge with them. it is so weird down here, though—all you see on the streets are people emulating the 'uuungas, which of course means emulating their hosts, since we've yet to see anything remotely, natively, intrinsically 'uuuunga from__them__yet, so what you basically have here is japan², sort of like what happened to mtv when it started cloning itself on digital cable, come halloween (which is still a big holiday down here, despite the pervasive bible-belter-down-with-paganism mentality, and the occasional local and county ban on in-school costumes/candy/masks), all you see in the dark are kids dressed like 'uuuungas, down to the rectangular slits in their masks, and the stiff-hair wigs, which are already pretty close to the hairspray hayseeds you see down here anyhow, which all goes back to my disgust and amaze-ment and all-around-pissed-offedness over the powers that be here not allowing the 'uuuungas entrance into any of the "lower thirty-one" (which is a pretty damn stupid nomenclature, since all 31 states are "lower"! alaska's part of canada again (as if it was somehow not attached to it for over fifty years!), hawaii's been an independent nation for the last three years, and the three "fingers" which dip down on the east, west and great lakes areas are all new canada, so...what's up with this "lower" crap?!?!?

but wanna know the truly absurd thing? despite the "no aliens" interdict, what have i seen since being transferred to the "lower 31"? (as in one of the lower rungs of hell!) scooter's sakaya shop, formerly scooter's liquors and beer, izakaya__ everywhere__, usually two doors down from the courthouse with the ten commandments planted on the front lawn, and three doors down from the beauty salon ("this week's specialty— 'uuuunga extensions and backcombing!"), and across the alley from the karaoke joint/skating rink, what amazes me is that these folks can even__spell__izakaya, which is a whole lot harder than "saloon." now I've been to real karaoke-skate rinks, in new canada, and once in japan itself, and aside from the chance to rub elbows with the 'uuuunga for real (there, not here), you get to see people who actually know their axels from their assholes, and the difference between a lutz and a flutz. the combination of a decent karaoke kamikaze and a skater who knows his or her kariography can be a sublime thing, almost as good as watching the 'uuuungas watch it. sure they hire ringers to keep things going on and off the ice, but compared to the shredders and virgin software you get__here__plus the human zambonis and butt-magnets who polish the ice with their asses before they *midori ito* into the boards surrounding the ice stage, i'll take ringers and wylies and manleys (i.e. those folks lucky enough to skate the skate of a lifetime coming out cold onto the ice in those rented skates, in front of about fifty drunken shouting strangers) over what passes for skate-aoke here in big hair-ville. but what i miss most of all is watching the 'uuuungas taking in the whole spectacle/ with those vague half-smiles on their faces, and that nodding/touching/head cocking/cooing patter between them, it's so funny, how we've never been able to find the verbal rosetta stone to crack their language, that supposed real piece of 'uuuunga writing which got yanked from ebay before i could bid on it was just a scrap someone fished out of their trash, (i heard it was a bag person.) who knows what it meant, if anything, (i doubt it was page one of "how to serve man"—so far they seem happy to eat their "let's party!" roasted sugar crabs, and slurp down tubes of hello kitty gelatin in between meals of sushi and sake.) but they sound happy, at least to me. whatever we show them, they'll watch it. but they won't buy it for themselves unless someone in the movie is lacing up a pair of ice skates, or golfing (__if__there's also some skating involved, so sorry, adam sandler, they're not after you, just the scene in happy gilmore where the zamboni guy is singing "endless love" while you kiss that girl who used to push cosmetics on tv), or bill murray is doing anything__ but__chasing ghosts, why they didn't like those two films is beyond me—i for one thought they would've liked the walking statue of liberty in ghostbusters ii. but i heard those two movies did sort of freak them out, if them getting up and leaving the room as a group when one of the slimers came on screen is any indication. me, i think akroyd was maybe too much for them. which is why i suppose no one ever showed them coneheads. (or maybe it was the french connection thing?) although i doubt they went for all those wes anderson films for the wry direction or the witty screenplays—if that was the case, why not invest in a copy of bottle rocket, too? the proof is in the bill, there... no bill in bottle rocket, no sale, (not that it isn't a funny film.)

i suppose it shouldn't be surprising that they have a jones for bill, though...who can forget those close encounters of the third kind aliens passing up all those beefed-up-sunglasses-wearing uniformed studs and studettes for richard dreyfuss? like he even looked anything like them, (which may have been the point, or else__they__were into the whole "to serve man" bit, and he just happened to look like "an eater," to borrow a cup of monty python...) i just can't help but think that__maybe__guys like me might have a better chance with all those 'uuuunga females if i looked more like bill murray (instead of the guy__everyone__ [nudge, nudge, wink, wink] says i look like, jude law. or brad pitt if i don't shave, if you get my drift!)...world weary, rumpled in a i suppose sexy way, and ironic in spades, hey, maybe all us guys should try working on__that__...it would beat the hell out of doing crunches in the gym!

Listing on the Find-A-Mate® site, January 5, 10:

Do you like golfing with the Dalai Lama? Singing "More Than This" while Skate-aoke Kamikazes form Donuts-on-a-Stick? Or are you mourning the fact that your ex does, indeed, smoke? If you are, come roam the high (and even the low) seas with me, on my houseboat off the FL Keys. I may be stuck in a No-Aliens Zone, but my heart is ready to soar. Chicks who dig the 'Uuuunga look are a plus, but chicks who don't aren't a minus, either. To hear a voice clip, press # now. To see a video clip, press + now. To leave a voice message....

Seen on the illuminated sign in front of the Greenville Baptist Church, Greenville, SC CSA Sunday, May 19, 10:

THE ALIENS HAVE NO GOD, NOR ARE THEY GODS! TURN THY SIGHT FROM THE GODLESS, CAST OFF THEIR INFLUENCE!!!

Graffiti sprayed on the side of the Greenville Baptist Church, Monday, May 20, 10 A. A.:

MAYBE GOD SENT THE 'UUUNGAS TO TEST US ALL! IF SO, HAVE WE FAILED

8.

"Pay at the Pump, Please"

THE ALIENS HAVE LEFT US. ALL THE ALIENS
ARE GONE, AS IS THEIR SHIP.

**Breaking News—all TV and On-Line services, September
22, 10:**

THEY ARE GONE—MANKIND IS ON ITS OWN
AGAIN

Headline, *The New York Times*, September 22, 10:

"Half submerged bouquets of flowers ring the spot on the
Japanese Ocean where the Alien ship sat for a decade, a familiar
silver landmark easily visible from commercial shuttlecraft
passing overhead."

**Caption for *Life Magazine* newspaper insert, for 360°
World Photo, October 2, 10:**

"—given the lack of *quid pro quo* between not only their
Japanese hosts, but between the Aliens and all humans they
encountered, it is—in retrospect—understandable that absolutely no exchange of scientific ideas, theorems, or knowledge
of any usable sort took place during the time the Aliens roamed
our planet. Thanks to the Japanese efforts to prevent possible
terrorist acts, no one was able to get close to the Aliens' ship.
Guarded by round-the-clock sea and air patrols, no one was able
to inspect the ship inside or out. There was no known effort to
study the ship via satellite lest the wrath of the host country be
invoked. (In any case, the smooth ovoid shape of the ship would
doubtless have revealed little.) Considering the vast amounts

of energy needed to power such a machine, an internal power source other than solar power had to have been in use. Scientists have speculated that the ship may have been taking on deuterium and tritium from the salt water itself as a fuel source.

"If this was the case, it may be argued that the length of the Aliens' stay may have been predetermined by the processing time for fuel extraction. They may have simply "parked" it on a suitable site, much like a car pulling up to the pump at a gas station, then went inside the station itself for snacks, a video rental, and a much needed bathroom break while the car was gassing up. Once the tank was full, they were able to take off. The implications of this scenario are doubly tragic to the human race, as well as to the planet; in the most obvious sense, we were an amusement of the most temporary and banal sort, while in a more tangential sense, we allowed ourselves to be a mere pit stop in the heavens, a source of fuel, period. The future implications are more troubling. The Aliens never attempted to establish any kind of meaningful communication with us. As such, we have no idea if there are any other Alien ships out there, multi-generational ships in all likelihood, with whom the recently departed-from-our-planet Aliens might be in contact. If so, might Earth merely become the nearest 7-11, rather than the cherished home to our species?"

**From: "Pay at the Pump World" by James Lederer, Ph.D.,
Scientific New Canadian, August, 18:**

New in Paperback: *How It Changed: The Alien in Popular Culture Following 1 A.A.* (Second Edition, with a New Afterword) by Toshio Sato. $25 in all Muji, Barnes & Noble, and Amazon.Com Sites

From the daily blog of Capricorn-Eyes-Man, July 27, 11:

—coming back to new canada should've been a happy homecoming, but now that they're gone, what's the use? and seeing all the places where they were so welcome, so expected, so anticipated, all the while knowing that they are gone, probably for good, is worse than not seeing any evidence of their being here at all. i took in the latest 'uuunga film festival, all their favorites in a five day showing, plus as much anime as the promoters could squeeze in, but looking at those females, the cartoon cuties, all i could do was cry inside over all the times i could have made a move on one of them, but was afraid to...i wonder if they realized how beautiful, how solidly erotic they were? i see women on the streets now, with legs thickened by trips to the gym, and lots of protein eaten, and wearing those white socks they loved, but it's just not the same, not when one of them broke my heart with a simple wag of one finger...they aren't__them__.

somehow, what they left behind them has made their all-too-brief presence here all the more poignant, all the more unbearable in the now. everywhere i look, i see japanese-influenced artwork, food, drink, clothing, even candy wrappers left in the gutters, only, the more i think about it, i realize that none of it is truly 'uuunga, nothing of the aliens themselves, remains, just what they used, what we all think they liked simply because they watched it or ate it or just looked at it for more than a few unblinking seconds, and no one has been able to decipher what they said on those audio or video tapes which remain of them either, ditto that scrap of paper which is now locked-up in some cia vault, along with all the other hush-hush stuff we're not supposed to know, like who really killed jfk out on the grassy knoll, or who the voters in ohio actually voted for in 2004. all we know is, they really seemed to like some movies with bill murray in them, and they liked to sit and listen to karaoke while watching ice skaters waxel and flutz. or at least they paid attention to those things, which may or may not mean anything in itself, if you think about it.

we thought they were gorgeous, we wanted to look like them, i have no idea what they thought of us. if they thought about us at all. maybe all they had on their minds was that ship of theirs, sitting like a drop of quicksilver on the choppy ocean, sucking chemicals and precious metals out of our water like gas from a pump. like that one guy wrote in that science magazine.

all i keep wondering is: were we regular or diesel?

Afterword for "What Falls From the Life"
A. R. Morlan with John S. Postovit

Initially, I wrote this one as a solo work, but upon reading it over, I realized it needed some scientific tweaking, as well as a male point of view in certain spots (not to mention some general editing here and there), so, after asking my pen pal John P. about it, I sent him the ms...and then I didn't hear from him in a long time. He's a math teacher, so I knew he was most definitely busy with his classes, so I didn't really think any thing about it; I did write to him and just asked in passing how work was going on the story, if he'd found time to get to it, then I got a postcard from him—he'd been in a bike/car accident, and broke his pelvis!! Yikes!! Naturally, I just decided to let the story wait (it had to wait) and went on to another project, but after he recuperated, John did get a draft of the story off to me, which included the needed fixes for the science sections, plus a new segment, which became Chapter 5 of this novelette (all of the writing there, save for the title of Cook's book, is John's), and which, in turn, affected some other sections of this piece, in that I merged the blogger and Cook into one person, and added in the part about the alien woman breaking his heart with a simple wag of her finger. This novelette wouldn't be what it is now without John's contribution; it was worth the wait getting his input on this....

One thing which did come from me and not from John is the Chapter 3 riff on dini surfaces—I found the trigonometric formula in an issue of *The New York Times* Sunday magazine and shoehorned in the formula—but John left that section as-is when going over the novelette, so I was rather surprised that it worked within the context of the story...especially since math is perhaps my worst subject (along with some sciences and phys. ed....I also managed to flunk home ec in the seventh grade, but that's another story!), and I never was able to pass Algebra One, and barely squeaked by in my school's Algebra B class (aka Algebra for Morons)—in college I took both remedial math (which ended up being a huge class; I was part of the generation which was exposed to the dreaded New Math in the 1960s, one of the biggest education disasters of the decade...I failed Mr. Counting Man, I was that bad at it!) and a course in Algebra designed for those students in the liberal arts track, so me actually using a trigonometric formula properly was something of an (admittedly minor) achievement for me as a writer.

The whole Bill Murray aspect of the story came about from seeing him in *The Royal Tenenbaums*—his character is laid back, quiet, and almost without emotion or passion; in one famous scene, after being confronted with a private eye's evidence of his much younger wife's checkered past (as in she smoked from the age of twelve, ran away from home at fourteen, got married at age nineteen to a Reggae singer, then proceeded to have sex with virtually anything with a Y-chromosome), he pauses, then says flatly, with no affect: "She smokes?" That is the sort of thing which would make the goat-eyed aliens swoon...or whatever such low-affect beings do which equals our notion of swooning. What can I say, the guy is brilliant. (I've seen *Caddyshack* over a dozen times.)

Plus, if we were to be confronted with aliens who offered up virtually nothing about themselves, but who did embrace the culture of the land which happened to shelter them, might we not instead embrace all those things which delight the aliens, sort of a trickle down effect on a cultural level? Something like people flocking to stores to wear clothes "designed" and marketed under the names of assorted musicians and actresses. I mean, do these people even wear their own clothes most of the time? But yet, we gotta have 'em, don't we? (Well, not me, and probably not you the reader, but somebody is buying that stuff!)

Personally, I enjoyed telling this from multiple points of view, and I especially loved how John added in the part about the aliens using our harvested gold to pay for items they bought—deliciously ironic. This one was a little long for all the editors who saw it (and not being what they consider a "name" author, no one was going to shove aside works from best-selling writers to even consider making room for it), but I still am fond of it...but the part about my friend John having that accident still sucks, though!!

ETAMIN AT EAST 47th

In dreams, Masahiro could sometimes still see his mother, even though he'd been far too young when she'd left to remember her features—with or without clarity. Always, she was on the verge of turning away, so that all he could dream-see-imagine was the smooth shell-rounded curve of her face, from cheekbone to chin, just before her head and body turned away from his father...and him.

Masahiro would tell himself upon waking that her dream-words *were* real, were something he'd managed to remember:

"I cannot touch him...or you, Hitoshi. *Burakumin*—it is too much to bear, too much to contemplate. I did not know... knowing, I cannot continue to suffer this...."

Had his mother said more? If so, perhaps it was out of his earshot, words said somewhere beyond the translucent maze of sliding screens and foot-fall deadening matting which made up the world beyond Masahiro's infant bedding. Words only his father heard, and chose to keep secret in his heart, his mind— along with that other secret, the one which drove away his mother.

Burakumin.

An invisible, tacitly taboo barrier between his mother and his father...yet one which was as tangible and as elephantine as a wall fashioned of un-faceted diamond, glistening in the harsh sunlight.

Only, when clouded by passion, that wall had remained invisible....

As Masahiro Takeguchi stepped out of the elevator at the Vanderbilt YMCA, his footfalls muffled by the low-looped carpeting which covered not only the floor itself, but nearly half of the hallway walls around him, he almost bumped into one of the aliens who was rounding the nearest jutting corner of the maze of interior walls which made up this wing of the YMCA's residential floor. The alien, his (?) face half-covered by those quasi Arab head-shoulders-upper chest drapes he (?) and his (?) fellow aliens usually wore, ducked said draped head-shoulders upper chest in that gesture of contrition/humility likewise uniformly affected by his (?) race: a quick, semi-circular dipping and raising of the head, accompanied by the left "arm" crossing and uncrossing the bottom of the chest.

Having taken a couple of courses here at the Y in the alien's body-language, Masahiro was able to make the correct physical response to the alien's show of contrition—bob his own head sharply up and down, while letting his right hand and arm sweep out until his briefcase thudded against the carpet-wainscoting on the near wall. No exchange of words was necessary (or even acceptable, as he dimly recalled from the course), and the alien strode past Masahiro with a scissoring snick of discreetly covered thin lower limbs and lashing rear appendage.

(Even thinking of this posterior appendage as a *tail* was likewise a taboo concept when dealing with the aliens.)

He could hear the oily whoosh-snick of the elevator doors opening and then softly closing as he continued to walk quickly but without obvious hurry to his deluxe room down the same hall from which the alien had been walking. Vaguely, Masahiro wondered if the alien had merely been visiting a friend here at the Y, or if he (?) was going to become the next alien living in that group room down at the far end of this floor; it seemed to Masahiro that that particular room was already filled to capacity, with the two bunk beds and one (two?) single beds already claimed by the draped and swathed beings who had come and stayed here (as in "here" being Earth, North America, and specifically New York City) just a couple of short years ago.

Not that he minded the thought of sharing the floor, the Y, with more of...them. They (still oddly nameless, merely tolerated by virtue of their willingness to attempt to blend in, while gradually sharing their scientific and mathematical knowledge with their human hosts) made little noise, caused virtually no problems either here or in the city proper. All they basically asked for (and got, thanks to whatever secrets they chose to divulge to NASA and whoever else was willing to pay for their knowledge) was privacy...no one was to speak to them without being spoken to first, and only then under specific, almost maddeningly intricate rules of alien etiquette, and likewise, no one other than another alien could share "close space" with them.

That so many of them had chosen to roost at the Y was something Masahiro found deliciously ludicrous; where else would one be more likely to bump into another being in relatively close (not to mention abundantly carpeted) quarters?

"Only in America," he whispered, as he slid the silvery Y-key (stamped "Locksmith—Do Not Copy!") into the lock on his door, and as he locked the door behind him, he began to chuckle dryly, a soft chortle that echoed dully in his small but highly personal living space. Aside from the Y-supplied television (an early HD model that was little better than a pre-HD model when it came to broadcasting high definition programming), scarcely anything besides the wood-look steel bed, chipped desk and motel-standard chair reflected what might be considered "American" interior design.

Virtually all of the wall space was transformed, softened, with overlapping sheets of rice paper embedded with flecks of ragged color and subtle sparkle, over which Masahiro had hung watercolor and pen-and-ink reproductions of Japanese artwork, from ancient etchings to modern advertisements, while he'd overlaid the nubby Y-carpeting with rectangles of rush matting, now dotted with some knife-edge pillows from his homeland. And on the metal bookshelf which jutted from the wall close to the bracket-mounted TV, he'd arranged all those Kodansya and Margaret Comics, still in their original dust-covers, which his ex-girlfriend had left behind, almost six years earlier. The graphics on the slick dust-covers were misty-hued, doe-eyed, often impossibly blonde stylized representations of Western Youth, the kind of adolescents young women like Yuka still swooned over back home, yet to Masahiro, they were still not so blatantly foreign, unapproachable, as the actual West was to him even now.

On his batik-decorated patchwork quilt (another left-over from his days with Yuka) rested a copy of Shimizu Yoshinori's *The Dreamy Hippopotamus*, the blue and yellow colors of the dust-cover almost screaming for attention against the muted blacks, reds, browns and waxy, cracked golds of the quilt squares. He longed to toe off his black wing-tips and rest himself, fully clothed, on top of that quilt, and continue reading his book, but just as he'd been unable to let go of his familiar Japanese way of living (when by himself, at least), Masahiro Takeguchi could not let go of that other ingrained personal ritual—bathing fully before taking his final rest of the day.

Not that the shower in his deluxe, albeit semi-private room was a truly fitting substitute for the sunken bath of his childhood, but it *was* still private (for now, at least), and the water was exceptionally hot. Even in the toilet when one flushed that.

But before he began to undo his tie and shake off his suit jacket, something undeniably *western* had invaded the sanctity of his own small rectangle of eastern culture, something which caught his eyes as he started to reach for his robe draped over the desk-chair: A raw sienna-colored sheet of paper, overlaid with the brown YMCA logo, had been impaled on his wooden bathroom door with an incongruously bright kelly green push-pin.

"*No...,*" he whined, not needing to read the message printed on the sheet to realize what it meant. No more fully private bathroom, no more lingering in the shower for as long as necessary to rinse away the grainy miasma of the city from his pores...no more ignoring that hook-locked other door in his bathroom.

"Not another roommate," he continued to fret to himself, as he scooped up his robe with one hand, and continued to loosen the knot in his tie with the other hand. But as he stepped closer to the paper, the tightly-packed words formed thoroughly horizontal sentences and paragraphs:

"Dear Mr. Takeguchi,

As of this afternoon, you will be sharing your bathroom with another guest. This individual is a member of our visiting society, and as such, there are certain additional rules of timesharing etiquette which will need to be followed:

1) In addition to knocking on the other guest's door, prior to using the facilities for an extended period of time, you will also have to be prepared to expect no reply as such from your new 'roommate.' Therefore, prior to using your side of the bathroom (i.e. the connecting door), please knock from your side, wait, then knock again if necessary, then WAIT for the sound of your 'roommate' unlatching your door, then closing the other door. Under NO circumstances are you to speak to your 'roommate,' nor continue to knock beyond a series of two or three knocks. This is a violation of the visiting society's concept of 'close space.'

2) Prior to using any facility in the bathroom (commode, shower stall, sink) please use the cleaner in the green bottle which has been placed there by the maid. Allow cleaner to dry on all surfaces before using item(s). Likewise, again spray the surfaces after use, and prior to vacating the room.

3) You are not to place the latch on the 'roommate's' bathroom door while the 'roommate' is occupying the connecting room; this is another social taboo among

the visiting society. If, however, the 'roommate' does not answer in kind to your knock (i.e. knock back), then it is acceptable to latch the other door, provided you are relatively certain that the 'roommate' is not present.

4) Guests at the Vanderbilt YMCA are discouraged from speaking to 'roommates' from the visiting society, either face to face or otherwise; however, should our new 'roommate' choose to speak to you through the door, it is acceptable to answer, if a reply is requested. This sort of situation is most likely to come under the circumstances of an emergency, in which case it is advised to contact the Manager immediately, since direct aid is also taboo.

5) If the latch is still in place on your bathroom door, and no one has removed it, please feel free to use the group bathroom down the hall, provided that it is not in use by the members of the group-room now occupied by the members of the visiting society.

6) Should you have any questions, please present them to the Manager, NOT to the 'roommate' from the visiting society.

Please co-operate with these additional rules; in this case, the actions of One reflect the actions of our own Society as a whole. Thank you.

Ms. Retsina Passero, Manager"

Rubbing his eyes, as if by doing so he could somehow rub some sense or even a bit of order into the mass of rules and subtly conflicting regulations he was now expected to follow before doing something as simple as urinating in his own toilet ("the commode"—as his oddly named Manager had dubbed it), Masahiro groaned aloud, stopped rubbing his eyes...then closed them tightly when he saw the dark, yellow sheet of paper was still covered with near-endless lines of drivel.

(While his eyelids shielded him from the surrounding room, and the offending rectangle of paper, they also served to trap him in the regulatory darkness of his memories—both personal and racial—as the remembered words returned to echo and reverberate with painful exactness:

("Son, you are *burakumin*...as am I. True, the law now says it makes no difference, but by blood the difference will always be there—"

("'Difference?' I see none—it if cannot be seen, why should it matter? We do not live in a *buraku,* so why must we be called people of a hamlet? Your words, they make no sense—"

("To your mother, they did...to one who does not know that he or she has had unwilling contact with a *burakumin,* it can matter greatly."

("That our people lived in a *buraku?* Is that not a place like any other to live?"

("The *buraku* of our time is not that of our ancestor's time... what others might call a *hamlet* in English, we knew then as a *slum*—"

("So? Being poor and needing to live in a slum should not impart such a difference—"

("It was not the mere living in the *buraku* that was the... problem. It was the *why* behind them living there that made all the difference....")

Turning himself around before opening his eyes, Masahiro pulled out his desk chair, then cleared a space directly in front of him before lifting up the phone—normally kept well out of sight behind some of his paperwork from the Metropolitan Museum of Art—and setting it down in the exact center of the cleared-off space.

The telephone line was scratchy, but he could still hear the cultured veneer of civility cracking audibly as Ms. Passero politely snapped, "Mr. Takeguchi, I'm only following the rules of etiquette followed by *your* new roommate. Yours was the only deluxe suite left with an available bathroom—a semi-private bath, per his request. I'm sorry if that offends your Japanese dignity, but he's paying for his rent the same as you are, so I should hope you'll be inclined to grant him some show of respect. After all, he's a visitor here, just like *you.*"

Following the western custom of counting to ten before speaking, Masahiro said with as much of his "Japanese dignity" as he saw fit to waste on a woman whose parents had named her after a resinated Greek wine rather than a Goddess or whatever it was Europeans named their girl-children after these days, "I am only curious about the inherent contradiction here...my 'roommate' is allowed to latch my door whether or not I am in my room, yet I cannot latch *his*—"

"Save it for the playground, Mr. Takeguchi. I don't make the rules, either ours *or* theirs. Maybe you'll luck out and he'll explain it to you while taking a leak or whatever the hell it is his kind does in there, okay? Just don't blame the messenger for the message—all I did was tell you what his 'people' asked me to write down. If *you* can get him to explain it better, you're free to—"

With infinite slowness and deliberation, he let the receiver descend from his ear to the base of the unit, listening with solemn satisfaction as Ms. Retsina Passero's thickly accented voice grew fainter and tinnier, until that final satisfying *click!* of the receiver hitting home. He hoped that the cut-off sounded as loud to her as it did in his imagination—and that it had been every bit as unexpected.

Masahiro fumbled with the cache of felt-tipped pens in the open lacquer-ware tray on his desk, until he found one with the broadest tip; bracing himself against the bathroom door, he slowly, carefully, inked over the sixth clause on the sienna sheet. The tip of the pen made fingers-on-wet-glass squeeging noises, as he brought the pen over the words again and again, until the edges of the blacked-out section began to bleed into the very grain of the paper.

He only stopped grinding the pigment into the sheet when he

heard something unfamiliar on the other side of the door...the infinitesimal metallic jingle of something small and hard hitting softer wood. Followed by the muted rustle of fabric-rubbing-fabric, and then, seconds later, the hollow retort of wood hitting wood.

Wondering if he'd made enough noise to signify more than a couple of knocks, Masahiro tossed the pen onto his desktop, then scooped up his robe and natural-bristle wooden bath-brush, before opening the bathroom door and stepping inside the white-tiled room.

The faint odor of an unfamiliar spray cleaner hung in the air; tiny glistening drops of it were still visible on the toilet seat and the outer edges of the rim. Apparently his "roommate" had been using the room while Masahiro was speaking to the manager... or wanted Masahiro to think that that was what he'd been doing.

It was beyond difficult to tell, with these aliens. Perhaps if they were to ever look a human in the eye, it might not be so difficult to at least guess what it was they were thinking...at least their eyes did have discernible pupils set in the over-large, oddly coppery irises. Not the solid black eyes of previous alien lore. But still, no one knew what any unusual changes in the size or shape of their pupils might mean, even if anyone could have witnessed those changes personally. That they could speak English upon arrival eliminated any chance to try and study their own tongue for aural clues as to their possible emotional state. To Masahiro, at least, the voices of the aliens sounded like the distorted, subtly garbled bray of a pull-string talking doll, lacking the nuances of syntax and emotion, even as every word remained isolated in its enunciated perfection.

Surrounded by the drumming shower-water, which ran off his soaped body in foaming sheets, Masahiro braced his hands palm-out against the slick tiles before him, and let the water pummel his head and upper back, while he wondered if the alien even needed to take a shower—he'd never seen any of them in the Y's gymnasium or pool areas, nor had he ever come across one of them in the downstairs laundry room, washing his or her spare billowing robes and head-coverings.

He smiled under the streaming water as an image appeared in his mind—the aliens, *sans* their clothing, looking like formless stick figures, devoid of musculature, or even skeletons... simply angular thin bodies, like rolls of clay formed between two swift-rubbing palms. Surmounted by a cupped-palms-balled blob of that same clay, pressed down hard without need of a neck onto the equally thin, formless body.

But his smile became a grim horizontal line across the bottom of his smooth face when another image came unbidden to him... that of the aliens' clothing, moving of its own volition down the streets of Manhattan, supported by nothing but its own forward momentum, even as it continued to billow and flap with short, sharp rasping bursts of sound in the fitful city breeze.

As he reached up to turn off the spray of water, Masahiro realized that *that* was his problem with the aliens. Not so much their alien presence, but the inherent wrongness of their clothing. Much like the thought of a Western woman wearing the clothing of a geisha...nothing overtly wrong, yet nothing about the sight was quite right, either.

Once the water was turned off, he toweled off with unaccustomed speed, not bothering to perform the majority of his personal post-bathing rituals, lest his unseen "roommate" misconstrue the meaning of whatever sound he might make. Drying himself quickly, missing most of his back and upper thighs in the process, Masahiro found himself mouth-breathing, fish-like and desperately silent, as he high-stepped around the tile floor, lest his feet make any unforeseen smacking sounds on the hard surface. Yet, while maintaining *his* silence, Masahiro found himself listening for any sounds from the other side of the unlatched door opposite his own bathroom door, almost hoping he'd hear the sound of something crouching in stiff, harsh-whispering fabric down near the level of the small keyhole...for what good was his own curiosity if it was not matched?

Padding quietly around the room barefoot (a hold-over from the days of his *burakumin* ancestors, the ones who were not allowed to so much as wear clogs, like other *non-burakumin* Japanese...not that such a restriction even existed anymore; he simply felt a need to follow it) Masahiro picked up the bottle of green spray from the top of the toilet tank, and began spritzing the liquid on all the surfaces he'd used, wincing slightly as the spray nozzle made a moist, raspberry-like noise with each pumping motion of the bottle's handle.

The sound reminded him of bad duck calls.

Aiming the bottle at the corners of the shower stall, as he wondered whether or not the places where the water ran off his body might count as a spot which had been "used" by him, Masahiro suddenly stopped spraying when he realized that he'd forgotten to do this before using all the "facilities:"—the sight of the still-moist spray on the shining white surfaces had made him forget about the second clause on that damned sheet of rules the manager had left for him. A feeling of guilt far out of proportion to the nature of his transgression surged over him, almost smothering in its pressing weight, and unconsciously, he hung his head down, as his own father's voice mentally scolded him:

You must try harder, be better...because so little is expected of our kind. They will think you inferior, because you are *bura-kumin.* And, being naturally inferior, such mistakes therefore come naturally to you. Because you lack self-esteem. Because you are apathetic to the ways of the *non-burakumin.*

Because you are not like them—

"Everything-all-right-in-there?-Have-you-had-an-accident?"

The blatty tones of the alien lacked any note of overt concern, or even urgency, just a series of fired-off words with the barest hint of curiosity in the slight upbeat end of each sentence. But a small glow of satisfaction coursed through Masahiro as he first swallowed, then said in a near-casual voice, "No, no, everything's fine...I just forgot to use the spray before I used the bathroom...clause two of that sheet Ms. Passero left in my room. The one your...society gave to her." For a second there, he almost forgot the accepted nomenclature for the aliens. For his part the alien didn't seem to notice the odd lapses in Masahiro's speech patterns; perhaps their kind wasn't attuned to such verbal nuances yet.

"I-will-not-worry-then-But-it-is-no-violation-not-to-spray-No-need-to-be-sorry-for-Bathroom-not-unclean-?"

The questioning note at the end of the alien's short speech gave Masahiro pause; gently resting the spray bottle on the toilet tank lid, he padded closer to the alien's door, and said, 'The bathroom was just fine...it didn't even look as if it had been used,' all the while hoping that he wasn't unwittingly committing yet another *faux pas*, one which might anger the alien enough to compel him to place his own call to their snide manager.

"That-is-a-relief-This-is-the-first-time-I-have-quartered-with-an-Earthly-I-do-not-wish-to-intrude-."

Unable to discern a questioning tone in the alien's voice, Masahiro simply gave a grunt of affirmation before gathering up his things and quitting the room. However, once he'd closed his door, Masahiro had to smile to himself as he re-read the fourth clause...either the rest of his "roommate"'s people had neglected to clue him in about the taboo concerning "direct aid" or his unseen next-door-alien had decided to put concern ahead of cultural circumspection.

Regardless of the reason behind the alien's question, Masahiro still found himself smiling even as he pulled back the quilt his old girlfriend Yuka had left behind, prior to crawling into bed; once he'd plumped his Y-issue pillow into a head-roll behind his neck, and settled down to begin reading Yoshinori's tale again, he couldn't concentrate on the rows of vertically-printed words, but instead found himself twisting the thin brown glued-in ribbon bookmark between his right thumb and forefinger, as he listened to the delicate metallic click of his door latch being secured, followed by...sounds which were, unfortunately, much too soft to be easily discerned.

At least not without him first getting out of bed, and moving quietly to the opposite side of that latched door.

True, *The Dreamy Hippopotamus* could wait, but then again, he supposed that he'd have plenty of nights not to go to bed, but instead sit quietly in his room post-bathing, waiting for the sound of that silvery lock falling into place....

It might even be worth it to listen, should he ask me why I was doing it, he told himself as his eyes wandered aimlessly over the rows of words which hung down like banners on the thin ivory pages....

"—it-is-too-much-to-bear-too-much-to-contemplate—" came his roommate's voice through the filtering maze of sliding screens in his father's house, and the dream-Masahiro tried to rise off his bedding, tried to aurally track the source of that blatty drone, but Yuka's left-behind batik-square quilt was holding him down flat against the futon, and the thin brown ribbon bookmarks of her discarded teen comics were like-wise restraining him, pressing him tight and helpless against the floor-level bed. "—I-did-not-know—Knowing-I-cannot-continue-to-suffer-this-?"

At last, a question, freeing him to respond:

"The list of rules Ms. Passero left, it did not say I had to reveal that I am *burakumin*...I'd thought my using the spray would cover that transgression. So few people in Japan even remember what the *burakumin* are anymore. I did not realize that I needed to tell...the visiting society what I am. It was so long ago that my ancestors performed the unclean tasks...it was their livelihood, to do that which was unclean, to butcher animals, to tan and work their skins, to handle corpses and dig the graves which were to receive them...they were only doing what others refused to do, things which were nonetheless necessary to all.

"For those social transgressions, they paid, over and over... for those violations, they gave up their very worth as people... only worth one seventh of a real person...forced us to look different, so as to somehow distinguish us from whole people who looked just like the rest of us *burakumin*...we who were called *Eta,* for the much filth we were forced to wallow in, live in, die in....

"For that, I am sorry for fouling our common place, for violating your close space...I did not know it was taboo to your people—"

Behind the nearest screen, Masahiro could make out the barest hint of the alien's shadowed visage, just the curve of a rolled-clay head, a subtle slope of upper cheek and jaw, before the silhouette glided out of sight with a murmur and lingering susurration of silky billowing robes. No answer, no retort. Just the receding echo of the alien's passing, always, always away, from him....

The latch on Masahiro's door was unlatched when he awoke; by standing just so, he could make out the unbroken sliver of light along the doorjamb on the latch-side of the door, and by pressing one ear to the ligneous barrier, he satisfied himself that the bathroom and the other deluxe room beyond were both empty.

Aside from an uneasy vulnerability he felt while urinating, his back defenseless against the unlatched door to the alien's room (he was reluctant to get too close to that other door, lest his "roommate" had simply forgotten another of his society's taboos and left Masahiro's door unlatched by mistake), Masahiro's morning bathroom ritual remained virtually unchanged that morning...only when he was about to leave their common bathroom did he again remember, with not a trace of guilt this time, that he'd forgotten to pre-spray all the facilities before using them.

Then again, the alien *had* said there was no need to be sorry....

Although Masahiro Takeguchi had worked in the Metropolitan Museum of Art's Concerts and Lectures Box Office for seven years now, he'd never found the time to visit the Arms and Armor room just a sharply winding corridor away from his workplace. Oh, he'd been through it, just as he'd walked or nearly ran through every room and exhibit in the museum (save for the women's rooms off European Sculpture and Decorative Arts and Islamic Art, on the first and second floors respectively) at one time or another...but he'd never taken the time to stroll with deliberate slowness though the collection of ancient human and animal armor, at least not until after the alien began to share his bathroom back at the Y.

Before yesterday, the concept of armor, of such extensive and protective personal shielding, had seemed inconsequential, even superfluous, to him. Perhaps it was that daydream about the clothes of the aliens moving about by themselves that prompted him to wander through the displays of empty armor, much of it positioned on horse armor worn by artificial steeds. Perhaps it was his own newfound status as a reluctant sharer of subtly violated space that piqued his interest in additional protection from the unknown.

"Perhaps I'm just tired of looking at the Far Eastern Art exhibits on the second floor," he blurted out, to the eyes-rolling surprise of a group of college-age women who stood in a tight knot near the corridor which ran parallel to the Art and Book Shop. Virtually as one, the jeans-and-sweat-top-clad women moved into the corridor proper, out of Masahiro's line of sight.

He had met Yuka in that same corridor where the young women now gathered, their voices a bright muddle of whispers and stifled giggles. She'd been looking for the Sackler Wing and the Temple of Dendur, which lay well beyond the Arms and Armor room, down the very hallway which abutted his work area, then a ways past his office—and even though he knew he'd passed through this room of stilled weapons and engraved body armor, as he looked at it now, Masahiro could not say with any degree of honesty that he'd actually looked at anything in the room, save for Yuka.

Was she still studying art in the City? Or had she made good on her half-threat, half-vow to return to Japan, to her beloved Tokyo? "How old would she be now?" he whispered rhetorically to one of the improbably small hollow suits of armor, knowing full well that since she was four years his junior, she had to be close to thirty by now. But the notion of Yuka actually turning thirty seemed as foreign and as impossible as the thought of real people actually donning the garments of beaten and embellished metal which surrounded him—and then being able to move with any semblance of normality, or practicality.

When he'd known her, Yuka had almost seemed too young to be reading those lurid, boy-meets-girl Kodansya comics, the digest-sized bright covered books she'd tuck so nonchalantly into her backpack already loaded down with Turner art books and sketch pads. Even though he knew that she was almost twenty-four, and working toward her M.F.A.... Yuka, who hadn't even known what a *burakumin* was, and who thought that a *buraku* was someplace you moved when you were just starting out and needed a place with relatively cheap rent.

And she hadn't cared when he did get around to explaining the concept of the *burakumin* to her, although her acceptance of him was tempered by her rather flip remark about his mother: "Was your father so sure it was him being a boo-RAH-koomin" (inexplicably, she always had difficulty pronouncing the word) "which made her leave him? Or was she just using that as an easy excuse?"

He hadn't told her of his dreams, not then. It was only when she was ready to leave him that he mentioned them—and was treated to yet another stinging castigation:

"Get off it, Masahiro...you said yourself that a lot of us back home chose to ignore the taboo, or even flaunt it. Why make your mother's problem our problem? Does anyone here care about it? You're making good money, for an immigrant. Better than a lot of Americans...so why do you insist on living in *this* Y-*buraku*? To keep on punishing yourself for something your father's people did a thousand years ago? That would be like the blacks here insisting on living in slave quarters, or putting prices on their own heads—"

"Yuka, it is not the same...here, the blacks look black, so they can move beyond it...people see them, feel sorry for what was done to them against their will. But for me, for my...it is different. We are...invisible blacks. So the hurt is so much more when the rejection ultimately comes. Or the quiet look of shock in the eyes—"

"Good-bye, Masa...and whether or not you choose to believe it, I don't give a *damn* what your people did a dozen generations ago. It does not matter to *me* at all."

The ringing slam of the door cut off the rest of her words; he had heard her swearing and mumbling to herself as she toted her heavy knapsack of art books and soft-sided nylon suitcase down the carpeted perplexity of hallways and dead ends on his floor, until the sound died out long before she reached one of the two silvery elevators in his wing.

She'd left him about five months or so before the aliens had arrived, in their globular silvery-dun ships, which had hovered like those ubiquitous Mylar balloons sold by seemingly every florist, novelty shop, food vending cart and stationery shop in the City over the entire continent. Within a year of her departure from his room, the aliens were making their first tentative advances into the streets of midtown Manhattan, striding in an undulating phalanx down the Avenue of the Americas, where Masahiro first saw them as he was waiting to cross West 51st Street near the Time and Life building.

And as only native (or pseudo-native) New Yorkers might be expected to behave when confronted with aliens *en masse*, nobody paid much attention to the tallish beings with the scissoring stride; they might as well have been an Arab tour group, or a *clique* of artsy-trendy fashion types, out for a stroll between gallery showings. No one would even write about them for the *Times*' "Metropolitan Diary" feature. Only he had been *gauche* enough to stare openly at them, at their gently swaying tails (this was during the time before the Y began offering those body-language courses), and continue to stand and stare as they spoke among themselves, and their thin upper limbs moved in ways unfamiliar to Masahiro—either in his homeland, or in his adopted land. He'd only stopped staring when a cab driver slowed down and yelled out his window, "How would you like it if they was starin' at you? Dontcha have a TV set or cable? They've *been* here awhile," before continuing down the Avenue of the Americas toward the old RCA building.

That was his first taste of the taboos which surrounded the aliens ("visiting society" came a year or so later)...and now, as he rested his head against his upraised right hand, while listening to the ever-fainter echoes of the chattering college-women he'd in all likelihood scared out of the room, Masahiro dimly wondered what sort of alien (as he persisted in considering them) would deliberately break the taboos set down by his own race. Two breeches of etiquette within roughly half a day...what might be next, the alien barging in on him while he was barely hidden by the clinging drape of the shower curtain?,

Masahiro wished that his commode did not face the alien's door, or that there was some kind of an interior barrier between the toilet and the other door. A privacy screen, at the least.

Or what should he do if the alien spoke to him again, yet did not ask the all-important question which he would then be allowed to answer? Perhaps he could break one rule of etiquette for each one the alien had broken...but he quickly dismissed that notion; he loathed the thought of somehow being answerable to Ms. Passero down at the main lobby registration desk. A public dressing down would be much to her liking...

Only when he knew that he'd stayed away from his desk for far too long a time to use some sort of rest-room-related disaster as an excuse for his prolonged absence did Masahiro reluctantly leave the room of long-discarded breast plates and shields, and return to the vulnerability of his daily routine.

Without quite wanting to think about the *why* of what he was doing, Masahiro near-jauntily swung out his briefcase-carrying arm as he walked down the carpet-lined hallway, allowing his case to thump against the nubby wainscoting with each forward step. In his wake, several doors cautiously opened, heads half-poked out then withdrew to the safety of the rooms behind the now-locked doors. While he'd been a permanent guest of the

Vanderbilt Y for what was probably far too long a time, he'd yet to fully figure out the odd-branching floor plan of each residential wing, including the exact layout of the rooms...especially that of his "roommate." But despite the sound-deadening qualities of the carpeted walls, hard, sharp blows still carried quite well.

Only when he inserted his key in his lock (but had yet to give it the half turn needed to open the door) did the full import of his wall-whacking filter into his consciousness: Please be gone from my room, he mentally begged the alien, Don't let me catch you in there. Remember your "close space" taboo....

At first glance, everything seemed to be untouched, unrifled. No revealing disturbances, no hastily replaced items glaringly out of sync with everything else in the room. Still, as he stepped slowly into his own space, unable to overcome a sensation of a more ethereal disruption, of a violation more mental than physical. Luckily for the aliens, they left off no strange odors, save for the after-scent of too much fabric bunched and folded oddly on their bodies. But something...some *thing* was quite wrong in his room.

Not the alignment of his framed prints hung over the rice-paper. Nor was it the casual tossed aside folds of his turquoise and paisley Windex Pro hooded ski jacket, the one he'd brought from Japan, as it rested in a shining pile of fabric and fake-fur trim against the base of his bed. All of Yuka's cast-aside comics were in place, ribbon bookmarks hanging down like tiny braided tails over the edge of the shelf itself. The TV was still set on the same channel. His drapes hung in the same precise, rounded folds from the curtain rod. None of the fruit he'd set in the deep windowsill behind the drapes had been so much as moved a fraction of an inch.

Yet...the alien had been in here, doing something more than merely looking. Of that Masahiro was certain. Why he was so sure, he still had no clear idea.

Was the air moving too much? Had the alien's feet moved the floor mats a hair's width out of place? Or had it folded his belongings without actually disturbing them, letting its fingers just graze the outermost surfaces of all that pleased or puzzled it?

(*Him*, Masahiro reminded himself, *He* was in here. Looking for...men-things, I wonder?)

Warily, he pulled out his desk chair to a position roughly in the center of the room, sat down, then slowly began to change position on the chair, moving in five degree increments, until he was sitting with the back of the chair wedged between his spread legs, looking, looking, searching for that one missed thing that was nonetheless out of sync with his last memory of the room—

The Dreamy Hippopotamus now wore a forelock of fraying brown ribbon, which cut across the green-ringed thought-bubble protruding from the left temple of the blue ceramic hippo which graced the cover of the novel. Masahiro was certain it had not been there when he placed the book on top of Yuka's batik quilt. No, the bookmark had been curled between pages thirty-eight and thirty-nine, just where he'd left off reading. He never allowed it to show outside the book while he was in the middle of reading something.

A violation of the slightest order, but the encroachment pained him, made him long to rip the sienna sheet of bathroom rules off his door and...shove it rudely, unexpectedly, under the other bathroom door, some equally small but significant show of protected privacy now broken.

Instead, he merely plucked the bright green push-pin from the surrounding wood, letting the message from Ms. Passero flitter to the floor, where he purposely left it. Face side down.

Still obligated to at least follow the surface niceties of room-sharing, he did obediently knock on the door, twice, then jangled the knob before opening the door...which hadn't been latched in the first place. Yet another bending of the other...man's rules. He supposed that the alien felt *he* was entitled to break what was his to begin with—

"I-forgot-to-first-latch-door-but-it-doesn't-matter-now-I-suppose-?"

"No, it doesn't matter," Masahiro found himself replying with a mildness of tone he didn't quite feel: as he unzipped, he did keep one eye aimed on the barely-visible door behind him, added as he reached into his gaping trousers, "As long as you don't mind both doors being open...so to say. Figuratively," he added, uncertain of just how much English subtext the alien actually understood.

"As-long-as-it-does-not-bother-you-?" The rise in the alien's droning voice was unmistakable. Shaking off, Masahiro started then stopped to speak a couple of times, before saying in time with the upward *zurrpt* of his zipper moving back into place under his trouser button, "I suppose it depends on what you mean by 'bother'...there is a matter of 'bother' in the sense of being annoyed, and then there is the matter of 'bothering' one's possessions, one's personal space—"

Without ever having actually heard it before, Masahiro realized that the alien behind the closed door had gasped. Covering the alien's ensuing silence by splashing water around in the green-sheened sink, thrice-rinsing his hands before purposefully turning off the faucets, Masahiro waited for the alien to respond, but he was on the verge of turning the doorknob before he heard:

"Is-it-a-taboo-with-your-people-?-To-bother-that-which-is-merely-owned-?"

"Not actually a 'taboo'-taboo...just a thing which isn't considered polite," he replied with a stiffness both literal and emotional. "A thing to be avoided, like...visiting someone's house, and taking a peek in their bathroom medicine cabinet. Which too many people do do...alas," he added, hoping for a reason he couldn't wholly understand that the alien would be able to detect the irony in his tone.

"Medicine-chest-taboo-?"

"That which is *in* it might be considered that...that's just an example, though. What we...natives own is considered to be an extension of *us*...a part of our 'close space.' Even when we are not around to protect it. What is ours is a reflection of our wants, our needs...our inner selves. Definitely 'close space.'"

"Inner-self-also-taboo-?"

In all the years that the aliens had been roaming around the city, including all the times they'd arranged group tours (albeit through the most convoluted verbal and written means) through his office at the Museum, Masahiro had never encountered such a...verbose member of their race. Isn't he welcome in that group room down the hallway? he found himself wondering, even as he sighed, then patiently replied, while still keeping one hand on the doorknob, "Of course each person's inner self isn't taboo *per se*...just prying into it unannounced is...impolite. Something strangers don't go doing to each other. Even friends have to be...careful in that regard. That goes for just about all the different cultures on the planet, all the peoples...in case you were wondering. I...suppose you realize that I'm not a native of this particular country?"

There. He'd broken one of the alien's taboos, and asked his own question. He paused, hand still encircling the now quite warm metal knob, waiting for a reply, or even the sound of the alien angrily pushing the buttons on the phone to place a call down to the Manager's desk.

"I-realize-now-"

That English-American-Western saying about curiosity and the cat flickered through Masahiro's mind, making him smile... especially when the line about satisfaction bringing the cat back came to him.

"I-also-realize-what-is-your-'inner-self'-what-is-your-taboo-is-being-boo-RAH-koo-min-But-why-is-that-taboo-to-you-?"

Belatedly covering his mouth with his free hand, Masahiro realized that he'd been literally speaking while dreaming last night...and that he should have instead sat by his closed door, making sure that the alien wasn't listening in on him—

"What-*Eta*-?"

Masahiro slowly uncovered his mouth. Obviously, the alien

had only heard fragments of his dream-plea, his self-denunci-ation. Enough to form a vague impression of Masahiro's pain, but not enough to fully comprehend its origins.

Ignoring the earlier, probing question, he instead said softly, "*'Eta'* is Japanese for...'much filth.' A word, like for refuse, or offal. It is...seldom if ever used in my country anymore. At least not in polite company. There is no longer a need, you see," he added too quickly.

"No-more-offal-in-Japan-?" Masahiro almost believed he'd heard a note of incredulity in the alien's flatly enunciated words.

"Oh, of course there is...humans just *do* that," he explained, hoping that the alien hadn't picked up on his unintentional play on the emphasized verb, his unconscious reference to the American slang.

"But-no-one-in-Japan-speak-of-it-?"

Was the alien confused or simply bored enough to keep bothering him? Sighing, he replied, "Not in those exact terms... we're more specific than that. Just...don't ever use that word, the E-word, around people of my race, all right? Consider it an Earth-Japanese taboo."

"Why-offal-taboo-?"

Wondering if the other aliens down the hall didn't want this one around because he was too dense or too obnoxious to be tolerated, Masahiro said, "I didn't say *that*, exactly...I suppose I must explain, or we'll be here all night discussing this. In my country, there are—were—social classes, each different, according to what the people in those classes did for a living, how much they earned. Like the classes in America, for instance. Well, there was a class, in Japan, many centuries ago, which...did things which were essential, but disdained. Unclean things. Things looked-down-upon by those who none-theless needed those things done for them. And...the people who did these things lived in special hamlets—*buraku*—which lent these people—*min*, in my tongue—their name. And...*Eta* was another term for these people, back when such differences mattered."

Why was it that such an explanation almost made the whole situation sound...normal? Understandable? The way it did for Yuka, when he'd used virtually the same words to describe his pain to her?

"Was-ancient-Japan-enclosed-?-Like-generation-ships-of-my-people-?"

Enclosed? For a second, Masahiro couldn't—or wouldn't?—see the connection, then, with a fluttery sense of uneasiness, began shaking his head, until he realized that the alien couldn't see him doing that. "Yes, in a sense. It is an island nation—"

"Then-no-one-else-do-deal-with-offal-and-disdained-things-?"

Such transcendent clarity—

A nod of the head, before he mumbled, "No, no one else."

"Then-no-where-else-to-put-what-which-was-unwanted?"

"No...no other way of dealing with any of it." That barely whispered.

"And-no-other-means-of-eliminating-that-which-was-offensive-?"

"Not unless the animals started butchering themselves prior to being eaten. Not unless the dead could bury themselves—"

"Bury-dead-?-In-ground-?-Only-?"

"Yes, Yes, in Japan, then, people buried their dead," he replied, as the problem the alien seemed to be hinting at became clear to him—of course, on a multi-generational spaceship, dealing with the dead had to be an entirely different matter: No hope of storing the bodies, yet someone had to either burn them or jettison them from the ship. In all likelihood, a "taboo" occupation in the alien society, as well as in ancient Japan—

The alien paused behind his door, as if mentally digesting this information, while Masahiro began to feel the first glimmer of understanding: *That* was why his "roommate" was occupying not a group room, but a deluxe single at the Y—either he, or his people, had been in charge of something like burial detail, or whatever it was the aliens did—had to do, while en-route here—with their dead.

So even the visiting society had their own *burakumin*—

"But-after-ripening-those-who-dig-them-back-up-still-despised-?"

"'Ripening'?" Could he mean decay? As in picking the bones from the earth? Masahiro's mind raced through the more acceptable options, as the alien blatted on:

"Once-ready-for-eating-do-your-people-also-despise-the-one-who-prepares-the-food-as-they-despised-those-who-handled-it-in-death-?"

Swallowing hard, while trying to ignore the yammering of his heart, the hard-pounding of his over-worked aorta, he chose his next words carefully:

"I believe you have a couple of the *burakumin*'s...tasks confused here. Killing for food, and burying their dead were considered unclean jobs, but they were also separate tasks. The taboo did not extend to those who prepared the butchered animals. Only those who had...blood or dirt on their hands were unclean."

"Different-on-generation-ship-those-who-bury-responsible-for-after-burial-Also-responsible-for-preparation-of-dead-after-So-others-absolved-of-dishonor-"

I am not really hearing this...he is confused. Our ways are too confusing for him. Too complex. Living virtually all of his life on a generation ship has made...adjustment to planet life too difficult for him to reconcile with ship life. He is merely confused by our ways.

"Only-a-generation-ship-necessity-to-exhume-dead-not-our-planet-custom-Great-dishonor-Greater-need-For-sanity-of-all-some-assume-ignominy-willingly-Being-despised-better-than-no-one-left-to-do-the-despising-"

(*True, the law now says it makes no difference, but by blood the difference will always be there—*

(*It was the* why *behind...that made all the difference...*)

When did your kind begin this cycle of despised/despiser? Three, five, ten generations into your voyage? Before or after you realized the dead were somehow worth more after their passing? Or was the hunger too great to continue living with dignity, but no resources?

"But you're no longer on the ship," he found himself whispering, so softly he actually heard the stiff rustle of the alien's garments as he moved closer to the other door out of aural necessity. "You...you were only doing what was essential...it went beyond a matter of choice. If you...your kind...didn't...all of you would've died. Surely, there had to be a reconciliation among all of you, afterward—"

(*...it is too much to bear, too much to contemplate...knowing, I cannot bear to suffer this....*)

He was touching my belongings. He, who buried and exhumed the dead for the sake of the living. For the life of the living. Not just dirt, not just blood, on his hands. *Eta,* on his hands....

My father's hands, touching my mother. Her, unknowing. Then, knowing.

"A-taboo-of-my-kind-To-touch-to-acknowledge-Is-to-admit-Is-to-remember-that-which-now-best-not-to-answer-By-not-seeing-Deeds-as-if-never-done-"

My people had to make themselves look different, act differently, live differently, all because we *were* no different from those who looked down on us, those who considered us only a seventh of a human—

(*I don't give a* damn *what your people did a dozen generations ago.*)

Yuka, Yuka, the memory, the memory of it is what *does* matter—

"But if they didn't partake...of themselves, in essence, they wouldn't be here to deny it...how can it be better to *be* despised?" Masahiro's hand grasped the doorknob tight enough to whiten his knuckles and turn his fingertips deep carmine.

"To-be-despised-must-be-here-What-is-not-here-cannot-be-contemplated-No-longer-is-To-be-is-preferable-"

To *be* in the slums? To *be* Eta, all the negative expectations hovering over one like a balloon tied to a person's hand? *Can* that be preferable?

"To-not-be-is-never-perferable-to-my-kind-To-be-despised-*is*-to-be."

The unexpected emphasis in the alien's voice was poignant in its raw simplicity. He...liked being despised, in a twisted sort of way Masahiro could not contemplate without coming too close to the essence of his own inner self. His *burakumin* being....

"No...no...," Masahiro whispered, far too softly this time for the alien to be able to hear him. "Yuka...they weren't your people for you not to give a damn about—"

"Everything-all-right-with-you-?-Are-you-in-there-?"

The doorknob gave way silently, quickly, under Masahiro's clenched fingers. Just as quietly, he shut the door behind him, even as the alien's voice continued to bleat out:

"Not-intend-to-violate-inner-space-Not-intend-breaking-taboo-"

Masahiro glanced around his room, his violated close space, moving his head so quickly he felt and heard something grate and pop in his neck, before reaching for the other doorknob, the silvery metal cool under his throbbing fingertips.

"Are-you-here-?-I-did-not-mean-to-"

(...*so why do you insist on living in* this Y-buraku?)

The carpeted walls muffled some of the sharpness of the door slamming hard against the surrounding jamb, but yet, they could still not quite mask the now almost plaintive drone of the alien's voice:

"Did-not-intend-to-violate-Did-not-understand-Did-not-empathize-"

My room. My belongings. He befouled them. Touched them with hands spoiled by the taint of *Eta*...hands he does not hold close to himself in shame, in humiliation. Hands which reached out to—

Fainter now, the voice echoed, softly in the maze of carpet-walled hallways, much louder, though, in Masahiro's mind:

"Must-explain-Must-rectify-"

Was this how she felt, when she left my father? Did his voice resound in her ears, as she walked away from the both of us? Was she frowning in dismay, or smiling in anticipation of her liberation from the taint of us? Or...was the sorrow a live thing in her, too?

The voice of the alien was a mere whisper now, a lingering yet strangely inorganic susurration almost indistinguishable from the shuffling sound of Masahiro's feet scuffing along the nubby industrial carpeting. Only when he stopped before one of the burnished metal-doored elevators did the sound of the alien's voice become something unique again, albeit still undefined, still a meaningless bleat of pure noise.

But it wasn't until Masahiro looked up from the floor, and into the softly gleaming burnished surfaces of the doors, that he finally saw the face of his mother....

Afterword for "Etamin at East 47th Street"

Back in the fall of 1979, I bought a seat on the bus which had been chartered by the choral group/brass quartet at my college for their series of church concerts in Illinois, Indiana, Ohio, Pennsylvania, New York (both the city and another site in the state), London, Ontario Canada, and finally southern Wisconsin, taking off two weeks of school time in the process, just so I'd have a once-in-a-lifetime chance to see New York City. My family has never been into traveling, at all (due to no one in my mother's family being able to drive—her father was legally blind without glasses, had only a fourth grade education, and had never driven a vehicle of any sort in his entire life, while her mother had been kicked out of high school in the ninth grade, after having spent two years in eighth grade, and since neither one of her parents could drive, she never learned how, either), so the opportunity to get to see NYC, a place I'd dreamed of for many years, was too good to pass up. Plus driving myself anywhere was impossible, since I flunked behind-the-wheel three times in high school (partly because I had no chance to practice between lessons, and also because of vision problems [no depth perception] and learning disabilities) so I willingly paid out over $300 in late 1970s money for one of the three extra seats on the bus.

For me, the absolute best part of the trip was New York City—while most of the other kids disliked the Big Apple (being from very tiny Wisconsin farming towns, many of them considered the city to be too violent, evil and dirty to be appealing), I loved it. I even enjoyed the YMCA where we stayed, the same one featured in this story. All the descriptions gibe with the place as it was in 1979—I have no idea if the place is even there anymore, or if it is, that it looks anything like that inside today. I do remember that a couple of the farm-kid chorus members went into a screaming, shrieking fit when one of them saw a cockroach (their reaction brought people out of their rooms into the surrounding hallway, and when the others found out it was only a roach, their scorn was palatable...and quite justified), plus the choir-teacher's bitchy wife (who had formerly been one of his students years before) gave me the Evil Eye when she and I were down in the basement laundry room, and I struck up a conversation with a thin, earnest, and barely dressed young man from India (he was literally washing all his clothes at once, and only had a pair of swim-trunks and a bathrobe on), since Ms Bitchazoid and her Old Coot hubby had spent most of the bus trip telling everyone what an evil, dangerous and frightening place NYC was, and how none of us were to speak to the locals there. (By way of partial explanation, he was a Texas native, and she was from Pennsylvania, and although they'd actually lived in the city for a few years, neither of them felt it was a Nice Place....) I do remember the fellow from India to be most polite, charming and modest—he was simply grateful to have found a place to live which was cheap, had a pool, and a place to do his clothes. I never knew his name, but he seemed like a nice enough guy. I think of him from time to time, and wonder if he's still living in NYC.

During my college years (all three and a half of them; I amassed enough credits to graduate a semester early, and never looked back—nor did I attend my own graduation ceremony), there were a lot of Japanese students in attendance, victims of Japan's stringent and unforgiving version of the SATs—a bad score meant no college for that person for a year. So many of them opted for a foreign school, including mine. While I was only fairly friendly with one Japanese woman (I still have the brown-paper Origami elephants she made for me), the rest of the students stuck to themselves, not learning much English, and in general creating a little slice of Japan in my town via Japanese language magazines sent from home, manga comics (hardbound ones), short novels in their native tongue, and lots and lots of Japanese clothing. Most of which they'd throw out behind their in-town apartments come the time to go home for vacation...and being a born scavenger, I'd go through what was thrown out, and lug most of it home. Thus I happened upon all the books mentioned in the story, including the intriguingly titled *The Dreamy Hippopotamus*, which I still have shoved in a box in my office closet. I came across articles about the *Burakumin* long after college, and gradually, this story pieced itself together in my mind. I'd also had a weird dream about aliens walking around, in clothes that resembled those worn by the aliens in my story.

I suppose the basic message here is hypocrisy, plain and not-so-simple. I figure if there are aliens, they'll be as petty and hypocritical as we are.

'RILLAS

So-Baba, she say, Started with the cigarettes, it did. Took them away they did. Off the tee vee. Off the pages of the reading things. Out of the hands of the people in the big buildings we throw the rocks at and spray the words on, the big empty buildings.

Started with the cigarettes, she says, nodding her grease-face at me when I was *real* small, sitting on her lap playing with the cracked buttons on the old lilac sweater, and Ma, *she* say, So *what* Baba, so *what*? So they took away the cigarettes. Who can find them anyhow? Can't eat cigarettes, Baba.

So old So-Baba, she say real soft, hard to hear because her teeth cracked when the yellow plastic dish fell off the table, so she talks with half a mouth, Didn't stop with the cigarettes. Didn't stop with the liquor. Didn't stop with the books, or the tee vee or the ray-de-o. Didn't stop with santa claus or the—

And Pa, he say, Baba! and makes the mad eyes at her and she don't speak, but her grease-face nods. And nods at me. I didn't have the *'rilla* things then, so I couldn't hold onto them when Baba say the mad-eyes from Pa things, couldn't rub the *'rilla* things in my fingers and say the *'rilla* words soft in my head.

I do that now. But So-Baba don't *say* anymore, only Du-duh-uh and paws at the grease-face with yellow curved nails in the bed under the pink blanket with no shiny strip along the top. Ma puts the grease on So-Baba's face for her, to keep away the wrinkles, like So-Baba wants. But So-Baba is old anyway. No wrinkles, but no *say* anymore because she's old and her mind kind of *fell,* like her teeth did in the yellow plastic dish, only we can't see the crack. But it broke up there, under her limp hair gathered in the big-holed net, makes her say Du-duh-uh, only I know it means *Didn't,* but the rest of it I don't know. She already *say* about the cigarettes. And the tee vee and the ray-de-o.

The things Ma and Pa wouldn't tell me what they were. Because they were banned. By the men in the big buildings that have the broke windows, and the big words on the sides. The men who took away the things I hear Ma and Pa whisper about when they think me and Bobby are asleep.

The *cross* and the *good book,* things like the tee vee and ray-de-o, the things Bobby and I tried to picture in our minds, only it is like trying to do the *'rilla* sign without *knowing* the *'rilla* sign. So we can't make the pictures of the *cross* and *tee vee,* or the other Don't say! things.

But we have the *'rillas.* Them we've *seen.* And the *'rilla* things we have in our pockets, that make the *'rilla* thoughts and words come easy.

Maybe So-Baba's mind cracked because she kept trying to say about what she couldn't *see* anymore.

If I had had the *'rilla* words and things to rub in my fingers when her mind cracked under the big hairnet, she could say more than Du-duh-uh.

Because *'rillas* have big *power.*

Me and Bobby and Jerrie from down the hallway, we found the *'rillas.* Because the hall wallpaper was coming down in the big curls, like it always does when outside is cold and inside is steamy wet near the heat places and shivery cold away from the heat places. Ma and Pa were in our place, taking care of So-Baba, and with the big door with the locks and bars closed, me and Bobby couldn't hear So-Baba say her Du-duh-uh or hear Ma say So *what?* anymore. Jerrie was making little thin curls out of the big fat curls of paper, ripping them and putting them on her head, to cover the places where her hair was so thin it was gone. Me and Bobby don't need curls, but girls like them.

All our Mas, they wear big squares of cloth, tied under their chins. They don't sit in the halls and make curls of paper for their heads. The hair in So-Baba's net, it comes off when the net comes off, or most of it anyhow. So Ma keeps the face-grease away from the net, so it can stay on.

Me and Bobby, we sat down on the floor of the hall and ripped little curls for Jerrie too, taking turns putting them on her head. Some fell off, but most didn't. Another big curl peeled down while we ripped, and Bobby pointed at the wall behind and say, Look! *Hairy*! And we all looked, and say, So big! Like our Pa but *hair*. Look at the *hair*. And Jerrie brushed off all her flaking yellow-backed curls, and say, I want hair like *that*, and pointed at the picture on the wall, the one the paper had been hiding.

The picture of the *'rilla*, only we had not learned the *'rilla* word then. Or found the *'rilla* things. Or learned the *'rilla* signs.

More heat come through the heat things set in the floor, and the picture curled off the wall, only we did not rip it into curls for Jerrie. We held it out flat on the dirty floor, and Jerrie tried to read the words next to the hairy thing there. Her Ma and Pa, they write the words on their kitchen wall, because they don't *say* to each other anymore. They make mad-eyes and write on the greasy wall with hard words of black, and their *say* hangs in the air like memories. Sometimes they say to Jerrie, sometimes they say on the wall to her, so she can read. Or sometimes she might not eat if she can't read her Ma's say about where to get the food. When So-Baba was young like me and Bobby and Jerrie, she say Pas and Mas like Jerrie's could stop being a Ma and Pa together, and live in different places like they had never been a Ma and Pa in one house. In one bed. But then, she say, that too was banned. Like the cigarettes, and the tee vee. All banned, she say, and nobody protested because they hadn't when it started, with the cigarettes and the taking away of santa claus, so when di-vorce was banned, no one *could* protest. Because, she say, the people *couldn't*. So-Baba she start to say, And when they said there was no G—but me and Bobby, we don't hear the rest of her say because Pa say loud, So what? What is gone is gone, Baba, don't do worrying about it! It won't bring anything back. Bringing back your god won't change things, Baba. And he made the mad-eyes at me and Bobby, and So-Baba sat and nodded her grease-face, and made sad-eyes for the things we couldn't picture in our minds. And me and Bobby could say nothing, not even the *'rilla* words, because we hadn't *seen.*

When the picture from behind the curls of paper was flat, Jerrie bent down near the floor and almost touched her nose on the paper, and finally she start to say the Broo—ooklin Z—z—*oo pr*—oudly announces the a-a-*rrival* of the nuh-*new*est guh-guh-*'rilla* in the monkey hau-*house.* Then she couldn't say anymore because the paper under the picture was eaten at the bottom, tiny crescents bitten away.

We all sat back among the ripped paper curls from Jerrie's head, and watched the *'rilla* paper curl up a little when we took our fingers off the edges. In the middle the *'rilla* stood big, and hairy, and upright, like our Pa in the rooms inside, but *not* like Pa either.

There was a man, like our Pa only with hair and fat on his body, and he stood next to the *'rilla*, only there were bars with space between them in front of the *'rilla* and behind the man. And the *'rilla*, he stood taller and heavier than the man, and had so much hair he needed no clothes. That was the first Sign, of the *'rilla*'s power.

Me and Bobby and Jerrie and our Mas and Pas and So-Baba, we all had almost no hair, and very little fat on the bones. And we shivered *in* our clothes, even when the trees had the curled leaves on them in the courtyard, in the few weeks when the sun shone down almost warm, and in the weeks before the curled leaves turned funny gray and fell in crackling piles that we'd jump in after scooping them into a bigger pile. Even then we needed clothes. Lots of clothes, in layers like So-Baba wore her slip and her nightgown and her old dress and her lilac sweater with the yellowing buttons like horny fingernails and yet she still said she was cold. Even when the wet heat comes through the heat hole in her room.

But all the *'rilla* wore was lots and lots of thick hair, and pads of fatness on the bones.

(So-Baba, she say before her mind cracked like old teeth, before the sickness came, we were *all* fat on the bones. We wore clothes to ac-*cent*-you-ate the fat, because the fat places were considered to be *sexy*—and Ma she say, Shuttup, Baba! For shame, saying the banned words! And to the kids! And later Ma wouldn't let So-Baba have the last of the grease from the pan for her face, just to *show* her. And warn her, too.)

And me and Bobby and Jerrie, we began to say, The *'rilla* was lucky, not to be cold in the outside. Because when we looked at the man, he had clothes on, only not so many as our Pa wore. But clothes anyway. Not thick hair and fat, not the freedom from smelly layers of clothes that itched in the places where the tiny dark things crawled, or stuck together, where the food had spilled on them.

And me and Bobby and Jerrie, we all say The *'rilla* must feel good to have air on his body all over, not just the face and hands.

The *'rilla*'s face was not like ours. It was dark, shiny in places, with the nose pushed big and flat in the middle. But the eyes were like ours, and that was all that mattered. Some people, in our building, they had worse faces to look at, all slipped down and funny colored, or mottled like the skin of the dog me and Bobby and Ma and Pa and So-Baba ate for three nights in a row. Some of the people, they had no *skin* on the bones, which was worse than having no fat on the bones. Some hid. Some didn't. We didn't look anymore either way. Some of the people didn't have eyes to look back at us, so it wasn't *fair* to look if they couldn't do the same back to us.

But the *'rilla* had eyes, nice eyes like ours, and dark like Jerrie's. So we could look at the picture because it might have been able to look back at us. If it hadn't been just a picture. The man in the picture, we couldn't see his eyes. They were bit away, along with half his head and face. What head there was had hair though. Looking at the picture, me and Bobby and Jerrie decided that this was another Sign, one of the *'rilla*'s power, because the *'rilla*'s face and body were not bit away. It was like the small things that squeaked and crawled in the halls, making the layers of paper ripple with their passing couldn't eat away the image of the *'rilla*.

Jerrie she say, Look at the bars. My Pa, he write on the wall that the heat from below us is captured in a big metal drum, because it is so powerful. If it wasn't held in, it would get out and overpower us all. The *'rilla* is held in. See? He must be powerful, or else he'd be out with the man. Bobby he say, And wearing clothes. Then I say, He has thick hair and fat on the bones, they are warm enough. Bet he doesn't itch all the time.

Not itching and smelling bad was a wonderful thought. Maybe the thick hair of the *'rilla* kept away the sting and burn of the rain that makes lines in the glass of the windows, until sometimes the rain ate through the windows and Ma and Pa hurried to throw the plastic table cover over the window, to keep away the cold burn of the rain. Maybe on the *'rilla*, the rain would only carry away the smell and the hard biting things on the skin, leaving soft thick hair that shone in the weak light of the sun. If me or Bobby or Jerrie went out in the rain without our clothes, our skin would blister and peel and make the red sores; and even if we did wear our clothes, *they'd* get holes and ragged places in them, but we'd have to wear them like that unless Ma or Pa could find us some different ones in the rubble and jagged wood near the outskirts of our big housing place. And the new ones might not fit, or might smell worse.

So, the first Sign of *'rilla* power was a strong one, and it became the first of the Signs we wrote on the wall, only *that* came later.

When our Ma and our Pa called me and Bobby inside, and Jerrie hears her Pa and Ma bang on the floor of the hall, but the *'rilla* picture was safe inside the layers of Bobby's clothes, because he had *seen* first.

Come our next time in the hallway, seated next to the heat hole in the floor, Jerrie say, My Pa, he write of the *'rillas*. On the wall by the stove. He write that the zoo was a place of animals, all so powerful they stay behind bars, in cages. He write that *'rillas* were strong, and loud like the rain sirens. But gentle. He write that when he was small like us, a *'rilla* saved a boy like Bobby when he fell into the *'rilla* cage in a zoo. The *'rilla* was big and powerful, but he did not hurt the boy. Many were afraid that the *'rilla* would show his power and overcome the boy, but the *'rillas* left the boy alone. My Pa, he write that on the wall. By the stove.

When Jerrie say that, me and Bobby could think of no say of our own. Then we could not read, but Jerrie could, and if she say it was written on the wall by the big cooking stove that *'rillas* did not hurt small ones such as us, enough though they had big power, we knew that *'rillas* must have the *biggest* power. The power *not* to use power.

(Our Pa, he say, The sun is so dim because some people had a power only it was a bad power because it got *too* powerful and it got away from the men in the big empty buildings who thought they'd caged the power, and when it got away the sun went dark and the sky burned and even the air burned and stung on open skin. Like only the rain does now.)

Thus we figured out the next Sign of the *'rilla*, that its power was a good power, not a dumb power that got away.

We did not rip apart big curls into little ones, and while we all sat and sat, our heads were bare of much hair or paper curls. But we had better than hair. We had the *'rillas,* even if we didn't have the words or things yet

The *'rillas* were *known* to us, and that was all that counted anymore.

Me and Bobby, we made the next *'rilla* find. On the wall of So-Baba's bedspace, where the wallpaper curled like a mossy tongue away from the corner of the wall. By the floor. Up on the bed, So-Baba made her say, Duh-uh-uh, and waved her yellow nails at us but when I saw the picture on the wall under the curl of limp paper, me and Bobby didn't listen to her say, but pulled the wallpaper away carefully, so as not to rip the picture below.

Because we could see the arm of the *'rilla,* all hairy over the fat on the big bones. And there were words, not too bit up. The picture on the paper was big, and when me and Bobby pulled it off the gray plaster of the wall, So-Baba she try to say Uh-uh-uh but even her fingers they didn't move, and me and Bobby smoothed the wallpaper back over the open plaster, so the cold wouldn't come through So-Baba's layers of clothes and chill her fatless bones. The picture we hid in our clothes, and took outside into the hallway before our Ma or Pa could see what we done. Out in the hallway, under the better bulb up on the ceiling, the one with more light than the sun outside, we looked at the *'rilla,* and saw the little cat baby it held in its big arms. We hadn't had a cat around since that orange-furred one we ate last year, at the time when the curled leaves dropped in crackling piles against the curbs. But the *'rilla* wasn't eating the cat, even though it looked to have sweet fat on the bones. It was *holding* the cat, like our Ma held Bobby when he was too little to remember when So-Baba could say plainly.

There were words under the *'rilla* picture, not too bit up, but we had to wait for Jerrie to come out before we knew what the paper write below the *'rilla* and the cat.

Jerrie look and look then say, The words they say that this *'rilla* is named Koko, and the cat is her *pet.* The words not say what *pet* is, but it is held like a baby, see? Like your Ma held Bobby. And the words they say...they say this Koko *'rilla* can *say!*

Me and Bobby both say, No! *'rillas* can say?

Jerrie nodded, her few strands of hair tossing back and forth under the yellow shine of the bulb above. Putting her finger under the words, Jerrie say, Here, it say that Koko uses *sign language.* She say with her *hands.* Say *signs* that mean words.

And it was that afternoon that we learned of the *'rilla's* next Sign, that the *'rilla*-animal could *say.* Like So-Baba, like Ma and Pa and us too. Only with its big hands. The dogs and cats and mottled things that barely walked that Ma had to cook until the fat on the bones didn't need chewing couldn't *say*. Either with their mouths or hands or paws.

And with that picture we learned the next Sign, could *see* it for ourselves. The *'rillas* like cats, kept them as *pets*. Which was something like the way Ma held Bobby long ago. Like he might break inside, and she didn't *want* him to.

(Jerrie say too, The words are part gone, but this Koko she lost another pet, and was sad. Then there was this pet and she was something that has been bit away. We couldn't tell from the *'rilla* Koko's face what that something was. Koko looked the same as the *'rilla* who stood behind the bars with the man. *'rillas* didn't smile, but that was all right. We had all seen many people who had no smile, some who had no lips. But Koko *'rilla*'s eyes were kind.)

It was then that we got the idea of keeping the *'rilla* things, only we didn't have the things. Yet. But Jerrie, she say, Maybe, if we held onto a cat, *we'd* be powerful too. And hairy.

Bobby, he say, Our Pa, he kept the skin from our last cat. All of a piece after taking it from the fat and bones. We could hold that. And rub it. For power.

For hair, Jerrie say, then patted her bare scalp where the hair was falling out in strands that clung to her first layer of clothes. Me and Bobby say, For *lots* of hair, and we all giggled. Then Jerrie, she say, Besides the hair, we should rub the fur for *good* power. Like the *'rillas* have. Maybe the hair goes *with* the power.

That made sense, since the hair and the power and the liking of cats was all a *part* of the whole *'rilla*. Like skin and fat and bones were all a part of something living, and something was wrong if something was missing. Then that person had to hide away, inside their home and only reach out for food brought to them. And *'rillas* didn't need to hide, so they were *complete*. So the hair and power and cats all went *together*. Plus saying the signs with the hands.

Our Pa, he didn't notice when me and Bobby cut the bits of

fur and stiff white flesh off the edges of the cat skin, since Pa was looking out the window with only bits of glass in the frame, and our Ma was cooking what she'd found that morning out near the rubble pile.

When me and Bobby and Jerrie each had a piece of cat skin, we found places to hide the bits of orange-striped fur, places where we could reach in and feel the silky smoothness of dense hair under our fingertips, and think about Koko and *her* cat while we rubbed the fur under our fingertips. Only the cat Koko stroked was warm and alive. But the bits of fur and skin were a *Sign* of the cat, the best we could do.

And the *'rillas,* being full of good power under the fat on the bones and the thick hair on the skin, *they'd* understand our sign. Jerrie say that the words on the paper say so. Since that was how they said themselves. In *signs.*

Soon the cat fur sign was joined by the food signs, not *real* food, but the plastic pretend fruit that Jerrie's Ma showed her. Jerrie's Ma, she showed Jerrie the odd pieces of brightly colored, waxy to feel fruit, and she write on the wall, This is what fruit used to look like. Before the power got away from the men in the big buildings. Before it turned warty and the skin slid around over the meat inside. This fruit was to look at always. But not to eat. You kids play with it now. I cannot look at it anymore. There is no more fruit like it to *eat*, and I cannot eat wax. Jerrie she say, My Ma cried a little after she write the last part. But my *Pa*, he write on the wall by the big stove, Those *'rillas* you say about Jerrie, *they* eat fruit. No cat no dog no slow walking things. Only fruit. This wax fruit if they want to. Jerrie she say then, My Ma cry and cry and Pa laughed, only he made no sound, but his mouth was open and his finger pointed at Ma and it was like laughing anyway.

Me and Bobby and Jerrie, we each took a piece of the fruit, which felt like candles on the outside only there was no wick for the flame to eat up. Me I took an *apple,* Bobby he took a round orange thing, and Jerrie she took the long string of little green balls with the uncurled waxy leaf on one end. We each say about the 'rillas eating fruit, no meat, and each of us then say all at once 'rillas don't eat the cooked fat from the bones, yet they have hair and good power. And keep cats. And we thought something more, something we only say later to each other, that maybe eating the soft cooked fat from the bones wasn't a 'rilla thing to do. Maybe eating the cooked fat made us hairless and weak. Not like the way 'rillas were.

At first, our Ma and Pa, they don't notice how me and Bobby just play with the food on our plates, and put it on So-Baba's plate when our Ma and Pa have their heads turned away. We take double of the steamed weeds from over by the rubble piles, so our bellies don't rumble. All So-Baba she say, Uuuhh....and make the slurping sounds when she sucks up the gray cooked fat off the white bones.

But one meal, Bobby he say, I don't want the cooked fat before he realized that we wasn't just with me and Jerrie, and our Pa he say, This food isn't good enough? You better eat it unless you can find something better. Now *eat*, but Bobby he pushed the plate away and say, 'rillas they only eat fruits so I can't eat the cooked fat or gnaw the bones.

Pa he say, 'rillas? So-Baba, you say about gorillas to the boys? *Shame,* So-Baba! And So-Baba she drool and say, Uuuuhhhhhh...and Ma she say, Baba can't *say,* about gorillas or anything. Who say about gorillas to you boys? Jerrie? Her Ma or Pa? They write about gorillas to you?

Me and Bobby we rubbed our cat fur under our fingertips where Ma and Pa couldn't see, and each of us say, We heard no say about 'rillas. Just a silly say, that's all, but Pa he didn't believe me or Bobby, and say, Just tell me who say about them. You two shouldn't listen to stranger's say, out in the streets. A stranger say about gorillas to you? Me and Bobby say, No, and look down at our empty plates.

Ma, she say, Oh forget about it...the boys had to hear say sometime of this. Any day the gorillas might come here, to this dwelling building. Next door, the woman say her sister say the gorillas have been in the outskirts of the city. Looting, shooting, taking the cooked fat from the kitchens. And worse. Better they hear say of it before it happens here. Better to know so that they can hide in time.

And while our Ma and Pa and So-Baba sucked fat from dead bones, me and Bobby chewed on tough weeds, tasting the bitter tang of the cooking water, and thinking of the richly colored wax fruit hidden in our clothes, the round orange thing and the apple so red and smooth.

Jerrie she say, My Ma and Pa, they write to me to beware of the 'rillas, only they write it funny, g-u-e-r-r-i-1-l-a, but maybe they have eaten so much of the cooked fat they can't spell anymore. Ma's been losing more hair. Her cloth fits closer to her head. But Pa, he write, The guerrillas are dangerous. They kill and maim, and steal cooked fat from stove tops. Me and Bobby, we say, Our Ma and Pa say the same thing. But they never say about the thick hair or good power. Or the cats or fruit But the paper, it *say* and it *show* different.

Me and Bobby took out the pictures, and all three of us bent bare heads over them, looking at the kind eyes and cradling arms of the 'rillas, and we didn't see our Ma as she came out of the big doorway and watched us for I don't know how long before she say, What are you kids looking at?

All of us say Nothing, but she didn't believe us and bent over and snatched up the 'rilla pictures. She looked and looked, and then laughed until the sound turned sour in our ears, and she tore up the 'rilla pictures and say, Stupid kids...stupid 'rillas. No wonder you two wouldn't eat your supper. Get your minds off these animals, the last of them has been dead for years. Dead and rotted down to bones and dust. Worry instead about the guerrillas, listen to what people say. Because someday, the guerrillas will come and get you, every last stupid one of you! And the only way to fight them is with your hands and brains. Not with stupid pictures of gorillas. Throwing the shreds of paper to the dirty floor, our Ma went back into the dwelling and slammed the door shut behind her with a sound we could all feel in our bones.

Without a single say, we scooped up the bits of *'rilla* paper, each of us putting a few pieces of it next to our fruit and bits of cat The hallway wasn't safe, we couldn't say in private. And only Jerrie could write then, so we couldn't write on the walls. But we had hands, and the *'rilla* things wound around us, safe in our clothing. And the shreds of paper, they say that *'rillas* say with signs, so me and Bobby and Jerrie, we worked out the signs (not the Signs, which were something different, those we would say to ourselves, in bed before we slept) between us, and soon we could say with no sound, yet by seeing we understood the say and could say in return.

And as we did the hand says, we hoped that the *'rillas* might be able to understand too. Because when Ma say that the *'rillas* were nothing more than bones (which may have been true, when Jerrie say to her Ma and Pa, What were zoos? they write back, The place where the animals used to be kept, before most of them died or were eaten) we each say to each other, Bones are powerful too. They last after the fat is cooked and eaten and the skin and hair shrivel into a small hide.

So even if the *'rillas* were dead, all of them, we still had seen them, so we could think about them in bed at night. Not like the things So-Baba say of, the tee vee and the ray-de-o and santa claus. The things that had been let to die without bones left over. The things that had been *banned*, like our Ma say.

Our Ma, she say, The *'rillas* or gorillas or guerrillas have been *banned*. Like the *cross* and *good book* she and Pa whisper about because they remember them but can't say out loud anymore. Because they're *banned*.

The *'rillas* might have been dead, but not being banned, they couldn't be *bad*, like the banned things were say to be by Ma and Pa, but not So-Baba.

Me and Bobby, we got to thinking about that part of it, how So-Baba used to say of things banned and bad, and Bobby he say Maybe So-Baba would understand about the *'rillas*. Maybe they could help her. Like they've helped me and you and Jerrie.

(Bobby, he say about the first of the good powerful things the *'rillas* did for us. A few weeks after we all stopped chewing the cooked fat, a soft fuzz of hair appeared on our heads, not long or thick like *'rillas* but *something* where *nothing* had been. Which made the *'rillas* all the more real in our minds and hearts. We loved the *'rillas*, for helping us that way, through their Signs.)

Me, I say, So-Baba she liked to say about the old things, and *'rillas* are very old, bones I think. She'll like the *'rillas*.

In the darkness of the room we shared, me and Bobby got out our *'rilla* things, the bits of paper, the fruit, the scraps of orange fur and skin, and hugged each *'rilla* thing to us, like Koko *'rilla* had done with her live cat, before taking them into So-Baba's room off the kitchen. In the near dark, with only a sliver of faded moonlight to illuminate the service, we softly say the *'rilla* Signs over So-Baba, and made the *'rilla* signs with our hands.

First we say, The *'rilla* has hair so thick the rains do not sting, and fat on the bones so thick the clothing doesn't come in layers.

Second we say, That which crawls in the walls and squeaks cannot eat the image of the *'rilla*. It remains so that we can see the *'rilla*.

Third we say, The *'rilla* has the biggest power, the power not to use power, in his hands and in his body.

Fourth we say, The *'rilla* say with signs of his hands, and the *'rilla* holds his own without hurting or crushing it. *'rillas* like cats too.

Fifth we say, The *'rillas* don't eat cooked fat off of bones, but eat fruit, and their hair doesn't fall out and their skin is fat over the bones.

And while we both say, me and Bobby make the *'rilla* signs, which were secret, and both of us kneeled down by So-Baba's bed, the *'rilla* things on the worn carpet between us, and then the bulb came on above us and our Ma she say, Crazy kids! Doing banned things in front of the open window! *Shame*, Baba, giving them bad ideas! while So-Baba grunted and say,

Uuuuuuhhhhhh through the thick yellow drool in her tooth-less mouth. Ma she took the *'rilla* things away and threw them down the trash chute in the kitchen near the stove, and she say soft but real mad, You do things like that and they can come up and take you away! To the place where the banned go! They watch below, where they say what is and what is not right. They hear and they see, and they take away those who say bad. Baba, she say bad things, and she got the broken mind. If they come and get you for say the bad thing, they do worse than Baba's broken mind!

But after Ma put us back to bed, after So-Baba tried to say something that had that G-sound So-Baba had tried to say a long time ago, me and Bobby found out that the *'rilla* words were still with us, and we missed the *'rilla* things but didn't need them, either. Not like we thought they would be missed.

Nobody could take away our *'rilla* pictures, or *'rilla* feeling inside.

Soon after So-Baba heard the *'rilla* words that night, Jerrie say to me and Bobby, My Ma and Pa they write to me Danger coming. The guerrillas are in the outskirts of the dry. They all say so. You can't go out, into the hall when they come near. We have to hide. Everyone hide, and hide the cooked fat and dead bones. When Jerrie finished her say, she pulled out some of her round green pieces of fruit, plus a new one we had not seen before. Long and yellow it was, with a gentle curve. Smiling under her fuzz of darkish hair, Jerrie say, My Pa, he write that *gorillas* like this fruit best of all fruits. More than cats. He write that the bad guerrillas like them too.

Me and Bobby, we say to her that the *'rilla* things aren't needed anymore, but Jerrie she say back, But if they come for us, they'll see right off that we *believe* in them. She then say, Maybe our Pa and Ma have it *wrong*. Because they eat the cooked flesh and have no hair. Maybe the *'rillas* had so much good power the rain didn't kill them, or they didn't let people eat them. Maybe the *'rillas* made their signs at each other and nobody else understood their say so no one knew where they went to. Maybe their cages got ruined like the buildings people write on.

Me and Bobby thought about it, and decided it might be a true thing. If the 'rillas could say, they had to think too. Otherwise there was no point in saying *anything* in the first place.

And maybe the 'rillas never ate the cooked flesh, and never lost their thick hair and fat on the bones. *Then* they could live in the rain without layers of clothes, moving free and clean-smelling in the outdoors, not having to pick through bad rubble for clothes that smelled and itched.

We had to say so much we ran out of signs, and used words when we had to, until our Ma opened the door and loudly say, Be quiet! And stop saying about you-know-what, it might be a banned thing. And the slam of the door shook all our fatless bones.

Soon everyone on our floor say, Guerrillas coming! and after a few days, people shorten their say, to g'rillas coming! and one morning all they had to say was 'rillas! and no one would venture forth from behind locked and barred doors, and the candles were brought out against the coming of the dread 'rillas! that people say of with such rolling of what eyes they had and such shuddering of the bones. It was say that 'rillas liked to break light bulbs for sport, if they were lit.

Finally came the day when people say the 'rillas were coming, and our Ma scooped up me and Bobby and made us go in the house and all we could do was make a 'rilla sign at Jerrie as *her* Ma saylessly pushed her into her house, and Jerrie made the sign in return, a smile playing on her lips under the faint coating of hair on her scalp. She knew what took me and Bobby a while to know—the 'rillas were coming, but they didn't want cooked fat or to shatter light bulbs. Just the day before Jerrie say, I dreamed about the 'rillas. They were big, and had a smell like sweat and cat fur, but not too bad a stink. And small things crawled in their thick hair, and when those small dark things were eaten, they popped between their teeth like crisp bits of fried fat. And they would pluck small crawling things from each other's fur, as a sign of companionship. And in their arms they carried cats. All colors, all sizes. Their *pets*. And they didn't eat the fat on the bone of their pets. And they understood the signs we say with our hands, and knew of many more besides our few hands says. And with his hands the biggest he say to me, Come, be free under the sun, and safe from the sting of the rains under your coat of hair and thick fat on the bones. And then I climbed up on his shoulders and went away with him. To a place where the weeds were raw and the soft white wiggling things that crawled without legs tasted juicy in my mouth.

Me and Bobby had almost gagged over that last part, but it didn't sound too much worse than the gray shreds of cooked fat clinging to the dead bones. And Jerrie had say, They understood the sign of our hands.

It *had* to be true. The *'rillas* were coming for the ones who *believed* in them, and understood the signs and the Signs. *If* they could get to me and Bobby and Jerrie.

Because all the grown-ups, they say, Hide, hide from the *'rillas*! If they find you, you'll die!

And so there we all were, me and Bobby and Ma and Pa and So-Baba, who say, Uh-uh-uhhhhh....from her place under the bed, and we were all wedged tight in the dark, with only the candle and matches nearby, and down in the courtyard we could hear the sound of the coming of the *'rillas* through the rain-ruined window, and the say of those who hadn't hidden, No, no, go away! and garbled screaming says that rose high and thin all the way up to our window. And in a low, shaking say, our Ma began, My Ma, she say to me that the *'rillas* were filthy, with guns at their sides and hate in their eyes, and they roamed in search of places to give pain and steal cooked fat and other things which are banned from us now, and while Ma say, So-Baba nodded her grease-face in the close darkness and I could feel the bob of that hair-netted head near my shoulder, and in my head I began to say the *'rilla* words, and soon my mouth began to say them too, and then Bobby began to say and this time Ma didn't say to shut up, not to say the banned words because she was sorely afraid and Pa kept saying, We're all dead meat, oh *God* we're all dead meat, but it wasn't like he *believed* anymore, so it didn't sound like a banned thing he say, but just a *thing*, a plain old word. But our *'rilla* words were better says, *because* we knew that the *'rillas* were real.

Because we'd seen the pictures that were not bitten away.

Because we'd given up on the cooked fat, and our hair grew again.

Because the *'rillas* had kind eyes, and could speak in hand says.

Because they had been real, and could be real again.

If we believed in them, and kept hold of the pictures in our minds, and made the signs when they came, we'd be able to join them. Like in Jerrie's dream.

The sounds of the *'rillas* was a terrible thing outside our door, as they went down the long hallway. At first I thought I heard says from the *'rillas*, guttural sounds of says in a tongue I didn't know, but I *knew* that true *'rillas* only did says with their *hands*, making the *'rilla* sign by which me and Bobby and Jerrie could understand them, and make say in return.

And as I thought that to myself, and mouthed the *'rilla* words, my Ma and Pa and So-Baba wailed and made horrible-sounding says deep in their throats, and shook under their layers of stinking clothing, not stopping when me and Bobby tried to lead them in a say of the *'rilla* words and did the *'rilla* signs before them in the thick semi-darkness.

And the footsteps of the *'rillas* made a deep booming sound that traveled through the floor and into the marrow of our live bones, and as me and Bobby did our say of the *'rilla* words out loud, plain so the *'rillas* could hear, something happened out there in the dank hallway which spilled a thin scattering of light into our dwelling through the space at the bottom of the door.

Something wondrous, but not unexpected to me and Bobby. And Jerrie, over in her Ma and Pa's home down the hallway.

The heavy thud of the *'rilla*'s clumping footsteps grew soft, hair-padded, and while heavy, the footsteps were slower, less resonant in our bones. And the lights did not shatter in the hallway.

Somewhere down the hallway, a door clicked open, the hinges making a scree of noise. The footsteps stopped, then began again, coming close to *our* door, and Ma and Pa and So-Baba began to really say in voices of terror and fear, and behind me and Bobby they clustered together, and the last clear thing I heard was Pa, and he say, Better to go now than let them kill us, and soon the says of Ma and So-Baba were nothing more than bubbling gurgles like cooked fat bubbling in the foul water on the big stove, then Ma and So-Baba were silent and did say no more.

The light along the bottom of the door was broken by chunks of blackness, and me and Bobby got out from under the bed just as Pa's big hands closed on our collars and pulled hard, and with a rending of rotted cloth me and Bobby broke free and crawled under the bed, and from under the stinking sweat-sour place we could hear Pa gurgle as he did something terrible to himself, and he too was to say no more, but we could barely hear his last burble because the locks opened noisily as the door broke inward from the middle, the door splitting from the top to the bottom down the middle, letting in the hallway light in a blaze that hurt me and Bobby's eyes. But we could smell the *'rilla* smell, and felt the big strong hands upon our arms and legs as they lifted us high up into thickly furred, fat boned arms and onto broad shoulders, where the crackling crawling things hide under the thickness of the hair.

And me and Bobby and Jerrie rode out of that hallway, littered with guns and holsters and bullets that came from we knew not where, riding high and safe on the shoulders of the *'rillas*, where we rode unblemished through the stinging rains out of doors, and made the *'rilla* signs to each other as we rode, popping the hard brown chewy things with our teeth.

And me and Bobby like the way the little crawling brown things sound when we crunch them, but Jerrie she say she likes the soft thick crawling white things much better than the cooked fat from bones even.

And the *'rillas* smile and make the sign of that which is good before each of us. And the cats in their arms purr loud in the sunlight.

In memory of Dian Fossey...and all the 'rillas.

Afterword for "*'rillas*"

When this novelette first appeared in print, it included a short forward I'll repeat here...and then expand upon: "Some of the more obvious influences (in this novelette) include the life, work, and murder of Dian Fossey, the murder of her gorilla friend Digit, Koko the signing gorilla and her cats (especially All-Ball, who died in kitten-hood), the increasingly restrictive nature of our society and culture, growing up poor, and listening to stories about members of my family (and family friends) whom I never had a chance to meet while I was growing up; some of these people had unusual quirks which eventually found their way into the novelette. As for the less-obvious influences, all I can say is this "*'rillas*" best captures the way my childhood felt while I was growing up, more so than anything I have written before or after, regardless of the fact that this piece is anything but autobiographical." I wrote that back in 1990-91 or so; since then, I've become less reticent about sharing the details of my childhood, especially after a therapist I once saw for a few months (due to major depression and a whole lot of other problems in my life at the time) told me that what I'd told her about my childhood made her sick, and then added that I would have been better off being raised in a foster home, an orphanage, or (and she literally said this part) by wolves, rather than the way I was brought up. Poverty played a big part in my upbringing, plus my parents' need to stay under the radar because of the fact that following a bitter visitation war between my father and my mother and her mother (which entailed them not letting him spend enough time with me during his court-ordered visitation time), my father finally had enough of their antics, and asked the judge in the divorce proceedings to rule on the matter—and after a social worker interviewed my mother (during said interview, she mouthed off to the woman, something she rather proudly admitted to doing), it was decided that my father would have sole custody of me. The court was obligated to notify my mother in writing that she was about to lose physical custody of me, and during the two-week window between her notification and my father coming to claim me, the two of them hurriedly moved to California, thanks to my not-so-*grand*mother working for a major airline in Chicago, and being able to apply for a fast transfer to their Los Angeles site. And when my father arrived at their former apartment house to legally claim me, they were gone, and no one knew or would say where they went. All of this happened when I was three and one-half years old. During our time in California, I was the weird only child from a divorced home who never saw my father, plus I was forbidden to mention anything in public about him, which in turn made the school curious about why there was no visitation involved, etc.

Even before they moved to Inglewood (then Hawthorne, later on), they were poor—my family (on my mother's side; as far as I've always been concerned, my family tree was whacked in half early on) came here from what is now the Czech Republic with virtually no money or prospects/skills/ability to acclimate to life in the United States, and proceeded to stay poor. Almost no one on my maternal grandmother's side could drive, and most of the elder relatives spoke no English. They lived in a Czech enclave, and associated only with their "kind." As it was, my maternal grandmother's mother and older siblings almost didn't get to stay here once they docked at Ellis Island—two of her older brothers failed the march-up-the-stairs rickets test, and were going to be shipped back to Bohemia on the next ship out, only there was another woman from my great-grandmother's village (a much richer person) who heard the commotion which began when my great-grandmother learned the news that two of her kids would be forced to return to Europe and began screaming in horror, and bribed one of the Ellis Island officials to let the two boys stay here. So my great-grandmother was able to rejoin her husband, who'd immigrated here a few years earlier, in Chicago...where they both died quite young from cancer, but not before five of their ten children also died in childhood/infancy. Neither of them spoke English, and my great-grandfather never could drive.

My grandparents (on the side of my family tree which still remained after my mother's divorce) were the duds from both their respective families—my grandfather was born with cataracts in both eyes, and was blind until early childhood, when someone in the neighborhood donated the money for his eye operation, and only attended school though the fourth grade. He worked for Wilson Meat Packing, as the person who put the casings (aka animal guts) into a barrel of brine, prior to them being used for sausage casings. Given his inability to drive, and his lack of education, it was a decent job, but despite the fact that he came up with two different money-saving innovations for the company (he concocted his own recipe for the brine in the casing barrel, which kept his casings whiter and better-preserved than his fellow workers' casings, plus he came up with a technique to pack far more casings per barrel, which he was later instructed to teach to his fellow workers), he supposedly never got any raises (which I think was a lie on his part), and ended up spending most of what he did bring home in the neighborhood bars. He was a drunk. And he whored around. And he beat my grandmother, and seriously neglected my mother. And as for my grandmother—for some reason, her own parents literally couldn't stand her, and when her mother was dying and going off to the hospital for the last time, she hugged all her kids but my grandmother—all she'd do with her was shake her hand. I don't know why, but my grandmother just didn't look anything like her siblings—I've seen photos of the family, and it was like looking at one of those "Can You Spot the Differences?"

pictures you sometimes see in Sunday magazine supplements. She looked nothing like her parents or her siblings. And she didn't act like them, either. Out of all the kids in her family, she had to repeat the eighth grade twice, so she was almost sixteen by the time she made it to high school...and was then kicked out because she couldn't keep up with the other students. She was a physically ugly person, but thought she was some sort of goddess—if she saw anything bipedal with Y chromosomes, she just *had* to flirt with him. Regardless of whether or not he was single, married, or had his significant other standing right next to him while my grandmother made a blatantly sexual pass at him. Somehow, she managed to get engaged to some dude named George, who later became the luckiest guy in Chicago when his parents, after meeting her once, demanded that he break off the engagement, now, and get his ring back pronto... but not pronto enough for (Lucky) George, for after he broke the news to my grandmother, she and one of her sisters took a hacksaw to the ring, and sawed it *almost* all the way through under the stone, so whoever might put it on next would wind up wearing a broken ring. After that, no one wanted anything to do with her, until her family hooked her up with my grandfather... who was the underachiever of *his* family. They were both rather old by the standards of their day when they married (mid-to-late twenties), and my mother didn't come along until her mother was twenty-seven (ancient, by late 1930s standards).

Their parenting skills were practically nil, and by the time I came along...well, living with two divorced, bitter women, with no male influence whatsoever, was emotionally difficult, especially when all my classmates had fathers, boyfriends or other male figures in their lives.

But it was the being poor part that really helped to set me apart...if I wasn't wearing clothes that were designed for older kids (thanks to having very premature puberty, from age seven and a half through nine years—at which time I looked like an adult among fourth-graders), I wore these god-awful sack-like things my mother made for me, which, after I outgrew them, she turned into pillow-cases by just stitching up the arm and neck holes. I wore size nine shoes from age eight or so, *adult* size nine, and in general, was a complete outcast. I looked weird, I acted even weirder (I was tested for neurological conditions more than once in elementary school, tests which I much later learned were for autism), and I dressed like a freaking garage sale had exploded and rained down mismatched clothes on me. And on top of all that, my mother was unable to get any sort of aid for us (or for me), since her decision to take me away from Chicago in defiance of the court's termination of her custody rights made my legal status somewhat nebulous.

But my family was good at scavenging—we lived in an apartment house, and the big old Dumpster out back was like a magnet for them. I played with a lot of toys other kids threw out (my only real Barbie doll was something with a chewed off nose and chewed up fingers, and hair that had been torn out by the roots; I did have new toys, but they were all knock-offs...dime store stuff...nothing I could take to Show and Tell, though), wore stuff that was thrown out (including those home-made dresses, which were sometimes sewn from fabric that had been tossed out by a tenant who sewed a lot), and even ate stuff that other people threw away. But the thing which sticks in my mind the most was this brown vase my mother and grandmother wanted, which was way in the middle of the huge Dumpster, too far for them to reach with their hands or hooks fashioned from hangers. So they hoisted me up into the Dumpster, and stood on the sidelines as I made my way across cardboard boxes, bags of who knows what, some broken glass (they did tell me to watch out for it as I unsteadily crawled through that minefield of trash toward that god-damn vase they wanted) and stuff I really don't want to think about, until I had that vase. It was pretty...it was about a foot high, with a round bulbous bottom, and there were flowers in cream and white on it, in some sort of raised thin applied material, either clay or thickened paint. And then, when we were about to move to Wisconsin in 1969, they left the damn thing in our soon to be vacant apartment. After I crawled through trash and broken glass to snag it for them!!!

That is what it felt like to be poor, for me at least. Getting lifted up into a Dumpster when I was about seven or eight years old, being told to stay clear of the broken glass before me, while I picked up this freaking vase that eventually was left behind when we moved out of the state.

I was their Dumpster-monkey. A means to an insignificant end.

Maybe that therapist was right. I don't think wolves make their young crawl through broken glass.

The ending of this novelette is deliberately ambiguous (did the children die, or did the marauders magically turn into real apes?), but personally, for me, the ending is quite specific—the children are dead, and they are in an afterlife consistent with their newly-created religion. I'm an atheist myself, so I have no expectations for an afterlife, but...if I could somehow choose where my spirit (if I even have one) goes once I croak, it would be to a place I've dreamed about many times. There's an endless green field, bisected by a thick brick wall about four feet high and one foot deep. On one side is me, and on the other are all my cats, the ones who have died. Sometimes one of them will jump up along the thick wall, and I can pet him or her, but not take them into my arms to hold them. They jump down to the other side before I can grab them. They're happy, over on the other side of that big brown brick wall. I want to be with them, but cannot climb over the wall. That's how the dreams end. I'm on the empty side, and they're all together.

But come to think of it, some gorillas on the cat side would be cool, too. I like gorillas (and elephants, too); they're what we should have kept on being before mankind developed into something capable of destroying ourselves. An afterlife spent with them and all my cats would be something to look forward to, if I was a believer. Which I'm not. Still, it *is* something pleasant to think about....

ABOUT THE AUTHORS

A. R. MORLAN WAS born in Chicago, IL on January 3, 1958, and moved with her family to the Los Angeles area in 1961, where she lived until 1969, when her family moved to Wisconsin, where she still lives.

Morlan has a BS degree in English (Liberal Arts), *Magna Cum Laude* from the now defunct Mount Senario College in Ladysmith, Wisconsin, which folded shortly before a F3 tornado tore apart her town of residence in 2002. She has been a free-lance writer since 1983, and has had fiction and non-fiction published in over 130 different magazines, anthologies, collections, and e-zines in the US, Canada and parts of Europe, in addition to two novels, *The Amulet* and *Dark Journey* (both available from Borgo Press), a story collection (*Ewerton Death Trip*, Borgo Press), a Romanian-language collection called *Femia Coperta* (*Cover Woman*) which came out in 2004, a couple of upcoming collections from Borgo Press, a co-edited (with Martin H. Greenberg) anthology called *Zodiac Fantastic* (DAW, 1997), and assorted introductions for various short fiction collections by other authors. She is single and childless, but a proud pet-parent of a varying number of cat-children.

JOHN S. POSTOVIT was born on December 18, 1962 at Grand Forks, North Dakota. He edited *Alpha Adventures SF*, and has been an occasional collaborator on several of Morlan's stories. He currently lives in Boulder Creek, California, and makes his living as a teacher and gallery artist.